Will Bark for Pizza

WILL BARK FOR PIZZA

BLUEBELL SPRINGS BOOK 1

CAROLINE STONE

Copy Editor: Write Girl Editing Services

Cover Design: Alt 19 Creative

Proofreading: FictionEdit.com

This one's for you, Bubbies. You saved me in more ways than you'll ever know. I hope they have lots of pizza in heaven!

I promise the dog lives.

CONTENT WARNING

This novel contains themes and events that may be distressing to some readers. Please proceed with care if you are sensitive to any of the following:

Panic attacks
Narcissistic abuse and trauma
Alcoholism
Toxic family members

ONE

KIRA

WHEN THE GOING GETS TOUGH, *the tough choose sugar.* Every single time.

At least, that was my philosophy. The half-eaten frosted sugar cookie sitting in my passenger seat could attest. The cookie was the size of a deep-dish pizza when we left Omaha eight hours ago.

To be fair, I didn't eat *all* of it. Husker wore a purple frosting smudge on the side of his nose that his lolling tongue hadn't yet discovered. The overstimulated Alaskan Husky, who was currently pacing the back seat of my Jeep like a caged lion, didn't need the sugar boost. But we shared everything that was deemed dog-safe. It was an unwritten rule.

We were a pack, he and I.

Narcissistic losers need not apply.

The dashboard was covered in dog hair, the windshield was splattered with the corpses of flying insects, and I hadn't turned on the radio since the backdrop of mountains appeared on the hazy horizon. Travis would have complained about all of it.

"Asshole," I muttered.

Husker's pacing came to an abrupt halt with the single word, a sloppy substance that hinted at dog breath smacking my cheek. He stared at me expectantly, head tilting.

"Not you, Bubbies." I wiped away the drool with the back of my hand before I could overthink it. "Never you."

We maintained eye contact in the rearview mirror for an extra-long beat before he resumed his pacing. I was so damned lucky I had him, this wonderful, quirky, lovable dog. He'd saved me, in more ways than one. Especially these past couple of years.

No matter what happened once we hit the town limits of Bluebell Springs, at least I had Husker as an ally.

The thought created a lump in my throat. I didn't know what to expect with this unannounced visit. Would we be welcomed with open arms or met with disapproving glares? Suddenly, I wanted another bite of cookie.

As though in tune with my craving, Husker jerked his attention to the passenger seat, leaning his chest into the net I'd bungeed between the front seats. It was supposed to discourage his notorious habit of standing on the center console, like a lion appraising his pride lands. But that didn't stop him from stretching his neck as far over the top of the netting as he could, his nose pointed expectantly at the snack in the passenger seat.

"Don't you think you've had enough already?"

His big brown eyes flickered from the cookie to me with an air of incredulity that rivaled any human I knew.

Probably a good thing dogs couldn't talk. The words were written all over his face. *Stupidest question ever, Mom.*

He had a point.

I reached over, fingers digging beneath the plastic covering, and Husker's mouth clapped shut on a held breath.

"Easy," I warned, breaking off a piece for us to share.

The giant cookie was the last thing I picked up in Omaha before we hit the road this morning. Even if my life was imploding, I wasn't going to mess with tradition. I wasn't all the way superstitious, but I was enough. I didn't want to add some weird curse to the list of shit I still had to fix. I needed this book launch to go well. It was very likely my last.

Besides, it was a damn delicious cookie. To be honest, I was surprised there was any of it left after eight hours on the road. Maybe I'd spent more time clutching the steering wheel for dear life than stuffing my face with sweets.

Small wins.

"Well?" I said to Husker, who was still standing. He knew the rules.

He immediately plopped his butt down in the center of the back seat, waiting for his portion.

I took a bite right out of the purple frosted B of *Books*, glancing in the rearview at Husker's reaction. His spine straightened, eyes shining with genuine concern. Whether that was for my oversized bite or his fear of not getting his fair share was up for debate. Either way, he looked so damned cute.

I smiled, relieved that after the hell I endured, I could once again find joy in the little things. I broke off a tiny corner of the dessert and tossed it over my shoulder. Husker caught the terrible throw as though he'd been training for this all his life. Really, he had.

To be fair, the cookie *was* to die for. But the sugar sat a bit heavier in my stomach as we passed a green road sign announcing my hometown was a mere five miles ahead. The mountains were no longer just background. When had they snuck up on me? The tree-covered layer of mountains closest to the water felt close enough to reach out the window and touch. The snow-dusted layers behind them were no longer white smudges, but distinct patterns. A silent declaration that the point of no return was fast approaching.

Fuck. Was I really ready to face all this?

The urge to turn around gripped me, but I fought through it. I replayed the dream to drown out the impulse of running. Mom wouldn't summon me home if it wasn't important. At least, I hoped that's why I'd dreamt of her last night.

Husker, typically the world's quietest Husky unless pizza was involved, started to whine, his excitement escalating. It didn't matter that we were still three miles from the fork in the road; he recognized the landmarks. The marina with the pontoon rentals, the enormous house perched on the highest hill this side of Glimmerstone Lake, the metal statue of a moose at the edge of a driveway that Husker always found suspicious.

Guilt gnawed at me. Bluebell Springs was hands down his favorite place, and we hadn't been back since Aspen's wedding last summer.

We hadn't been much of anywhere.

Cracking the back windows diverted Husker's attention away from the cookie, and shifted my guilt to more manageable levels. He resumed pacing at twice his previous frenzied speed, darting from window to window every few seconds, as though he didn't want to miss a single scent.

I slowed, much to the annoyance of the car behind me, who took the first opportunity to pass on the narrow, winding road. Damn tourist. Husker deserved to take in all the smells. Fur swirled around the interior of my Jeep, forcing me to also roll down the front windows, just so I could see the road ahead.

Maybe I should call Dad, and warn him I was coming.

I glanced at the dashboard screen. My fingers hovered above the call button for several seconds before falling away. "I think it's better to surprise him, right?"

And everyone else.

Husker didn't answer me. He was too busy freaking out.

He recognized the familiar fork up ahead. Left, and you drove through downtown Bluebell Springs, accessing all the touristy shops and local businesses. Or, take the right, and bypass the main strip in favor of a straight shot to Glimmerstone Lake.

The painted wood sign surrounded by a colorful array of flowers had welcomed residents, newcomers, and tourists alike to my hometown for decades. It was disarmingly stationed in the center of the fork, but angled just a bit to the left—as though beckoning anyone headed toward the bypass to reconsider a visit to the small town before heading out to the popular lake. The sign grew bigger through my windshield at an alarming rate.

Anxiety officially set in, my chest heavier. I felt my throat close. But before full-on panic hit, a fiber of dog hair tried its damnedest to sneak up my nose, and I sneezed.

An odd reset button, but I wasn't complaining.

My eyes squinted shut for a fraction of a second, but when they re-opened, my gaze landed on Kat's Place, right on the outskirts of the fork. The parking lot was three-quarters full, a notable sign that tourist season was well underway.

My stomach twisted into a knot. I was ninety percent certain I was still on the *do not serve* list.

I wouldn't miss the drinks. After Travis, I no longer touched alcohol. But I'd certainly miss the burgers and crisp French fries seasoned with what I could only describe as crack.

"Here we go," I said to Husker, tapping the brake to slow us down, and taking the left fork into downtown.

I didn't know how this was going to unfold. I didn't exactly leave town on great terms last summer. I said plenty of mean, fucked-up things under the mixed influence of heartbreak and the bride's special cocktail.

"They never should've given me that microphone," I mumbled. Though Aspen had forgiven me, I'm not sure anyone else did. How could I blame them? It was quite possible that the second my tires hit asphalt downtown, I'd get a police escort right back out, courtesy of my oldest brother.

But I had to risk it.

Mom hadn't been in my dreams in months. She'd been

gone for four years now, and I could count on both hands the number of times she appeared in my dreams since the day we lost her. Each time, something significant happened. Sometimes good. Sometimes really fucking bad.

Now, when she showed up, I paid attention.

I hoped Dad was okay. That my brothers weren't in any trouble. Oh God, I hoped nothing had happened to my niece.

"Connor would've called me," I reassured Husker. Which of course made his ears perk with interest. He loved both of my brothers; he loved my niece even more. "Or, at least, *someone* would have called me."

I glanced at my dashboard screen again, tempted to make the call and just rip off the Band-Aid, but my fingers didn't move from their death grip on the steering wheel.

In my dream, I lay flat on my back on a paddleboard in the middle of the smaller, lesser-known Ghost Lake. Husker was perched on the end of my board, relaxed and taking in the sights and smells.

Mom floated on a board next to me. Books floated all around us. So many books.

It was magical and incredibly peaceful. I had so many things I wanted to say to her, but I was so comfortable just lying there, the sun warm on my skin, the gentle rock of small waves tranquil. I stayed silent. It was enough just to have her near again.

But then the wind picked up.

The calm waters turned choppy.

One by one, the books sank below the surface.

I sat up on the board, watching entire stacks of books

plummet right through the water. Mom locked eyes with me for a single beat, her expression pleading.

And then, she disappeared.

I woke up in a cold sweat.

After that dream, I felt compelled to come back home. So much so that I started packing in the middle of the night. Husker was not pleased. He liked his lazy mornings. But he liked the threat of being left behind even less, so he stayed glued to my side as I paced around my apartment, filling bags.

I could hardly fathom that Mom had been gone for so long. I yearned for a few lazy days hanging out in her bookstore, reading in the corner nook, soaking up the sunlight. Lazy bookstore days were the cure to life's toughest ailments—skinned knees, disappointing news, and broken hearts.

"Add a mini life crisis to that list," I mumbled as we passed what the locals called Gift Shop Alley, eyes peeled for my brother, the police chief. He liked to park in the alleys, barely noticeable until it was too late to hit your brakes without him noticing. Luke wouldn't hesitate to pull me over in a heartbeat. His grumpiness knew no bounds, on the best of days. If he was in a bad mood, he might just find a reason to arrest me.

"At least Aspen doesn't hate me," I said the words over my shoulder, in Husker's general direction. But he was too focused on a golden retriever walking past Bert's Shirts to hear me.

Aspen was the rarest, most wonderful kind of friend.

It's why I set my sights on her bakery down the street.

I certainly didn't need more sweets, but I craved a friendly face before my family got hold of me.

A block from Frosted Peaks, I noticed a new pizzeria beside the veterinary clinic. Its sign was purple and whimsical, set against the typical log planks that adorned nearly every business exterior in town. Pizza Patty's. The logs had a freshness to them, as though they were recently re-stained. They glowed like toasted marshmallows against the sunlight.

The place looked busy, and there was a water bowl outside its door. *Dog friendly.* I hoped I'd be in town long enough to try it. The way Husker stationed himself at the window, hoovering up great whiffs of pepperoni-scented air, suggested he did, too. That dog lived for pizza.

Before I could catch a glimpse of the patio that snaked around the corner of the building, my gaze snagged on a large window sign directly across the street. The bold red letters seemed to reach into my chest, twist around my heart, and squeeze, like a woman giving birth with no drugs.

Going Out of Business Sale.

My foot slammed on the brake in the middle of Main Street.

I couldn't breathe.

My throat closed, as though hands were strangling it shut.

I stared at the sign in red letters, taking up more than half the display window of Brenda's Book Nook, and I couldn't fucking breathe.

What the hell?

Communication with my family certainly dwindled

over the past year, but it wasn't nonexistent. No one had said a damn thing about Mom's bookstore fucking *closing*.

Husker whined from the back seat as dog hair drifted around me, as though someone had shaken up a snow globe. I felt frozen in time, stuck in a moment I wanted no part of. Why the hell did no one *tell* me?

I gripped the steering wheel tighter, certain it was the only thing keeping me from a waterfall of tears and a bloodcurdling scream sure to alert the entire town.

The dream suddenly made a lot of sense.

Someone honked behind me, and I hit the gas.

TWO
BECKETT

"WHAT DO YOU THINK?" Luke Mason asked, stepping inside the lakeside cabin and flipping on a couple of lights. I threw one more glance toward the general direction of the lake, but it still wasn't visible. I followed him inside.

It was like walking into a time capsule. Wood panel walls, olive green carpet, and a burnt orange floral-print couch jumped right out at me. If I didn't know better, I'd swear I was back on the East Coast, in Nana's old basement. The cabin felt cramped and compact with its closed-off rooms, but open concept wasn't trending when it was built.

"I know it's a little dated," Luke added, thumbs anchored in his gun belt as I moved around. The police chief was working today, but he agreed to meet me and show me the place before his shift officially started. "But it has good bones."

"Nothing I can't handle," I admitted. The cabin appeared to be well maintained, even if it was a time-traveling experience into the seventies. It was also furnished, which was a plus since these days, I didn't have much in the way of material possessions. Just what little I'd packed into a storage unit. I was in no hurry to pull any of it out.

I walked through the rooms, counting seven with the bathroom. Eight, if you added in the covered outdoor space with picnic tables, just off the kitchen. I wasn't surprised to find a green toilet and wall-mounted sink that matched the living room carpet in the tight bathroom. Hell, the gas range in the kitchen matched it, too.

"Lots of green," I remarked.

"Grandma Pebble," Luke said. I pieced together that she was the grandma on his dad's side, as I'd been living with his other grandparents for the couple of months I'd been in town. "She refused to let Karl and Wendy change a thing when they bought it from her. No one had the balls to touch a thing after she passed. If there was ever a woman who'd haunt your ass, it's Grandma Pebble."

"I'm not enacting some kind of curse if I rip out the carpet, am I?" I asked on a laugh.

Luke clapped me on the shoulder. "I'm afraid that's a risk you'll have to take."

I didn't believe in ghosts, so I wasn't worried about some woman I'd never met haunting me.

"The family won't mind?"

"Hell, I think they'd throw a party."

My gaze snagged on a framed family photograph hanging just above the hideous couch; it was taken in front of the cabin. I instantly recognized my friends, among the gaggle of kids piled in front of nearly a dozen adults. A short, stout woman with gray hair tied up in a red bandana and a lopsided smile that promised trouble stood in the middle of the chaos—Grandma Pebble, I presumed.

What would it be like to have a family that size? To have family gatherings out at the lake with siblings and cousins? To spend holidays with laughter and banter instead of hyperawareness and disappointment? Hell, I'd even take the bickering.

"That was the summer I turned fourteen," Luke said, nodding at the photo. "Same summer Dad refused to teach me how to drive, so I taught myself and drove his truck right into a stream."

"Bet he was pissed."

"Only reason he let me come on that camping trip was because no one wanted to stay behind and babysit my ass. But I was grounded until Christmas."

I'd heard a few stories about their family camping adventures at Ghost Lake. How Luke pranked his little sister by putting a snake in her tent one summer. How she got even by putting it in his sleeping bag. Connor, ever the peacekeeping middle brother, got caught in the crossfire when the two started throwing the snake at each other. Their cousin Thoren sat back and watched the whole thing he'd instigated unfold, laughing himself stupid.

"Thoren doesn't want this place?" I asked, staring at the picture and wondering if the girl with blonde pigtails was Luke's sister. I'd never actually met her, despite following Luke to Bluebell Springs on a couple of our joint leaves. Bad timing I guess, because I always wondered what kind of woman a snake-throwing girl grew into.

"I'm not sure you could convince him to move back here unless you hogtied him and tossed him in the back of your truck. He and his dad don't exactly see eye-to-eye. He'd sooner bear crawl buck-ass naked on broken glass than ask Karl for shit. Including this cabin."

"Guess he's a lifer, then?" Thoren was the only one of us four still active duty.

"Lookin' that way." Luke checked his phone, then dropped it back into his uniform pocket. "Uncle Karl said he's open on rent-to-own options if you're not ready to buy something."

"That could work." I had money tied up in several investment properties, including my first commercial building. It was a big step for Campbell Enterprises. Renting sounded more my speed while I focused on establishing this new side of my business.

"I have to warn you, though. Karl might change his mind. He's done that before."

"He's not sure about getting rid of it, then?"

"If it were up to my aunt, the place would've been sold ten years ago. But Karl . . ." Luke let his sentence trail off with a shrug. "And look, if he does change his mind, my grandparents are happy to have you as long as you need a place to stay. Hell, you're the favorite grandkid at this point. If you wait it out long enough, they might just leave their house to you in the will."

He meant it as a joke, but my laughter was forced. I didn't want to overstay my welcome with the Westons.

I parted the dusty curtains on the opposite wall of the couch, wondering whether they'd always been ivory, or if they just needed a good wash.

Dirty curtains or not, the view sold me.

"That's Ghost Lake," Luke said.

The private lake hadn't been visible on the mile-and-a-half drive up and down a rough dirt road. But through the picture window, it was framed in perfection. Deep blue water with hardly a boat floating on it and a backdrop of mountains. Thick woods all around, like walls. A few houses nestled in them. Luke wasn't kidding when he said it was quiet. Compared to the larger, touristy Glimmerstone Lake on the other side of Bluebell Springs that was already littered with boats, jet skis, and pontoons, this place was deserted.

"Only locals live out here?"

"For the most part, yeah. There won't be any asshole kids out here throwing parties. Just families camping on occasion."

That explained the orange tent off to the far left.

"Why is he looking to get rid of the place?"

"Karl doesn't come out here anymore. Hasn't for years." Luke cleared his throat. "Not since Aaron."

I never met his cousin, but having served in the Army with some of his family, I felt as though I knew him. He was the reason Luke, Connor, and Thoren enlisted together more than a decade ago. The reason I met any of them.

"You don't want it?"

"I don't need another place to keep up, and I can't live here twenty-four seven. It takes too long to respond to calls from out here."

"No one else in the family wants it?"

"Anyone here is set up. Everyone else has moved away and isn't interested in coming back or being responsible for a property that'll sit empty most of the year."

"Has it been empty long?"

"Aspen lived out here for a few years," Luke said of Karl's daughter. "But not since she got married." By my calculations, the cabin had only been vacant a year. "She still comes out here to clean once a month. I check on it to make sure there're no squatters."

In other words, the house wasn't neglected. It was looked after, and hopefully wouldn't need major repairs. I didn't mind a personal renovation project, but I didn't anticipate having time for something extensive when I was just getting settled with my new commercial ventures.

"C'mon," Luke said, nodding toward the back door off the kitchen. "You need to see the rest of it."

I followed him through the enclosed outdoor space, noting an old charcoal grill in the corner. Though it needed a solid scrubbing and possibly a power wash, my stomach growled at the thought of a burger grilled over coals.

"The property goes all the way past the clearing," Luke said, pointing toward a dirt area through the trees. The ground was hard-packed around what appeared to be a small wood-planked dock, but no boats or any water toys were tied to it. "The road dead-ends there. It's also your best lake access."

"It's private?"

"Yeah. You might get someone turning around once in a while. Occasionally, a lone fisherman avoiding his honey-do list. But they're harmless. They won't bother you if you don't bother them."

The full acre on the quiet lake was exactly the kind of property I hoped to find. The cabin could be updated, and until then, it was perfectly livable. It didn't have a garage or shop space, but it'd probably be easier to store my materials in town anyway. It was the perfect setup.

We walked down to the edge of the water, and serenity greeted me like an old friend. Nana would approve, even if I wrote Karl a check for the whole thing today. We had a long chat about me putting down roots in this town. Yet the permanence of even a rent-to-own situation made my stomach tie in knots. If I backed out of buying it down the road because I found something better, what kind of rift would that cause? How would that affect my decision to make this town my own? This wasn't a property I could simply flip.

"See? Quiet."

I stepped right up to the edge. The ground dropped off a few feet into the lake, a tangle of tree roots and boulders making it a less than ideal place to get into the water if I felt like taking a swim or getting in a kayak. I could see the boat dock from here, though, down a dirt-packed trail. And I had a pretty good view of the entire lake.

"Does anyone here *use* the lake?"

A kayaker paddled off in the distance, a fisherman was camped out on a dock directly across, and a gaggle of geese enjoyed the calm waters. But otherwise, the lake was empty.

"Oh, yeah." Luke pulled a vibrating phone from his uniform pocket. "But it's all locals out here."

It was a random Tuesday afternoon. "They're working."

"Fuck me," Luck groaned, staring at the phone cradled in his hand. "I have to go. Some tourist got into a fender bender with Dana Wilcox downtown. She's all bent out of shape. I better go defuse the situation."

I couldn't place the name to a specific person. But I also didn't grow up in the small town like Luke did. He knew everyone. Some he liked, many he tolerated, and a special few grated on his last nerve. Judging by his expression, Dana was one of those special pains in his side.

But he vowed to serve and protect, so that's exactly what he did. And while he might pretend it inconvenienced him to deal with the thorns, I knew better. I served downrange with Luke Mason during two deployments. He felt a personal duty to protect them all, as though the citizens of Bluebell Springs were an extension of his family.

"Mind if I hang out for a while?"

He handed me the keys, already on the way to his police SUV. "Lock up when you're done?"

"Yep."

"Hey, Beckett," he said, pulling open the driver's side door. "Stop by and talk to my dad soon."

I stared at him, dumbfounded. "He's going to sell it, then?"

"Yeah, he decided last night. He's giving you first right of refusal. If you want the bookstore, it's yours."

THREE
KIRA

I SPED past the bakery and took a sharp right down a street filled with real estate offices, a museum, and a haunted tour guide business that wasn't there on my last visit. Husker whined in confusion, but I didn't slow until we left the city limits.

I couldn't go back to Omaha. Not yet. But I sure as hell wasn't ready to face anyone. Not even Aspen.

Why did no one fucking *tell* me?

I wove through backroads until I found the familiar rutted dirt road I'd been running to since I got my learner's permit. The weathered *private road: no trespassing* sign greeted me like an old friend.

I turned onto the rough road, grateful that I splurged on my Jeep after my most popular book series went viral on TikTok. This road wasn't maintained or intended for regular vehicles; I learned that lesson the hard way.

"Connor still gives me shit about towing me out that summer," I threw over my shoulder to Husker. But he was back to bouncing from one window to the other, sniffing at the crack of fresh air as he tried to decipher my plan. It felt so . . . normal. My erratically beating heart calmed. "But I guess you were there, weren't you?"

We'd been together since Husker was nine weeks old, when he was small enough to fit inside a cat carrier and ride under the seat on the plane. He was a hellion of a puppy that summer, when I broke my axle on this so-called road.

A particularly rough bump elicited a grumble from the back seat. My seven-year-old pup was slowly aging into a grumpy old man dog.

"Sorry, Bubbies."

The road was in worse shape than I remembered. Uncle Karl liked it that way. Left it rough on purpose. He claimed it kept the tourists away from the *good side* of the lake. Never mind that they rarely sought out the smaller, less exciting lake at all. And when they did, the locals chased them off.

As a kid, I remembered bumpy rides in the backs of pickups. It was a game to hold on and not get thrown from the bed of the truck. Mom *hated* that game.

A mile and a half later, the smaller, lesser-known Ghost Lake came into view through a clearing of trees. The road dead-ended at the water. Houses dotted the lake on the opposite side, each one separated by thick forest. Unlike the popular Glimmerstone Lake that was packed with lake houses so close you could reach out your window and touch your neighbor, Ghost Lake was for those locals who preferred a quiet, separate existence.

The backdrop of mountains, lit up by the early

evening sun, delivered the serenity I so desperately needed.

Husker, on the other hand, lost his ever-loving mind.

"We're overdue, don't you think?" He couldn't hear me over his excited Husky chatter, demanding I let him out of the Jeep immediately.

I parked near the boat dock I was happy to see still standing. Even better, it appeared as though someone replaced the rotted planks with fresh ones. Was Uncle Karl finally staying out at his cabin again after all these years avoiding it? I chose to believe he was, and it soothed the worst of my frustration.

I clipped a long leash onto Husker's collar, hooked the handle to the trail hitch so he couldn't chase any wildlife, and set to work digging out an inflatable paddleboard I nearly didn't pack.

Because of the dream I had.

I looked up at the sky. "Thanks, Mom."

Husker watched as I used the hand pump to fill the purple and gold paddleboard we hadn't put on the water in nearly three years. A gut punch of sadness struck me, but I took a deep breath and willed it away. I'd deal with that emotion another day. I had enough emotions in line ahead of it.

Starting with the frustration I currently felt with my family.

I took out my irritation on the hand pump. I wasn't able to find my electric one while loading up this morning, and right now I was glad for the manual labor. Husker tilted his head in confusion with each mumbled curse. My anger made the grueling task go faster.

How did no one *tell* me?

The board was taking shape. It was faded in places, and I was mildly concerned the inflatable board might leak from being neglected all this time. I listened for a hiss of air once it was filled. Nothing. At least, I *thought* it was nothing. Hard to tell with how hard I was panting.

"It's good!"

Husker popped to all fours, tail wagging. His excitement was enough to convince me we wouldn't sink in the middle of the shallow lake. Considering the water was probably sixty-five degrees—sixty-eight if I was lucky—that was a good thing.

As I was putting the hand pump back into the car, my phone rang.

Instantly, Husker's large ears dropped, and I swore.

I owed this dog a lot for everything he went through with me while I was in what I now referred to as my Dark Ages. The mere sound of the phone ringing or a text chiming could cause him undue stress. I'd changed the tones a dozen times, but it didn't matter. Husker was reacting to me. Would I ever not tense at the sound of my phone? Just another reason Travis could go to hell.

"Sorry, Bubbies." I tapped *answer* when I recognized the caller.

"Happy twenty-fifth book release!" Lila's chipper tone sang through the speakerphone. Husker perked at the sound of her voice, earlier stress forgotten. *Small wins.* "I hope you're doing something exciting to celebrate."

"Does paddleboarding count?"

"Come again?"

"I'm about to get on the lake with my paddleboard." I

feigned nonchalance, but inwardly I felt guilty for keeping yet another secret from yet another person. Lila Quinn was my personal assistant and currently, the only close friend still treating me like one. She was the reason anyone even knew about today's book release, because I sure as hell wasn't on social media shouting it from the rooftops.

I met her at a local writers' conference two years ago, and we hit it off immediately. She was a godsend on the marketing that overwhelmed me when my author career really took off. Without her, I'd have drowned long before now.

"Where did you rent a paddleboard?"

"I own one."

"Since when? And where are you? Standing Bear Lake? I can meet you there in half an hour."

I let out a heavy breath, deciding it was best to just spit it out. "I'm in Colorado."

"Colorado?" she repeated. "Is everything okay? Is someone sick? Oh, God, did someone die?"

"Everyone is fine." *Everyone but me.* "I had a dream. About my mom."

"Oh." Understanding and compassion warmed her tone, stripping it to the equivalent of a verbal side hug. She was one of the few who knew about my Mom dreams and what happened the last time I ignored one. "She wanted you to come home?"

"Yeah, I guess so." Now, I knew why. But I wasn't ready to tell Lila the bookstore was closing. I wasn't ready to face that reality myself.

"You didn't want to invite your PA?" she asked, tone hinting at hurt and confusion but still hugging me tight.

Best PA ever. Best *friend*. "You know I love a good road trip. And we could've gotten some epic social media footage."

If it hadn't been for Lila, I'd have no social media presence at all.

"It was super last minute."

"I can still come meet you out there," she offered. "Oh! You could do a book signing at your mom's bookstore! I'll bring everything. All you have to do is show up and smile."

I let out a laugh, because we both knew I'd never do it. I kept my author identity a secret. My profile picture was merely my author logo, and I never posted a single picture on any platform that showed my face. I liked the anonymity. It'd come in handy when I eventually confessed to my readers that I was done writing paranormal romance.

"Just think about it," she encouraged.

"No one here even knows I'm Diana Davenport."

"No one?"

"Just my cousin, Aspen. I'd be mortified if anyone found out what I write."

"You make it sound like writing sexy vampire romances is some sort of crime," she chastised.

I couldn't imagine the book club Mom started before I was born would be excited to find out I wrote paranormal smut. They'd show up to a book signing for Brenda Mason's daughter, but once they read the first chapter, they'd be horrified and concerned for my soul.

"Trust me, it's better this way."

"Promise me if you ever do an in-person event for Diana Davenport that you'll bring me along. Kidnap me, if you have to. I do *not* want to miss your coming-out party."

"I promise."

It was easier than explaining that I'd never reveal my secret pen name. Or that my author career as I knew it was about to be on a downward spiral. I hadn't dredged an ounce of inspiration since the Big Breakup. I was almost certain that part of me died a swift death along with the most toxic relationship I'd ever experienced. The price for peace was high, but I'd happily pay it again.

I'm not sure my readers felt the same way, though.

"How long will you be out of town?" Lila asked.

"Not sure." I didn't give much thought to this plan when I loaded the car this morning. I packed enough clothes, dog food, and reading material to last me a solid ten days. Being an author had been my full-time job for the past three years, and it afforded me a flexibility I certainly took for granted until now.

I'd miss that the most when the money inevitably ran out and I had to return to reality. Thanks to Lila, I might have a couple of years of freedom ahead of me before that day arrived.

"You okay?" Lila asked, her concern genuine. "Because I can pack a bag and be on the next flight—"

"I'm okay."

"You're lying."

"I'll *be* okay," I corrected.

"Is that what the paddleboarding is for?"

"Yeah." I half dragged, half carried the board to the edge of the shore before digging out the paddle with one hand, and balancing the phone with the other.

My dog was pacing, convinced I would leave him behind. He did the same thing when I filled my suitcase this morning, just a bit more dramatically.

"I'd never leave you behind, Husker," I said, returning to my Jeep. I unsnapped the tether from the purple paddle and left the cord behind. I'd be fine without it in water this calm. But Husker's life jacket was nonnegotiable. "You know that."

"Wait, Husker's going with you?" Lila's tone perked up.

"Of course."

"I didn't take him for a swimming dog. He likes the water?"

"Actually, he hates the water."

"Okay, I'm lost."

"He loves being on the board, just not the getting wet part."

I set the phone on the Jeep's bumper and crossed my fingers that the doggie life jacket still fit. Though I felt fairly confident he could swim without it, it made me feel better for him to have one.

After letting out the straps, the bright yellow and black jacket snapped closed around his torso with just enough give. Husker gave me the most pitiful look, as though the other dogs would make fun of him for this. But he'd forget all about it once we were on the water.

"Maybe you'll get some writing done while you're out there," Lila said, her tone both encouraging and nonchalant, as though she didn't want to push me, but knew I needed a solid nudge. "With the change of scenery, and all. Your Veltori vamps do like mountains."

"Maybe." I told her I was suffering from writer's block, because it was easier than admitting the truth. Diana Davenport would never write another book. I just didn't know how to tell her, or anyone else. "Do you need anything from me?" I asked her of the book launch.

"Feel free to respond to reader comments. They're loving this latest book and already begging for Mateo's story. Seriously, babe, a love triangle?" *Fuck, I did that, didn't I?* "But otherwise, I've got it covered."

"Thanks, Lila. You're the best."

"You wouldn't have hired me otherwise," she insisted. "Send me a picture of Husker in his life jacket. I *need* to see it!"

"He's allergic to pictures on a good day, but I'll see what I can do."

Once the call ended, I made a few pitiful attempts to fulfill Lila's request. Husker refused to look at the camera for a single one, and all of them were blurry. Maybe I could try again when we got back to shore. Until then, I slipped my phone into the center console of my Jeep. It was better for my sanity if I left it behind. Better for my bank account if I didn't drop another one in the lake.

"Ready, Bubbies?"

I locked up the Jeep, slipped my keys into a waterproof bag I'd secure to the board in a minute, and led Husker to the edge of the lake. He waited on the shore until I got into the chilly water; thankfully I'd chosen to wear shorts. There was nothing worse than soggy jeans, especially when the sun dropped and the temperatures cooled.

I let out a hiss at the icy water making contact with my

bare skin, but it was a welcome shock. Like a reset button on my fried emotions.

I turned the board so it paralleled the shore, giving Husker more real estate to hop onto. I waited until he was mostly settled before I knelt onto the board. Even with no wind, it was too risky to stand until I felt confident my dog wouldn't capsize us.

After unclipping his leash and tossing it onto the dock, I used the paddle to push us away from the shore.

The lake was mostly deserted, aside from a stray boat on the opposite end where the water was deeper. Ghost Lake held true to its name. If I didn't know some of the locals who lived in the houses across the water personally, I'd suspect they were ghosts themselves, for how little they were on the water.

I caught a glimpse of a couple of tents farther down the bank and was instantly taken back to the countless family camping trips we enjoyed out here on Uncle Karl's land. Life was so much simpler back then. My brothers didn't hate me, Mom was still alive, and my parents were happy.

The bookstore wasn't fucking going out of business.

It felt like a lifetime ago.

Out in the center of the lake, Husker settled into a lying position, like a sphinx affixed to the front end of my board. Alert but relaxed.

Not a single book floated in the lake.

I took my first deep breath since I hit the road this morning.

I don't know how long we stayed out on the water—*minutes, hours, days?*—only that when I seemed to blink for the first time, the sun had dipped behind the mountain range and goosebumps danced across my bare arms.

"Shit, we better get back to shore," I mumbled, carefully standing. I paddled faster on my feet than on my knees.

It wasn't until I turned the board around and pointed us to the shore that I noticed the second vehicle. A black truck tucked against the trees, nearer Uncle Karl's cabin, but it wasn't his. Karl had been stubbornly driving the same 1991 Chevy pickup for decades. As a mechanic, he had plenty to say about the newer models and all their fancy computer components.

My pulse doubled. Had I been in such a trance that I didn't hear a truck pull up? Or were we simply on the other side of the lake? Maybe the truck was there the whole time, and I didn't notice it.

A man walked out from the clearing of trees and onto the dock. He was on his phone, reminding me that my own was locked inside my Jeep.

I sucked in a deep breath, refusing to let fear take hold. Travis made me afraid of everything. At one point, I was too scared to make the trip home by myself, as though some terrible fate might befall me should I travel alone. It was one of the reasons I almost didn't attend Aspen's wedding last summer. Which reminded me, I owed my bestie, Alyssa, a call too.

"I'm done being afraid," I said, quietly but firmly.

Husker looked up at me, then back to the man. Though he was an incredibly affectionate dog who would more likely lick an attacker to death than bite one, he looked more like a German Shepherd than a Husky. It was often enough to make someone think twice.

I took in all the details I could—jeans, a gray T-shirt that stretched over earned muscles, work boots, short dark hair, tattoos on one arm, probably in his thirties, around six foot if I had to guess.

Husker, who was content to stay in one position the entire duration of our paddle, chose *that* moment to fixate on a suspicious growth of pondweed. A low growl followed his tenuous lean over the edge of the board.

"Bubbies, leave it!"

One minute I was upright on the board.

The next, I was underwater.

FOUR
HUSKER

Splash!
I'm wet.
Why am I wet?
It's just my tail.
But it's wet.
Yuck.
Where did my mom go?
Why is my tail wet?
I don't like being wet.
I want a towel rub.
Mom, can I have a towel rub?
Wait, where is my mom?
This stupid water is cold!
Abort!
But there's some weird leafy thing in the water.
Looks suspicious.
Mom says leave the pondweed alone.
Is that pondweed?

Ugh, my whole nose is wet.
Dumb idea.
Mom?
Wait, what's that smell?
It smells sweet.
Ooh, frosting!
Did I get it all?
Better swipe my tongue out once more.
All gone.
I wish there was more.
Why is Mom in the water?
Does she like being wet?
No, being wet is stupid.
Who's that?
It's a man on the shore.
He looks nice.
I bet he gives good belly rubs.
Is he coming to save my mom?
Where is my mom?
Uck, my nose is still wet.
My tail's wet too.
I want my towel rub.
And treats.
I definitely deserve treats.
That pondweed looks weird.
Where did my mom go?
Did she go get pizza?

FIVE
BECKETT

WHEN I SPOTTED the redhead with a dog standing on a paddleboard in the middle of Ghost Lake, that should have been my sign to turn the hell around and go.

I'd lingered out at the cabin long enough, convincing myself that purchasing this cabin was the perfect way to put down roots in this town. Nana, whom I was talking it over with on the phone, grunted as soon as the words left my mouth.

"There's a redhead on a paddleboard."

I didn't need to say more. Nana was there through two of the blowouts that occurred after my *interactions* with redheads in the past. Chaos and a string of bad luck always followed in their wake.

"It's an omen," Nana said, right before the woman fell into the lake.

"Yeah. Probably."

I simultaneously ended the call and kicked off my boots, before stripping out of my shirt. Luke mentioned

Ghost Lake was shallow compared to the larger Glimmer-stone Lake, but that didn't mean someone couldn't drown in it. And so far, Red hadn't resurfaced.

A blond shepherd dog whined and paced on the paddleboard, pressing his nose into the water on each side. He didn't seem eager to jump in, but he was definitely concerned.

The woman was still under.

Fuck.

No time to remove my jeans, I emptied my pockets and waded into the lake. I swam straight toward the board. The water was colder than I expected, but I blocked out the discomfort and focused on the mission at hand: save Red.

The dog wearing a bright yellow and black life vest silently paced from the front to the back of the board, looking down at me with big brown eyes, urgently begging me to do something about his human.

I dove under, the setting sun no fucking help in the darkening waters. I scanned the area, mostly with my arms, and came up empty. I refused to let panic set in, refocused my search, and dove back down.

There, on the opposite side of the board, a sea of red hair and long, bare legs gave her away. She was headed to the surface. Only when her head broke the water did I follow suit.

"Husker, you okay?" she choked out as she propped her elbows on the board, fear heavy in those blue eyes. Despite her coughing and panting, her concern was more for the dog than herself. That much was evident in the way she looked at him. Had I ever met a redhead who came with a dog? I quickly shook the question away. She already showed me she was chaos. Having a dog didn't change the redheaded curse I'd endured since the fifth grade.

The dog lay down on the board, his head next to hers, nosing her face in obvious concern.

"You okay, ma'am?" I asked from the opposite side of her board, announcing my presence as my foot found purchase on the slippery bottom. The water was just shallow enough that I could balance on my toes and keep my chin above the surface without having to tread water.

"Shit," she sputtered, her eyes doubling in size when she spotted me. "Where did you come from?"

"Sorry. Didn't mean to startle you. You okay?"

"I'm fine." She ran her fingers along the back of the dog's neck. The gesture seemed protective, as though she'd fight me if I threatened her dog. I had to admit, in his doggie life vest, the pup didn't seem all that intimidating. The mama bear warning in her narrowed eyes made sense. "Really, I'm good. Just a little wounded pride."

"You hurt?"

"You ask a lot of questions," she fired back, understandable suspicion in her gaze.

I took a few steps backward, finding firmer footing. My aching toes thanked me.

"I saw you go under," I explained, brushing water from my forehead before the droplets could roll into my eyes any worse than they already had. "You weren't coming back up."

"I'm fine."

"You were under long enough for me to swim out here."

"My foot got tangled in pondweed." She looked at the dog. "Seems like it got us both, huh, Bubbies?"

"I can call someone—"

"I appreciate your concern, but really, I got it from here."

If I had any sense, I'd leave well enough alone. Swim back to shore, hope like hell I had a towel to sit on until I could get back to the farm to change, and forget all about the frustrating woman anchored on the other side of a paddleboard. But around redheads, I seemed to be a special kind of stupid.

"At least let me help you back to shore," I insisted.

"You don't need to do that."

"I'm not a serial killer or anything."

"That's something a serial killer would say," she pointed out.

"Fair point." I scanned the lake, the shoreline, the houses, the nearby tents. "If I were a serial killer—which, to be clear, I am not—there are too many witnesses. This would be a really bad place to murder you."

Husker looked at me, his head tilted at an angle that shouldn't be physically possible. Add in those big brown doe eyes and pointed ears large enough to pick up a radio signal, and I strongly suspected this dog was good at wielding his cuteness to get anything he wanted.

"Witnesses?" Red sputtered a laugh that ended in a coughing fit. Her eyes watered, mascara smudges running.

I wished I could take away the taste of lake water in her throat. Fragile was the last word I'd use to describe this mystery woman, but a near-drowning scare could rattle even the toughest of people. Something I knew all too well. I wouldn't wish it on anyone.

"This place is deserted," she added. "It's perfect serial killer ground."

"There are two tents over there," I said, pointing to the family camping just on the other side of Karl Hayes' property line. A fire roared, and laughter carried across the lake. "Two adults in that family. Both have been watching since I swam out here." I waited as her gaze snagged on the campsite. She released an exhale, her shoulders dropping the slightest.

In case it wasn't enough, I went on. "Across the lake, there's a couple in their garden. Been there for hours. Green house with the kayaks tied to the boat ramp. The woman's been off her knees since you went in the water. I bet she's even called someone by now."

"What are you, some kind of secret service or something?"

"Or something."

I'd always been observant, a survival skill I honed at a young age, thanks to an alcoholic father. My military training only sharpened those skills. I couldn't turn it off if I tried.

"You think she called someone?" Red's expression was less the relief I expected and a whole lot more like dread. I needed to get this woman and her dog back to shore so I could leave with a clear conscience.

Before I did something reckless, like ask her out.

It didn't matter that I swore off the opposite sex after my last incident with a redhead cost me a solid job and uprooted my comfortable life. My brain went stupid around these women. All the more reason to steer clear of the entire female population until I was comfortably established in my new life.

Even then, I might get a dog before I entertained getting tangled up with a woman again. Or maybe a plant. Wasn't that the first step in proving you had your shit together? Make sure you can keep a plant alive for a year, or something like that?

"I bet the police chief is on his way," I said, to reassure her and get my head on straight. Dana Wilcox's fender bender probably took a back seat to a potential drowning. Once I got Red and her dog back to the shore, I'd shoot him a text. "I'd be arrested before I could dispose of your body."

"Police chief," she mumbled, a flash of panic in her eyes.

"Wait, *you're* not a serial killer, are you?"

One corner of her mouth lifted so subtly I wouldn't have noticed it if I weren't staring.

Fuck, stop staring!

"Not a serial killer."

"I hope that if you're lying, you'll let me live on account of me swimming all the way out here to save you."

"I'll take it into consideration."

A hint of a full smile danced across her lips, but it was the shivering that most caught my attention. The water couldn't be more than sixty-five degrees, and the sun had already dropped behind the mountain range. It'd be dark within the hour. Probably sooner. Though it might take a while for hypothermia to set in, I didn't want to test the theory.

"As long as you're feeling generous, can we please head back to shore before my family jewels shrivel up and disappear?"

"The water's not *that* cold," she scoffed playfully, a full-body shiver giving her away.

"Tell that to my future children."

I gripped the nose of the board and tugged it toward the shore. Husker popped to his feet and stood at attention, as though he were the one steering us to dry land. Red held on by her elbows, pushing the board from the opposite end.

I focused on the red Jeep parked near the boat dock. The one with Nebraska plates. The name Husker made sense now, but not why she was out here in the first place. I hadn't been in Bluebell Springs long, but Luke was pretty adamant: Ghost Lake was a private lake. How did she even know about it? The turn off the highway to Karl's property wasn't announced. It was overgrown, and littered with no trespassing signs. Hell, I drove past the turn the first time.

"Can you grab him until I can get his leash?" Red asked, wringing out her long hair that went past her shoulders, before she stepped out of the lake.

Noting the handle on the back of the doggie life vest, I slipped my hand through it. Not that he needed the anchor. Husker stayed still, watching his human with an unbroken stare as she retrieved the leash from the dock.

"Actually, give me just a second." She hurried to her

Jeep, threw open the passenger door, and reached in. I shouldn't stare at those long legs, but *damn*.

A colorful tattoo snaked around one lower calf, but before I could make out what it was, my gaze zeroed in on the redness wrapped around her other leg. If I had any regrets about swimming out to her, they were gone now. If she hadn't freed herself from the pondweed, she might have drowned.

"Will you hold him still?" she asked me, nodding at Husker as she held up her phone.

"Strange time for a photo op," I pointed out.

She lifted the camera a little higher, letting me know I was captured in the frame. "In case you *are* a serial killer," she said, a flirty flicker in her eyes that I may or may not have imagined.

She set the phone on a rock and stepped her toes into the water so she could clip the leash onto Husker's collar.

The pup looked at the water between him and the shore and started to whine.

"Does he really not know how to swim?"

"Of course he does. It's more of a preference."

I held the board as still as I could until Husker hopped off. His back paws sank into the soft shore and a gentle wave rocked up to his hocks. He bolted forward as though he'd been bitten.

"That's a pretty serious preference," I noted, unable to blunt the chuckle that followed.

"There's a reason he's the dry one." Our gazes met and held for several seconds, and something inside me stirred. It was possible it was the gas station quesadilla I had on the way out here, but it was far more likely the redhead and her far too enticing smile. Because I had to focus on her smile to ignore the way her wet T-shirt and shorts clung to her skin, revealing curves that could haunt me for days—probably longer. "Most huskies I know don't like the water."

"He's a Husky?"

"He's an *Alaskan* Husky."

"Is that supposed to mean something special?"

"It's the reason he doesn't look like the typical Siberian Husky. He's a mixed breed, bred to be a sled dog. In Alaska."

I looked at the dog, who had his head tilted so far to the right it should hurt. But he didn't seem in pain. Just curious about what his mom was up to as she collected flip-flops and her phone from the shore.

"Bet he loves the snow."

"You have no idea." Her smile caused her blue eyes to sparkle. It made me forget where I was or that my soaked jeans clung uncomfortably to my legs. Or that I really should send Luke that text. Hell, I'm not sure I could recite my full name at the moment.

But I sure wanted to know hers.

Against my better judgment, I asked, "Am I allowed to ask your name, or is that against the serial killer code?"

"That would take all the fun out of it, don't you think?"

She flashed me a flirty look that had *Danger! Danger!* shouting inside my head. I knew all I needed to know. She was a redhead, she was trouble, and she wasn't from here. It was best if I detangled myself now before I did something half-witted—like ask for her number.

I carried the board back toward her Jeep—of course it was red, too—and set it down as she led Husker to the back and hooked his leash on the trailer hitch. "Where's your paddle?"

"What?"

"Don't paddleboards normally come with a paddle?"

"Dammit," she hissed, looking back at the lake. It was too dark to tell if it was floating out there somewhere.

"You're supposed to attach the paddle to your foot, right?"

She held up the aforementioned tether with its Velcro ankle strap. "I took it off."

"I might have an extra one. A paddle, that is."

She glanced back through the trees, where I parked hours ago. "In your truck?"

"No, back at the place where I'm staying." *Shut the hell up, Beckett.*

She let out a laugh, the gentle chime of it almost rusty with disuse. It sent my thoughts spinning, coming up with ways to let her practice.

"Nope," she said, still smiling but also shaking her head. "That's just another thing a serial killer would say to lure me to my death—where there are no witnesses."

"Actually, there would be a lot of witnesses."

It wasn't just Luke's grandparents there. It was Connor and his daughter, too. Though I appreciated my solitude—something Karl's cabin could afford me should I decide to pull the trigger—I thoroughly enjoyed the bustling nature of the quaint homestead the family called a farm. It was crawling with people and chickens alike. Somehow, I suspected it was the last thing she'd want.

"Thanks, but no thanks. It's just a paddle." Red pulled a towel from the back of her Jeep and dried herself off. "I can get another one."

I forced myself to turn all the way around and stare out at the lake. Forced myself to think about anything else other than the way water droplets clung to her skin. For a beat, I pictured the view ahead of me as my own. The way the mountains turned to shadowy silhouettes after the sun was behind them. It was a view I'd get to enjoy every evening. I could easily imagine spending time out here, enjoying the serenity and isolation on what little down-time I might have. Despite my hesitation and the possible walking omen behind me, something about this place felt right.

"You want me to deflate your board?" I asked, deciding Karl wouldn't mind if I slept on the decision, considering his penchant for changing his mind. Besides, it was late enough as it was.

"I appreciate you saving us and all, but really, you can go now." She reappeared at the side of her Jeep wearing a hoodie. She made a subtle, not-so-subtle shooing motion with her hand. "I got it from here."

It was the out any sane man who was eager to avoid a curse would take. I almost did. I started to round her Jeep, headed back toward the cabin for my truck. But then I spotted a giant half-eaten cookie in her front seat. If the interior light wasn't on, I wouldn't have noticed it at all. "atulations ook 25?"

"What?"

"The cookie. Or what's left of it."

Red rolled up her deflated paddleboard and tossed it

into the back of her Jeep. "It's a celebration cookie, if you must know."

"What are you celebrating?"

She opened the back door and Husker hopped right in. "Do you have a towel?" she asked, scanning me up and down. I'd collected my shirt and boots, but I hadn't put them back on. They were piled on the dock, which, I realized as I started to shiver, was a dumb place for them to be.

"Yeah, I'm sure I do." I was pretty sure I didn't.

"You should use it," she said, her gaze lingering on the tattoos on my bare chest. "It's cooling off."

"You sure you're okay? You don't need to get checked out by a doctor or anything?" I didn't even know why the hell I was asking, considering it was clear she was fine and eager to be rid of me. It was only that her rounding the Jeep to her driver's side door felt too final.

I should leave well enough alone. Let her drive away and forget all about the odd encounter. Count my blessings that I remained untangled from a redhead for once in my life.

She hopped into the driver's seat, closing the door but leaving the window rolled down. Husker stuck his head out the partially opened window in the back, staring at me expectantly, as though I should have a treat, or at least, offer him a head scratch.

"Thanks for the assist," she said, cranking the ignition.

"You have somewhere to stay?" The questions sounded desperate, but I couldn't seem to stop them. When she drove away, I might never see her again. Especially if she was just passing through.

Nana would smack me upside the head for prolonging this.

"That's another question a serial killer would ask," she answered with a smile before she backed up and drove away.

I stood on the shore, jeans still soggy, and watched the red Jeep disappear around the wooded bend, into the dusky darkness.

"What a weird fucking night," I mumbled, collecting my T-shirt and boots from the dock. I shot Luke a quick text to fill him in, and save him the trip. I sent one to Nana as well, but I had to reassure her I didn't ask the redhead on a date to keep her from calling back and lecturing me.

The last light on the horizon faded into night. Dozens of stars overhead transformed into hundreds. Then thousands.

Yeah, I could call this place home.

A yawn assaulted me so strongly my eyes watered. I should go. I was exhausted down to my bones, and I had a long day ahead of me tomorrow. I looked out at the peaceful lake one last time and noticed something long and narrow wash up to the shore.

I trekked back down toward the water's edge. Sure enough, a purple paddle that matched the pad of Red's board had wedged itself in the rocky sand.

She and her dog might be miles down the road by now. If I left the paddle on the dock, she might come back and find it.

But because I just couldn't seem to help myself, I carried the paddle back to my truck for safekeeping. At least, that was the lie I told myself.

SIX
KIRA

SIX UNBLINKING BLACK eyes stared at me from the corner of my pillow, four out of eight legs visible and twitching. The last remnants of sleep shredded from my system as I screamed, and the spider leapt away from the crazy lady—aka *me*—who launched said pillow as far across the attic as humanly possible, while wrestling out of a sleeping bag that had seen better days.

My knee banged against the hard floor as I kicked the sleeping bag free, a string of muttered and varied fucks punctuating every panicked breath.

Husker popped to his feet, pacing around me as I frantically searched for the nearest blunt object I could find to take out the hairy-legged demon. There were stacks of boxes everywhere, but not a crowbar to be found.

Hiding out in the bookstore's upstairs apartment for a night had been a risk, but I wasn't ready to face anybody. Not Dad, not my grandparents, and definitely not my brothers. Though Aspen would've taken me in no questions asked, I didn't want to disturb the newlyweds with a late, unannounced visit.

I had the key to the bookstore, as did the rest of my family. It'd been on my keychain since the day Dad distributed them to each kid, shortly after Mom's funeral. I also packed a thermal sleeping bag—perks of having military veteran brothers. One night of roughing it in the old, dusty apartment before I decided who to face first seemed doable.

I didn't think about the *fucking spiders* that would take up residence in the vacant space.

A big, hairy spider that was currently MIA.

"Where'd it go?" I whimpered, spying my flip-flops and snatching one up. I didn't want to sacrifice my favorite pair, but desperate times and all that. Charlotte and whatever web she had going on up here definitely had to go.

Morning twilight bathed the mostly empty space, but it wasn't enough to track down the eight-legged asshole.

To be fair, she probably thought *I* was the asshole for intruding on her cozy, quiet space.

Either way, I wasn't waiting for the sun to fully rise. I needed to be out of here before the bookstore opened.

I had a sinking suspicion that my archnemesis was either lurking inside my sleeping bag or hiding under my second pillow. It would be a lot easier to prove or debunk my theory if I could risk turning on the overhead light. But the moment I did, one of the early-morning coffee drinkers would no doubt notice and call Margene. Or worse, Dad. Spider or no spider, I wanted to stay incognito every minute I could get away with.

Husker looked at me, then at the sleeping bag, then back to me.

"Leave it, Bubbies," I said, quietly but firmly. The last thing I needed was the heart attack I'd surely have if my dog tried to wrestle a wolf spider the size of a damn bowling ball.

I scanned the studio apartment for inspiration, and discovered a yardstick propped against the wall. With it and the flashlight of my phone, I sucked in a deep breath. I scrunched up my face as my pulse raced off the charts, but pretended I was brave—because New Kira could do "hard things"—and poked the yardstick toward the opening of my sleeping bag.

Just as the shaky stick lifted the fabric, thunderous pounding echoed in the empty room.

I screamed again.

Husker paced in circles, whining.

"Police, open up."

"Oh, for fuck's sake," I grumbled, recognizing Luke's *official* tone. I started to call out to him, but then I remembered the door was deadbolted. I didn't need him busting it open and breaking the damn door.

I slipped on my flip-flops, flipped open the deadbolt, and stepped out of the way. I knew my brother would charge into the room like he owned the damn place. He'd been banging on the door like he was prepared to raid a known drug den.

"Calm down, Rambo. It's just me."

"Kira?"

I flipped the light switch on as Husker weaved through the stacks of boxes and rushed my brother, pressing his body against Luke's legs. I had to admit, I wasn't upset that those black uniform pants would be covered in blond fur. To his credit, my brother bent over to give Husker pets. He might be a grumpy pain in my ass most days, but my brother did have his redeeming qualities.

"Why are you here?" Luke asked, his tone an understandable mixture of annoyance and confusion. He scanned the stacks of dusty boxes littered throughout the room, his gaze finally landing on my makeshift sleeping area. I spread a blanket over the floor—only now able to see exactly how dirty it was—and put my sleeping bag on top, leaving room for Husker to curl up beside me.

The spider—Charlie, I decided—chose that moment to scurry out of my sleeping bag and make a beeline for the dark bathroom doorway. Dammit, I really had to pee.

"Why is the bookstore for sale?" I shot out.

"How did you get in?" We were both good at sidestepping the questions we didn't want to answer. It was a dance we did well.

"My key?"

"Dad changed the locks a month ago. Your new key is sitting on his desk." His tone was harsh, and his scowl an accusation.

"You think I broke in." Not a question, because he wasn't asking it.

"I know the place was locked," Luke said, folding both arms over his chest. Most might find the pose intimidating, considering his height and muscular build. But I'd never been rattled by him. Call it emotional calluses from years of handling both my brothers. "I checked it myself."

"I don't know what to tell you. I used the key. Maybe you didn't do a very good job of checking it."

"I check it every night," he said, his words a defensive growl.

"How did you even know I was here?"

I was careful to park a couple of blocks away, in an overflow lot that was filled with local and tourists' cars alike. No one in the family knew about my red Jeep. It was a recent purchase, and I didn't think to text anyone the news. I didn't think anyone would be all that happy for me.

"Silent alarm was tripped."

"Wow, you need to work on your response time."

"I came right over, before you could finish making camp. Did you think no one would find you here when the store opened?"

"Before I could—" I shook my head, already exhausted with my brother. Five minutes had to be a new record. Clearly, my calluses had softened with disuse. "Does it matter if someone finds me here?" I fired back. "There's a reason we have keys."

"*You* don't have a key."

I covered my face with both hands and groaned. I needed an iced coffee stat. It wasn't fair I was being forced to face my brother on low caffeine levels. My lower back ached from a rough night on the floor, my stomach was rumbling, and I felt like I could sleep for two days if everyone would just leave me the hell alone. Why did I keep running into irritating men?

"Can we not do this right now?"

I stuffed the few loose items I had into my duffle,

including the clothes I was wearing when I fell into Ghost Lake. I couldn't decide whether this confrontation was better before or after a near-drowning experience.

I shuddered at the memory of the pondweed wrapping around my foot when I went under. For a moment that felt like an eternity, I was certain I was going to die. That Husker would be floating around solo on a paddleboard, and no one would even know I was in the lake.

"Why are you here, Kira?" Luke asked, his tone gentler.

"You wouldn't understand." I'd tried to tell him once, about my Mom dreams. But he scoffed as if I were crazy.

"Well, whatever the reason, you can't stay here."

"Who put you in charge?"

It was Luke's turn to groan, and he scrubbed a hand over his face.

Small wins.

"I wasn't planning to move in," I said, meaning to lighten the mood.

"Did he hit you?"

"What?"

"Where's The Asswipe?"

It took me several beats to realize my brother meant Travis, and the glacial layer around my heart thawed a sliver.

"We broke up," I told him.

Though Travis never actually hit me, I didn't know what Luke would do if he found out he cocked a fist right at my face the day I came home from Colorado last summer.

"I hope you mean that."

The words hit me like a blow, but I couldn't pretend I didn't deserve it. I lied before when it came to Travis, especially to my family. I thought I was protecting someone I cared about. But it turned out, I was just stupid.

"Why is Dad selling the bookstore?" I tried again as I rolled up my sleeping bag. I had half a mind to leave it behind in case the eight-legged demon invited a friend over when I wasn't looking. Did Charlie have friends, or did she just eat them for a snack?

"You'll have to ask him."

An answer I should have anticipated.

"Right."

"How long you staying?" he asked, arms folded again as he leaned in the doorway. It was obvious he wasn't going anywhere until he followed me out of the building.

"Haven't decided."

"Typical."

Defensiveness rose in my chest, but I forced myself to take a couple of deep breaths before I spoke. My brother knew how to rile me up on the best days. On the days I had shitty sleep and drowning nightmares, I was extra susceptible to his bullshit.

"Want a coffee?" I asked, trying to be the bigger person. Trying to extend an olive branch.

"Why would I want a coffee? I just got off my shift, and I'm fucking wiped. I was almost in bed when—"

"You know what, forget it."

I shouldered my backpack, wedged the sleeping bag under my arm, and clipped on Husker's leash. Luke stood in the doorway, like the roadblock he was, until I glared at him to move. Smart man that he was, he stepped to the side and let me pass.

"Kira?" he called from the top of the stairs.

"Yeah?" I turned to look back at him, hoping he had a change of heart about the coffee. If I could get through to Luke, the rest of the family would be a cakewalk. Or so I hoped.

"If I find out you're lying about Travis—"

I resisted the urge to give my brother the middle finger, mostly on account of not having any free hands, and rushed out the back door.

Maybe coming back was a mistake.

SEVEN
BECKETT

Madeline: Dad didn't show up for court.

I STARED at my phone screen for a long beat, rereading the words a second, and then a third time. Leave it to my sister to skip small talk or any form of pleasantries first thing in the morning. She'd always been a rip-the-Band-Aid off kind of person, even when we were kids. But fuck, this was not the way I wanted to start a day that was already overflowing with to-dos.

"Everything all right, dear?" Connie Weston asked, carrying a full plate of pancakes to the table and setting it in the center. Where Nana was tell-it-like-it-is sassy and full of vinegar, Luke and Connor's grandma was sweet as a peach pie.

I scrubbed a hand over my face, hoping to rub away the frustration that had no place here. "Yeah, just family stuff."

"If there's anything we can do to help, just say the word."

"Thanks."

There wasn't much anyone could do to help when it came to my family, unless they could convince my sister that my parents were a lost cause. I sure as hell couldn't get through to her. Thirty-plus years had proven that.

I took a long sip of coffee, and shot off a quick reply just as Dale joined us at the table.

Beckett: How bad is it?

Madeline: They're being evicted in three days.

I didn't want to care. I spent too many years hoping Dad would get sober and stay that way. Or that Mom would kick him out for good, and stop taking him back. But the cycle never broke. No matter how much Madeline and I tried to intervene, it never mattered. Those two were an inevitable, unavoidable train wreck destined to collide over and over. It was best if we stayed the hell out of the way.

My saint of a sister, however, kept putting herself right in the middle. She still had hope.

I stayed in Richmond until she got engaged to Kyle. My brother-in-law was the best kind of human there was. I owed him a lot. The day after they married, I enlisted in the Army, and got the hell out of Dodge. I'd only been back twice to see their twins. I went no contact with both my parents years ago. Madeline was the only reason I even knew they were alive. And—at least *currently*—out of prison. Dad for DUIs; Mom for writing bad checks. Most days, I really wasn't sure how Madeline and I turned out so normal.

> Madeline: You have any rentals coming available?

Fuck. This was not a conversation appropriate for the Westons' breakfast table. I put my phone face down on the table, and took the offered plate of bacon.

Growing up, breakfast was always cold cereal—if we were lucky enough to have milk in the fridge. Mom only ever made a fuss about meals when she and Dad first reconciled. By the end of one of their toxic cycles, we were lucky if the bowls in the cupboard were still intact.

The Westons had spoiled me these past two months.

"Joe called," Dale said as my phone buzzed. I ignored it. "Said the drywall is in for your latest project."

I was grateful for a shift of focus, allowing a mental to-do list for the Kniffen Street house to run through my head now that the drywall order finally arrived. "Thanks. I can swing by and pick it up while I'm in town today."

"Luke told you about the bookstore?" Connie asked, her expression fragile as she spread butter onto a pancake and slathered it in her homemade strawberry syrup. No one spoke it, but I pieced together that Connie hadn't stepped foot inside her late daughter's bookstore since her passing. I imagined it was too hard, but I didn't know if seeing it sold would be harder.

"He mentioned it yesterday, when we were out at Ghost Lake."

Instantly, the image of the feisty redhead in the wet T-shirt that clung to her skin trespassed across my thoughts. She was wearing a red lace bra underneath. Whether that was true, or now part of the fantasy I conjured up overnight, I was no longer sure. I spent the night tossing and turning, wondering what became of Red and her quirky dog with his sonar-capable ears. With any luck, they were a hundred miles down the road by now, and I'd have nothing more than her purple paddle to assure me the encounter was real.

"What did you think of the cabin?" Dale asked, obviously sensing his wife's uneasiness about the bookstore, and moving the topic away from Joe. I felt like an ass, thinking about a woman I barely knew, instead of extending compassion in this delicate situation.

"It has good bones."

"It's never been updated," Dale pointed out. "It would be another project, if Karl is even willing to sell it. He's been known to change his mind."

"Luke mentioned that."

"You're more than welcome to stay here as long as you like," Connie said, her words almost a plea. "We love having you."

"I appreciate that."

My phone buzzed against the table again, and I shoved it into my jeans pocket without reading the new slew of texts my sister sent. I wasn't going to offer up one of my rentals, but I wasn't ready to have that argument with her, either. She'd beg me to give them a month—to buy them time until they found somewhere else to go. Or she'd offer to pay their rent, though I knew Kyle would quickly put a stop to that idea.

"You sure everything is all right?" Connie asked again.

"Yeah." I didn't share much about my family with anyone. Luke knew more than most, but even he didn't know the brunt of it. I planned to keep it that way. After a lot of thinking last night, I could finally see myself settling in Bluebell Springs, at least for a good, long while. I didn't need to taint that vision with toxic family baggage. "Just some family business. It can wait until after breakfast."

"How's Millie doing this morning?" Connie asked Dale of their rescue cow who'd been limping for the last two days.

"The same. Vet's coming out later to check her out."

I was thankful the breakfast table conversation shifted to farm topics as I cleaned my plate. Connie turned down my offer to wash the dishes, as she did most mornings. I promised to be back this evening for family dinner, and headed into town.

I knew Joe *needed* to sell his late wife's bookstore, but I was equally sure he didn't *want* to. This wasn't going to be an easy conversation.

EIGHT
HUSKER

What's that smell?
Is it popcorn?
It's quiet.
Everyone's sleeping.
I like sleeping.
Who made popcorn?
I like this bed.
I don't want to get up.
But I like popcorn.
And I'm hungry.
Mom left me food, but she didn't put anything good in my bowl.
Maybe I should wake her up.
She's making a funny noise again.
She tells everyone she doesn't snore.
But she does.
Mom, why are you snoring?
Oh! Is that popcorn under the couch?

I should find out.
But I like sleeping.
I'm so tired.
Too comfortable.
I didn't like sleeping on that hard floor.
It was dirty.
And it smelled funny.
Good thing Uncle Luke saved us.
Mom was really afraid.
But she wouldn't let me get the spider.
We're safe now.
I need to eat that popcorn.
Before someone else eats it.
But it's stuck way under the couch.
Can I reach it?
I don't want to get stuck again.
That was scary.
Maybe Uncle Luke put something good in my breakfast bowl.
Should I wake him up?
No, he's too grumpy.
Stupid popcorn.
Wait, I got it!
Chomp, chomp, chomp.
Ooh, butter!
Mom, do you have more popcorn?
Why are you making that funny noise again?
Maybe there's more popcorn in the kitchen.
Mom says I'm not supposed to be in the kitchen.
But this is Uncle Luke's house.
He didn't tell me to stay out of the kitchen.

No popcorn in my breakfast.
Rude, but okay.
I'm hungry.
Chomp, chomp, chomp.
Okay, so this is still pretty good.
Would be better with gravy.
Chomp, chomp, chomp.
Or pizza.
Chomp, chomp, chomp.
It's all gone.
Why is it all gone?
What's that sweet smell?
Oh!
Where's that cookie?
I know Mom brought it with us.
Uh oh.
Mom's snoring louder.
I should wake her up.
To make sure she's okay.
And then she can share her cookie.
I'll use my nose.
Press it right into her cheek.
Yeah, that should work.
Mom, wake up!

NINE
KIRA

IF THERE WAS A BETTER cure for a sour mood than a cupcake from Frosted Peaks, I hadn't found it. Was I over-doing it on the sweets lately? Yes. Yes I was. Did that stop me from heading to Aspen's bakery? No, it did not.

My stomach had been growling since Husker woke me from a desperately needed nap on my brother's couch with a wet nose to the face. Preferable to a fucking spider on my pillow, but still.

Of the two of us, Husker was the only one to have breakfast, as evidenced by his empty travel bowl. Since Luke's fridge was emptier than the ski slopes in July, I left my grumpy brother a note and the remnants of my cele-bration cookie on his kitchen counter as a peace offering.

I was semi-relieved that he went back to bed since grudgingly offering up his shower, and firmly reminding me I needed to find another place to sleep tonight.

Once I worked up the courage to talk to Dad, I'd head to the farm. I suspected Grandma Connie would happily offer up a guest room once she realized Husker was along for the ride. Those two had a special bond. Even if she was sore with me, she'd never turn him away.

But first, cupcakes.

I missed the ability to walk everywhere.

In Bluebell Springs during the height of tourist season, it was faster to walk downtown than navigate the sheer number of people from my car. I'd left the Jeep in the over-flow lot earlier this morning when I walked the few short blocks to Luke's condo.

As soon as I got my hands on one of Aspen's legendary desserts and a desperately needed iced coffee, I'd stop by the hardware store to face Dad.

A bowl filled with water sat outside the bakery, welcoming dogs. Though her cupcakes were the most popular, Aspen made an array of goodies, which included homemade dog treats. At the moment, Husker was the only four-legged customer in line.

"Kira?" Aspen did a double take from behind the counter when she spotted me through a steady crowd of customers.

"Surprise."

She rounded the counter, adorned in an apron covered in sunflowers and flour, and went right for a hug. Instantly, my blood pressure lowered. Of anyone, Aspen had the right to be the angriest with me. And yet, she was the one to keep in touch. To hint at the end of every conversation that it'd be really nice to see me.

Until this moment, I didn't know if she really meant it.

"What are you doing here?" Her elated expression dropped in a heartbeat as she knelt to greet Husker. "The bookstore?"

"You knew?" I asked, trying to hide the hurt in my tone, but certain I failed.

"The sign only went up yesterday. I was going to call you, but one of the ovens went out and it's been a total disaster. I'm so sorry, honey."

"Yeah, me too." I cleared my throat and scanned the crowded shop. "Where's Tango?" I asked of her dog.

"Owen's off today, so they're at home, working on that back deck. Well, Tango is probably supervising. You'll have to see it when it's—"

"Kira Jane Mason, you get over here right this instant and give your Aunt Wendy a hug," Aspen's mom ordered.

I was so thoroughly in my own tiny bubble, shrinking into the background avoiding the overwhelming crowd of strangers, that I didn't even notice Wendy was working today. She moved around the counter with purpose and enveloped me in a solid hug. I melted into her, sucking in a deep inhale. I did not want to lose my shit in the firm but comforting embrace I didn't feel I deserved.

"Does your dad know you're back?" she asked before letting me go from her stranglehold. Husker pressed his weight against her legs the second I moved, but whether he thought he was protecting me from her wrath, or suspected there were treats in her apron pocket, was a toss-up.

"I'm headed there next. Did you know he was going to do it?"

"Yes, sweetie. But he only talked to me night before

last. He didn't call you, did he?" She shook her head and mumbled something under breath about her brother being stubborn. "I told him to call you before the sign went up."

"What happened?" I asked.

Wendy shook her head, the bandana adorned in kittens tied at the top of her head bouncing with the movement. "This isn't my conversation to have. And even if it were, I'm still disappointed in you."

"Mom," Aspen said, her tone a plea.

I felt the onslaught of eyes on us. I didn't recognize anyone in line, but I felt the judgment all the same. I owed Wendy an apology, too, but this wasn't the time or place to get into the nitty-gritty of it all.

"You should be upset with me," I agreed, owning up to my shittiness, despite the intense urge to run out the door and never look back. As much as I wanted to blame Travis for the collateral damage he caused, my actions were my own responsibility. "I'm going to be in town for a few days. Can we grab a coffee soon?"

Wendy's hardened expression softened as she fished a treat out of her pocket, and offered it to Husker. "We can. You still drink iced coffees?"

"I'm pretty sure there's more iced coffee running through my veins than blood these days."

"I'll make you something to-go."

"I want more than a coffee date," Aspen said as Wendy returned to her place behind the counter. The line of customers had grown out the door since I came in, but my dear friend didn't seem in a hurry to dismiss me.

"I'd like that."

"I'm off Friday afternoon. Maybe we could go paddle-boarding?"

Instantly, the image of a certain sexy stranger flashed in my mind. His intense, yet kind hazel eyes. The heavy stubble dusting his chiseled jaw. The tattoos snaking up his left arm and covering his chest—*had there been a black panther?* The water droplets clinging to his sculpted muscles. The way his wet jeans hung low on his hips, revealing—

"Kira?" Aspen's chuckle brought me back to reality.

"Yes. Friday. Sounds great. So great."

"You okay?"

"Yep!" Husker tilted his head at my higher than usual octave. With any luck, I'd never run into the sexy stranger ever again. I wasn't here for that. After everything I went through with the last *sexy stranger* who managed to charm me, I officially swore off men for the foreseeable future. Until I had my own shit together, I didn't need the complication. I didn't *trust* the complication. Maybe I never would again.

"You look good as a redhead," Aspen said. "How long ago did you do that?"

"A couple weeks ago." During our paddleboarding adventure, I'd tell her why. But I could tell by their growing line of customers that it was time for me to scoot. Two women I didn't recognize dashed around behind the registers as though there were rockets on their shoes. There was no chance of Aspen escaping for a short break right now.

"I like it."

"Thanks. Mind if I grab a cupcake to-go?"

"I know just the one you need," Aspen said, her smile genuine.

Wendy set two iced coffees on top of the bakery case as Aspen boxed up a cupcake. "One for your dad."

"Thanks," I said, meaning it, the dread from earlier returning.

"Can I give you a word of advice?" Wendy said.

"Of course."

"Just listen."

Aspen handed me a pink box with the Frosted Peaks logo on top.

"I think this will hit the spot." I nodded. "How much—"

"See you Friday," Aspen said, sending me a warm smile before she returned to the crowd of customers, and all but ignored any attempts to do more than leave a tip in the jar.

Husker zigzagged his way down the sidewalk, weaving between amused tourists as we headed toward an outdoor area with several picnic tables down the block. The only open table was tucked in the far corner near a wall of hedges separating the makeshift community picnic area from an alley, and we made a beeline for it.

First, the cupcake. Second, the hard conversation with my dad.

Husker plopped his butt on the ground, his gaze darting between the box and me. Not to my surprise, Aspen included a couple of her dog-bone-shaped treats, even though she knew I'd share my dessert too.

"Take it nice," I said semi-sternly to Husker.

As if I hadn't said anything, he went in for the chomp too quickly, and I snatched it back.

"What did I say?"

He looked at me, those pitiful brown eyes promising he'd do better if I'd just give him the damn treat already.

This time, he was gentle in his pilfering of the bone-shaped morsel.

I returned my attention to the cupcake—some type of lemon concoction by the look and intoxicating aroma of it —but before I could successfully tug it free from its cardboard holder, a voice from the nearby alley caught my attention. I froze, certain I was hearing things.

"I'm not doing it, Madeline."

Husker perked instantly, popping to all fours as he scanned the area for a voice he recognized as well.

"No fucking way," I murmured.

I didn't have to turn around to know who it was. The gruff baritone voice was the same one I heard when I surfaced from my near-drowning experience last night.

I had pegged him for a tourist, though reassessing that assumption now, I couldn't peg why I thought that, other than he mentioned having a place to stay. He knew how to get to Ghost Lake, on Uncle Karl's hidden road, nonetheless. It'd been a number of years since I called Bluebell Springs home, and even then, I didn't know everyone in town. He might be a transplant, or simply someone who graduated years ahead of me.

"Kyle would never let you do that, and you know it," he continued, gravel crunching beneath heavy, pacing footsteps.

I slowly peeled back the wrapper from my cupcake, and Husker snapped his attention back to me.

"Don't bring the twins into this."

Twins?

Huh. I hadn't pegged him as a dad. I snuck a peek over my shoulder to try it on for size. It would be an incredible imbalance in the universe if this incredibly attractive man was also a father. At least, my readers would certainly think so.

I swallowed away that thought with another bite of cupcake, not ready to face how disappointed they would be when the news about my inability to write eventually reached them.

The man stopped in his tracks, his gaze snagging on mine. My heart skipped a few beats, and messed up a few others. Dammit, those eyes were gorgeous. The *man* was gorgeous.

"I have to go," he said, lowering the phone and ending the call. "Red?"

Husker darted for him, the loose leash I forgot to anchor trailing after him. The sexy stranger knelt to greet my dog like they were old friends. My heart squeezed without permission. Had Travis ever greeted Husker that way? Even once? No. He was too concerned about getting dog hair on his precious fucking pants.

"Everything okay?" I asked, rubbing my thumb along the sweating cup of iced coffee so I had something else to focus on besides the way my dog was practically fawning all over him.

"Yeah. Just family stuff."

"So, you're a dad?" I asked.

"A dad?"

Hell, even his confused expression was attractive. If I had any sense, I'd pack up my cupcake breakfast and head straight for the hardware store. Facing my own father seemed less intimidating now that I was again in the orbit of my reluctant hero. Though I hadn't actually needed saving from drowning, I did need saving from myself. Little did Mr. Sexy Stranger know, but I was on the verge of a panic attack. One averted because of him.

"Is it just the two kids, or are there a bunch more?"

"I don't have any kids."

"Are the twins code for something?" Maybe I misunderstood. I was a romance author, after all. I was certain at least one of my heroes had used twins in the context I was now implying. Except, they were excited, not irritated as he was a minute ago. "Never mind."

"Oh, ha." A smile broke across his lips, and my breath caught in my throat. That smile should be against the law. "My niece and nephew are twins. I was talking to my sister."

"Madeline?" I guessed.

"How much of the conversation did you overhear exactly?" he asked, rubbing a hand at the back of his neck. His easy expression hardened a fraction.

"Not much."

"Cupcake for breakfast?" He nodded at my dessert. "You really do love your sweets, don't you?"

I tensed, my body instantly ready for battle over the criticism. "You have something against sweet treats?"

His eyes flashed wide for a beat, and I realized my tone was quite harsh. *Perceived criticism, Kira. Perceived.* I really needed to work on my defensive reactions, and toning them the hell down. It'd been a reflex for so long, that undoing it was proving difficult.

"I love sweets," he offered.

I studied him—his tone, his expression, his posture. All pointed to casual, and most importantly, genuine. My racing heart rate lowered.

"Sorry," I said, my eyes dropping to Husker, who leaned against the sexy stranger's legs, taking in all the booty scratches he could get from his new best friend. "You want to try a bite?"

"Oh, I know it's good," he said, waving off my offer. "I've sampled pretty much every flavor over the past couple of months."

Maybe I hadn't been all that off about him, though that didn't explain how he knew about the private road to Ghost Lake.

"You new to town?"

"Assessing how many people will miss me if you chop my body up into little pieces?"

His eyes twinkled with amusement, and dammit if my pulse didn't skip and stutter.

My gaze snagged on a tattoo peeking out of his shirt sleeve. It reminded me of a military crest, but I looked away when he caught me staring.

"How do you know that's my method of choice?"

He caught Husker's loose leash in his palm, and walked him back to the table, offering me the handle. I reached for it, and his fingertips grazed my skin. I sucked in a breath at the contact that had no business causing the delightful tingles that skittered up my arm. It awakened nerve endings I thought might remain dormant the rest of my life.

"The way you're so protective over what you care about most tells me you'd be a little vengeful if provoked."

"Are you planning to provoke me?"

The words slipped out without permission, laced with flirtation. I was surprised how the urge to take them back didn't come. Since the Big Breakup, I shut down at any male attention. All of it made me wish to be invisible. But with this man and his twinkling hazel eyes, heart-stopping smile, and delicious cologne that promised to be better than my cupcake, I realized I wanted to be seen.

I watched in rapt attention as one corner of his mouth lifted in amusement. I bet those lips could do amazing things.

"Maybe I am."

A chipmunk scurried across a boulder. Husker yanked on the leash, ready to launch himself in pursuit like a furry missile. My arm went swinging.

Right into the two iced coffees.

Mr. Sexy Stranger had the quick reflexes to jump back, out of the path of destruction. But that didn't save my lap. I hopped off the picnic bench with a quick scream of shock, coffee and ice cubes flying off my thin leggings in every direction. Husker's leash had rubbed my wrist raw, but at least he hadn't run off into traffic after that damn chipmunk.

"Husker," I scolded.

He whimpered once, his head whipping back and forth between me and where the chipmunk had vanished.

"Get over here," I said, quietly but firmly. This time, he listened.

"I really need to carry a towel if I'm going to keep running into you," Mr. Sexy Stranger said, his tone both flirty and apologetic. "I can run and get you some napkins—"

"It's okay." I shook my head, brushing off the loose liquid from my clothes with bare hands.

This was what I got for flirting with the opposite sex. It was as though the universe were scolding me. Didn't I learn my lesson when it came to strange handsome men who were capable of making up any story they wanted about their life? Charming men who pretended to be everything you were looking for, until they had you good and snared in their web?

"He has a thing for chipmunks, I take it?"

"Squirrels or squirrel-like critters, yes. Whatever it is, it's personal." I picked up the empty cups and carried them to a nearby trash receptacle. Guess I wasn't going to see Dad this morning after all. "C'mon, Bubbies."

"You're leaving?" Mr. Sexy Stranger called after me.

"Yep."

"Without saying goodbye?"

"Yep," I answered over my shoulder.

"Can I at least get your number?"

"That's something a serial killer would ask."

"Or a man who's interested," he fired back.

At the corner, we locked gazes. Before I could do something reckless, like give in to his simple request, I sent him a flirty wave and disappeared behind the building, rushing back to my Jeep.

TEN
BECKETT

"This'll have to be the last one for this round," Joe Mason said, shimmying a sheet of drywall onto the high stack in the bed of my heavy-duty truck.

We were both sweating our asses off after hauling this out the back of the hardware store and into my truck. The humidity in Bluebell Springs was far lower than I was used to, but once that sun came up over the mountains, everything warmed up fast. I wished this was all there was, but the Kniffen Street house was a gut job. I'd have to come back tomorrow to get the rest.

I went around the side of my truck to fish tow straps from the built-in toolbox, catching sight of something purple tucked beneath it.

Red's paddle.

Red.

She caught me off guard this morning, right in the middle of an argument with Madeline. As I suspected, my sister begged me to put my parents up in one of my rentals, and she did her homework to know which one was currently sitting empty. Madeline was a pain in the ass when she set her mind to something, which explained the dozens of text messages and two voicemails since this morning's *discussion*—including one from my brother-in-law.

Seeing Red eating a cupcake with her dog eased some of the tension. For those few minutes, I forgot all about my headache-inducing family.

Until Husker spotted a chipmunk and iced coffee went everywhere.

I really needed to stop running into Red in wet clothes. Lake water. Iced coffee. It didn't seem to matter. Fuck, would it be a torrential downpour next? All possibilities were responsible for showcasing the shape of her perfectly curvy body, and left my imagination running wild. I tried to convince myself it'd be different if she were a brunette or a blonde, but I suspected that was a bullshit lie.

Something about that woman had my full attention.

A woman with a red Jeep and Nebraska plates who I might never see again.

"I'm going to grab you a box of drywall screws."

Joe slipped inside the back door of the store before I could tell him I already had plenty, so I set to work on the tow straps. The trip to the Kniffen Street house was a short drive from here, but it was up a steep hill. I wasn't risking any of the drywall falling out on the three-minute trip over.

"That's everything," Joe said upon returning. "Got enough straps?"

"Yeah, plenty."

"My boys helping you out with this?" Joe asked, leaning his arms against the side of my truck as I tightened the straps.

"Tomorrow."

"Good. Glad you have some help."

I could tell Joe was stalling, but I didn't want to push him into a conversation about his late wife's bookstore if he wasn't ready. I checked all the ratchets once more to buy him time.

He pulled off his ball cap and scrubbed a hand through his thick silvering hair. He'd been infantry; growing out his hair now was a point of pride. He wore it well, except when he was stressed. His finger combing often left it standing on end until his ball cap tamed it back down.

"You're here about the bookstore, right?" he asked.

"I am."

"I don't have a price yet," he admitted. "Waiting to hear back from the appraiser. Might be a couple days, but could be early next week."

"You're skipping a realtor, then?"

"I already talked to Owen," he said of Aspen's husband. "It's an expense I'd rather not add to the list. He understands. But if you want to utilize him, I'm not opposed."

I'd only purchased one other commercial property to date, with Owen's help. Nana might smack me upside the head for it, but I could figure this one out on my own. The end result would be a better, stronger relationship with a family that meant a great deal to me. It would firm those roots I so badly wanted to put down.

"You sure you want to sell it?" The entire family was pretty tight-lipped about the whole thing. I couldn't begin to guess what prompted this decision, and I didn't ask. It wasn't any of my business. But the weary expression on Joe's face suggested finances were at play.

"Want to? No." Joe shook his head. "Don't exactly have a choice, though. So, if you want it, I'm offering you first right of refusal."

"Why me?"

"I know you'll do a good job with what needs fixing up. You'll do it *right*."

"There's no one else in the family who wants it?" I was pushing here, and I knew it. This felt like the same conversation I had with Luke yesterday about the cabin. I just didn't understand how no one seemed to care about keeping family things in the family. If I had the kind of tight-knit family they did, I'd hold on tight to them. Maybe Joe sensed that about me. Trusted I'd take care of the bookstore as though it were a family heirloom, regardless of what it became once I leased it to a new tenant.

"It's too far gone to burden anyone with now."

I waited, giving Joe the chance to decide whether he wanted to fill me in or not. I wouldn't push any more than I already had.

"I have a daughter who's an author. Did you know that?"

"I didn't know she was an author," I admitted, trying to place her name but failing. Kayla? Kendra? Something with a K. I always thought of her as snake-girl.

"She isn't interested in coming back here, though," Joe said, his expression hardening a little more. "She made that pretty clear last time I saw her."

Another thing the family was tight-lipped about.

"Well, if you're sure, I'm definitely interested in seeing the place."

"We can do a walk-through this week, with the appraiser."

"I look forward to it."

"You just have to promise me you won't lease it to any of those fucking gift shoppers with their cheap-ass trinkets. Those money-hungry city slickers are only interested in exploiting tourists. Brenda wouldn't have wanted that."

"You have my word."

"You're one of us now, so I'm holding you to it."

One of us.

I made the decision to move to Bluebell Springs just over three months ago.

I'd been visiting my Army buddies after that disaster with Amy—aka the last redhead I inadvertently got tangled up with. Though to be fair, I did my best to steer clear of her from day one. My troubles with her were all because I *wouldn't* go out with my boss's daughter. Rejection activated a special kind of vengeance in her toward me. But not like any of that fucking mattered now. She left me no choice but to walk away from a life I considered quite comfortable.

Another reason I should know better than to ask another redhead for her phone number. What the hell had I been thinking this morning? It didn't matter that Red didn't give it up. She'd been flirting with me, and I liked it. Too damn much.

I shook away the thought as I finished securing the drywall.

What was supposed to be a long weekend away earlier this spring turned into the decision to relocate to the small lakeside Colorado community near friends I considered family. *Real* family. The kind of family who had your back, no matter what.

I was no stranger to collecting income properties. I had a few in Richmond, and a handful more in Fayetteville, outside the base. But this would be different. I wasn't buying some random house in a city too large for anyone to care. Each transaction could be taken personally, in a town that boasted a population just shy of a thousand. This was more than just business.

"Let Connor know I can put that tile order in whenever he's ready to get started on that bathroom remodel," Joe said, closing the tailgate after I hopped down.

"You're not coming over for dinner tonight?"

"Afraid not. I have a phone call to make. Let Connie know?"

"She won't be happy," I said, half teasing to lighten the mood. But Connie Weston took skipping the weekly family dinner as a personal offense. I learned that the hard way, the first week I stayed with them.

"She'll understand this one."

I nodded.

That was my cue to leave. To head back over to the Kniffen house and offload this drywall before the threat of a late afternoon rain shower came to pass. But I couldn't seem to help myself.

"Do you know anyone in town with a red Jeep? A redheaded woman with a dog?"

"Doesn't ring a bell. Why?"

"Just want to return something she lost." It'd been a long shot. The Jeep had out-of-state plates. It stood to reason she was a tourist, but I couldn't shake away one detail: she knew how to get to Ghost Lake, and she seemed quite comfortable out there.

"I'll keep an eye out."

"She might be gone by now," I said, waving away the question as I hopped into the driver's seat. "She had Nebraska plates."

"Nebraska?" Joe asked, his attention snapping to me as I closed the door and hung an arm out the open window. "With a dog? Almost sounds like . . . But a redhead, you said?"

"Yeah."

"Never mind. Wrong person." Joe lifted his ball cap once more and scrubbed a hand through his hair. "I'll give you a call about that walk-through. Might be able to squeeze it in tomorrow."

I nodded, and headed for the Kniffen Street house, eager for the manual labor that would help me avoid my sister's annoying persistence. I'd work until I had to head to the farm for family dinner. With any luck, the sun would set after I successfully avoided any and all red Jeeps.

ELEVEN
KIRA

"Husker, stop stealing my asparagus!" Grandma Connie scolded—not that she meant it. And Husker knew it, as evidenced by the way he trotted off with the stalk he pilfered from her picked pile and lay down in the grass to munch away on his treasure.

I didn't bother intervening. What was the point? That dog didn't listen to a damn thing I had to say when Grandma Connie was around.

"All that dog hears is *free treats*," Grandpa chimed in, plucking weeds from the vegetable garden with a hoe.

God, it was good to be back.

After the iced coffee incident, I decided it might be best to secure my room at the farm—and another shower. Dad would be over tonight for the weekly family dinner, and I could talk to him then. We'd go for a walk around the property, away from distractions and my nosy brothers.

"When did you get the new Jeep?" Grandma Connie

asked, tossing a few more stalks of asparagus into her bucket.

"Last winter."

"Looks expensive," Grandpa said.

I tensed, ready to defend my frivolous purchase. My family knew I wrote books, but they didn't know under what name. Because I wrote paranormal romance, no one pressed me too hard for information. I was okay with that. But I still felt awkward admitting those books afforded me a very comfortable life, as though I somehow found a glitch in the matrix and happened upon success I didn't quite deserve.

"Get off her back, Dale," Grandma Connie said. "Means the girl is doing well. I'm proud of you, honey."

"Thank you." The compliment felt like a warm hug I didn't know I needed. I was embarrassed that I thought my family would be so upset with me that I wouldn't be welcome home. I was so over being afraid of worst-case scenarios. I wondered if that fear would ever go away. "I can take you for a ride later?"

"Ride?" Grandma Connie shook her head. "I want to drive it."

"What do you know about driving a Jeep?" Grandpa asked her.

"More than you're giving me credit for."

"If she drives your Jeep into the lake, don't come crying to me," Grandpa said.

"What reason would I have for driving a perfectly good car into a body of water?"

"Ask me that again when Connor's towing you out. Because it won't be me."

Their back-and-forth banter was soothing. They liked to jab at one another, but it was never in malice. Their voices never raised. Their tone always hinted at playfulness. They'd send each other off with a kiss before one walked away.

For a long time, I convinced myself that was what Travis and I did. We bantered. But when the bickering turned to all-out screaming matches, I couldn't seem to remember how it happened. One day everything was the storybook version of the love I always wanted. The next, it was a special kind of hell I didn't know how to escape.

"Kira?" Grandpa called, as though he'd said my name more than once and I missed it.

"Yeah?"

"You still writing books, then?" he asked, his tone gentler than before.

"Just published one yesterday, actually." A non-answer was better than an outright lie. Or the truth. Because if I admitted to anyone that the words had dried up and shriveled into nothingness, they'd worry more than they already did.

"*Huh.*"

Husker trotted over from his spot in the shade and sniffed around Grandma Connie's bucket. Before I could warn him off, she tossed him an offering. He refused eye contact with me as he tracked it down.

"We should cook steaks to celebrate," Grandma Connie suggested. "Probably too late to pull them out of the freezer for tonight. But we'll do that before you leave. How long are you staying?"

"At least through the weekend." I wasn't in a hurry to

head back to Omaha. Other than Lila, all that waited for me there was a writing desk void of sticky notes, an apartment I no longer enjoyed, and a bunch of bad memories. "Maybe a little while longer."

"You *have* to stay longer," Grandma Connie insisted. "The book club's meeting next week. I know they'd love to have you."

A heavy silence fell over the conversation. I wanted to ask, but I already tried that when I first showed up. Apparently, everyone had formed a consensus. The only person who was going to fill me in was Dad.

"Husker, don't do it," I called to my dog when I noticed him sizing up a chipmunk perched on top of a boulder across the yard. I'd granted him off-the-leash privileges because I knew he wouldn't stray far from the garden where his favorite snacks were kept. At least not while Grandma Connie was there to schmooze.

Unless a squirrel-like creature was involved.

"Bubbies," I said, my tone another warning.

He darted a look at me then refocused on the chipmunk.

Abandoning my weed-picking post, I reached for the leash . . . but I wasn't fast enough. Husker sprinted after the chipmunk as though it represented the Iditarod finish line.

I held my breath as the Alaskan Husky came within inches of clipping the tail of a really pissed off chipmunk, seconds before it scampered under a giant boulder. Husker stood near the base, looking quite proud of himself as his tail wagged in earnest at my approach.

"C'mon, Bubbies," I said, reaching for his collar.

But before I could successfully clip the leash on, his head snapped to something else entirely, and he bolted.

"This is your fault, you know," I said to the chipmunk in hiding.

I spun on my heel, prepared to run in case he'd spotted a chicken on the loose. Connor would not be pleased if Husker terrorized one of his precious hens. But it wasn't a chicken. It was my eight-year-old niece, Opal.

Her laughter rang out as she dropped to the ground and Husker smothered her with kisses.

"She must taste like bacon," Grandpa said, shaking his head.

"Probably pizza," I said.

Husker looked right at me, expectantly.

I held up my hands to show my dog I did not, in fact, have any pizza on me. His ears were extra sensitive to that word. Convinced I was telling the truth, he resumed his obsessive licking of Opal. She was the only one he willingly gave a kiss to. And I'd resorted to begging.

"Dale, why don't you order us some pizzas for tonight?" Grandma Connie said. "I can make lasagna another night."

"Husker, let the girl breathe," I said.

Opal giggled some more as she pushed back to her feet and sprinted for me. She attacked me in a hug, her tiny arms wrapping around my waist and squeezing surprisingly hard for an eight-year-old. I nearly went backwards. "Aunty Kira, I'm so glad you came."

"It's good to see you, kiddo."

Husker circled us a few times, until he spotted my middle brother.

"Kira?" Connor's confusion was warranted. But at least he, the peacekeeper in our family, was bound to be nicer about my surprise visit than Luke.

"Hey, Connor."

After Husker got all the booty scratches out of Connor he could, he returned to Opal's side to lick one of her hands again. She giggled, and the two trotted off toward Grandma Connie and her asparagus bucket.

"I didn't know you were coming," Connor said, sounding almost hurt.

"I didn't tell anyone."

"Everything okay?"

I studied him, searching for any sign that he was still peeved with me. I'd said some hurtful things to him, too. But his eyes held only compassion.

"Want to take a walk?"

"I need to check on the chickens," he said, his statement an invitation.

After I secured Husker to a long lead and Opal promised to keep him out of trouble, I followed my brother toward the chicken coop that stood in the middle of the two houses on the expansive property. Aside from the rescue cow, Millie, the chickens were the only animals on the piece of land we'd all called *the farm* since we were kids. And they were new, within the past few years. It was Grandma Connie's gigantic garden, more than anything, that gave this place the feeling of a farm. I couldn't remember which of us kids had started the nickname the entire family adopted.

The chickens were Emily's idea. My late sister-in-law had designed the elaborate chicken coop that resembled a hobbit house the year before she passed, and I knew Connor would never change it.

"I'm sorry for all the terrible things I said last summer," I said, before I lost my nerve. "I was in a bad place. It's not an excuse. I just—"

"Travis gone?"

"I broke up with him that night," I admitted.

"You didn't say anything."

"Oh, I did."

I gulped a swallow, feeling a fresh wave of anxiety threaten to undo me. I was done crying over this shit. At least, I really wanted to be. I watched as he grabbed a basket for the eggs just outside the enclosure, and then followed him as he crouched through the circular door just to navigate it. Emily had been nearly a foot shorter than him and used to tease him about being a giant.

"I said all kinds of things. I just didn't say any of it well."

"I figured the breakup was a recent thing, considering the hair."

I combed my fingers through my long hair, tucking it behind my ear. Travis hated me as anything other than a platinum blonde. Dyeing my hair red was the latest silent middle finger I gave him, right after he changed his number yet again and gave me another thing to block. Not that he ever knew it. But it felt good, all the same.

"The hair was a more recent decision."

"You're really done with the guy?"

"I've been no contact for almost a year."

It didn't mean Travis respected that boundary. He blew up my phone with hundreds of text messages at first, saying anything and everything to get my attention. Eventually, I found the courage to block his number. But he still found creative ways to bother me. Most recently, he Venmoed me fifty dollars for my birthday. I used it to buy a steak dinner, and then blocked him there, too.

"Are you okay?" Connor finally asked.

The question nearly broke me, but I pulled back the tears before they could fully form.

"What I care about more is, are *we* okay?"

Connor collected an egg, looking back at me as he placed it in the basket. "We're family, Kira. We were always okay."

I wanted to hug him, but I didn't trust the chickens. I preferred to wait outside the coop in the enclosure, where it was safe. The hens and I had a complicated relationship, on account of me being Husker's mom.

"I really am sorry."

"You done apologizing?" he asked, coming back out with a dozen eggs in his basket, and closing the rounded coop door behind him.

"Yeah, I guess I am."

"Good."

I glanced back across the spacious yard—some grassy, some rocky—that separated our grandparents' large log cabin and Connor's smaller three-bedroom home. Husker was behaving himself, sitting like a sphinx beside the garden with Opal. Grandma Connie tossed something to him, and he caught it. Opal's laughter echoed softly. She'd grown so much in the past year. She was at least two inches taller, her hair longer. I made a silent vow not to wait so long between visits ever again.

"How have you been?" I asked Connor.

"Come on, Kira. Is that what you really want to ask me?"

"I'd ask if you knew why Dad was selling the bookstore, but I'm guessing you're not allowed to tell me, either."

"Margene." He answered so quickly, I hardly had time to register he did anything other than blow me off.

"Margene? Is she buying it?" Margene was the bookstore manager who took over after Mom's passing.

"Buying it?" Connor shook his head as he set the basket of eggs just inside the back door of his house. "More like robbed it clean."

"What?"

"She's been stealing from the bookstore for years," Connor said, heading back toward the family garden. "It's on the verge of bankruptcy. So, go easy on Dad, okay? He has his hands tied here."

Halfway back to the garden, my phone rang. I shivered at the name on the screen.

"It's Dad."

"You should probably take it."

I hung back, swiping to answer the call just as a black truck pulled in. It seemed vaguely familiar, but everyone in this town either drove a truck or a Jeep-like vehicle. Probably just some local wanting to chat it up with Grandpa. I turned away to focus on the call.

"Hey, Dad."

"Kira, there's no easy way to say this, so I'm going to come right out and tell you."

"I know."

"What's that?" he asked.

"I know you're selling the bookstore."

"You do?" He let out a heavy sigh, and I felt the weight of his decision echo. If Connor hadn't given me a heads up, I might've gone off on him and made this so much worse.

"Yeah. I'm in town, actually. Are you coming to family dinner at the farm tonight? We could talk after—"

"Maybe it's better if you and I have a chat by ourselves. How about I pick up a couple of steaks and you come on over to the house?"

"Yeah, okay. I'll be over in half an hour?"

"See you then."

I stood frozen for several beats. Something about his tone at the end left me with an overwhelming sense of dread. I had a feeling I wouldn't much care for this conversation. But I'd come all this way, at Mom's beckoning. The least I could do was hear him out.

As I approached the garden to ask Grandma Connie if she'd keep an eye on Husker, I noticed Connor greet the man in the black truck. Maybe he was a delivery guy?

"Who—"

"I'll watch Husker," Opal said, as though I asked her to do just that. I looked at her, wondering if she'd developed a mind reading ability in the past year.

"Thank you, Opal." I looked at Grandma Connie and added, "I'm going to head over to Dad's."

"Probably a good idea."

"Don't feed him too much P-I-Z-Z-A," I said to both of them as I followed everyone inside the house. Husker went straight for the kitchen—no surprise there. "And absolutely no onions."

"I ordered the supreme without them," Grandma Connie reassured me.

I washed my hands, grabbed my keys, and headed to my Jeep.

"Hey, Kira," Connor called to me, waving his arm from the opposite side of the black truck.

Though I planned to stop by and pick up Dad's favorite local brew on the way to his place, I was still running early. Maybe Connor had some more advice to give me before I walked into this heavy conversation. It was worth hearing him out, so I walked over.

"I can't remember. Have you met Beckett?"

When my eyes locked on the other man, my heart stuttered a few beats. It was Mr. Sexy Stranger.

"You again," I said, shaking my head in amusement. Because, of course it was too much to hope I'd be able to steer clear of this mysterious man who kept popping up everywhere I went. Including my family's farm.

"Red?"

"It's Kira," I said, admitting defeat.

"I should've known that was you," he said, nodding toward my Jeep.

"You two have met?" Connor guessed, his eyebrows drawn in confusion.

"We've run into each other," I admitted, my gaze still locked with Beckett's. God, even his name was sexy.

"You must be the author."

I snapped my gaze to him, instantly feeling uncomfortable that he possessed that knowledge when he only just learned my name. My heart rate spiked before I could stop it. It took several beats for the irrational paranoia to pass. If he was friends with Connor, it wasn't impossible to think I came up in conversation at some point. Connor bragged about his family more than any of us. I willed my pulse to chill the fuck out, silently cursing Travis for the tenth time today.

"And you must be?"

"He served with us," Connor explained. "Beckett Campbell?"

"*You're* Campbell?" My brothers had always referred to their *fourth musketeer* by his last name. They talked about him all the time, especially during deployment calls. I'd never seen his face, but in many ways, I felt as if I knew him. I didn't know what to do with that information now.

"Afraid I am. Is that a bad thing?"

I remembered how observant Beckett was out at the lake. Suddenly, it made a lot more sense. He had military training.

"Guess you're not a serial killer after all," I said, letting out a single laugh.

Connor gave me a funny look, but it was Beckett's amused smile that captured most of my attention. Just because he was no longer a complete stranger did not mean this was okay. If anything, it made Beckett Campbell completely off-limits. Probably for the best, considering I was still a certified train wreck. Though my wandering eyes—that were currently sneaking up-and-down glances of the man in his dusty jeans and tight-fitting shirt—hadn't yet gotten the memo.

Beckett shrugged. "Sorry to disappoint you."

"Did I miss something?" Connor asked as Luke's police cruiser came up the driveway. Definitely my cue to leave.

Beckett and I shared a conspiratorial glance that seemed to say *I won't tell if you won't tell.*

"Not really," I said.

"I can assure you that your new roommate is not a serial killer," Connor said. He also said something about him being a helluva guy, but I didn't make much out after the word *roommate.*

"I better go," I said, turning on my heel and power walking to my Jeep, suddenly desperate to get off the farm as quickly as possible.

Roommate.

Well, shit.

TWELVE
BECKETT

HEADLIGHTS SLICED THROUGH THE DARKNESS, illuminating the gravel drive. Husker perked from his spot beside my camping chair as the fire crackled in the metal pit I'd been poking at for the past hour, unable to sleep.

"I think your mom's home," I said to the dog.

I had another long day ahead of me tomorrow, considering I didn't get to half the things on my list today. But despite my best efforts, sleep eluded me. I was still in mild shock. Red was Luke and Connor's little sister. Red was the girl who threw snakes right back at her brother without an ounce of fear. I scrubbed a hand over my face, wondering how she felt about this recent revelation. Wondering why the hell I cared.

It shouldn't be a big deal. If anything, it should be the reminder I needed to steer clear. Redhead or not, she was clearly off-limits now that I knew who she was.

And yet, somehow, that made her all the more enticing.

I added *talk to Karl about the cabin ASAP* to my mental to-do list. The damn thing was a mile long, but this particular item would need to move to the top before the redheaded curse struck and ruined yet another good thing.

The Jeep's engine quieted, and Kira pushed open her door. Husker tilted his head at that severe angle again, which made those damn ears seem taller somehow. I couldn't help but chuckle. He did that a lot over dinner, using those big doe eyes and quirky head tilt to sucker almost everyone out of some of their pizza. Including me.

Kira Mason hopped out of her Jeep, headed straight for us. The sliver of moonlight was not enough to illuminate her face, but the gentle flames of the fire were.

Even exhausted, she was beautiful.

And totally off-fucking-limits, I reminded myself.

"Hope he hasn't been too much trouble," Kira said as Husker ran up to her, tail wagging uncomfortably close to the firepit. Though it had a lid, flames licked up from the openings. Kira noticed immediately and repositioned him.

"We've just been chilling."

We'd been outside for over an hour. Though Husker was sleeping at the foot of Connie's bed when I slipped downstairs, he trailed after me when I headed toward the back door. I clipped on the leash that Kira left in the mudroom.

I'd never had a dog of my own, but I always wanted one.

"I'm surprised Opal didn't steal him tonight."

"She tried," I said. "But one of Connor's hens got out—"

"Bubbies!" Kira said, her tone both a scold and a laugh.

"He didn't catch it," I added. "But it was enough to make Connor more than a little sore at him."

"Not surprised." She looked up at me. "Guess everyone is asleep?"

"Yeah."

"Grandpa passed out in his recliner?"

"With reruns of *M*A*S*H* playing? Yep."

We shared a smile, and dammit if my heartbeat didn't skip. There was something about this redhead that just messed with my internal workings. I barely knew her, but now that the connection was made, I realized I knew her a lot better than I should. Her brothers talked about her all the time while we served. She was a part of their childhood stories, woven into their history.

"Have a seat," I offered.

She wrapped her arms around her chest, revealing a hint of shape beneath the oversized sweatshirt that hung nearly to her knees. I couldn't quite make out the words on the front of it, but it had something to do with being a writer and the warning that came with it.

"I really should get to bed."

"Your bed's not going anywhere."

What was I doing?

She glanced down at Husker, then at a chair next to mine, and finally, she came closer and sat. Husker circled her chair and ended up in the gap between our seats.

"I'd offer you a beer, but I don't drink."

She ran her hand along the back of Husker's neck. "I wouldn't accept it if you did."

"I thought we were past the serial killer accusations," I teased, poking a stick through one of the larger openings in the grate to move around the burning sticks and keep a healthy space between us. Husker helped, but I didn't know if that'd be enough to ward off the magnetic pull that seemed to exist between us.

"I don't drink. Anymore."

I wanted to ask why. Hell, I wanted to ask a whole lot more than that, but I sensed her hesitation. Instead, I offered up a piece of my story I rarely shared, hoping it would put her at ease.

"My dad's an alcoholic," I said. "It made him mean and unpredictable."

"So you've never touched a drop?" she guessed.

"I wish I could say that." I let out a heavy sigh and sat back in the chair, gazing up at the star-filled sky. It wasn't as though I'd never seen a night sky like this one, but until Colorado, I'm not sure I ever appreciated the peace it offered. I had the overwhelming urge to share everything with Red, but the good sense not to. "I haven't touched a drop since my first deployment. Ten years ago."

"Do you miss it?" she asked.

"No."

"I don't miss it, either. But it's only been a year." She stole a side glance at me I pretended not to notice, as though waiting for me to admit I knew something about her. I was curious, but offered up nothing. She went on. "I don't think I'll ever miss it, either. There's something incredibly freeing about that, you know?"

"Yeah," I agreed.

Because I did know. My father was a prisoner of alcohol, among other things. I wondered many times what his life would have become if he'd been able to control his drinking. Been able to stop after *just one beer* like he said so many times. Maybe we could have been the happy family I always wanted.

But despite the disease I knew it was to him, he had a choice to give in or to fight it. He chose not to fight it.

"What about your sister?" Kira asked.

"She drinks socially. Or she did, before the twins."

"How old are they?"

"Just turned four. Lexi and Liam." I nearly pulled my phone from the pocket of my flannel jacket to show her the latest picture of them, but I caught myself before my fingers wrapped around it. It was better if we kept things as impersonal as possible. I didn't know how long Kira would be in town. I learned over dinner that she resided in Omaha, and surprised everyone with her unannounced visit. I just had to survive the few days she was here without doing something reckless.

"Your mom?"

"You ask a lot of questions," I said, firing her earlier accusation from the lake back at her. It came out flirtier than I intended, but that didn't seem to stop me from flashing her a half smile.

She tucked her knees beneath the oversized sweatshirt, her painted toes dangling from the edge of the chair. I still couldn't make out what the words said because she kept her arms wrapped around the front of it.

"It's only fair," she said.

"How's that?"

"You know my entire family."

"I just met most of them a couple months ago."

"I haven't met any of yours."

"You're not missing much. I mean, Madeline and her family are great. But my parents . . ."

I let the sentence trail off as I stared into the dancing flames. A silence fell over our conversation as I reached down to stroke the back of Husker's neck. A silence that I feared might give Red a reason to call it a night and leave me outside alone. I threw out another question.

"Where did you sleep last night?"

"What?"

"Last night. You weren't here."

"It's a long story."

"I'm not in a hurry." The words seemed to spill out of their own accord, too quickly for me to decide whether or not I should actually speak them. "But if you're tired—"

"I am," she said, freeing her legs from the inside of her sweatshirt and slipping her feet back into the rose-gold flip-flops at the foot of her chair. I could make out the beginning of the tattoo that snaked around her right calf. Some type of purple flower peeked out from the hem of her leggings.

"C'mon, Bubbies. We should get to bed," she said to Husker, bending to reach for the leash. Her fingers brushed against mine, and we both froze at the electrifying contact. I knew she felt it too, or she wouldn't be staring back at me.

My gaze dropped to her lips. I sucked in a breath when her tongue slipped out to wet them. Her fingertips rested atop my hand, alerting every nerve ending in my body. Oh, this woman was trouble all right. Trouble I wanted to get intimately acquainted with, consequences be damned.

A wet nose wedged itself under my arm hard enough to make it jerk away from the arm of my chair.

The moment shattered with the contact.

Husker stared at me, as though asking why I stopped petting him. And then he stood, backing his rear end against my legs with a shove.

Kira let out a soft laugh, standing and tucking her hands into the front pocket of her hoodie. I finally made out the embroidered words. *Do not annoy the writer. She may put you in a book and kill you.*

"He wants booty scratches."

"Is that what this means?" I asked Husker, obliging.

"It's only second to belly rubs."

"And pizza?" I guessed.

Husker snapped his head at me, those giant eyes staring expectantly.

"You said it," Kira said, holding up her hands to alleviate herself of any guilt.

"So you *are* a serial killer, but only in your books?" I guessed.

Kira slid me a sly smile, those blue eyes twinkling against the firelight.

"Trying to find out the hard way?"

"Do you write murder mysteries?"

"Not exactly," she said. "But I have been known to kill off characters who had it coming."

"The cookie," I said, a sudden revelation dawning as Husker trotted back to her side.

"What?"

"You were celebrating. It said, '*Congratulations on your 25th Book*', didn't it?"

She crouched down to scoop up the leash. When she stood, her devious gaze flickered to mine.

"Maybe."

I knew I nailed it.

"Is that what you do?" I asked, my curiosity knowing no bounds.

"You already know I'm an author."

"But, do you write books for a living?"

"Yes." This time her reply was more stretched out and unsure. As though the answer required an asterisk for further explanation. "And before you ask, I will not tell you my pen name."

"Pen name?"

She turned part way, facing toward the back door. But before she took a step, she said, "You didn't think I wrote under my real name, did you?"

"If there's one thing I've come to learn about you, Red, it's to expect the unexpected."

"Goodnight, *Campbell*," she said, turning away completely and leaving me with a wiggling finger wave.

Because I was a glutton for punishment, I watched her walk away, the sway of her hips barely visible beneath her blanket of a sweatshirt. It was enough to cause my blood to rush south.

The back door closed, and I dropped my head to the back of the chair, searching for a shooting star. Yeah, I was that desperate. Because how the hell was I supposed to sleep tonight, knowing Red was right across the hall?

THIRTEEN
HUSKER

I smell bacon.
Bacon's my favorite.
Pizza's my favorite.
Bacon pizza.
Is Grandma Connie making bacon pizza?
Mom, wake up!
I need bacon pizza.
Mom's making that funny noise again.
Doesn't she care about bacon pizza?
I'll go get us some.
The door is closed.
Why did Mom close the door?
Maybe if I push it.
With my butt.
Bump.
Why didn't the door open?
Should I try again?
What's that noise?

Not snoring.
Footsteps!
Someone's in the hallway.
Smells like pine needles.
It's my new best friend!
Hey, New Best Friend, let me out!
Maybe if I stick my paw under the door—
"Husker?"
That's me!
Why are you talking so quiet?
Oh, Mom.
Don't worry.
I'll save her some bacon pizza.
Maybe.
I'll try.
"You need to go outside?"
Yes!
And bacon pizza from Grandma Connie.
She lets me in her kitchen.
Even though Mom says no.
Mom, are you coming?
Mom's still asleep.
Should I wake her up?
"C'mon, Husker. I'll take you out."
What's that, New Best Friend?
It smells like the lake.
Sniff, sniff, sniff.
"That's for your mom."
For Mom?
That's my mom's.
It's for the lake.

So we don't get wet.
It smells like pondweed.
Abort!
"Let's go outside, okay?"
Okay!
Bye, Mom!

FOURTEEN
KIRA

THE SUN SLICED through my bedroom window, laser beaming right into my sleepy eyes. I didn't want to close the curtains last night. I was searching the sky for a shooting star, hoping to wish away this special brand of hell.

But I doubted even a dozen shooting stars were enough to save Mom's bookstore after what Dad told me.

I reached for my phone on the nightstand behind me, cursing at the time.

"Five thirty?" I grumbled, turning my back to the open curtains.

I expected to find Husker, curled up in his dog bed. The older he got, the more sleeping in became his life's purpose. But his bed was empty.

The door was cracked open, though I distinctly remembered closing it last night. I didn't want to risk any accidental glances of Beckett Campbell when he finally decided to head to bed. I had enough trouble keeping those trespassing thoughts at bay.

A faint hint of campfire hung in the air, the memory of me flirting shamelessly with it. What had I been thinking?

I groaned into my pillow. It was too early for any of this.

Against the will of my very tired body, I shoved aside the covers and forced myself out of bed to find my wandering dog.

But before I made it into the hall, I found a purple paddle propped against the doorframe.

My purple paddle.

How did he find it?

I was too tired, too stressed, too overwhelmed, to wrangle any of this so early in the morning. I placed the paddle inside my room and closed the door behind me.

Days started early at the farm. The sizzle of bacon and the light hum of conversation traveled to me as I came down the stairs. I expected to find my grandparents sharing breakfast, Husker mooching off of their plates.

He was mooching, all right. But not from Grandpa or Grandma Connie.

From Beckett.

"Sit," Beckett said, his voice soft but stern as I peeked around the doorway.

Husker plopped his bottom down immediately, staring intently at the piece of bacon Beckett held between his pinched fingers.

"Good boy," he said, a smile gracing his lips that caused a quiver low in my belly. He still hadn't shaved, and I secretly hoped he wouldn't any time soon. I'd be willing to bet Beckett with a full-on beard was even sexier than Beckett with three-or-four-day stubble.

He turned his attention back to his plate, and nearly caught me peeking. I quickly spun, hiding behind the doorway, my back plastered to the wall as my pulse raced erratically.

I couldn't face him. Not before I had my morning coffee—and at least two more hours of sleep. I needed my wits about me, and my shields up.

Because I shouldn't be flirting with a man who considered *both* my brothers his closest friends. The same man who'd made himself at home with my grandparents for the past three months. Everyone in this family loved him. That much was clear.

The last thing I needed to do was go and mess that up.

Or make a complete and total fool of myself when he rejected me.

But the way I felt seen last night was screwing with my senses. That, and my severe lack of sleep.

Beckett hadn't pushed me to say a single thing more than I wanted to as we sat by the firepit. He didn't trick me into revealing my deepest, darkest fears so he could later weaponize them against me. There were no passive-aggressive digs. He simply accepted what I had to offer, and expected nothing more.

And he definitely flirted back. Exhausted or not, I didn't misread that.

Since Travis, I'd wanted nothing to do with men. My heart was wrung dry after that nightmare. I never wanted to wonder again why my love wasn't enough. I didn't need to feel the painful sting of rejection that left me lost and humiliated. I recognized it now for the manipulation it was, but that didn't mean I'd be signing up for it again.

I was safer on my own, just Husker and me.

Yet all Beckett Campbell had to do was flash me one of those easygoing, sexy half smiles, and I had to fight the urge to fling myself at him. Oh God, how I wanted to crawl right into his lap last night to see if he'd kiss me breathless. He seemed like a man who knew exactly how to work those lips.

"It's all gone, Husker," Beckett said, a low chuckle escaping his throat. I stole another peek and found Beckett rubbing the back of my dog's neck with vigor. As though he didn't mind at all if he was covered in dog hair for it. My nipples tightened, reminding me I wasn't wearing a bra beneath my oversized T-shirt.

Husker tilted his head, and caught sight of me.

I flung myself behind cover again, but the jingle of his collar warned me he was coming.

Shit.

I couldn't be seen like this, with yesterday's makeup no doubt smeared all over my face. I hadn't even bothered to brush my hair that was strangled in a ponytail holder, and I was wearing a pair of Scooby Doo pajama shorts I had since college.

I took the stairs two at a time, Husker dead on my heels like it was a game of tag, and hurried down the hall.

Husker hopped onto my bed, and I closed the door.

"Bubbies, you traitor," I teased.

Husker rolled onto his back, disguising the demand for belly rubs as submission. I crawled back into bed, and gave in.

I didn't know at what point I fell back to sleep, only that I woke to repeated chimes from my phone. The sun was higher in the sky, and my stomach was rumbling in objection. I wondered if there was any bacon left. How long had it been since I had a homemade breakfast that wasn't a protein shake?

Wiping sleep from my eyes, I unlocked my phone.

> **Lila:** Are you up?

> **Lila:** Please tell me you're up!

> **Lila:** Kira?

> **Lila:** I'm too excited to wait, but I don't want to wake Growly Kira.

> **Lila:** Do they have DoorDash there? I can send you coffee.

> **Lila:** Please call me!!!

I wasn't exactly a morning person. Lila knew me well.

Before I could save her the trouble and call her back, I noticed one other text message from a number I didn't have saved. One with a Nebraska area code.

> **Unknown:** I know u luv me kare bear :)

I tossed my phone as though it were on fire. Husker hopped off the bed as though we were under attack.

Dammit, Kira. Rein it in.

"Sorry, Bubbies." I had to stop reacting this way, at least for his sake.

I rubbed both hands over my face and forced myself to breathe through my panic spike. Travis hadn't bothered me in over two weeks. It was a record. I blocked his latest number, his email on three different email accounts, and even Venmo. He didn't have most social media, on account of him being too damned paranoid. But it'd been almost two months since he changed his phone number. I was foolish enough to think he was through with phone number roulette.

I focused on deep breaths, and my racing heart slowed.

I reached for my phone and went through the motions that, at this point, were automatic. I didn't respond to his text. I'd learned that nothing I said mattered. I could tell him I still loved him or tell him to go straight to hell, and it had the exact same impact—it created an opening. The words didn't matter. Only the response.

I hadn't responded since the night we broke up, almost a year ago.

That didn't stop Travis from trying dozens of tactics to get a rise out of me. Anything from begging me to give him another chance, to telling me how horrible a person I was to hurt him.

I stopped reading most of them.

After this new number was blocked and the text deleted from my phone, I called Lila.

"Kira!" she shrieked, her excitement overpowering, reminding me I had yet to find coffee. I rarely drank anything other than iced, but today, I was willing to make an exception.

Husker hopped back on the bed, head tilted as though searching for his friend. Lila was one of his favorite people.

"Hey, Lila. What's the big news?"

"You don't know, do you?" She sounded giddy, like she was about to explode with barely contained excitement.

"Know what?"

"Oh, my *eeeh!*"

Husker tilted his head all the way to the side at the high-pitched squeal, staring straight at the phone I'd since put on speaker and dropped beside me.

"You hit the top ten."

"What?"

"Top. Ten. In the *whole* store."

She paused, no doubt giving me time to let what she was saying soak in, but I could still hear a faint tapping noise. Something like a woodpecker on a sugar high. Or the patiently impatient tap of her perfectly manicured nails against her kitchen table.

The image it conjured pulled a reluctant smile as I dug my laptop out of its bag for the first time since I packed the car, and powered it on. I held my breath as I waited for everything to load, and the Wi-Fi to connect.

"Are you looking?" she asked.

"Yeah. It's loading."

I pulled up my browser and typed in *Forever Forbidden* in the search bar. It populated Diana Davenport, along with the book title.

On the listing, I scrolled down to the ranking.

Then *I* squealed.

Number nine.

Husker hopped off the bed and paced around it, his tail wagging. He didn't know why we were excited, but he wasn't about to be left out of the party.

"This is real?" I asked, my words almost a whisper. Tears threatened the corners of my eyes. How long had I hoped for this kind of success? It seemed like years since I added *make the top ten* to my vision board. Back when I was a newbie author hardly anyone knew. My books did well, especially after that viral TikTok several months ago, but this was a whole new level.

"It's real, babe! I've taken, like, a million screenshots."

"How is this possible?"

"You mean, how is it possible your book is doing so damn well, besides the fact you have the best PA in the entire world doing your release marketing and running your ads? And before you ask, no, I have not gone over budget."

I let out a strangled laugh. "Yeah, besides all that."

"You might have blown up on BookTok again. I'll send you the video."

I pulled up my sales dashboard and nearly screamed. "Holy shit. I could buy another Jeep," I joked.

"Keep this up, and you could buy your own fleet of Jeeps."

Her words were a sucker punch to my excitement.

There wouldn't be a next time.

There wouldn't be another book, or another series.

I tried for months to write after my Dark Ages ended, and the few hundred words I managed to force from my fingers were garbage. I hadn't attempted to write something new in almost four months. My characters wouldn't talk to me, and the ones who did were too bitter to redeem.

I closed my laptop, suddenly choking back tears.

I should tell Lila.

I *would* tell Lila.

But this conversation deserved in-person care. "When I get back to Omaha, we'll have to do a dessert date," I said.

"What's wrong?"

"Nothing."

"Kira," she said sternly.

"I'm just overwhelmed." It wasn't a lie, but it definitely wasn't the full truth.

"You sure you don't want me to come to Colorado?"

"No. I still have to finish my apology tour."

"How's that going, by the way?"

"You know? Better than I expected." I told Lila about my long conversation with Grandma Connie out in the garden yesterday. There'd been fewer tears than I expected, and a whole lot more understanding. "Connor doesn't even seem fazed," I added, remembering my very brief and easy chat with him. "I can't tell if Luke's forgiven me yet. I feel like I'm on probation with him."

"What about your dad?"

My chest tightened, and tears threatened all over again. I swallowed them back, and replaced the sadness with anger.

The conversation with him last night was emotional, to say the least. But it had nothing to do with the terrible things I said last summer. He cut right to the topic of the bookstore, before I even set down the six-pack on his kitchen counter.

I'd never seen him cry, aside from Mom's funeral. But he teared up last night when he told me he had no choice but to sell it after the financial ruin that was Margene Miller.

That woman better pray I never found her.

Dad and I spent most of the evening talking about the state of the bookstore, and why he had to sell not only the business, but the building too. Connor was right. He had his hands tied. He'd dipped into his retirement fund to avoid affecting the hardware store's bottom line. He couldn't even afford to pay anyone to staff the bookstore, which was why, despite the going-out-of-business-sale sign in the window, it wasn't even open.

We were both too worn out after all that to clear the air about my last visit.

"That's a work in progress," I admitted.

Tomorrow morning, I'd meet him and an appraiser there.

He agreed to let me be a part of the selling process, but I had no inclinations that the role was anything more than a way to appease me. An olive branch. I couldn't change his mind. I couldn't change what had happened in my absence. And Dad warned me it was highly unlikely anyone would want anything more than the building.

The bookstore as we knew it would cease to exist.

"They'll forgive you, Kira."

"I hope you're right."

"You have a family who actually gives a shit about each other. Don't take that for granted."

I wanted to tell her about the bookstore, but I couldn't

bring myself to talk about it yet. Instead, I deflected. "Travis texted me."

"He what?"

"Changed his number again."

"Kira, this has to stop."

"You know I can't respond. It'll only make it worse."

"But you could get a restraining order."

"I blocked the number. Deleted it from my phone."

"That's not going to stop him. And you know you can retrieve deleted texts from the last thirty days."

We'd argued about this a few times. Lila was less than thrilled that I was deleting the text messages, but the idea of them existing on my phone at all gave me the worst kind of anxiety. The only thing they would prove was that he'd been inundating me with messages I never answered. Travis' most important priority was self-preservation. He was careful not to say anything that could be construed as threatening. I'd never be granted a protective order.

"Hey, I forgot to send you that picture of Husker in his doggie life jacket," I said, hoping like hell to change the subject. "I actually got one while he was on the board."

"You did?" Lila was kind enough to drop the restraining order talk—for now. "Send it! I have to see this."

I attached the picture, and hit send. "It should be there any minute."

"Um, *who* is that?"

Shit.

"Kira Jane!"

Relieved to be off the hook about Travis, my fingers had moved too quickly. I meant to send her the first one I took of *only* Husker. But instead, I sent her the second one. The one with Beckett smiling in the background, shirtless, and covered in tattoos.

"I repeat, *who* is that?"

"It's a long story," I said, biting my bottom lip. My stomach was growling, and I desperately needed a shower. "My grandma's waiting for me downstairs."

"Is he your next book inspiration? Oh my God, he'd make such a sexy vampire. Is that your inspiration for Mateo?"

"He's a friend of the family."

"A very delicious-looking friend. Look at all those tattoos," she cooed. "Are you sure you've sworn off men?"

"I have to go."

"You're calling me back later with details."

"There are no details."

"You're such a liar."

"Am not."

"Babe, who's taking the picture?"

Damn Lila and her uncanny ability to notice details with detective-like accuracy.

"I'll call you this weekend."

"If you don't, I'm coming there myself to meet this *friend of the family*."

"Bye, Lila." It was a good thing I avoided FaceTime. I could feel the blush heating my cheeks and neck. It was just a harmless little crush. One that would lead to nothing. One no one needed to know about—Lila included.

"Or you," I said to Husker. Though, I suspected my dog had a bigger crush on him than I did.

FIFTEEN
BECKETT

My arms fucking ached from moving around sheets of drywall for the past two days. I was fortunate enough to have both Luke and Connor's help this afternoon. Both of them seemed to enjoy hanging drywall. Both also hated taping and mudding, so I knew what the next few days held in store for me. One day, I might have a team of my own assembled. For now, I was grateful for some help over no help.

"Last one?" Luke asked, nodding at the board leaned against the living room wall.

"Last full sheet."

He looked at the drywall board, then at the staircase it needed to go up, then back at the board. "Let's just fucking get it done."

I looked forward to the nice hot shower in my future tonight, almost as much as I looked forward to having the least favorite part of this flip done.

When I first moved to Bluebell Springs, I focused on

buying homes that needed minimal work. They were quicker to convert into rental properties, and all but one I purchased was a quick flip. This house, a short three-minute drive from downtown, was a complete gut job. But the location in this tourist town couldn't be beaten. It was close to the restaurants and shops, as well as an easy distance to Glimmerstone Lake. I hadn't decided if I'd rent it to a long-term tenant, or make it a vacation rental.

Madeline would quickly volunteer herself as tribute if she got to decorate a vacation rental. My sister had many talents. Which reminded me, I needed to give her a call. She'd gone eerily quiet today. Madeline quiet was much more concerning than Madeline blowing up my phone.

Luke and I lined up the last full sheet of drywall in the main bedroom, holding it still while Connor knelt to screw it into the studs.

"Owen show you that house on Blue Spruce Lane?" Connor asked.

"Going to see it early next week. They're not quite ready to show yet."

It was convenient having a buddy who was a realtor in town. I often got the scoop on new listings before they hit the market.

"You're going to buy up the whole fucking town before the year's over," Luke said, shaking his head in amusement.

I'd only purchased three houses, one condo, and the commercial building that was recently converted into Pizza Patty's. Though Bluebell Springs barely boasted a thousand residents, there were hundreds of houses. Some in town, some on the outskirts, and some around the lakes. That didn't include the dozens of commercial buildings.

Until Nana insisted I was overlooking a stellar opportunity, I didn't consider adding commercial rentals to my portfolio. She was the reason I might be adding the corner bookstore building to my list of current projects. Though I wasn't sure it'd remain a bookstore for long.

For Kira's sake, I hoped it did.

I couldn't help but wonder how she'd feel about it being sold. It was entirely possible Connie or her dad warned her I was a possible buyer. Either way, she deserved to hear it from me. *Tonight*, I promised myself. I'd tell her tonight. If I had an ounce of energy left when I crawled into the house anyway.

"You going to buy Karl's cabin too?" Connor asked.

"Considering it," I admitted, though I was still holding out for that rent-to-own option. I left him a voicemail yesterday but hadn't heard back.

"I hate to break it to you, but Dad's not going to sell that cabin."

All three of us turned at the male voice in the doorway. Thoren Hayes held up a stack of pizza boxes in one hand, and a small cooler in the other. "Boys ready to take a break?"

"What the hell are you doing here?" Luke asked, crossing the room and relieving Thoren of the pizzas. He slapped him on the back of his shoulder hard enough that he dropped the cooler to the floor with a loud *thunk*.

"Surprise, assholes!" Thoren wore the signature shit-eating grin he sported so well.

"How long you back for?" Connor asked, helping

himself to a Gatorade from the cooler. Whether he didn't feel like a beer or was skipping out of respect for me, was anyone's guess. I told them all I didn't care if they drank around me. My disdain for alcohol had nothing to do with any of them. Even drunk, they were good fucking people who'd never dream of harming a fly.

"Just for the weekend." Thoren swiped a large slice of meat lover's pizza and took a big bite. "This shit is *good.*"

"It's Beckett's place," Luke said.

"I'm just the landlord," I explained. "I can't take any credit for the food."

"Shit, if I'd known that, I would've name dropped you. Might've gotten free pizzas."

After washing my hands in the connecting en-suite—I hadn't ripped out the pedestal sink yet—I pulled up an empty five-gallon bucket and flipped it over to sit on.

"You want your Dad's cabin?" I asked.

Luke shot me a look that said *your funeral* as he stripped off his gloves and served himself a slice of cheeseburger pizza.

"My old man would never sell me that cabin. Not if I paid him double what it's worth."

"Do you *want* it?" I asked again.

"Nah. What would I do with it anyway?"

Of the five of us—Owen was missing from our impromptu dinner—Thoren was the only one still active duty. We all got out before twenty years for one reason or another. But Thoren was a lifer.

"It's been sitting empty since Aspen moved out," Connor said, drying his wet hands on the inside of his T-shirt.

"Because my dad is one stubborn son of a bitch."

"You have an issue if I buy it?" I asked him.

"Nope," he said. "But Dad won't sell. It's like he thinks selling it would be selling what's left of Aaron. Makes no fucking sense since he won't step foot on the property. But good luck."

"What's the special occasion?" Connor asked, no doubt sensing the heightening tension, and trying to ease it.

"Mom's birthday is Saturday. Aspen begged me to come back. Thought if I showed up, Mom would decide *I* was her surprise and not suspect they're throwing her a big-ass party."

Maybe *that* was why Kira was in town. From what I was told, she and Aspen were close. Not only because they were cousins, but because they were best friends. If she was here for the party, she'd probably leave, like Thoren, when it was over.

I only had to survive the next few days without doing something stupid. Like pressing her up against the wall and kissing her senseless. Fuck, I really needed Karl to call me back about that cabin. I'd find a way to convince him.

"Now it makes sense," Luke said, shaking his head.

"What?" Connor asked.

"Why Kira's back."

I shot a look at him, wondering if he read my fucking mind. Hoping that if he did, he didn't read the part where I imagined slipping my hand up Kira's oversized pajama shirt in search of her supple breast that I strongly suspected would fit perfectly in the palm of my hand.

"Kira's in town?" Thoren asked, sounding surprised.

"Yeah," Luke said. "Been nothing but a pain in my ass. Did you know I found her sleeping in the goddamn bookstore apartment the night before last? On the fucking floor in that sleeping bag Connor gave her."

"What?" Connor nearly choked on his pizza, and reached for his drink.

"Said she didn't break in, but Dad changed the locks a month ago."

"Maybe he mailed her a key?" Connor suggested.

"He didn't," Luke fired back.

"Has she been back since . . ." Thoren didn't finish his sentence, but the brothers looked at one another, filling in a blank I wasn't privy to.

"No," Luke said.

"She apologized," Connor said.

"And you let her off the hook, right?" Luke grumbled.

I shoved another bite of barbeque chicken pizza in my mouth to keep from asking the half dozen questions swirling around in my brain. Why did she need to apologize? What happened last summer? Why was she sleeping in the bookstore when she had family and friends all over town?

"C'mon, Luke," Connor said. "You know why she lashed out."

"Lashed out?" Thoren let out a loud laugh that drew everyone's attention. "She stole the fucking microphone from the band."

"To give a toast?" I tossed in a guess.

"It was at first," Connor said, as though coming to her defense.

I understood why when Luke chimed in.

"Then she basically told everyone in this town to fuck off. That she was better than all of us."

"That wasn't *quite* what happened—"

"The hell it wasn't," Luke said, cutting off his brother. "I was on call."

Meaning he was sober and had a better memory than most. But Luke was also harder on people than they sometimes deserved. I wanted to believe this was one of those times. It seemed all too possible there was a side of Kira I hadn't experienced, because I'd only known her a few days.

"She was lit that night," Thoren said, his eyes sparkling, as though he was enjoying the conversation. He looked at me. "Drunk Kira is *unhinged*."

"She was going through a hard time," Connor again came to her defense.

"Yeah, yeah. Because of The Asswipe," Luke mumbled, fixing himself another slice. "Still not a good excuse."

"Who?" I asked, hoping my question wouldn't get too much scrutiny. I certainly didn't want anyone to mistake my curiosity for the interest it was. But something didn't fucking add up here.

"She was dating this asshole for a while," Connor explained. "She broke up with him the night of Aspen's wedding. Did you know that?" he directed at Luke.

"Doesn't give her the right to take it out on everyone else." Luke shoveled in the rest of his pizza and stood, rubbing his hands together. "We going to cut up the smaller pieces of drywall tonight or what? Because if you girls want to keep on gossiping, I'm fucking out."

SIXTEEN
KIRA

Armed with an iced caramel coffee, I headed for the bookstore half an hour ahead of the time I agreed to meet Dad and the appraiser.

It didn't matter that the sun was shining brightly this morning, or that Husker was happily zigzagging on the sidewalk in front of me, blissfully unaware of what this all meant. Dread filled every cell of my body.

I hated this so much.

Yesterday, I mostly hid in my bedroom and caught up on all the work I neglected over the past several weeks. I responded to reader comments and emails—avoiding the most popular question: *When is Mateo's story coming?* I ran numbers, and reevaluated my budget. Lila was thrilled I gave her more ad money to play with to capitalize on *Forever Forbidden's* spike of success.

I also spent an embarrassing amount of time staring at the picture of Husker, with Beckett in the background, smiling right at the camera. Zooming in, and memorizing the tattoos I could see. A unit crest. A panther. A moose skull? I had so many questions.

Though I'd never own up to it—Lila would never let me live it down if I did—I hoped he provided writing inspiration.

But any attempts to write and salvage Diana Davenport's career were a complete flop. After two hours and several deleted sentences, the single page in my document sat empty.

That was it.

I was done writing.

And Mom's bookstore was nearly done existing.

"This isn't fair, Bubbies," I said to Husker as the *going out of business sale* sign came into view, causing my heart to sink clear into my toes. I hated that the store was closed because Dad didn't even have the funds to staff it.

Husker looked at me, then at the door. He knew exactly where we were.

Despite knowing it was closed, I reached for the door handle and tugged. It was my final prayer that I'd been living a nightmare reality. That with one tug of the handle, the door would open, the familiar sounds of chatter and laughter would filter around me, and everything would be the way it should be the second I stepped across the threshold.

But the door didn't open.

The nightmare was real.

Mom would be heartbroken to know her bookstore was closed on a Friday morning. It was one of the busiest of the week, and one of her favorite days. Friday mornings were for coffee drinkers, those who read the local newspaper from cover to cover, and her famous buy-one-get-one-half-off sale that tourists absolutely loved.

This was wrong.

I dug my key ring from my purse and inserted the key into the lock, relieved when it turned easily.

I needed a sliver of time to stroll leisurely down the aisles of books, before Dad showed up with the appraiser and shattered my nostalgia once and for all.

Husker tugged me inside, and the old book smell rushed me instantly. At least *one thing* was the same.

I pulled the door closed behind me and simply stood, taking it all in.

With the exception of the missing staff and customers, it looked exactly as it did last summer.

Floor-to-ceiling bookshelves along every wall, still full of books. Display tables set up for new releases, bestsellers, and fun monthly themes—Whodunnit for June. Though, upon closer examination, the display was . . . a little tacky.

Okay, so maybe not *exactly* the same.

The puzzle corner where Mom collected the most unique jigsaw puzzles and brainteasers with a half-completed floral puzzle on the square table was a complete mess. I set to straightening it without fore-thought. But it didn't take long before my attention was pulled away.

The children's section toward the back, equipped with beanbags and stuffed animals from the classics, was in disarray. Books were strewn everywhere, as though someone left in a hurry. A couple of the covers were torn. The beanbags that once were vibrant and new looked to be on their death bed. Someone had stuffed a

Clifford dog in a kennel made of books on a lower level shelf.

"What the actual *fuck?*"

After freeing the stuffed animal, I kept moving about the store.

The old register Mom found at an estate sale and refused to get rid of, even when they upgraded the payment system to a digital one, was still here, and positioned on the front counter. At least Margene didn't steal that. Probably because it was too damn heavy to carry out of the store.

The cushy, mismatched chairs stationed around the bookstore so people could hang out and enjoy their books and the coffee they picked up down the street were in decent shape, though they were certainly more worn than I remembered. Okay, maybe "worn" was being generous. Some were actually torn in places, with stuffing sticking out. One had a broken leg.

The table in the middle, where the coffee drinkers and book club members gathered, was scratched and marked up, as though someone had let a classroom of kindergarteners loose with permanent markers and butter knives.

Mom would be sick.

But perhaps the most heartbreaking discovery of all was that the corner reading nook I spent so many days hiding in was missing its eclectic mix of throw pillows and folded blankets. It wasn't even a nook anymore. It was now filled with racks of cheap touristy trinkets Mom would never be caught selling in her store.

"What the fuck, Margene?"

Husker sniffed every surface and book as I paced

throughout the store. I ran my fingers along the spines, catching dust the farther back I went, and my anger for Margene Miller instantly renewed.

Mom would never allow dust in her shop.

Mom would never allow any of these bullshit changes.

Margene was the assistant manager when Mom was still alive. They were *friends*. She took over after Mom's passing. No one thought anything of it. Why would they? Hell, she was invited to family dinners at the farm, and even showed up for a few. Dad relied on her to keep Mom's dream alive. He *trusted* her. We all did.

And now the greedy bitch was likely hiding out somewhere in Mexico with all the money she stole.

I wasn't a vengeful person by nature, but if it was the last thing I did, I'd find her and make sure she answered for the way she wronged my family. Maybe I didn't have enough money to buy the bookstore myself—not that I had a damn clue how to run one—but I had enough saved to hire a private detective, and a good lawyer.

"Hell, maybe that's how I'll get back on Luke's good side," I said to Husker. He looked at me, his quirky head tilt suggesting he was trying to make sense of what I said. Or maybe he recognized my brother's name. Husker was a momma's boy through and through, but he sure loved his *guy time* with my brothers.

And now Beckett.

Warmth filled my chest as one of the forbidden scenes I considered writing this morning flashed in my mind. One where my heroine's hands were tied to the bedposts with silk scarves, and a shirtless, tattooed, bearded hero was above her—

"For fuck's sake, Kira," I grumbled.

Where the hell did that come from?

Sure, the man was sexy. But even if he weren't incredibly off-limits, considering his connection to my entire family, I wasn't ready to go there with any man. Not even one as tempting as Beckett Campbell was proving to be.

I might need to consider cutting this trip short.

But dammit, I couldn't fathom leaving now. Not after seeing what a mess Margene made of the store. Not without knowing the fate of Mom's special place. I felt a personal conviction to stay and see it through, no matter how fucking bad it hurt to watch. I owed everyone that much.

As I circled back toward the front, I noticed a single paperback sitting on the large book club table. A book I felt certain wasn't there a minute ago. Or was it?

I took a healthy sip of my iced coffee, hoping for a desperately needed caffeine jolt. I hadn't managed a good night's sleep since the night before Mom appeared in my dream and insisted, in her own way, that I come home.

"What should I do, Mom?" I asked, looking up at the ceiling.

It didn't matter that the store was closing, or that Dad would be holding a big going-out-of-business sale that would leave the shelves looking ransacked. Years of calling this bookstore a second home had instilled the habit of putting away any book that was left out.

I reached for the book and nearly dropped my coffee.

It was mine.

The only book not on a shelf in the entire store, and it was *mine*.

Husker sat, looking at me expectantly, as though the book were a treat.

"This is the first book I ever published, Bubbies," I explained, feeling tears well up in the corners of my eyes. "And no, you can't eat it." I'd caught him licking a book more than once.

My Diana Davenport career didn't really take off until after Mom passed. But I published my first book, *High Stakes*, before then. Besides Aspen and Alyssa, Mom was the only other person in Bluebell Springs who I shared my secret pen name with. She was sworn to secrecy, but she sent me a long, gushing text after reading my first book, begging me to do a book signing at her store.

Before I could tell her yes, a man passing through town on his way home to Boulder slid through a stop sign. There were a lot of accidents during that ice storm, but that was the only fatal one that day.

I carried the book to the paranormal romance section, searching alphabetically by last name, and gasped.

I thought there might be a couple of Diana Davenport titles, but I certainly didn't expect an entire shelf dedicated to her.

Not a single book was dusty, either.

"Have they been *selling*?" I whispered, finding it hard to believe. Sure, Diana did well digitally. She'd sold more e-books than I could ever count. But being an indie author, my books rarely made it into bookstores, even independently owned ones. The few that carried them were Lila's doing. And she had to lay the charm on thick to convince bookstores to carry my books when the author was adamantly opposed to doing in-person events.

The rattle of the doorknob snapped my attention to the front. I quickly re-shelved the book, and led Husker to the front to meet Dad and the appraiser.

"Kira, how'd you get in?" Dad asked, his expression one of genuine surprise.

"My key."

"Did I—" He lifted his ball cap and ran his fingers through his thick hair. "Thought I forgot, but guess you got it. Anyway, this is Phil Clausen. He's here to do the appraisal."

I shook hands with the man a few years my dad's senior. Whereas Dad was in his usual work pants and blue shirt with his name stitched into the pocket—he likely came straight from the hardware store—Phil wore dark-wash jeans and a gray polo. He held a heavy-duty clipboard against his chest, looking much too professional for my liking.

It's not his fault. The voice in my head sounded a lot more like Mom's than my own.

"This is a great location," Phil said, wearing a smile that felt both professional and genuine. "Lots of possibilities here."

I forced a smile in return, but my stomach was tying in knots at what this all meant. The iced coffee no longer sat well—my fault for avoiding breakfast once again to avoid Beckett. Probably a good thing, considering the sudden and violent flip my stomach just managed to complete.

"You okay?" Dad asked.

"I'll be right back." Husker trotted alongside me as I beelined for the restroom in the back. I didn't lose the coffee, thankfully, but I was sweating as though I were trapped in a sauna, despite the chill in the bookstore.

My vision blurred. I braced my back against the cool tile wall opposite the door and slunk to the floor.

Husker placed his head in my lap, and I focused on stroking his head, his soft fur grazing my fingertips—the only sensation grounding me to reality.

This wasn't my first panic attack. I experienced them when I was faced with the sight of my own blood. And during my Dark Ages, I had panic attacks for a variety of other reasons that had nothing to do with blood. But the familiar territory was never pleasant.

"Breathe, Kira." I whispered the command.

My temperature increased to inferno levels. Sweat poured from me profusely. I wanted my sweatshirt off, but I couldn't muster the strength. The spinning room was fading to black.

"Kira, are you all right?"

"Here come the hallucinations," I murmured, working harder to breathe, and finding little to no relief. Because Beckett Campbell was definitely *not* on the other side of the door. Maybe Dad, but not the military veteran I'd been hiding from, and shamelessly fantasizing about.

"Kira?" Husker popped to his feet and stared at the crack between the floor and the bottom of the door. *Huh.* Maybe I wasn't imagining it.

"Yeah?"

"You okay?"

My shirt was soaked beneath my sweatshirt. I didn't have the stamina left to pull off the top layer. I was quickly losing consciousness. I let out a laugh that turned into a sob.

"Not really."

"Can I come in?"

"Why not."

The room went dark.

My head rolled back, landing on a very firm ledge. Did this bathroom have ledges? Why was this one curved just right to support my head? It was hard, but not like tile. What was this magical surface? And why did it smell like pine needles?

"Breathe, Kira."

This warm ledge had warm breath, too. It tickled my neck. Or maybe Husker turned the fan on. Did I teach him that trick? I felt the weight of his head against my folded legs, his cold nose pressing against my bare knee. The wall behind me was warm. Not quite level. *Ha.* Maybe the appraiser would have something to say about the state of the wavy walls, and Dad would decide not to sell after all.

"Take a deep breath," Beckett said again, his voice soft against my ear. Something cool pressed against my forehead and held.

The relief was instant.

"Thank the vampire gods." My words were more of a moan than anything, but I didn't care.

"Vampire gods?"

"The Veltori five," I told him. "Seth, Vincent, Dameon . . ."

The damp cloth against my head turned from cool to molten lava. I groaned, unable to open my eyes to see where it fell.

"Hold on."

Water rushed from the faucet for a few seconds, then the cloth was replaced against my forehead.

Finally, my eyes fluttered open.

Two jean-clad legs stretched out on either side of my folded thighs. Tan work boots with yellow and black laces touched the door. Husker lay between those legs, his chin resting on my crossed legs as those big brown eyes looked up at me in concern.

"You back with me?" Beckett asked. His low voice gently rumbled against the side of my head, just behind my ear. His lips brushed against my hair as he spoke.

"Um, yeah?" The first rush of embarrassment hit me. I remembered Beckett's voice on the other side of the door, but not him coming in or propping his body behind me. I squirmed, desperate to get up, but my wobbly legs were protesting hard.

"Take your time," he said. "I'm not in a hurry."

Now that my body temperature was no longer a thousand degrees, his warmth was comforting. Like the safety net I always craved when these stupid panic attacks hit. Part of me wanted to sit right here until the day was over. Or at least until the appraiser left. How the hell did I think I could handle being a part of the selling process?

"How are you here?" I asked, pulling away the wad of damp paper towels from my forehead and forcing myself to sit up straight, breaking the contact of his chest to my back. I ran my fingers along Husker's head, but it wasn't enough to distract me from the absence of Beckett's heat.

I liked it.

Too much.

"You ready to go back out there?" Beckett asked.

I looked over my shoulder at him, which was a huge fucking mistake. Those hazel eyes from a distance were dangerous. But this close, they were deadly. I was both locked in a trance and too intimidated by the intensity of his stare.

But something didn't sit right.

"Beckett, why are you here?"

"I'm guessing you don't know," he said, his expression regretful. "I've been trying to tell you, but we kept missing each other—"

I bristled, and my tone turned cold. "Tell me what?"

"I'm the prospective buyer."

SEVENTEEN
HUSKER

Mom is mad.
Why is Mom mad?
We're leaving.
But my new best friend wants to come.
"Don't follow me."
Oh, boy.
Mom is extra mad.
Sorry, New Best Friend.
Mom says you can't come.
Ooh! I smell pizza.
Why aren't we going the way of the pizza?
Car ride?
Okay!
Hop.
Mom slammed the door.
Mom is really mad.
Maybe she needs a treat.
New Best Friend, give Mom a treat.

Wait, he can't come.

Why can't he come with us?

I like him.

He gives good belly rubs.

And he shares bacon.

And lots of pizza.

We're moving.

Where are we going?

I should stick my head out the window.

But the other window is open too.

I don't want to miss the smells out the other window.

Or the other window.

Or the other window.

Or the other window.

All those smells.

Pizza.

Donuts.

Mini squirrel.

"You can't chase the chipmunks, Bubbies."

But he's looking at me funny.

I can't fit through the window.

I need to get him.

Where did he go?

He's fast.

I'm fast too.

"Want to go to the lake?"

Lake?

Is that where the pondweed lives?

I don't want to get wet.

But I want to find the pondweed.

Being wet is dumb.

There are chipmunks at the lake.
And deer.
Big, giant deer.
I hope Mom brought treats.
Maybe I should rub my nose against her neck to ask.
"Sit down."
Still mad.
I better listen.
Plop.
"Thank you."
Mom is sighing.
"Sorry, Bubbies. I'm not mad at you."
Crinkle, crinkle, crinkle.
Is that the treat bag?
It's the treat bag!
The treat is flying.
It missed my mouth.
Where did it go?
Oh, there it is.
Ooh, bonus treat under the seat!

EIGHTEEN
BECKETT

I'D NEVER EATEN mashed potatoes on a pizza, but today seemed as good a day as any to take a risk. Not like I could fuck up any more than I already did.

The invitation to join Joe and the appraiser at the bookstore this morning was last minute. I was always eager to learn more about the different aspects of buying and selling all types of properties, and the timing was perfect.

But he didn't warn me Kira would be there.

If I hadn't caught a glimpse of Husker's white tail swishing at the back of the store, I might not have known she was there at all.

I wouldn't have been there when she needed me.

For a woman I barely knew, it was fucking unreal how this one thought kept unraveling my best defenses.

The icy glare and utter look of betrayal etched into Kira's expression when I confessed I was the prospective buyer would forever be seared into my brain. She stormed out of the bookstore without a backward glance, warning me *not* to follow.

Despite how badly I wanted to run after her and make this right.

But I couldn't make this right.

I couldn't go back to last night, to knock on her bedroom door after she was asleep, so we could talk. And though I tried to hang around the farm as late as possible this morning, neither she nor Husker emerged before I was due to meet the plumber at the Kniffen Street house.

I couldn't rewind time and stop any of this from happening.

The family was pretty tight-lipped on the bookstore overall—most days it seemed like a taboo topic—but it shouldn't have come as a surprise that it would mean so much to Kira. Hell, she was an author. A bookstore from her childhood might have inspired her career. And here I was, like some greedy-ass land baron, come to destroy something special to her.

It wasn't my decision to sell the building or liquidate the business. From the conversation between Joe and the appraiser, there was no changing Joe's mind. I still felt like an asshole for not putting the pieces together before Kira had a fucking panic attack on the bathroom floor.

Worst of all, I couldn't make an ounce of sense of why the urge to fix everything for a woman I'd known all of three or four days was so overpowering. Nana would cuss me out for my stupidity in all of this.

I reached for my glass of soda, and nearly drained it. Probably should save some for when the pizza arrived, but apparently, today wasn't about making sensible decisions.

Moving to Bluebell Springs was an opportunity for a fresh start. For the first time in my adult life, I felt ready to put down roots.

And Kira Mason . . . would be gone in a few days.

None of this should matter.

I shouldn't feel so damn guilty.

I thought saving properties from outsiders was a good way to become a part of this community. It wasn't as though I was buying the bookstore out from under Kira or anyone in her family.

But fuck, it *felt* like I was.

"Need a refill?" the server asked, reaching for my nearly empty glass.

"That'd be great, thanks."

I didn't know her name. I wanted to fit in here, yet I didn't know anyone but Patty herself. Was I getting anything right lately?

"We can't have the meetings at my house," a tall, elderly woman who sounded like she smoked two packs a day said, pulling out a chair at the table behind me. "I don't have enough seating, and I'll be damned if I'm listening to Carol Ann complain about sitting on the floor. That woman spends most her days on the floor."

"Be nice, Thelma," another woman said, her gentle tone laced with amusement. "She's a yoga instructor, not a drunk."

My shoulders shook with silent laughter.

"Well, don't look at me," a third said as layers of jewelry clanged together at her approach. "Frank outlawed book club meetings ever since *Fifty Shades of Grey*. Poor man is scarred for life."

"We told him to leave," Thelma said unapologetically.

"What about the library?" the second woman said.

"Jodi kicked us out last time. Said we were too disruptive," the third woman said. "Plus, our picks aren't exactly story-hour friendly."

"Shit, it is summer, isn't it?" Thelma said.

"Your mashed potato pizza," the server said, startling me out of my eavesdropping.

"That any good?" Thelma asked.

I looked back, but her gaze was on the server.

"It's one of our best sellers."

"Really?" I asked, surprised. *Huh.* Maybe it wouldn't be the worst decision I made today after all. Not that the bar was set all that high.

"It's really good," the third woman, the one adorned in several layers of jewelry, reassured me. "Though I only got to try one piece because Frank inhaled the rest."

Because everyone was staring at me, I took a cautious bite.

Well, damn.

It wasn't just good.

It was delicious.

"See?" the woman with dozens of necklaces hanging around her neck said. "We should order a mashed potato pizza."

"I was craving the BLT pizza," Thelma said.

"I wanted to get the buffalo chicken," the other woman, dressed in a purple track suit and matching purple tennis shoes, chimed in.

"No way. We're not going to finish three pizzas," Thelma said.

"I could share?" I offered without forethought. I hadn't come to Pizza Patty's to socialize. If I had, I'd be sitting at the bar. Or outside in the sunshine to chat it up with the locals and tourists alike. But I *was* trying to fit in. It had nothing to do with these women being tied to a local book club.

Probably not.

"Pull up a seat," the woman in purple offered.

"I'll bring more plates," the server said.

"Say, you're that real estate investor handyman guy," Thelma said, assessing me with an up-and-down gaze. "The one staying with the Westons?"

Handyman. General Contractor. I didn't think these women gave two shits about the distinction. Somehow, I admired them for it. Maybe I needed my head examined.

"Beckett Campbell."

"I'm Thelma."

"I'm not Louise," the second woman said.

I cracked a smile.

"Oh, good. You understood the reference."

"That's Lotti," Thelma said, nodding at the woman in purple.

"And Dylann," Thelma added about the woman adorned in necklaces, bracelets, and rings.

"My dad really wanted his oldest to be a boy," Dylann said with a carefree shrug as I set the mashed potato pizza on the table. "He got me instead."

"My dad never wanted me at all." The comment slipped out unbidden. At least the women had the decency to laugh, even if the suspicious look in Thelma's eyes suggested she didn't buy it as a joke. "You three lived here long?"

"Most of our lives, actually," Lotti offered, helping herself to a slice of my pizza.

"Heard you were in the Army with the Mason boys," Thelma said.

"Yes, ma'am."

"Oh, he's a gentleman, too," Lotti cooed, green eyes twinkling in adoration. Or maybe it was just the sunlight catching on one of Dylann's many necklaces. "Just like the hero in *Forever Forbidden*."

"Is that a book?" I guessed.

"It's our current book club pick," Dylann explained. "Brand new release from Diana Davenport. Do you know her books?"

"Can't say that I do."

"Oh, you're missing out!" Lotti said.

"Does he look like a man who reads vampire smut?" Thelma asked.

"It's not smut," Dylann said, giving me a little shoulder nudge. "It's just really sexy."

"Same thing," Thelma said, rolling her eyes, looking very much like she'd like to have a cigarette.

The server returned with small plates, and a round of drinks for the ladies—a margarita on the rocks, a blended chocolate martini, and a Long Island iced tea. Though I'd never met any of these women, I'd be willing to bet my truck that book club was a *very* entertaining time.

"I haven't read much lately," I admitted, "but I'm always up for a good book recommendation."

"Better get your ass down to the bookstore and grab a

copy before it closes for good," Thelma said. "Fucking shame, that is."

"It wouldn't be closing if Margene Miller wasn't a colossal ass weasel," Lotti said, surprising me. She seemed the most soft-spoken of the bunch. But judging by the grim expressions worn by all three women, they shared an equal animosity for this woman.

Despite my incessant curiosity, I shoved a bite of pizza into my mouth to prevent the questions from slipping out. I didn't do the gossip thing, but something told me these women had more than secondhand rumors to share.

"I still think we should organize a manhunt," Lotti said, her tone too gentle for the fierce suggestion.

"My passport expired," Dylann said.

"We can sneak you across the border," Thelma said, her confidence slightly alarming. "But we might have trouble sneaking you back in."

"Frank would run out of clean underwear long before I figured out how to get back home," Dylann said, shaking her head.

"We should hire one of those sexy PIs," Lotti offered. "But only if he's willing to come to a meeting and report his findings."

"By PI, she means stripper," Thelma explained to me.

Lotti shrugged, reaching for her chocolate martini. "I wouldn't be upset if he had multiple careers paths."

"You need to get laid," Dylann said, shaking her head and taking a healthy sip of her margarita.

I nearly choked on my pizza and reached for my drink.

Thelma laughed, Dylann patted me on the back, and Lotti offered up her water.

"Say, you have military training," Lotti said.

"Back off," Thelma warned.

"What?" Lotti asked, her expression innocent. She reminded me of someone from a TV show Nana used to watch when I was a kid. But I couldn't quite place it.

"We're not asking Beckett to go to Mexico himself to hunt down Margene Miller," Dylann chimed in.

"Mexico?"

"For all the times that sorry excuse for a human brought up Cabo, we're pretty sure Margene headed down south the second she cleaned out the bookstore's bank account," Thelma explained.

"She's in Cabo?"

"Or maybe Cozumel," Dylann said. "If I had a dollar for every time that woman mentioned Cozumel, Frank could finally retire."

"You forgot Cancun," Lotti added. "Hey, Beckett—can I call you Beckett?"

"Of course."

"You're not also secretly a bounty hunter, are you?" Lotti asked.

"Afraid not."

"Do you *know* any bounty hunters?" Dylann asked.

I did not. But I had a strong suspicion Nana might. *Huh.* Maybe there was something I could do to make this whole bookstore mess right after all. Kira might hate me for buying the building—I couldn't let some outside assholes lowball Joe and turn it into a dreaded gift shop, so I had to buy it—but at least I could do something about this Margene Miller.

Maybe.

That's the excuse I'd cling to when Luke, Connor, or Thoren gave me shit for turning into a gossip queen.

I waited until after the server—Jamie—placed the additional pizzas onto the table, and asked, "What exactly did Margene Miller *do*?"

NINETEEN
KIRA

"HAVE YOU BEEN OUT HERE LONG?" Aspen asked as she and her dog, Tango, stepped onto the boat dock.

Husker immediately hopped to his feet to greet his lab friend, and my heart squeezed. If I didn't live six hundred miles away, they could spend time together. As it was, he was too used to being the only dog in my life worthy of pets. If I wasn't careful, Husker would turn all the way into a grumpy old man dog. He needed a friend.

"Just came out here to think," I said, greeting Tango with a firm rub along the back of his neck while Husker was distracted by Aspen's attention and the homemade treat she offered him.

"Everything okay?"

My legs dangled off the dock, and I kicked at the water with my bare toes. The water was cold, and they were numb by now.

"I don't really want to talk about it."

Except, I did. I really, really did. I was bursting at the

fucking seams, desperate to let out a long scream. But the locals wouldn't appreciate the outburst on their quiet lake, so I held it in.

"You know I love you, Kira." Aspen kicked off her flip-flops and took a seat next to me, dangling her feet into the lake.

"I sense a *but*."

"That's because I'm a little worn out with how much you seem to hold things in these days."

Despite the compassion in her tone, guilt gnawed at me. Of anyone who had a right to be upset about my outburst last summer, Aspen was the kindest about it from day one. I owed her more than silence.

"Beckett's buying the bookstore."

"Beckett *Campbell*?"

"Yeah."

Beckett *fucking* Campbell. The man who came to my rescue this morning and was my undoing, all in the course of a few minutes. How long would I have lain there, crumpled on the cold tile floor, if he hadn't found me?

"That's a good thing, right?" she asked.

My spite renewed. His kindness was costing me Mom's bookstore.

"No, it's not a fucking *good* thing," I snapped.

I gulped a hard swallow, well aware that I needed to dial back my anger. I hated how easily I could still be set off, especially around well-meaning people. This wasn't me.

Aspen, the ever patient friend I didn't deserve, simply waited, much as Beckett did the other night around the firepit. It wasn't fair to like and hate the man so much all in the same moment. It hurt my damn brain.

I took a deep, centering breath. "Sorry."

"You're hurting. I get it."

That didn't mean she deserved my misplaced anger. Especially when it was still so damn unpredictable.

Travis knew how to push all my buttons at once, and set me off like a fucking bomb. He worked me up until I exploded, and then got really calm, convincing me time and time again that I was the crazy one. The one who couldn't control their temper. That I was the problem in our relationship, despite him never once taking account-ability for a single thing.

Though I never got to that level of anger since I broke things off with him, I still dealt with a short fuse more than I cared to admit.

Maybe someday, it'd get better.

Maybe I'd even be myself again.

But today was not that day. Because the man I was secretly crushing on—the same man who served overseas with my brothers and won over the hearts of my entire family—was destroying the one thing that meant the most to me.

Served me right for letting down the walls I fortified and swore to never let falter.

"He's buying the building. Not the bookstore."

She frowned, as if trying to unriddle my words, and then shook her head in defeat. "What does that mean?"

"It means Dad's liquidating the business."

"Oh, sweetie. I'm so sorry. I—"

The hum of an engine turned both our heads. I

reached for the handle of Husker's leash so he wouldn't run off to greet our newcomer and end up chasing a deer. Husker was more than a little annoyed at the yank when he tried. He looked at me, then at Tango—who was leash-free—and back at me.

Not fair, Mom.

"So, I invited a stray," Aspen admitted, biting her lower lip the way she did when she did something sneaky and was hoping I wouldn't be mad at her for doing it.

A white Bronco rounded the bend, appearing from the clearing. Alyssa Bennett waved from her open window.

I tensed.

The three of us had been best friends since kindergarten. We had our share of fights throughout the years, but last summer, Alyssa reached a breaking point with me after what it took to get me to Aspen's wedding at all. We hardly spoke that weekend because she was so pissed. And that was all before Stupid Intoxicated Kira decided to steal the microphone from the band.

I couldn't blame Alyssa for being upset with me, but it didn't make me any more excited to see her today.

Though I planned to reach out to her—eventually—I wasn't prepared for this conversation right now. Not after the bomb that was dropped on me only hours ago.

"Did she move home?" I asked Aspen as she stood and slipped her feet back into her flip-flops.

"No. She's in town for the weekend. You heard about Mom's surprise birthday party?"

"Yeah. Connor mentioned it. But are you sure *this* is a good idea?" I muttered to Aspen as Alyssa hopped out of her Bronco. The second her gaze landed on me, her cheerful expression hardened. I could feel the laser beams from her narrowed gaze penetrating my bones. The urge to hop in my Jeep and run away was overpowering, but I fought my way through it. Like it or not, Alyssa was on my apology tour list.

"You didn't tell me *she* was going to be here," Alyssa hissed.

"Yeah, same," I said, defensiveness rising automatically. Husker didn't seem to care about the tension. Only that Tango was allowed to trot up to Alyssa without restraint and he was unfairly tethered by a leash. He gave me a look that said as much.

"Okay, okay," Aspen said, lifting her hands in surrender. "I tricked the two of you. But I had a good reason."

"You're going to help me make her body disappear at the bottom of this lake?" Alyssa guessed, a sinister smile spread across her lips as she gave Tango pets.

"Funny, I was just thinking the same thing about you," I fired back.

We stared one another down for several tense seconds, with narrowed glares and pinched lips. She had every right to be pissed at me. During the drive to Bluebell Springs for Aspen's wedding, she let me know exactly what she thought of Travis. She made it pretty clear that if I stayed with him, our friendship would not survive. Though deep down I knew she was well meaning, I never responded well to being told what to do. I was also at my fucking limit. There'd been tension ever since.

"If you two want to throw punches"—Aspen looked at me—"or *snakes*, leave me and the dogs out of it."

Light danced in Alyssa's eyes, and her tightly pursed

lips curled at the ends. Suddenly, I was fighting a smile, too.

We both burst into laughter at the same time, meeting in the middle and falling into a hug. The kind of hug I'd been desperately craving for what seemed like forever. The kind of hug that reassured me that though I may have hurt some feelings last year, my closest friends and family did not abandon me. I could fix this.

Husker wedged his way between our legs, insistent that *he* should be the center of attention now that Tango had his turn.

"I heard you ditched The Asswipe," Alyssa said, letting go and crouching to greet Husker.

"Have you been talking to Luke?" I asked on a laugh.

"I have my sources."

"Well, this was easier than I thought it would be," Aspen murmured.

"You thought you were staging an intervention again, didn't you?" Alyssa asked.

"Well, yeah."

The three of us laughed as we unloaded paddleboards from vehicles and set to inflating them. Thankfully, my friends shared their battery-powered pumps. My arms were still sore from my last encounter with a hand pump.

"You remember that time you tried to do an intervention because Alyssa and I got into a huge fight over Tony Nickles?"

I shook my head, remembering how big a deal that seemed at fifteen years old. How the world seemed to come crashing down when we found out Tony had made out with both of us.

"I did you both a favor," Aspen said, pulling off her sweatshirt.

It was an unusually warm day at the lake, not a cloud in the sky. The wind was nearly nonexistent, and the water still. But despite the warm sun, it still had nothing on the Nebraska humidity. I also remembered how chilly the water was and decided I'd rather keep my sweatshirt on this time.

"Have you seen what's become of dear ol' Tony?"

"No," I said.

I had to unfriend all the boys I went to high school with on social media. Travis was convinced they'd reach out and hit on me—none of them ever did—and I did it to prove I only wanted him.

I did a lot of stupid things to prove my loyalty.

"He was balding so badly he started shaving his head. He's also got a nice beer gut."

"And to think you two ended up mud wrestling over him," Aspen said, laughing.

"You could have picked somewhere dry to hold your intervention," I said to Aspen.

I anchored my paddle to my ankle with the tether, still amazed that Beckett found it. It made it even harder to be mad at him, and right now, I *needed* to be mad at him. Anything else was far too complicated.

We paddled out to the middle of the lake. I didn't dare do anything reckless like stand on the board like my friends. Tango simply sat on the edge of the board and watched, making it easy for Aspen to navigate without risk of crashing into the water.

My crazy dog, however, was pacing. Probably my fault

for giving him a pup cup early this morning—my pathetic attempt to remain number one when I knew damn well I was far down on the list.

He loved it here.

Would it be so crazy to . . . *move home?*

"How long?" Alyssa asked me when we stopped paddling and simply floated in the middle where the best view of the largest, snowcapped mountains was.

"How long am I home?"

"How long ago did you dump the sorry excuse for a boyfriend you had?"

"The night of Aspen's wedding."

Aspen looked at me, her expression revealing shock.

"I've been no contact with him since I picked up my stuff from his place the next day."

"That's why you left without telling anyone?" Alyssa guessed.

"Travis supposedly planned a romantic weekend away the same weekend as your wedding," I said to Aspen, since Alyssa already knew this part.

"What?" Aspen asked, her question a mere whisper.

"You still haven't told her?" Alyssa asked.

I ignored the prodding I deserved and went on.

"He claimed I never told him your wedding date, even though the save the date was on his fridge for months."

I took a deep breath, reminding myself that this was all in the past. Travis was in the past. These were just things that happened to me. Things I couldn't change. Things that no longer deserved my energy or emotions. But my closest friends deserved an explanation.

"In case it's not obvious, he's a narcissistic asshole. He

controlled every aspect of my life for three years, but I was too stupid to see it for a long time."

"You weren't stupid," Alyssa said, giving me a break I didn't expect. "You're a decent human being who never expected someone you trusted and cared about to be so fucking deceitful and manipulative. Give yourself some grace."

I sent her an appreciative smile as Husker finally settled on the board, pointed toward the mint green house across the lake in his Sphinx-like position. The same house with the garden and kayaks. I wondered if Luke was called out to the lake that night I fell in. If Beckett met him and told him some crazy redhead fell into the water and needed rescuing.

Did he know who I was then?

Impossible.

Or was it?

We never met until a few days ago, and his surprise seemed as genuine as mine. But I heard about him so much over the years that it felt as though I knew him. He probably heard about me. Saw pictures. But he pretended not to know me. Or was that real? Maybe the red hair threw him.

Gah, I hated how confused I was. I didn't know if it was because of the bookstore secret or because I was dredging up all this shit about Travis. Probably a combination of both.

"You okay?" Aspen asked.

"There's a lot I haven't told anyone," I admitted.

"You can tell us if and when you're ready," she added.

"Oh, I'm ready," I answered immediately. I held on to

Travis' secrets for too long, thinking I was protecting him when really I was enabling his shitty behavior. I understood now I'd been abused into silence. I owed him nothing. So, I told them everything.

I told them how he wasn't merely an alcoholic. How he gambled away thousands of dollars, chasing some high I didn't understand. How he convinced me the FBI was tapping his house so we could never have a fully honest conversation. How he always made my birthday all about him. How he ruined one Christmas by packing all my belongings—including fully un-decorating the seven-foot Christmas tree I bought—and left everything in the hallway of my apartment, all because I spent the day in Lincoln with my grandparents who were in state visiting.

"Why did you never tell us?" Aspen asked gently.

"It all sounds crazy. I thought *I* would sound crazy. That no one would believe me."

"He convinced you not to go to my wedding?" Aspen asked. "Because he planned a *romantic* getaway?"

"There was no trip." If I'd skipped the wedding, Travis would have made up some excuse about the hotel reservation getting canceled—through no fault of his own. I knew that now. "But I was so afraid of the consequences of not doing what he wanted that I wasn't planning to come."

"To be fair," Alyssa said to Aspen, "I basically kidnapped her against her will."

"The night of your wedding, Travis got super drunk and texted me a picture of a receipt from Berkenheimer's."

Aspen threw a hand over her mouth. "He didn't."

"He wanted to punish me for going to your wedding.

So he sent a picture of the receipt for an engagement ring he returned."

"Can we go hunt down this asshole right now? I'll bring the shovels."

"I'd been drinking too much," I admitted. "Because before that picture, he was blowing up my phone saying the worst things to make me feel bad about leaving him home alone. When that picture came through, I just . . . lost it. My ability to hold everything inside just disappeared."

"And you thought the best way to let it all out was to give a toast to the bride and groom that turned into a family roasting?" Alyssa asked, her question kinder than I deserved.

I met her gaze across the water between our circled boards, and we burst into laughter.

"You know, not *everything* you said was terrible," Aspen admitted.

"And some of it was pretty fucking funny," Alyssa agreed. "Like how Luke always has a stick up his ass, even when he's happy."

"I'm sorry for making a scene," I said to Aspen. Then I looked at Alyssa. "I'm sorry you had to fly to Omaha and kidnap me, but I'm really glad you did. If you hadn't—"

"Okay, okay," Alyssa said, holding up her hands. Both dogs looked at her, as though she might have treats. "That's enough. You're forgiven, but only if we can move the fuck on. And if you promise the only time you will ever see Travis again is if we're burying his body somewhere deep in the forest where no one will ever think to look."

God, I didn't deserve friends like this.

"Deal."

"I'm hungry," Aspen announced. "Let's go grab a burger at Kat's."

"Um, pretty sure I'm banned," I said.

"I called in a favor," Aspen said of her aunt. "But you owe me one."

I owed her a lot more than a simple favor. I owed them both. "Dinner's on me."

"If you want us to argue, we're not going to," Alyssa said.

Maybe I couldn't save Mom's bookstore, but at least my most important friendships were still intact.

"Anyone up for darts?"

"Only if you won't cheat," Alyssa said to me.

"I never cheat," I said, turning my board around but refusing to get off my butt. Partially, I was feeling lazy. Mostly, I wasn't eager to be tossed into the lake again.

"You *always* cheat," Aspen agreed with her. "But it doesn't matter. I'll still beat you."

Despite the shittiness of the bookstore situation, at least I still had my friends.

But I also still had to deal with Beckett Campbell and my conflicting urges to sneak across the hall tonight to smother him with a pillow . . . or crawl under his covers and mount him.

TWENTY
BECKETT

Cutting the ignition, I scanned the full parking lot of Kat's Place. I didn't recognize any of the vehicles packed into the gravel lot. No patrol car. No beater truck. *No red Jeep.*

Just as well. I could grab a late dinner to-go and head back to the Kniffen Street house to finally start mudding. I did some of my best thinking while mudding and sanding walls. And after the lunch hour that stretched to two hours and ended with dessert pizza and slightly tipsy book club members who had a whole lot to say about a certain Margene Miller, I had a lot to think about.

Before I could push open my truck door, my phone rang.

Closing my eyes, I took a deep centering breath as I pulled the phone from my shirt pocket. Some days, the temptation to throw this thing in the lake was stronger than others.

When I opened my eyes, it wasn't Madeline's name on the screen as I expected, but Nana's.

Small relief, though still more than I wanted to deal with tonight. But I didn't dare send her to voicemail.

"Hey, Nana."

"Well, how'd it go?" Nana asked, skipping the pleasantries just like Madeline always did. Guess it ran in the family, and I never noticed.

"I did a walk-through of the bookstore today with the current owner and an appraiser."

"And?"

"It's a good building. Great building, actually. Corner location in the middle of downtown. An apartment upstairs that could be rented out. Good bones. No obvious issues. It's been well kept up. There'd be no issue leasing it out. I'm told there's plenty of local interest. I have a meeting with my realtor next week to go over market rent rates."

"It's priced competitively, I'm sure."

"The appraiser hasn't given the owner a final number yet. He promised to have it by early next week, but I have a ballpark. I've been promised first right of refusal."

"You get that in writing?"

"No," I admitted. "Didn't think that'd go over well here."

"Ah, I forget you're in a small town."

Nana grew up in a town roughly this size and lived there until her first husband passed away. But once she remarried a couple of decades ago, she moved from major city to major city. Now that she was a wealthy widow, she traveled the world and bought real estate when she was bored. She avoided small towns as much as possible. Whether she liked being on the go, or was running from the painful memories of losing Gramps, I still hadn't decided.

"You have the capital to make this work?" she asked.

"That shouldn't be a problem."

The bookstore would require a hefty down payment and likely be the last property I acquired for a while, until I built my cash reserve back up—unless Karl did something shocking, like offer to sell me the cabin on the lake. It would mean frugal living for a while if he did, but I'd make it work. Maybe pick up some handyman jobs around town if I wanted to build that reserve more quickly. Joe promised there were plenty if I wanted them.

The book club ladies would get a kick out of that.

"That's why I'm leaving you everything in the will," she cackled. "You never ask for money."

She didn't have to say the rest. We both heard it. *Unlike my ungrateful, entitled daughter.*

"You can leave it to Madeline." It was my typical response.

"So she can give it all to your mother? Fat chance. Madeline's heart's in the right place, but her actions are a bit misguided. Heard she's been trying to con you into letting your folks live in one of your Richmond rentals."

"Yeah," I said on a heavy sigh. I didn't bother to ask how she heard that. Maybe Kyle filled her in.

"You're not letting them?"

"Not a chance in hell."

"Good. Doesn't do any good to enable people who

wouldn't lift a damn finger to help themselves, much less anyone else."

Though Nana sounded heartless, she'd tried as much as I did to help my parents. She spent a great deal more money doing it, too.

"It's too bad," Nana said, sounding as though she meant it. "Your mother could have had such a different life, but she had to go and get mixed up with that drunk." She never referred to my dad as *my dad*, for which I was grateful. "Ruined her whole life. But not my circus, not my monkeys. Not anymore. I bailed her out of jail once. She didn't learn her lesson."

Her comment sparked a thought from my earlier lunch conversation.

"Slightly off topic, but do you know any good private investigators?"

"What do you need a PI for? You in some kind of hot water?"

I instantly regretted my question, but I knew better than to weasel out of the answer now. "No, nothing like that."

"You trying to get the four-one-one on that redhead from the lake before you go and get mixed up with her?"

It shouldn't surprise me that she remembered that very brief conversation. I avoided that topic entirely.

"The old manager for the bookstore I'm buying stole a bunch of money and took off south of the border. It's the reason the owner is liquidating. They haven't found her."

"I thought you were buying the building."

"I am."

"Sounds like you're trying to buy a business, too."

"I don't think it's for sale."

And even if it were, what the hell did I know about running a bookstore? Not a damn thing. The only thing worse than the bookstore going out of business, per Joe's decision, was if some idiot decided to buy it and ran it immediately into the ground. I didn't need to be that idiot.

"You can't get emotionally invested, Beck."

"I know."

But I tasted the lie, and it tasted like lake water, iced coffee and, unsurprisingly, a little bit like dog breath.

Until moving to Bluebell Springs, I did a solid job of *not* getting emotionally invested with my investment properties. I always offered a fair price for any property I acquired, and I hired the best property managers to ensure my tenants were well taken care of. But the hometown of my closest friends and their family was a far cry from a city where everyone could easily become invisible if they wanted.

I was learning, very quickly, that *not* getting emotionally invested was the wrong way to go about things here.

"This about a woman?"

"What? No."

"Fuck. It is, isn't it?"

"She's one of the Masons, that's all."

"Christ on a cracker, is *she* the one who fell in the lake?"

It was eerie how perceptive Nana was. I suppose it was one of the reasons she was worth millions.

"That was a coincidence."

"The redhead, right?"

"Kira."

"You're picking me up from the Denver airport Sunday."

"You don't need to come, Nana."

"Just booked my ticket."

"Already?"

"I'll text you my itinerary."

"I don't have anywhere for you to stay—"

"I've got it covered. And Beck?"

"Yeah?"

"Keep it in your pants until I get there, mkay?"

The call ended as a motorcycle pulled into the parking lot, taking a narrow spot in front of my truck. Thoren pulled off his helmet and hung it from the handlebar. He caught sight of me and nodded a hello.

I turned my phone to silent, shoved it in my shirt pocket, and got out of the truck.

"It's fucking strange seeing you all over town," Thoren said, sporting a grin as we headed to the front door. "Beckett Campbell living in my hometown. Never thought you'd settle somewhere small."

"Small town life is growing on me."

"You haven't been here long enough for the town to decide they know all your shit. Tell me how you feel after that happens."

I held open the door. "You ever moving back?"

"Nah," Thoren said. "Nothing for me here."

Except his eyes zeroed in immediately on a brunette laughing in the corner. The woman I didn't recognize was huddled with Aspen—and Kira.

Fuck, Kira was *here*.

I froze behind Thoren.

"You two dumbasses coming inside or you just going to stand in the doorway and let in the flies?" Luke slapped me on the back of the shoulder, breaking the trance before Kira had a chance to spot me. "You're late."

"Took the scenic route," Thoren said, clearing his throat as I followed them both to a high-top near the bar.

"Who's that?" I asked Thoren.

"A ghost," he mumbled, taking a seat that allowed him to put his back to the brunette.

Kira glanced my way as I pulled out the seat adjacent to him, our gazes locking for a single heartbeat. Her long red hair was tied back in a wavy ponytail high up on the crown of her head. One side of it hung over her shoulder. I followed the path of that long hair down the side of her face, her neck, her collarbone, right to the low cut of her tight teal shirt where a silver necklace dangled into her cleavage.

Fuck, she was beautiful.

I yearned to explore every peak and valley with my fingertips.

The moment was shattered a second later when those blue eyes narrowed into daggers directed right at me. She spun away, putting her back firmly to me.

Message received.

"Heard you got assaulted by the book club today," Luke said from behind a menu he probably didn't need to look at but studied anyway every time we came here. He always ordered the same damn thing.

"I joined them for lunch," I offered, sneaking another glance at Kira.

"You sure you want to go there?" Thoren asked, his

voice low enough to be drowned out by the country music so Luke didn't hear.

Fuck, had I been that obvious?

"Not going anywhere."

Kira Mason was off limits.

Whether she hated me or not, that would never change.

But fuck, I was only a man. It was impossible not to appreciate the view.

"Guess we're both full of shit tonight, huh?" I asked him.

"They had some opinions about Dad selling the bookstore?" Luke asked of the book club ladies.

"When did you become such a gossip girl?" Thoren ribbed.

"It's not fucking gossip," Luke shot back. "I need to know what's going on in my town."

"Sure, *Glenda*."

Luke shot him a pissy look.

Kat Hayes broke the tension, arriving at the table with a tray of drinks—iced tea for Luke, who was in uniform, a water for me, and a lager for Thoren. She dropped a fully tattooed arm around Thoren's shoulders and squeezed him in a half hug. "You boys need an appetizer?"

"Surprise us?" Thoren said to his aunt.

"I got something I think you'll like."

"No jalapenos," Luke pleaded.

"I'll go easy on you. This time."

"I appreciate that. Say, you going soft, Kat?" Luke asked, nodding to the women in the corner by the dartboard.

"Don't you worry about me," she said to Luke. "Your sister's on probation, and I refuse to serve her any alcohol, even if she's on her best behavior."

"If she gives you any trouble—"

"I'll let you do the honors."

Thoren looked at me. "Luke put Kira in the back of his patrol car last summer, in the cage, and drove out of here with lights flashing."

"Seems excessive," I said.

Luke's expression soured, but before he could explain himself, Thoren chimed in.

"You should have heard what Kira said about him."

"Cut her some slack," Kat said, her firm tone hinting at gentleness.

Kat Hayes had a reputation for being a hard-ass. You had to be, to run a bar and grill in a small tourist town. But underneath that armor, I suspected she was a big softy.

"She was going through a rough time," she said.

"Still doesn't excuse the way she acted."

"Luke Mason, get off your damned high horse, or I'll put jalapeno seeds in everything I serve you tonight, iced tea included."

"Yes, ma'am."

I hid my smile behind my sweating glass of water. Thoren didn't bother hiding his at all.

I scanned the crowded bar and grill as Kat wove through the tables back to the kitchen, my gaze landing once again on Kira. She held a dart, her arm bent at the elbow as she lined it up, and fired. It hit somewhere on the inner circle. I didn't have to wonder if she was good. The confident smirk she wore when she pulled her darts from the board and spun around said she knew what she was doing.

I bet she was competitive. An idea was taking form in my brain—a really stupid idea involving darts and side bets.

"So, Alyssa's in town," Luke said, effectively wiping the cheeky grin right off Thoren's face.

"She's just here for Mom's party," Thoren said flatly, downing half his lager in a single long swallow.

"Is it really out at the cabin?" Luke asked.

"Shocker, right?" Thoren said.

"The cabin on Ghost Lake?" I asked.

Luke nodded.

"I thought—" I cut myself off before I sounded like a fucking gossip, too. Guess that meant Karl wasn't selling the cabin after all. Probably why he didn't return my voicemail. I could survive a few more days staying across the hall from Kira. Especially since she was doing everything in her power to avoid me.

"Fixed you boys up a sampler platter," Kat said, dropping a massive plate filled with nachos, quesadillas, poppers, wings, and three different types of dip in the middle. "If you still want burgers, I can get those going."

Luke ordered his usual to-go.

"Extra jalapenos," Thoren said to Kat.

"Not funny."

"It's a little funny," I added, remembering the jalapeno hoax we pulled on him in Afghanistan. He'd probably hold a grudge about that for the rest of our lives. But fuck, it was worth it.

Luke grumbled.

I helped myself to some nachos.

"I forgot how fucking good this food is," Thoren moaned.

Kat served bar food, but she had to have a few special ingredients up her sleeve. Like crack, because it was *that* addictive. Much better than any typical bar food I tried anywhere in the country.

"You reenlisting, then?" Luke asked Thoren, the question throwing me.

"It's what I do," he said on a shrug.

"Where you headed next?"

"Trying to get Alaska."

"You still like it?" I asked. When we all served together, we were Blackhawk mechanics. Some of us had also been crew chiefs. But I got out when they made me a platoon sergeant and told me I couldn't work on helicopters anymore.

"It's something to do," Thoren answered noncommittally, his head swiveling over his shoulder for another look at Alyssa.

I searched my memories but couldn't recall her name coming up in conversations when we served. But with the way they kept sneaking glances at one another, neither wanting to be caught by the other, I'd bet there was history there.

"And if I get Alaska, I don't care what they make me do."

Kat returned with Luke's to-go burger just as his phone buzzed on the table. A call, I suspected. She waited for him to stand before handing him the bag.

"You'll be there tomorrow?" Kat asked him about the surprise party.

"I will."

She patted him on the arm, probably because she couldn't easily reach his shoulder with them both standing. Luke towered over most people, me included. "Be safe out there."

Luke nodded on his way out the door.

"You boys good?" Kat asked, taking Thoren's empty bottle. "I can bring you another."

"Bring it to the table over there," Thoren said, pointing to an empty high-top near the dartboard. "And a round of drinks for the ladies."

"Play nice, Thoren," Kat warned.

"I always play nice," he said, sporting a mischievous smile that suggested I should talk him out of this.

But the truth was, I'd been thinking the same thing. Maybe Nana was right to get on a plane and come straighten me out. Because the draw to Red was too damn enticing, and even if she was pissed at me right now, tonight I didn't feel much like fighting the pull.

I felt like taking a risk.

TWENTY-ONE
KIRA

"Nope. No boys allowed," Alyssa said as both Thoren and Beckett filled a nearby high-top with a giant plate of food.

My stomach rumbled at the sight of it, despite having inhaled a bacon cheeseburger and Kat's special seasoned fries less than an hour ago. Considering dessert awaited us —courtesy of Aspen—I shouldn't be tempted to steal a nacho.

But I did anyway.

"Careful," Beckett said, one corner of his mouth tipped up in a half smile.

I shouldn't like it. I shouldn't like anything about the man buying Mom's bookstore. The same man who kept it a secret, and blindsided me earlier today. But tell that to the butterflies throwing a fucking rager in my belly, remembering the way he held me during my panic attack. They caught a whiff of his delicious scent—some unfairly sexy mixture of pine needles and manliness—and shut off contact with my logical brain.

"You wouldn't want to get kicked out for stealing."

"Wouldn't be the first time I was kicked out of here."

If I were smart, I'd call it a day and head back to the farm. Except, I didn't have a ride since I left my Jeep behind when I dropped off Husker.

"So I've heard," Beckett said.

"You ladies aren't afraid of a little friendly competition, now, are you?" Thoren's question was directed ninety-nine percent at Alyssa. They were locked in a staring contest.

Those two had a special love-hate relationship on account of Thoren breaking her heart over a decade ago when he enlisted in the Army without telling her. But I was too distracted with my own dilemma of the six-foot-two variety to unravel whatever was currently happening in their soap opera.

"You suck at darts," Alyssa said to Thoren.

"You're good, though," Beckett said to me, his voice low enough so only I could hear. I made the mistake of flickering my gaze to his, and my traitorous nipples tightened as a result.

"Stalking is totally a serial killer thing."

Dammit, was I flirting? *Stop flirting with the enemy, Kira.*

I averted my eyes, but instead of looking back at the dartboard, or the table of cupcakes, or at Aspen or Alyssa, they traveled of their own accord, taking in the delicious way Beckett's biceps strained the sleeves of his T-shirt. Maybe I should've let him dive underwater and save me from drowning the other day so I could experience exactly what those muscles were capable of for myself.

What the hell, Kira? You're supposed to be mad at him.

"I was being observational." Beckett nodded at the tabletop filled with an array of cupcakes. "What's the occasion?"

Aspen brought them along to celebrate my twenty-fifth book release. Something I forgot all about until Lila called earlier. I made the mistake of putting her on speakerphone in front of my friends.

But if I were being honest, I was secretly thrilled that my best friends wanted to make a thing out of it. I'd forgotten how much fun celebrating the little things could be, and made a vow to do it more often. Even if I never published another book, there would be other wins worth acknowledging.

I hoped.

"Who says there's an occasion?" I asked, my guard going up of its own accord.

The last time I shared my excitement for a book release with a man, he reached right into my chest, yanked out my heart, and stomped on it thoroughly.

"Oh, please," Alyssa said, rolling her eyes, reaching across me to steal a nacho. "Are you still keeping that a secret, Kira? Or should I say Dia—"

"Yes, it's a secret," I hissed between gritted teeth, feeling the heat of Beckett's curious gaze as I gently elbowed Alyssa in the side.

Alyssa rolled her eyes. "Fine. My lips are sealed." She made the juvenile gesture of zipping her lips with her index finger and thumb and throwing away the key. "You two playing or what? Aspen has to head home, so it's just the four of us."

"Sorry, kids. I have to open the bakery tomorrow." Aspen gave me a quick hug, lowering her voice as she said, "Enjoy your dessert." Her twinkling eyes glanced at Beckett, then back at me. "You earned it."

"I'm not—"

But Aspen didn't wait around for my rebuttal. Just as well. She'd rendered me speechless. Fuck, was I *that* obvious? I was supposed to be pissed at the man. If my best friends could see right through me, I had to be extra careful around my family. I came back to make amends for the drama I caused last summer, not cause more of it. And sleeping with my brother's best friend seemed like a good way to do exactly that.

"Well?" Alyssa asked again.

"What's the game?" Beckett asked.

"Cricket," Thoren volunteered. "But we'll play the easy way, without the order. That work for you ladies?"

"Sure. If you need the handicap, old man," Alyssa said to him.

"I'll play," Beckett said, looking at me expectantly as Thoren and Alyssa continued to quietly banter.

"Are you some secret dart shark or something?" I asked him.

"Or something."

The answer reminded me of something he said at Ghost Lake, and a shiver went through me from head to toe. But not the bad kind of shiver that should shock some sense into me. Oh, no. This was the sinfully delicious kind of shiver I'd written about in many romance novels.

You cannot sleep with Beckett Campbell.

Not tonight.

Not ever.

"I should warn you," Alyssa said to Beckett, "Kira cheats."

"I do not."

"I'm not worried," Beckett said, his gaze locked on mine again.

I should have asked Aspen for a ride. This whole exchange felt dangerous, and yet, I couldn't seem to help myself. I leaned into it.

"Your funeral," I said, giving him a flirty shrug before spinning toward the dartboard to retrieve my purple darts.

"Care to make a little wager?" he asked when I returned to the table.

"What do you have in mind?"

"If I win, you tell me your secret."

My heart pounded in my ears. I was good at darts, but I had no idea if Beckett was a secret world-class dart champion. Considering he'd been in the military, I suspected he had decent aim.

"And if I win?"

"What do you want?"

I wanted many things I had no right to want. I wanted him to push me up against the wall and kiss me breathless. I wanted to rid him of that fitted shirt and trace my fingertips over all those tattoos as he told me about each and every one. I wanted him to sneak me into his bedroom and put that mouth to other good uses, too.

My resolve to stay mad tonight was clearly shot to hell. I blamed too much time in the sun for scrambling my brain, since I was drinking Dr. Pepper and couldn't attribute my poor lapse in judgment to the alcohol.

To keep myself from saying anything stupid, I shifted focus.

"I would say a bookstore, but I don't think that's on the table."

"Kira," he said, his gruff tone so gentle it stirred something inside me.

Or maybe it was the compassion lingering in his eyes that threatened to undo me. Those damn eyes that were both intense and kind at the same time. It would be so much easier to hate him if he were rude, unapologetic, or selfish. But so far, Beckett Campbell proved to be none of the above.

"Looks like I'm not the only one keeping secrets," I finally said.

"I tried to tell you."

"When? When we were outside by the firepit the other night for almost an hour?"

"I should have told you then."

"Why didn't you?"

"I was distract—"

"Can you two stop bickering and start playing?" Thoren hollered over the music. "I have a bet to win, and it's boys against girls."

"Fat chance," Alyssa said to Thoren.

I knew this game well and was good at it, whether we aimed for numbers in order or not. I stepped up to the line, finding my center so I could focus on my shot, but barely. I could *feel* Beckett's eyes on me.

Why did I have to like it so much?

I took a deep breath, and focused on the twenty section.

My dart landed just above the triple twenty slot, in a single zone.

I let out a breath I hadn't realized I was holding. It wasn't what I was aiming for, but at least it was close. *Twenty was better than zero.*

"Not bad," Beckett said.

I aimed the second dart but missed the twenty by one slot section.

"I tried to find you last night," Beckett said as I took aim with my final dart of the round. "You were asleep."

Dammit, he was right. I was avoiding him.

I threw the final dart, but it bounced off the board and landed on the floor. *Shit.*

I retrieved my darts, but when I tried to return to the table, Beckett blocked my path. I put out a hand to avoid a full-on collision. Big mistake. My palm flattened against his chest, and there was no question that all his cut lines, hard muscle, and *man* were not an illusion. Not when I could touch them so easily.

I jerked my hand away as though I touched a hot burner. In some ways, I had.

"Do you *want* the bookstore?"

"I don't live here," I reminded him.

"That's not what I asked."

I didn't know how to answer that, so instead I said, "If I win, I want a favor."

"What kind of favor?"

"A future favor."

"Done."

"Just like that?"

"Do you want me to argue?"

"Nope."

He stepped up to the line, his first dart hitting the triple twenty I'd aimed for three times but missed.

Double shit.

Beckett threw again, hitting the double nineteen. This was not looking good.

I pilfered a cupcake and took a bite.

Alyssa squealed with excitement the next board over, throwing off Beckett's third throw. She hit a bullseye. Thoren looked at her with the same adoration he had at sixteen. Maybe someday, those two would figure out they were meant to be together.

Maybe not.

Was anyone ever really meant to be together?

I took a second generous bite of a confetti cupcake filled with some type of delicious cream I couldn't quite pin. Cake batter?

When I first met Travis, he seemed to be everything I was looking for in a man. He checked every single box. Except, he actually didn't check any of them. He pretended to be what I wanted, and only after I was completely ensnared in his web did I realize he fooled me.

The revelation was gradual at first. When the full truth finally hit the day I drove back to Omaha to break things off, it packed one helluva punch. It made me question everything I ever thought I knew about love.

About fate.

I used to believe in fate.

Now, it seemed to hold true only in the fiction I wrote.

Used to write.

I took another bite.

Maybe that's why I was stuck.

I couldn't bring myself to write the love stories I no longer believed in.

Shit, that's heavy.

Too heavy.

I finished off the cupcake and wiped my fingers on a napkin.

"You okay?" Beckett asked.

"Yep. Why?"

"It's your turn." He offered my darts to me. "Been your turn for a few minutes now."

"Oh." My fingertips grazed his warm hand as I took them. I was instantly pulled back to the bookstore, sitting on the cold tile, Beckett's warmth wrapped around me like a blanket as I slowly came back to consciousness. How he held a cold compress against my forehead, never once rushing me. He not only took care of me without me asking, he didn't expect anything in return for doing it.

Yeah, this whole being upset with him thing was on shaky ground.

And if I didn't start playing dirty, I was going to lose more than this game.

Maybe I want to lose.

I focused all of my attention on the dartboard, took a deep breath, and threw.

My dart hit the double twenty. Then a triple eighteen. And a single sixteen.

Oh, thank God, there was hope after all.

When Beckett was up again, I stepped up behind him.

Just as he threw the dart, I used a sultry tone and said, "You know the favor I want is open-ended right?"

Beckett stumbled his throw, and his dart hit the wall.

Alyssa laughed.

"I tried to warn you. She cheats."

"Playing dirty, Red?"

Another shiver, this one more centrally located, tingled inside. He hadn't called me Red since we were properly introduced. I didn't realize until now that I missed the nickname.

"Just keeping you on your toes."

He threw his second dart of the round and hit the bullseye.

Damn, he was good.

As Beckett took aim for his final throw, I ran my fingers from his hard bicep to his elbow.

"Don't miss."

His dart hit the edge of the board, barely holding on to the one spot he didn't need.

He looked down at me, those intimidatingly sexy eyes a mixture of mischief and heat.

"Is this how we're playing this game, Red?"

"I don't know what you mean," I said, feigning innocence.

I fluttered my lashes in exaggeration, and Beckett laughed. God, that sound was magical.

"Stop flirting and play," Thoren said, rolling his eyes as though they were any kind of innocent.

Heat flushed over my chest, reminding me that we had an audience. And though we might be somewhat shielded in our corner by the growing crowd, we were not invisible in this very public setting. I didn't need the lecture from Luke, if half the town told him his little sister was flirting with his best friend. He wouldn't buy that I was only doing it to win a game of darts.

He wouldn't be wrong, either.

Just as I released my dart, Beckett's hot breath tickled my neck. Thankfully, the dart still hit a seventeen. But barely.

"I'm going to get a refill," he said, holding an empty cup. "Need anything?"

"Dr. Pepper."

"Coming right up."

I held the second dart, but this time when I went to throw it, I knew better and held on to it. Because Beckett tried once again to steal my tactic.

"No cheating while I'm gone," he said against my ear, his breath a teasing caress against my skin. I shivered as I imagined his warm breath in other places on my body.

"I'll come with you," Thoren said to him.

My second dart landed in the double twenty, closing it out. But only because I waited to throw it until Beckett vanished into the growing crowd.

"Something going on with you two I should know about?" Alyssa asked, her expression all mischief.

"No," I said, shaking my head so vigorously my ponytail swished from side to side. "He's just—"

"Best friends with Luke, Connor, and Thoren," she offered.

"He's the one buying the bookstore," I added, hoping that straightened this out.

"So you're *flirting* with him to what? Convince him to let you buy it instead?"

"I can't afford to buy it," I said, the admission causing my stomach to plummet. I threw the third dart, and by some miracle hit an outer bullseye. *Huh.*

"You sure about that? From what I can tell, your last book launch was a pretty good one."

I considered it, of course. I tossed and turned last night, crunching numbers in my head. But every scenario had me coming up short, both in money and time. "Even if I could afford the building—which I can't—I wouldn't have anything left over to revive the business."

And I had very little knowledge of how to actually run a bookstore. If I found a way to take over and failed . . .

"Fucking Margene Miller," Alyssa grumbled. "Maybe our next girls' trip needs to be to Mexico to find her ass."

"Anyway, I'm headed back to Omaha in a few days. Probably after the going-out-of-business sale is wrapped up next week. I told Dad I'd stick around to help with that."

"You working on your next book?"

"No."

Alyssa's expression shifted from curious to serious. "Will there *be* a next book?"

"No way! You hit a bullseye," Beckett said, handing me a full glass of Dr. Pepper. "Tell me the truth," he said to Alyssa. "Did she cheat?"

"No. But if she did, I wouldn't tell you anyway."

"Fair," he said, picking up his darts.

The game resumed, and Alyssa dropped her question. For now.

I sipped on my Dr. Pepper as he threw three darts in a row and hit nothing that counted toward his score.

"Can't blame me for that round," I said, stepping up to the line again.

"Sure, I can," he said.

"I didn't do anything."

He glanced down at my lips for several beats, then at the straw in my cup. The one with a light pink lipstick tint toward the top.

"Sure, you didn't."

With each round, I played dirtier. So did Beckett.

When he pushed aside my ponytail to reveal the dragonfly tattoo peeking out from my tank top strap, my dart hit the board next to us. When I slipped my hand into his back pocket, his dart shot up at the ceiling.

"Christ, at this rate, you two will be here until morning," Thoren ribbed.

Alyssa had beaten him, but I suspected he let her.

"We're almost done," I shot back.

"She just needs a seventeen and a sixteen," Alyssa said in my defense. "Then it's game over."

"Not if Beckett hits the triple sixteen first," Thoren said. "C'mon. Shut her out, man. You're our only hope."

Beckett stepped up to the line, and I stayed off to the side at our small table, slowly unpeeling the wrapper of a cupcake. I traced my tongue along the cone of white frosting.

"Shit, man. Focus!" Thoren said after he hit the single nine with his first dart.

I bit into the cupcake, allowing the frosting to cover my nose.

Beckett's second dart landed in the regular sixteen spot, but barely.

I dipped my finger into the frosting and sucked on it.

Beckett's final dart hit the wall, just below the board.

"What happened there?" I asked, feigning innocence as I set my cupcake down. I used a napkin to wipe the frosting from my nose, fully aware that Beckett was starting at my mouth. It made me stare right back at his.

I really wanted to find out if he was the type of man to kiss a woman breathless. Because if I was wrong about that, there was no hope for me when it came to men. Not now. Not ever.

"Would you two stop looking at each other like you want to sneak away and screw in the bathroom so Kira can win this thing already?" Alyssa shouted above the music, turning more than a couple of heads.

I was past caring.

This friendly game of darts was doing some wickedly delightful things between my legs. I couldn't remember the last time I craved a man's touch. Even if this never went anywhere, it was refreshing to know that maybe I could date again . . . sometime . . . in the very distant future.

"Kira?" Beckett said, handing me the purple darts.

"Yeah?"

"You missed some frosting." He swiped his thumb along the side of my mouth, and a quiet whimper escaped my throat. I watched as he sucked the frosting from his thumb, and my panties dampened.

Triple shit.

I spun away and faced the dartboard. I had to end this

game. Not only because I wanted the satisfaction of beating Beckett, but because if this game didn't end soon, we'd probably end up making out in front of everyone. Or more. I didn't need to give Kat another reason to blacklist me from her bar. The fries were just too good.

"You got this, Kira," Alyssa cheered from the side.

Thoren made some remark intended to throw me off, but I couldn't make it out over the pounding in my ears.

I tossed my first dart and it hit the eight, just above the sixteen. Dammit.

Alyssa came up behind me, grabbing me by the shoulders. "I know it's hard, but focus. It'll be so much more satisfying if you beat him."

I remembered the open-ended favor that would be my prize, and it made hitting the seventeen spot easy.

"Yay!" Alyssa squealed. "One more, baby!"

Beckett had one elbow leaned against the high-top, his feet crossed at the ankles. "You got it, Kira."

"You're not going to try to sabotage me?" I teased.

He just answered with his sexy half smile.

I sucked in a deep breath and focused. I played darts a lot growing up, taught by both my brothers. I got good. Really good. If I missed this shot, I would never hear the end of it.

And if I hit this shot, Beckett owed me a favor of my choosing.

The dart sailed through the air and landed right where I aimed it—at the eighteen spot.

"Girls rule, boys drool!" Alyssa shouted as she grabbed me up in a hug and stuck her tongue out at Thoren.

"Rematch?" Beckett suggested.

"Sorry, man. I gotta head out," Thoren said to him.

"Me too," Alyssa said, her face turning a slight shade of red. "Beckett, can you give Kira a ride back to the farm?"

I shot her a look that said *what the hell?*

Alyssa ignored me.

"I got her," he said.

"Kira, try not to give Beckett too much grief about beating him? He didn't know what he was up against." Alyssa squeezed me in a hug. "I'll see you at the party tomorrow. But if I don't, I'll call you soon."

Just like that, I was alone with Beckett.

It didn't matter that the place was packed, that the music was almost too loud for regular conversation. I was only aware of Beckett and the fact I'd be riding home in his truck. Returning to a quiet house where everyone else was asleep.

"I have to get the cupcakes," I said to him as I cleaned up what remained of the dessert table.

I felt Beckett behind me and the breath froze in my lungs. All I had to do was take a single step back, and I'd feel his hard chest pressed against my back. Would he wrap his arms around me or slide them down my hips?

"I have a confession," Beckett said.

"Oh?" My hands wobbled as I placed the leftover cupcakes back in their container.

"I already know your secret."

"Doubtful."

The lid clicked shut on the container, and I spun around with it in tow, using it as a barrier. Beckett's gaze locked me in place.

"It took me a while, but I figured it out."

"Figured what out?"

"*Huh*, guess I missed some of that frosting," he said, reaching his thumb up to the side of my mouth again.

I fought the urge to turn my head, to capture that thumb with my own lips. I wanted to see his reaction when I sucked his thumb between my lips. But before I could follow through with that reckless impulse, his confession stopped me dead.

"You're Diana Davenport."

TWENTY-TWO
HUSKER

"Your mom is home."
Mom is home?
Opal, you give the best pets.
You also taste good.
Lick, lick, lick.
"You should go to her. She needs you."
Is she okay?
"I think she's confused."
Oh, I get it.
Mom needs to give me booty scratches.
That'll make her feel better.
"Yes, Bubbies. It will."
Lick, lick, lick.
Opal giggles are my favorite.
"C'mon, Husker."
Uncle Connor.
Does Uncle Connor have treats?

"In his left pocket."
Opal you're the best.
It's why I let you give me hugs.
Oh! Uncle Connor has the leash.
Are we going on a walk?
Click.
"Good boy, Husker."
Left pocket.
Treats.
I need one.
Please, now.
"Calm down, bud."
Uncle Connor has a good laugh.
He has better treats.
Chomp, chomp, chomp.
"Let's go."
It's dark outside.
Way past my bedtime.
Smells like funny walking birds.
Sniff, sniff, sniff.
*Uncle Connor doesn't like it when I chase his funny
walking birds.*
It's really dark.
It's past Mom's bedtime too.
Where is Mom?
Oh, there she is.
Wag, wag, wag.
She's with my new best friend.
She's not mad at him anymore.
But she's not happy either.

Hmm.

"Thanks for watching him."

Mom!

New Best Friend!

Mom!

New Best Friend!

Mom!

New Best Friend!

"Guess we know who he missed more."

Mom has jokes.

I always miss Mom more.

"Hey, Beckett, you have a minute?"

Uncle Connor wants to give my new best friend treats?

"Yep."

"We better get to bed, huh, Bubbies?"

Bed, yes.

Unless New Best Friend has treats.

We should see if he has treats.

"Red?"

"Yeah?"

"Don't worry."

"About what?"

New Best Friend is getting really close to Mom.

Maybe I should step between their legs.

Remind them I'm here.

I'll wedge them apart so I can fit.

I think they forgot I'm here.

Right here.

That's the perfect spot.

"I'll keep your secret."

Mom?
New Best Friend is walking away.
Mom, why are you frozen?
Mom?
"Let's go get you a treat, Bubbies."
Ooh, treat!

TWENTY-THREE
BECKETT

I TURNED onto the familiar private road as the sun lowered toward the mountain peaks in the distance. Cars, trucks, and SUVs lined both sides of the dirt drive leading out to the Ghost Lake cabin, leaving a questionable amount of room for two vehicles headed in opposite directions to pass one another.

As the drive to the cabin was blocked off, I found a spot past the cabin, closer to the lake, and pulled in behind a hunter green 4Runner. I couldn't see the boat dock from here, but I didn't need to. I remembered meeting Kira like it happened yesterday.

I could hear Nana's voice in my head. *You dumbass, it did happen yesterday. Stop thinking with the wrong head.*

The warning wasn't enough to ward off the memory of Kira's wet T-shirt clinging to the curves of her body, her red locks plastered to her cheeks and collarbone. Had she been wearing that necklace the day she fell into the lake? The same one she had on last night that kept disappearing into the V of her shirt. I imagined dipping a finger into the valley between her breasts to reveal what charm dangled on the end of the silver chain. Would she make one of those soft whimpers she made at the bar and grill when I sucked frosting from my thumb as my rough fingertips grazed her soft flesh?

"Oh, good!" The familiar female voice pulled me immediately out of my forbidden fantasy.

"Hey, Aspen."

"Beckett," Aspen said, a look of relief falling over her face. "Can I ask a favor?"

"Of course."

She gave me an apologetic smile as she opened the back door of her SUV, revealing a massive sheet cake with the words *Happy 60th Birthday Wendy* inscribed on it. "I hate to ask, but it's crazy heavy, and I don't think I'd make it to the cabin without tripping. It's literally the only task Dad asked me to handle tonight. I don't want to mess it up by dropping it."

"I got it."

"You are a lifesaver. I sent Owen ahead with Tango so we wouldn't have any mishaps in the car. But my phone died, so I can't call him."

"Really, I don't mind."

"Good. Because we only have about five minutes before my parents are due to arrive."

As I carried the cake and followed her off the heavily rutted road toward a path in the woods, she filled me in about the plan for Karl to pretend to take Wendy out for a special birthday dinner, but a surprise phone call would come in before they got to the restaurant, warning him there were trespassers out at the lake property.

"Think she'll be surprised?" I asked.

"I just hope she's not mad. They haven't been out here in a long time."

Aspen grew quiet as we followed the path through the thick trees toward a clearing. I didn't want to risk putting a damper on the night, so I joined in her silence.

The aroma of grilled burgers and brats hung in the air, and I wondered if someone had cleaned up the old charcoal grill or brought in another for the occasion.

"How late did you and Kira stay out last night?"

I nearly stumbled over my own two feet at the unexpected question. I gripped the edge of the tray beneath the sheet cake as though my life depended on it. I didn't release a breath until my feet were flat on the ground beneath me, and I double-checked that the cake was still fully intact on the tray in my clutches.

"We all left at the same time," I said.

Aspen laughed. "I wasn't insinuating anything."

"Right."

"Not that I'd be entirely against it. You two are grown adults."

This felt like a trap, so I stayed quiet.

"Just know that Kira's been through a lot." Her gentle tone was laced with warning, the sign of a true friend. "If you don't have any intention of treating her right, then maybe the kindest thing you can do is leave her alone."

"I wasn't planning . . . She's not staying."

"Maybe not," Aspen said, sounding as though she might know something I didn't. "But that doesn't give you license to use her and toss her to the side. If you're planning to stay in Bluebell Springs, you *will* run into each other."

"I'd never do that to her."

My admission slipped of its own accord. Kira wasn't just some fling I was pursuing. But she wasn't staying either, which meant anything more was off the table. Not that it mattered if she was staying. Because nothing would change the fact that she was off limits, out of respect for the family who made me an honorary member of their clan.

So what *was* she to me?

I didn't know how to answer that question.

"Good," said Aspen. "Treat her with respect, and I won't have any reason to bury your body at the bottom of a really deep lake. One where the water is too cold for you to ever float to the surface."

"Anyone ever tell you that you're a little scary?" I teased on a shaky laugh.

She directed a beaming smile at me. "Owen. All the time."

I followed Aspen through the clearing toward the cabin.

There was something special about the Ghost Lake property filled with laughter, music, and people that brought it to life in a way I hadn't been able to visualize when Luke showed me the property. Though I preferred my solitude, I could envision hosting the occasional gathering myself.

Too bad Karl wasn't selling.

Maybe I'd live in the Kniffen Street house for a while.

It wasn't as private as the Westons' farm or a quiet cabin on Ghost Lake, but it had a decent-sized garage where I could store materials and tools, and the neighbors were friendly. It could work until I found something more permanent.

"You can set the cake right over there," Aspen directed, indicating a table covered in a sparkly pink tablecloth.

I set the sheet cake beside a wicker basket filled with cards, catching sight of Red over the top of the rounded handle.

There had to be three or four dozen people gathered in the backyard, but my gaze landed on Kira as though I knew she'd be standing by the water. She pointed something out to Opal on the lake. Husker sat by their side, intently staring at a chipmunk perched on a nearby boulder, twitching its tail.

"She only bites when you ask," Aspen said, nodding toward Kira.

"That the vampire in her?" I teased.

Aspen looked shocked. "She told you?"

I shook my head. "I figured it out."

"Does she know?"

"Yeah."

"I'm sure she loved that," Aspen said, laughing. "Well, no promises about the biting thing, then." She patted me on the shoulder as she walked away.

Good thing, too. Or I might have said the quiet part out loud. How I might not entirely hate getting bitten by Kira.

What the hell am I doing?

I didn't know the answer to that, but it didn't stop my feet from moving in her direction.

On my way to Kira, I spotted Luke, Connor, Thoren, and Owen huddled around a stainless-steel gas grill I recognized from the farm. Their expressions were animated and uplifting. Some were laughing. It reminded me of the better nights overseas, when we were off-duty and telling stories.

None of them saw me.

I considered detouring toward the grill, but Connor would have everything under control. I'd just be in the way.

At least that's the excuse I clung to as I weaved my way through the crowd, nodding hellos to a few familiar faces, and made my way to Kira.

Husker saw me first.

He popped to all fours, tail wagging earnestly as the chipmunk scurried away. He looked from me, to the boulder the chipmunk dove beneath, and back to me, as though imploring my help in capturing the furry little beast who was taunting him.

"Uncle Beckett." Opal lit up at the sight of me.

It made me miss my own niece and nephew that much more. If only there were a way to get Madeline and her family out to Bluebell Springs without our parents following, I'd do it in a heartbeat. I liked being an uncle.

My gaze flickered to Kira's, catching the deep blue of her irises.

I might even like being a dad someday.

"I'm still mad at you, you know," she said, the warmth in her eyes suggesting the opposite.

I returned a look that called bullshit.

A gentle blush colored her cheeks as she looked back out toward the water. She'd been acting coy around me ever since I admitted I knew she was Diana Davenport. It took a little digging, admittedly. But after she mumbled something about Veltori vampires mid-panic attack, I'd been trying to solve that puzzle. I figured out she recently released a book—her 25th, according to that celebration cookie—and Alyssa had nearly revealed the name. I had enough to complete a quick Google search at the bar while I waited for our sodas.

Maybe someday, my sharp detective skills would impress her. I wasn't sure that day was here yet.

I directed a question to Opal. "What are we looking at?"

"Ducklings," Opal said excitedly

I spotted a string of six ducklings following a pair of larger ducks, one trailing far behind the group.

"Looks like one's a little confused," I said.

"That's Henry. He gets distracted easily," Opal explained matter-of-factly. As though she knew Henry personally.

Husker leaned his body against my leg, using his full weight. I reached down to scratch his head.

"Husker likes you," Opal said to me.

"I like him, too."

"He doesn't like many boys."

Kira's eyes widened, her lips parted but not moving.

"He likes Dad, Uncle Luke, Uncle Thoren, Uncle Owen, Grandpa Joe, and Grandpa Dale," Opal said. "And you."

Having recovered herself a little, Kira offered me a shrug. "She's not wrong."

"Husker didn't like the bad man," Opal added.

"Should've listened to him," Kira muttered under her breath.

"Husker protected you, Aunt Kira."

"Yes he did. Because he's a really good boy." Her smile seemed forced, not quite reaching her eyes.

I remembered what Aspen had said, and it fueled something inside me—a mixture of frustration, anger, and protectiveness. My fist balled at my side. Who hurt Kira?

"Husker seems like a smart cookie," I said.

The pup snapped his head at me at the word *cookie.* Oops.

"Sorry, bud. But in my defense, you have a lot of buzz words."

"In case you haven't figured it out, they all revolve around food," Kira offered.

"You should carry treats in your pocket," Opal said, producing one.

"You give sound advice for an eight-year-old."

"I'll be nine at the end of the summer," she stated proudly.

"You're growing up way too fast, kiddo," Kira said.

"Aunt Kira, will you come to my birthday party?" she asked, hope sparkling in her eyes.

"Absolutely, I will."

Was Kira . . . staying? Or would she simply make the trip back? Fuck, I shouldn't care what the answer was. It didn't *matter* what the answer was. We could never be anything more than friends. *Friends.* We could be friends.

"Hey, Grandma Connie wants you," Kira said to Opal, nodding toward the crowd closer to the house.

"Uncle Beckett?" Opal said, looking at me as she started to walk away.

"Yeah?"

"Don't overthink it." With those words, she sprinted toward Connie. I stared after her as she disappeared into a sea of people. Many of them I recognized; several I did not. It was easier to focus on that—on anything else—other than the gravity of what an eight-year-old just said to me.

"I swear, some days Opal is just an old lady trapped in a kid's body," Kira said, her gentle laugh uncoiling the tension I'd unknowingly collected in my shoulders. "Speaking of old ladies, I heard you met some of the book club members."

"This small-town life is sure something," I mumbled.

"You planning to stay in Bluebell Springs, then?" she asked, folding her arms over her chest, accentuating parts of her I had no right noticing. I focused instead on the gooseflesh spreading across bare arms, wishing I'd brought along the flannel jacket in my truck to offer her. I'd sneak away the first chance I had to retrieve it.

"Yeah, I think I am."

I followed Kira's gaze back to the water, to the straggler duckling currently being wrangled by a parent.

"What about you?" I asked, despite knowing better. "You ever consider moving home?"

She flickered her gaze to mine, the setting sun deepening the blue of her eyes, reflecting gold flecks. Shit, when had I moved so close to her? I took a subtle step back to preserve the space between us.

"Can you keep a secret?"

"I'd say I'm good at keeping secrets, but somehow I don't think that'd go in my favor."

"You should have told me about the bookstore," she said, agreeing with my statement. The malice from yesterday was missing entirely in this moment. "But maybe we just agree not to keep secrets from this point on?"

The request felt far more intimate than I think she intended, but I didn't hesitate to answer. "No more secrets."

"Good."

"So?" I asked, scratching Husker's head now that he was back to leaning against my legs as though anchoring me in place.

"There's nothing left for me in Omaha, other than Lila."

"Who's Lila?"

"My personal assistant."

"You mean *Diana's* personal assistant," I corrected.

Her gaze instantly darted around, but no one else was within earshot due to the music and light roar of conversation floating through the air.

"No one heard me," I reassured her.

She narrowed her gaze at me anyway, but her lips curled into a smile she wasn't able to fight for long. I liked this. Far too much.

I glanced back toward the grill, but only Connor and Owen were there now. If I had any sense, I'd tell Kira to have a nice evening and seek out my buddies. It wasn't as though she'd be alone. She had friends, too.

Yet my feet stayed rooted in place.

"Husker hates the apartment." Her gaze dropped to him, still pressed against my jeans. He looked up at me, those giant bat ears making him look extra goofy. "We go for walks, but it's not the same as having a yard or trails."

"Why an apartment, then?"

Kira bit her bottom lip, as though weighing how much to share with me. A churning in my gut told me this had something to do with the ex Luke commonly referred to as The Asswipe. "It's kind of a long story," she finally said.

"I have time—"

A loud, piercing whistle silenced the crowd. The music stopped.

"They're coming!" Thoren announced, his voice carrying effectively. "Get ready to make my mom cry."

"She's not going to cry," Aspen yelled.

I glanced at Kira, and we shared a silent laugh. It was fucking with my head how natural this felt between us. As though I'd known her for years instead of days. I guess in some ways, though, I'd known her longer—through her brothers and their animated stories about the fearless little sister who was not afraid to throw snakes, climb trees, or walk barefoot everywhere as a kid. She'd always intrigued me, long before I ever met her.

I was about to tell her as much when the crowd yelled, "Surprise!"

TWENTY-FOUR
KIRA

STARS ILLUMINATED the night sky as I walked Husker along a hard-packed trail that led to the boat dock. The party was still in full swing, more than three hours after Uncle Karl and Aunt Wendy showed up. Thankfully, the surprise was a pleasant one for Wendy. Maybe they'd start using the cabin again. It was a shame for it to sit empty.

But if they didn't, maybe *I* could buy it.

Or at least rent it, if they weren't ready to part with it.

Beckett's question about whether or not I thought about moving home played on repeat in my head all night, whispering in the back of my mind during every conversation I held with anyone.

There really was nothing left for me in Omaha but bad memories and writer's block. Lila was the only friend there who survived my Dark Ages. I pushed the others away too far, and I couldn't blame them now for ignoring my messages.

But could I truly be happy here if I had to watch

Mom's bookstore be dismantled and turned into God-knows-what?

Not for the first time, I wished I knew a way to save it. I didn't know shit about running a bookstore, which only frustrated me more. All those years I spent in Denver after college, I could have been home, learning the business. I could have stepped in after Mom passed instead of Margene.

Fucking Margene Miller.

Instead, I found a job in Omaha so I could follow Travis when he transferred from Denver.

I thought being in Colorado would be too hard after Mom left us. That maybe she brought Travis into my life as a way to ease the sting of her loss, and nudge me on a new adventure.

If I only knew the special hell that awaited me one state over, I'd never have left.

But even if I'd stayed close, it was never my dream to run a bookstore. I wanted to write the books that lived on their shelves. Once upon a time, I had aspirations of being a household name, scheduling book tours around the country, and someday seeing my books on the big screen.

I went from dreaming big to allowing outside influence to turn me small. Travis fed on every insecurity, cementing my fears that I wasn't good enough to make it. That my success was nothing more than a fluke that might unravel at any given time.

Now, I was too chicken to even own up to *being* Diana Davenport, much less travel the country on tour.

"What do you think, Bubbies?" I asked Husker as we stepped out onto the boat dock cloaked in darkness. It would be the perfect hiding spot until someone parked nearby turned on their headlights. "Do you want to move home?"

A nagging whisper in the back of my mind tried to convince me I was only interested in moving back because of Beckett. A man I barely knew. A very off-limits man.

I wouldn't hate being around him more, even if nothing ever came of it.

But he wasn't the reason.

At least, I was ninety-nine percent certain he wasn't the reason.

Ninety-five.

Okay, like ninety.

Beckett or not, it was the family and friends I missed most. The closeness. The connection. If I could find a way to preserve the bookstore before Dad sold the inventory—and maybe kidnap Lila—Bluebell Springs might make sense. Hell, even Luke wasn't being as cold to me as he had a few days ago.

Husker lay down at the edge of the dock as I kicked off my flip-flops and dangled my bare feet above the chilled water. I wished, not for the first time, that I remembered my sweatshirt. Despite the unusually warm evening, it was still much cooler here than Omaha's humid summer nights. I'd rather deal with goose bumps than swampy sweatiness, though.

I rubbed the back of Husker's neck, certain he appreciated the friendlier temperatures with all that Husky fur.

He was so happy here, surrounded by people he loved instead of being stuck with only me in the apartment, bored out of his mind as I spent my days writing—or stressing about not writing, as I had this past year.

"Bubbies, leave it," I warned him when he scooted farther forward, dipping his head over the side, no doubt catching a flicker of pondweed in the sliver of moonlight.

He grumbled in response.

"And what are you going to do if you fall in?" I asked him, as though he understood every word. "Do you *want* to get wet?"

He looked back at me, his head tilted at that sharp angle that made him extra adorable, and usually resulted in bonus treats. I was about to admit as much when I heard the light chatter of male voices.

I stiffened, hoping to remain unnoticed on the edge of the dock. After hours of socializing, I was a little spent. I craved my solitude. But I also wasn't ready to head back out to the farm.

"I wanted to give this place one last hoorah. For Aaron. He loved it out here." Was that . . . *Uncle Karl?* He had an unmistakable gruff voice that tended to travel in clearings. I leaned back, as though that alone would help me hear their conversation better. "But I don't plan to make this a regular thing."

I let out a sigh. That was too bad.

Or maybe it was exactly the permission I needed to ask Karl about renting it myself.

I was a couple of weeks away from having to make a decision on my apartment lease. Was this the sign I needed to take the leap and make the move?

"You're still planning to sell, then?"

Beckett?

What the actual fuck?

Why was Beckett Campbell having this conversation with *my* uncle?

"If you're still looking for somewhere to settle. I know you have other options—"

"I'm definitely interested in this one. Luke mentioned something about rent-to-own?"

Luke? I was going to kill my brother. He might still be a little sore at me for last year, but we were at least back to being amicable to one another. Why the hell didn't he say something to me about the cabin? Uncle Karl had talked about selling the place a few times over the past decade, but he always backpedaled. This time, it sounded serious.

"I'd rather be free and clear of the place, if I'm being honest," Karl said. "Wendy, too." Wendy? She didn't bring it up when we met for an afternoon coffee date the other day. "But I'm sure we can work something out. I heard you're also buying the bookstore, so I understand the timing isn't great."

"I can make it work."

What. The. Fuck.

This was why I didn't let my guard fall anymore when it came to a man. Because no matter how sweet they pretended to be, they were always looking out for themselves first. Beckett didn't give two shits about me or what I wanted. And why would he? He didn't know me. Not really. He'd been accepted into the family in my absence, and suddenly everyone was trying to sell him everything that meant anything to me. What was next? The fucking farm?

I wanted to march off to my Jeep and peel out of here. But I couldn't leave the dock without exposing myself.

"Why don't I give you a call next week and we can talk this over? I might have Owen facilitate the paperwork."

"Sounds good," Beckett agreed.

I wondered if Aspen knew her dad was selling the place. But of all people, she would have told me. Right? *Right?*

Gah, I hated how one twist made me question everything and everyone close to me. How I still struggled to trust anything.

"Would you mind keeping this between us, for now?" Karl asked. "Wendy and I want to talk to the kids first."

So, Aspen *didn't* know. I let out a breath.

"Of course," Beckett said.

"I better head back to check on Wendy."

I waited on the dock for Beckett to return to the party with Karl, willing my racing heart to slow so I could make a plan. Though a handshake among friends was as good as a signature in this town when it was among friends, I might still have time to talk to Karl before the deal was official. He might change his mind if he knew someone in the family actually wanted the place. *Maybe I should go back to the party and mention my interest—*

Splash!

"Husker!"

Fucking pondweed.

I didn't think twice. I jumped in after him, worried his leash would wrap around a pole and prevent him from resurfacing.

"Kira?"

Fuck. Beckett.

"Go away. I got this."

"You okay?"

"You're all right, Bubbies," I said to Husker, ignoring Beckett. I scooped my dog into my arms and walked him to the shore. He could probably swim, but I wasn't going to test that theory in the dark. His eyes were wider than normal, and he looked like a rattled, drowned hyena who'd eaten too much pizza. Startled, but otherwise unscathed.

"What happened?" Beckett asked, wading into the water to meet us, soaking his boot-clad feet in the process.

"I don't need your help," I growled.

"Kira," he said softly.

"Go away."

"You heard that, then?"

He took Husker from my arms and set him on the shore, catching the leash handle with one boot so Husker couldn't run off. Beckett offered a hand to me that I only begrudgingly took because the bottom of the lake seemed extra slick, and I was struggling to get to dry land on my own. With any luck, I'd slip and pull the jerk into the cold water with me.

"I thought we *just* agreed. No more secrets."

"Kira, I haven't even had a chance to tell you." I wanted his tone to be condescending. It would be so much easier to be mad at him if it were anything but the gentleness that it was. "Everyone told me Karl wouldn't sell. And after he decided to throw a party out here, I thought that was it. This conversation was a complete surprise to me."

"Is that why you were out here the other day?" I asked,

unable to quiet the chattering of my teeth as Husker shook off gallons of water.

"Yes." Beckett stripped off a flannel jacket he hadn't been wearing the last time I saw him near the cabin and draped it over my shoulders, shielding me from the worst of Husker's attempts to shed the lake water from his thick fur. "You really need to stop falling in the lake."

"Tired of saving me?" I shot back, heavy on the sarcasm.

"No more secrets?" he asked, as though seeking permission as he rubbed my arms to create warmth.

"No more secrets."

He leaned his head lower, until his lips were even with my ear. "I'm tired of pretending I'm not affected by seeing you in wet clothes."

A current of warmth swept through my body at the admission, my heart pounding for an entirely new reason. I wasn't imagining the attraction between us, of that I was certain. But I thought I was the only one with the dial turned up so high.

Until now.

I clutched the edges of the jacket with my fingers so tightly my vise grip threatened to rip the fabric. But if I didn't hold on, I'd certainly do something reckless. Like grab his face and pull him in for that breathless kiss I so desperately wanted.

"Do you want the cabin, Kira?"

"What?"

"If you want it, it's yours."

I looked up into those hazel eyes, the gold flecks illuminated by the sliver of moonlight. Fuck, a girl could get lost in those kind eyes. So lost, she'd never find her way back. If I had any sense, I'd run. Now.

"Why?"

"Because it obviously means something to you."

My gaze flickered to his lips for a beat. "That's it?"

"That's it."

"What's the catch?"

Beckett brushed back the soaked locks of my hair, and cupped my cheek. His thumb caressed my damp skin, his fiery touch igniting me from the inside out. I should totally run, but my bare feet cemented themselves into the rocky sand, refusing to budge.

"Red, there is no catch."

"There's always a catch."

"Not with me." I followed the path of his parted lips as he lowered his head toward mine. "Never with me."

I shouldn't want his kiss, but I craved it more than the air I breathed.

"You say that like you mean it," I said in a panted whisper. Our lips were a feather's width apart, our breaths mingling.

"Get to know me a little better, and you'll see that I only ever say what I mean."

I reached for his cheek then, pulling him toward me, erasing the last sliver of space between us and pressing my lips to his at long last.

I'd written about kisses that caused the world to stop, but until this moment, I didn't believe they were more than fiction.

Beckett's lips moved against mine in a perfect rhythm that ignited every nerve ending from head to toe. I slid my hand to the back of his neck, curling my fingers into his neck to drag him closer. He slid a hand over my lower back, pressing me to him. Our bodies molded together as if they were designed to click perfectly into place.

Beckett jerked. "Shit! Husker!"

It took several seconds to register that Husker had freed his leash from Beckett's boot and was running toward the parked vehicles.

"Everyone okay?" a voice hollered, shattering the moment.

Luke.

Fuck.

I jumped back, and nearly stumbled into the lake. Beckett caught me by his coat.

"Husker fell in," I called back, spotting my six-foot-four brother walking between two trucks. I'd never been so thankful that the rutted road out here wasn't sedan friendly. It was the only protection we had from being caught.

"And your sister went in after him," Beckett added, following my dog, who ran for my brother, robbing me of his warmth. I yanked the flannel coat tighter around me, feeling the chill of the water for the first time since Beckett helped me out of the lake.

If it wasn't for Husker, Luke would have caught me kissing his best friend.

I made a mental note to take Husker to Pizza Patty's tomorrow and get him anything he wanted.

"Of course you fucking did," Luke said, sounding exasperated. "You all right?"

"I'm fine."

"Karl find you?" Luke asked Beckett, moving on the second he confirmed I wasn't injured.

Beckett secured Husker's leash, wrapping the handle around his wrist. But not before my dog had a chance to rub his wet fur all over Luke's jeans. *Good boy, Husker.*

"Yeah, I just talked to him."

Luke nodded at Beckett, a silent exchange happening between them. One that renewed my earlier anger, reminding me that my oldest brother had prior knowledge of this but didn't think to mention it to *me*.

I resisted the urge to chew him a new asshole—or push *him* into the lake—and held out my hand to Beckett for the leash. It was best I head out before I had any more time to think about that kiss that had most definitely left me breathless. So fucking breathless.

"C'mon, Husker. Let's get home so we can dry off."

"Heading back to Omaha, then?" Luke asked, his tone smug as I retrieved my flip-flops from the boat dock.

"Maybe I will move back here," I said to Luke, poking a finger into his chest. "Just to spite *you*."

That shut my brother up.

Beckett shot me a smile, warming me in an instant. Yeah, it was definitely time to go. "Thanks for helping us out," I said to him, unable to meet his gaze as I hurried back to my Jeep.

TWENTY-FIVE
BECKETT

"That the bookstore?" Nana asked, nodding out the passenger window as we drove through town.

"Yeah," I said through a yawn, fighting the exhaustion that resonated in my bones. My own damn fault for *kissing* Kira last night and expecting I could get a fucking ounce of sleep before I had to head to Denver this morning to pick up Nana.

"It's not open."

"No, it's not."

"Funny thing about going-out-of-business sales. You have to be open to sell things."

"Joe doesn't have the staff."

"What's Joe doing?"

"Running the hardware store."

I slowed to take the turn past the bank, and headed toward the farm. When I told Connie where I was headed this morning, she sent me off with a to-go cup of coffee, a breakfast sandwich, and a request to bring Nana there for a family meal.

"What's he doing with a bookstore?"

"It belonged to his late wife."

"Brenda." Not a question. An easy observation.

"It's been a staple in this town for thirty years."

"Who's the redhead?" Nana asked as I turned off pavement and onto a dirt road.

"Kira Mason. She's Luke and Connor's younger sister. You'll meet her soon." Unless she went into hiding—or ran back to Omaha since I left this morning—there was a good chance that meeting was about to take place.

"Brenda's daughter?"

"Yes."

"I sure as hell hope you listened to me," Nana mumbled.

"She lives in Nebraska," I explained. "She's just here visiting."

Except, after last night, I wasn't so sure. She might stay. She might buy Karl's cabin, and move home. I didn't know how to feel about any of that yet. Did I *want* her to stay, or would that overcomplicate things?

"Good. Keep it in your pants until she's gone."

Christ, this conversation was too much for how fucking tired I was. I scrubbed a hand over my face to hide a yawn. How Nana, who'd been flying since late last night, was wide awake, was beyond me. I was still wiped from the drive to Denver to pick her up. But there was no nap in my future today. Nana wasn't the type of woman to take it easy, even if jetlagged. Which, I suspected, she wasn't.

All I did on the drive to the airport was think about

that kiss. That fucking axis-tilting kiss that had me all messed up in the head.

Kira Mason wasn't mine.

She could never *be* mine.

I had no fucking business kissing her.

Or wanting to do it again.

Even if she kissed me first.

It no longer mattered who initiated our kiss. We were both headed on the same collision course. If Luke had arrived a minute earlier, we'd have been caught. That alone should knock some fucking sense into me.

One kiss shouldn't have me so jumbled.

And yet, within only a few days of meeting her, I felt compelled to be around her every chance I got. To hear that beautiful laughter. Tease that heart-stopping smile from her lips. To cause that sexy barely audible whimper to escape her throat. To give her . . . *everything*.

Maybe it was a good thing Nana was here.

If this was a bad idea—and yeah, it fucking was—Nana would straighten me out before I ruined what I'd established in Bluebell Springs over a woman. She wouldn't let me fall victim to another redheaded curse. At least, I hoped not.

"Cute farm," Nana said, squinting and leaning forward. Before I could explain why they called it *the farm*, Nana kept right on talking. "Where are all the animals?"

"Connor has chickens," I offered.

"*Hmm.*"

"And there's a rescue cow named Millie."

As I parked the truck, I caught a blur of white shoot

across the yard. Husker was on the loose, and Red was running after him.

"And a dog, I see," Nana added as Kira caught the leash, much to Husker's dismay. He was clearly on a quest to chase down his chipmunk nemesis.

"That's Husker, Kira's dog."

"Oh, Beckett," she said with exasperation, patting my leg. "Looks like I got here just in time."

"Nana—"

"Hurry up, now," she said, pushing open her door. "I want to meet everyone."

I pulled Nana's second suitcase from the back of my truck, and closed the door. It was heavy, as though she'd stowed away a body or two. She'd be the first to tell you she wasn't known for traveling light. But this seemed excessive, even for her.

She hadn't mentioned a return flight, and now I understood why. Nana was planning to stick around for a while—as a welcome guest of the Westons.

I shouldn't be surprised at how easily she melded into the Mason-Weston clan. She came bearing thoughtful gifts for people I'd mentioned only a handful of times. She and Connie were swapping recipes within an hour of meeting, Dale was puffing on a specialty cigar near the firepit, and Opal listened in rapture as she shared stories of her world travels over lunch. The two spoke of Italy as if they'd *both* been there before, though Connor assured us all Opal had never traveled out of the country, and they had no idea where this sudden fascination came from.

Currently, Nana was in a full-scale conversation with Connor about his plans for rental cabins he considered adding to the farm.

Nana fit right in, as though she'd always known this family. As though she were a long lost member, finally returned home after years away.

It was all I could do to sit back and watch in awe.

"I like her," Kira said, picking up the smaller carry-on bag and looping the strap over her shoulder. "But I don't know how well she likes me."

"She likes you."

"You don't have to lie to spare my feelings, Beck."

Dammit, I liked the way she called me *Beck*.

"You don't have to help," I said to her.

"I know."

We hadn't talked since she left Ghost Lake last night. I stayed to appease Luke, and ward off any suspicion he might be harboring about me and his little sister, however warranted it may be. That was a battle I'd save for a future time, down the road. Her door was closed when I finally made it back, though. And I left this morning, before anyone other than Connie was awake.

Kira and I'd been stealing glances at one another since I arrived with Nana, the pull undeniably strong. I wanted nothing more than to tug her into my arms and kiss her again. To feel her body perfectly molded against mine as our tongues danced and the world around us disappeared.

I was in over my fucking head.

"Beckett, about last night—"

"Yeah, we should probably talk about that."

"I shouldn't have done that."

"You shouldn't have kissed me?"

Her eyes went wide. "Do you want to say that a little louder?"

"Relax, Red. Everyone's over there," I said, nodding toward the patio area with the firepit.

"Except, I have ninjas for brothers, and they tend to sneak up when you least expect them."

"I have eyes on both of them." I nodded toward the patio where Connor was immersed in conversation with Nana, and Luke was taking a phone call and looking a little pissed off about it.

"I'm sorry I kissed you," she said.

"Are you?"

We locked eyes for several beats, so much lingering in the silence between us. We both knew this was a bad fucking idea. That if things didn't work out, so much could go wrong. Aspen's threat alone should be enough for me to back off. And that didn't take into account that Nana's room was right next door to mine.

Not that I'd ever disrespect the Westons by sneaking around under their roof.

If I had an ounce of sense, I'd simply agree with Kira and let this go.

"I've made a lot of mistakes," she said, glancing at Luke.

"Kissing me was a mistake, then?"

"Would you stop saying that like it's a challenge?" she said, huffing out a breath. If I had to guess, she *wanted* to be annoyed. But the twinkle dancing in her eyes revealed the truth. My teasing was getting to her. "I'm a hot mess, Beckett."

"And?"

"And I don't want you to get tangled up in it."

She spun on her heel and headed toward the house with Nana's smaller bags, leaving me no choice but to grab the heavier suitcases, and follow. Kira was quick on her feet, but I caught up to her on the second-floor landing.

"I meant what I said last night," I said, following her down the hall to the guest room beside mine that Nana would be calling home for an undetermined number of days.

"The part about the cabin or the catch?"

"Both."

Kira set the floral-patterned carry-on bag on a sitting chair beside the bed and looked back at me.

"I appreciate that. I really do. But we both know that anything more than friends is a really bad idea. Especially if I decide to move home."

What Kira said made total sense on its own, but it was the fear lingering in her eyes that made me back all the way off. I prayed I never met the asshole who hurt her. I wouldn't trust myself around him.

"Friends, then," I said, holding out a hand to shake.

She stared at my outstretched hand. "Not friends with benefits," she clarified.

"Define benefits."

Kira rolled her eyes, but my teasing earned the intended response. A smile broke across her lips. "Friends. No benefits."

"Friends. Platonic benefits."

"Fine. But only because Husker has dubbed you his new favorite person."

And finally, after several beats of hesitation, she placed her hand in mine. Neither of us admitted to the jolt of electricity at the contact, though I spotted the flare of surprise in her eyes as clearly as I felt the current in my own body.

Being *just friends* with Kira Mason might very well be the death of me.

TWENTY-SIX

HUSKER

That was the best dinner ever!
Grandma Connie is the best.
Why doesn't Mom add special sauce to my dinner?
Grandma Connie calls it gravy.
Can I have more gravy, Grandma Connie?
"You sure you're okay, sweetie?"
I'm okay.
But I really want more dinner.
With gravy.
Oh, you mean Mom.
Mom, are you okay?
Maybe you need to pet me to feel better.
There, scratch my booty.
Booty scratches make everything better.
"Just tired."
"I know it's a lot."
What's a lot?
A lot of dinner?

That's not possible.
Never too much dinner.
"I just wish there was something I could do."
"We all wish that."
I wish for pizza.
Is there pizza?
"I've thought about moving home."
Home?
Mom, we are home.
"Don't do that unless it's what you really want."
"I miss this place."
Sniff, sniff, sniff.
What's that under the cupboard?
Bonus hamburger!
"You miss your mother."
Chomp, chomp, chomp.
"Yeah, of course I do."
Mom feels sad.
Mom, why are you sad?
Do you want bonus hamburger, too?
I'll look for more.
Sniff, sniff, sniff.
"We all miss her, you know."
"I wish . . ."
"Your mother was very proud of you."
No more bonus hamburger.
Grandma Connie's kitchen is clean.
Cleaner than Mom's kitchen.
But I'm not allowed in Mom's kitchen.
Grandma Connie lets me in her kitchen.
Grandma Connie, do you have more?

"Husker, you've had enough."

Silly Mom.

Grandma Connie, don't listen to Mom.

"Sweetie, I would love to have you home."

"Yeah?"

"Of course. We all would."

Grandma Connie's got something in her hand.

She's being sneaky.

Mom doesn't see.

Num, num, num.

"But?"

"But don't put your life on hold."

"There's not much to put on hold."

"What's that?"

"Nothing. I think Husker and I are going for a walk."

Walk?

Did you say walk?

Mom said walk.

Walk!

We're going on a walk!

Let's go, Mom!

Hurry up!

"Guess you better take him before he bursts from all the excitement."

Where's my leash?

I need my leash so I don't chase the mini squirrels.

Right, Mom?

Get my leash!

Walks are my favorite.

Let's go on a walk!

Walk! Walk! Walk!

TWENTY-SEVEN
KIRA

THE TRAILS in Bluebell Springs alone were nearly enough to convince me to move home. I'd forgotten the peace and serenity they offered, especially the lesser-known trails near the farm. The crisp mountain air recharged me from the inside out. It didn't matter that the sun was hidden behind a bed of clouds. For the first time in a long time, my overactive nervous system finally calmed.

I felt at peace.

Grandma Connie's words repeated in my head. *Don't put your life on hold.* She meant Mom wouldn't want me to stick a bookmark in the pages of my own book to save *her* bookstore. It was always her dream, and though she would have happily shared it with me, I never wanted it.

Until now.

Until it was days away from being erased from existence.

Except, there was nothing I could do to save it. The

day after tomorrow, the going-out-of-business sale would start and that would be the end.

I needed a miracle.

I needed Mom to tell me what to do.

But she hadn't revisited my dreams since the night that drove me to return home.

Husker's zigzag pattern lessened as the hard-packed trail narrowed, turning rockier. He pulled me up the slight incline as my breathing became more labored.

I was out of shape, and the higher elevation wasn't helping.

The cramps in my side were just another byproduct of hiding in my apartment this past year, struggling with the most severe case of writer's block, mixed with a heap of guilt that I was stupid enough to fall for every lie Travis ever concocted. If ever I put my life on hold, it was for that asshole.

Been there, done that. Got the T-shirt. Needed to burn said T-shirt.

Spotting a familiar wooden bench Grandpa made decades ago, I headed for it just off the trail. I poured Husker a small bowl of water he probably wouldn't drink on account of all the distractions around us, and sat to catch my breath and take in the view. I took the mountains for granted most of my life, until I moved away to a place that had little more than rolling hills. I loved the layers. The tree-covered mountains up close, the rockier, snow-dusted ones behind them.

If I moved home, I wouldn't have to drive to find a decent nature trail.

But I'd move home a failure.

What would I even do once the book royalties dried up?

I pulled my phone from my pocket, curious how the release of *Forever Forbidden* was doing. How much additional time this nice bump in sales might buy me.

Before I could navigate to my web browser, though, a voicemail notification popped up. Lila had tried to call, probably during family dinner. Grandma Connie had a strict no cell phone policy during the larger meals—which would now be all of them, considering Beckett *and* his grandma were staying at the farm.

I still didn't know what to make of Pauline Duncan. No one would argue she was a generous woman, considering the surprisingly thoughtful gifts she brought along. I thought Opal was going to faint from excitement at the coffee table book of Italy's history. But there was something about the woman that warned you not to cross her, as though she made a powerful ally, but a very bad enemy.

She told everyone over dinner she was here to check on her grandson and see how he was settling in somewhere new. Yet it felt like a half truth.

Or maybe I felt an enormous amount of guilt for *kissing* Beckett, and worried she somehow knew about it. Was she here to warn me not to hurt him? I suspected she had a pretty high standard on the type of woman who was good enough for her grandson, and I didn't make the cut.

I navigated to the voicemail box on my phone and listened to Lila's message on speaker.

"Hey! Hope you're writing up a storm because I haven't heard from you in a few days. No pressure or

anything, but your readers are dying to know when Mateo's story is coming. You ready to put up a preorder soon?"

Shit. My fault for writing a fucking love triangle and leaving one of the characters without a happily ever after.

"Anyway, I had an epic idea I wanted to run by you, so call me back soon. Love you!"

I meant to hit the call back button, but something caught my eye before I could.

"Blocked voicemails?" I murmured. I'd never noticed that feature on my phone before. *Huh.*

For curiosity's sake—or maybe I was procrastinating heading back to the farm—I selected it.

An explosion of voicemails appeared on the screen, all from the same 402 area code. I was fairly certain I blocked this specific number earlier this week, when an unwanted text message showed up in my inbox. I scrolled through the long list as disbelief warred with anger.

Anger won.

"Twenty-five. Twenty-fucking-five?"

My stomach plummeted into my toes, and I suddenly felt sick.

The bastard had called me *twenty-five* fucking times since I blocked his number *three* days ago.

After a *year* of me not responding to a single message, call, or email.

What the actual fuck?

I refused to listen to a single one, but I opened the transcript of the most recent one, to be sure I wasn't over-reacting. The cryptic message spelled out on my screen made my skin crawl. Most of it didn't make sense. Something about the FBI and how they were out to get him.

God, this again. It was obvious Travis was shit-faced drunk when he left it.

My hands shook so violently I nearly dropped the phone. I set it on the bench beside me as I felt my throat constrict. Husker paced in front of me, both eager to get back to walking and also concerned for me. I hated how this still affected me so strongly. How it affected Husker, too.

I should call someone.

Aspen would tell me to change my phone number. Again.

Alyssa would insist I get a restraining order.

Lila would—well, it was hard to tell what she would do. She was a little unpredictable. She might tell me to delete all the messages so they no longer took up energy on my phone, or she might offer to sneak over to Travis' house and put raw shrimp in his ventilation system.

Luke, if he wasn't in the *hating me* mode, would do something reckless like drive to Omaha.

Beckett—

I shook my head, warding off the thought. It was enough to stop the tears from falling.

Beckett would do something chivalrous. I didn't know how I knew, but I did. He would do or say exactly what I needed him to do or say. And that was the very reason I couldn't involve him in any of this. If I needed a sign, Nana's surprise arrival was surely it. It may as well be a blinking neon sign: *Leave Beckett out of your hot mess. He deserves better.*

Tears started to fall, and I knew what came next.

I braced for the panic attack that wrecked me, so

fucking thankful I was more than a mile away from anyone who might find me. Bonus points for the ugly sobbing noises doubling as bear deterrent.

Small wins.

I don't know how long I stayed there on that bench and cried. Only that the overcast sky grew darker, warning me I should head back to the farm before anyone came looking for me.

"Sorry, Bubbies," I said to Husker, forcing a hug on him. He hated them, but for two and a half seconds, he gave in and let me hold him close. "I'll make it up to you tomorrow."

We headed back to the house and snuck in the mudroom door, finding the place quiet. Everyone would be gathered outside, around the firepit off the back patio, for the s'mores Opal insisted were nonnegotiable.

I didn't know if I had the bandwidth for a large gathering tonight. Whether I could pretend everything was fine. But before I made that decision, I needed to wash away the makeup-smeared evidence.

A few feet before the staircase, I heard voices and froze.

"Spell it out for me, Joe. I like facts. What did she do?"

Pauline and *Dad*? He missed dinner, but he must have shown up while I was out on my walk.

"There's a second mortgage on the building. I don't know how she got a lender to approve it without me, but she found one of those online deals."

"That'll be forgery charges."

"Already filed."

"Good. Smart man."

"She cashed out the money before I ever knew about it."

"From a local bank?"

"She had a friend on the inside."

I glued myself to the wall just outside the formal dining room, hoping Husker cooperated and didn't give us away. Dad never told me about the insider at the bank. What else didn't he tell me? And why was he filling in a complete stranger about *our* family business? Giving her details he kept from me?

"Anyway, the bank account is empty. I had to deplete my savings to make the last payroll. That's why the place is closed right now. I can barely afford to pay for the utilities. She took everything."

"And no one can find her?"

"Not yet."

"Fuck, I'm sorry, Joe."

"Yeah, me too."

Me too. It broke my heart hearing all this from Dad a few nights ago. But the wound re-opened hearing him tell it again, and adding new details. As if this made it all the more final. There really was no hope. We'd sell as many books as we could this coming week, donate the rest, and close the door on Brenda's Book Nook. Forever.

Could this day get any fucking worse?

"I have vendors still sending me bills, threatening to send me to collections if I don't pay up. One even threatened a lawsuit. It's the biggest mess you can imagine. I can't let anyone take that on. It would be like handing over a sinking ship that has minutes left before it goes completely under. Who can save that?"

Take on what, exactly?

Was Dad talking to Pauline about selling *her* the bookstore? Was *that* why he was being so honest with someone he met all of five minutes ago? Or had Beckett already had the two in touch before tonight? Was Pauline in town to make a new investment?

No, that didn't make sense. Why would a woman who traveled the world on the regular buy a small-town bookstore somewhere she'd never been before? Beckett mentioned his grandma was a smart businesswoman who'd done very well for herself over the years. This didn't seem like a smart business move—for anyone.

Fucking Margene.

"Beckett will have a number of local tenants to choose from before the sale is even final. I can help him vet them. Give him insight on which ones to steer clear from."

"It's the best-case scenario in a really shitty situation."

"I'm selling to him below market value," Dad said. "It's just enough to pay off the second mortgage and maybe give the part-timers a severance check to thank them for sticking it out."

"And here I was, worried he was getting too emotionally involved in his business decisions."

"He's a good kid."

"Yeah, he is."

"His parents?"

"A problem he left behind a long time ago."

"He's lucky to have you, then."

I heard the clink of an ice cube, as though someone took a drink. It was my cue to leave, but the next thing Pauline said froze me right in my tracks.

"What's up with that daughter of yours? The redhead."

Her tone made me flinch. I held my breath, desperate to know what this woman had against me. Because with a question like that, she obviously had some reservations about me that weren't entirely in my own head. And why the hell did it matter? Beckett and I had agreed to just be friends. I didn't need her approval for that.

That didn't seem to stop me from wanting it, though.

"Still can't get used to that hair," Dad said, his tone amused.

"Beck's prone to the redheaded curse. Just want to make sure she's—"

The sliding door to the patio opened, alerting me I was about to get caught if I didn't move. *Dammit.* I scurried up the stairs, bribing Husker with the promise of treats so he didn't give us away.

TWENTY-EIGHT
BECKETT

"Where's Aunt Kira?" Opal asked as I set a couple of camping chairs between the metal patio furniture already stationed around the firepit to accommodate the additional guests. Connor's daughter insisted we have an epic s'mores night before she headed off to summer camp tomorrow so she'd be a pro at it, and no one, Nana included—I swear, that woman was immune to jetlag—had the heart to turn her down.

"I think she took Husker for a walk," I said, remembering the two disappearing into the woods earlier. Maybe it was a good thing Nana was here, because the urge to join Kira for that walk was overpowering. More so since we agreed to be *just friends*.

"They're back," Opal said, matter-of-fact.

I scanned the patio, but no one else seemed interested in Kira's whereabouts. Luke was chopping wood, and Connor was carrying the split pieces to the firepit. Dale was a dozen yards away, arms folded and deep in conversation on the phone.

Kira might be inside helping Nana and Connie with the s'mores fixings. Or she might be upstairs, hiding from everyone. She did that a lot, isolated herself, even though she loved her family. I didn't know much about her past, but I certainly knew a thing or two about healing from one.

I remembered the panic attack at the bookstore, and my pulse doubled.

What if something was wrong?

"I'll go check on her."

"Bring a treat for Husker," Opal said, reaching into her pocket and handing me a bone-shaped morsel, as though she knew I had yet to fill my own pockets.

"Thanks."

I took the stairs to the second floor two at a time, waiting until I reached the end of the hall to call her name. Her door was closed, but I knocked anyway.

I saw the paw under the door first.

"Beckett?" Her voice sounded off, and I went on high alert at the strangled sob. It reminded me of the times Madeline admitted defeat with our parents when we were younger, after they showed their true colors and broke her heart once again.

"Can I come in?"

"Please go away."

Hand resting on the knob, I leaned my head against the door. If she didn't want me to come in, I would leave her. But I had a sneaking suspicion she really didn't want to be alone right now.

"Please, Kira?"

After several beats of silence, she finally said, "Okay."

I gently pushed the door open, and was greeted by Husker. I offered him the treat Opal gave me, warding off his escape attempts. Kira was curled in the fetal position on top of the covers, her ponytail fanning the pillow. I didn't need to ask if she'd been crying. The puffiness around her eyes gave it away.

"It's time for s'mores," I said, biting back the urge to ask what was wrong. Because something was definitely fucking wrong.

"I might pass tonight. You can take Husker down, though."

"Opal will be really disappointed if you don't join us," I said gently, closing the door behind me.

"I can't go out there like this, Beck," she said, her words a panted whisper. Tears sprang to her eyes, falling down her cheeks.

Fuck.

I crawled onto the bed slowly, gathering her into my arms. She didn't fight me, just melted into me. Her tears soaked through the cotton of my shirt.

"What's wrong, Red?"

"Everything."

Husker hopped onto the bed, tilting his head at the two of us. I patted the spot beside Kira, and he plopped down at the back of her legs. *Good boy, Husker.*

I held Kira in my arms, allowing her to cry.

"You don't have to tell me anything you don't want to," I reassured her. "But I'm here to listen if you do."

"Why?"

Because you're important to me, and although I don't fully understand how that's possible when we hardly know each other, it's true.

"Because you deserve to be heard."

That made her cry harder, so I held on tighter.

"It's stupid," Kira said.

"I doubt that."

"It is." She sniffled, and I handed her a tissue. "My stupid ex."

"Well, I don't need a lot of context to know *he's* stupid," I agreed.

That made Kira laugh, and the sound calmed my racing pulse. "I went no contact with him last summer. You probably heard about the wedding toast."

"I did, but I haven't heard about it from you."

"I'll spare you the details. Just know, it was as bad as Luke makes it sound."

"Yikes."

"Tell me about it." She sniffled again, wiping away moisture from her cheeks as she nestled against me. It felt right to hold her, though I didn't know what that meant. *Friends, Beck. Just friends.* "I broke up with him that night. Last time I saw him was the next day, after I showed up to get what little stuff I still had at his place before he did something mean like throw it all away."

My fist balled against her back at the thought of someone disrespecting Kira so harshly, but I stayed silent. This was not my story to tell.

"I told him that night I'd never talk to him again, and I've stood by that. Blocked his number, his email, his Snap-Chat, his Venmo."

"Venmo?"

"He's tried everything he can to reach out, even after I told him I wanted to be left alone."

"He didn't listen?" I had an urge to drive to Omaha right fucking now and confront this asshole.

"He gets creative. Changes his number sometimes." Kira reached for the phone resting beside her, and I watched as she navigated to her voicemail. "I don't get it," she said, sounding more frustrated than sad. "If you block a number, why the hell can they still leave a voicemail?"

But it wasn't just one voicemail. It was several. At least a couple dozen. Maybe more. All with recent time stamps.

"Have you told anyone?"

"You?"

"Maybe Luke—"

"No," she said quickly.

"He cares about you."

"I know there's a heart somewhere beneath all those layers of ice," Kira said, "Which is why I can't let him know. He'll do something stupid like get arrested trying to make a point. Not a great look for the police chief, you know?"

Well, fuck. She had a point.

"Maybe it's a sign," I said.

"A sign?" she asked, an incredulous laugh slipping out.

"A sign to move home."

"Oh." She sniffled again, and I handed her another tissue. "Maybe. But what would I do?"

"Write more books?" I offered.

The tears that had dried started up again, and I wondered what I said that was so damn wrong. I wrapped both arms around her, pulling her tight against my chest once more. I pressed my lips to her forehead. "Whatever it is, Kira, it's going to be okay."

"There are no more books," she said on a shaky sob.

"What do you mean?"

It took her a few minutes to calm down enough to speak again. At some point soon, someone would come looking for us. And finding us together on her bed would not go over well with anyone downstairs. But I wouldn't rush Kira. Not now. Not ever.

"I haven't written a single word in a year. Not since I finished the last book. I—I can't write anymore."

"I'm sure that's not true."

"He *broke* me. He fucking broke me, and no matter what I've tried, I can't seem to fix it. I can't believe I was stupid enough to fall for him. Stupid enough that I pursued him and followed him to Nebraska when he got a job transfer. Stupid enough to believe he supported me when really he was jealous. He did everything he could to strip me down to nothing."

"Kira—"

"I've been rebuilding. I'm proud of how far I've come. But Diana—" She shook her head against my chest. "She's done writing. And once my readers find out, they're going to hate me."

"They won't hate you."

"You leave your readers on a love triangle book, and tell them the guy who didn't get the girl will never get one, and see how that goes."

"Maybe you just need time," I said gently.

"I've had a *year*. And before you say I'm being too hard on myself, I already know I am. It's not going to change anything. And the worst part? No one knows. Not my readers, not my friends or family. Not my PA. No one." She turned her head, looking up at me, her blue eyes shiny. "No one but you."

"I'll keep your secret," I said, pressing another kiss to her forehead. I should probably stop doing that, considering the friend pact, but I didn't give two fucks right now. I couldn't fix all her problems—only she could do that—but I could reassure her she wasn't in this alone.

"Thanks."

We should get downstairs soon, but instead, I tucked her head back against my chest.

"Beckett?"

"Yeah?"

"What's up with the redheaded curse?"

"Fuck," I said, laughing. "What did Nana tell you?"

"Nothing. I overheard her say something about it."

It was the last thing I wanted to talk about, but I could already feel the tension lightening in Kira, likely at the prospect of talking about anything else but her own life. So I swallowed my pride. "I have a thing for redheads, and they have a thing for messing up my life."

"No wonder Nana doesn't like me," Kira said, the vibration of her laughter rumbling against my chest. It took every ounce of restraint I had to keep my imagination from turning reckless with all the ways body-to-body vibrations could make both of us very happy.

"I'm sorry. The cards *are* stacked against you."

"When did it start?"

"In the fourth grade."

"Oh, wow, that young, huh?"

"Don't pretend you didn't have a crush in the fourth grade."

"I had a couple," she admitted. "What was her name?"

"Carly Mitchell."

"How did she ruin your life?"

"She kissed my best friend during recess."

"That's horrible."

"I was heartbroken."

"There were others?" she asked, the heaviness she'd held lightening a little more with her curiosity.

"Darci Peters."

"High school or college?"

"After," I said. "She was my first wife."

Kira pulled back from my chest to stare at me, and dammit if my gaze didn't immediately drop to her lips. I couldn't decide which was worse—never kissing her and always wondering what it would be like, or kissing her and having my world turned upside down in the best fucking way, only to know I could never kiss her again.

"First wife?"

"Only wife. Now ex-wife."

"Oh."

"Jealous?" I teased.

"Of course not." She nestled back against my chest, but not before I caught the flush spreading across her cheeks. "What happened?"

"We were too young. I enlisted in the Army and sent for her as soon as I finished Basic and AIT."

"That's the school portion?"

"Yeah."

"You were a Blackhawk mechanic, like my brothers and Thoren?"

"Yeah."

"I think it's really cool how the four of you were together from the beginning."

"Me too."

"So, she came out to Fort Lewis. Then, what?"

"We got married at the courthouse, and a week later, she ran off with an infantry guy."

"What?"

"True story."

"Geez, Beck. I'm sorry."

"I was devastated back then. She cleaned out my meager bank account, so that sucked. Stole my car and wrecked it. But I found out later she'd been sleeping around while I was in Basic. It would have been better if I knew before we signed the marriage certificate. But the judge was kind enough to grant an annulment, and save me a lot of headaches."

"I'm guessing Nana was not pleased."

"She didn't want me to marry her in the first place."

"She has good instincts?"

"Most of the time."

"There were more?"

"There have been a few others, yes," I admitted.

"Would it matter if I told you I'm not a natural redhead?" Kira asked, looking up at me again.

God, it would be so fucking easy to lower my lips to hers and kiss away her fears. To take my time showing her exactly how special she was. How well she deserved to be treated.

Husker rocked the bed as he hopped to all fours, the only warning we had before a quick knock came.

"Are you two decent or do I need to get the garden hose?" Nana hollered through the door.

TWENTY-NINE
KIRA

ARMED WITH AN ICED CARAMEL MOCHA, I headed for the bookstore an hour ahead of the time the book club was scheduled to meet. The store wasn't technically open today, as Dad wanted to preserve the book club's final meeting the best he could, but I had permission to sell books if someone walked in.

The big going-out-of-business sale would start tomorrow, and go through the end of the week. I agreed to stay through the duration of it, even if it was likely to gut me. This weekend, it was all hands on deck, with my brothers and the rest of my family to clear out whatever remained, bookshelves included.

Mom would want me here.

At least, I hoped so.

After the sale was over, and the business fully liquidated, I'd make an official decision about moving home. Because right now, my head was still a giant jumble all thanks to a very titillating kiss that played on repeat without my express permission. A kiss I shouldn't crave again.

If only Beckett hadn't been a fucking incredible man last night when I was at a low point, maybe the potency of said kiss would have worn off by now.

Maybe.

But doubtful.

How many times did I have a meltdown and just wanted a fucking hug from Travis, only to be met with a cold stare and the even colder *"I'm not enabling this behavior by giving you a hug"* bullshit he spewed.

Beckett held me. He listened. He asked for nothing. Never once did he make me feel like a burden or an idiot for the choices I made. He didn't try to convince me I did something to deserve this. That it was somehow all my fault.

Beckett Campbell was quicksand.

If I had any sense at all, I'd keep that in the forefront of my mind.

But the memory of that soul-awakening kiss on the boat dock had already booked a room. Seemed like it was planning on a long-term stay.

That kiss was all-consuming. Unlike anything I'd ever dreamed up.

I prided myself on writing great first kiss scenes in my Diana books—my readers would back me up—but kissing Beckett made me question everything I knew about my creative abilities. I could hardly find the words to describe what I experienced. The current of warmth that skittered through my body like a tingly caress and awakened parts of me I didn't realize existed, much less were dormant.

The way I felt as though I were floating out of my body and simultaneously more grounded than I'd ever been.

It seemed like fiction.

And yet, I could feel the sensation now, as though his lips were pressed to mine in this very moment.

It was so damn tempting to kiss him last night. To reach my fingertips to his jaw and pull his lips to mine for a taste of that drug-induced kiss once more as he held me.

Did I ever once feel that full-body buzz when Travis kissed me?

No.

Never.

Not even when things were good.

If Beckett could kiss like that, what could he do to other parts of me?

"Friends, Kira. *Just* friends."

The click of the deadbolt as I unlocked the front door of the bookstore brought me back to the present. I dropped the leash, allowing Husker to trot inside ahead of me.

The welcoming scent of books was almost enough to drown out the deafening silence.

Almost.

I missed the days when Mom left a dog bed out for Husker and any other furry visitors that might stop by the store. She once kept a jar of homemade dog treats at the counter as well.

If the store were mine, that was the first thing I'd bring back.

But the store would never be mine.

In a few days, it wouldn't exist at all.

A tremor threatened to rip through my body, but I

choked it back down. Dad wanted so desperately for the book club to have one last, normal meeting. I didn't need to drag down the mood with waterworks that may or may not be contagious. Many of the members coming today had known me since diapers. Members who were more like family members. I had to stay strong for them. I wanted today to be special.

"Let's get this place ready," I said to Husker.

I shot Aspen a text to check on the cupcake order she promised to have delivered, then set to work. Though a checklist waited in a binder at the register, I moved about the shop on muscle memory. I started the coffee pot, adjusted the chairs around the table, wiped down the dusty table, set pads of paper, an array of colorful fountain pens, and book tabs at both ends. I turned on white twinkle lights overhead, fighting my discouragement that half of them were burned out. Nothing I could do about that now. Some twinkle lights were better than none.

I grabbed dusting spray and a rag. I didn't have the time to clean properly, but I could at least address the areas closest to the community table.

While I cleaned, Husker wandered off toward the back, refusing to come back when I called to him.

"Bubbies, you better not be licking the books."

He looked up at the top shelf in the paranormal romance section, as though someone stood there talking to him. His head tilted at that familiar sharp angle as I approached.

"You better not be making friends with that fucking spider—"

As I approached him, I caught a whiff of something sweet. Something floral. Something *familiar.*

The hairs stood on my arms, as though I stood near a spot where lightning recently struck. I dropped my hand to my chest, feeling it fill with warmth.

"Mom?"

The bells jingled overhead, startling me from my trance.

"Special delivery for Kira Mason."

Husker sprinted toward the front, reaching Beckett two seconds before he pulled the door closed behind him.

I glanced once more toward the shelf that held *my* books, and whispered, "I'm glad you're here, Mom."

"Hey, Husker."

"I wasn't expecting you," I said, forcing myself to walk slowly despite the urge to copy my dog and run right into Beckett's arms.

"Aspen asked if I'd drop off some cupcakes," he said. "She said she's bringing the rest shortly."

"Thank you," I said, struggling to meet his gaze for more than half a second at a time. I might have only known this man for a week, but I was past being able to pretend I wasn't catching feelings. I'd take the secret to my grave, but the lie I told myself wasn't sticking anymore.

"You okay?" he asked, sounding like he meant it.

I moved behind the counter to unbox the cupcakes, desperate for the physical barrier between us so I didn't make any reckless decisions when it came to those very strong, very warm, very capable arms.

"Yeah."

"Are you sure?"

"I'd really like to pretend none of that happened," I said, plating the cupcakes.

My finger slipped and stole a smudge of frosting on accident. I automatically brought it to my lips and sucked the frosting away, realizing my mistake only when I caught Beckett staring.

"Sorry," he said, clearing his throat and turning his back to me. "The shelves are fuller than I thought they'd be."

"Sale starts tomorrow."

"Right."

"Would you believe there are more boxes of books upstairs?"

"Really?"

"Mom used to get deliveries almost daily. That was my favorite part of being here, opening the boxes to see all the new books. It was like a treasure hunt."

"You sure you don't want the bookstore? I hear the new landlord's a really nice guy."

"You're sweet," I said, setting aside a vanilla cupcake on a small plate and tearing off a corner for Husker. "But it wouldn't work."

The conversation between Dad and Pauline replayed in my mind, reminding me just how impossible it was. I had money, especially after this latest book release, but if I burned through half of it just to get the business back in the black, I wouldn't last the summer. Mom had good years, but I remember her stressing about the years when the profit was razor thin at best.

"What if it *could* work?"

Before I could give Beckett an answer, the bells jingled over the front door.

"I brought margaritas!" Dylann Jenkins announced, as half a dozen elderly women flocked inside behind her.

Husker slipped by me before I could grab his collar, but Beckett caught him.

"I got him," he said, reaching for the leash I left on the counter.

"You know I don't drink," Carol Ann Collins said to Dylann.

"That's why *I* brought virgin daiquiris," Lotti Daniels said.

"I smell coffee," Carlos Jeffries said approvingly, adjusting his purple, thick-rimmed glasses as he inhaled deeply.

"Wait. Is that *Kira* I see?" Thelma Anderson stood taller than anyone in the group, aside from Beckett. A slow, approving smile spread across her lips. "You're a redhead. I fucking love it!"

I was attacked with heartfelt hugs, some gentle, some borderline violent, all given with the utmost love. Tears I could no longer hold back trickled down my face as the women—and Carlos—chattered on top of one another.

"I love the new hair!"

"I'm so glad you ditched The Ass Weasel."

"It's so fitting you're here for our last Nook meeting."

"We've missed having you."

"I heard you fell into the lake and were rescued by that new hunky handyman."

"He's right there, Lotti."

"Oh, hey, hunky handyman."

"Your mom would love this."

"You look hot!"

"When are you moving home?"

"You should marry this hunky handyman and have his babies."

"Down, Lotti."

"I'll babysit."

"We've missed you!"

"Welcome home, sweetie."

Husker soaked up all the enthusiastic pets, and gobbled up what I sincerely hoped were dog treats, but highly suspected were not. As long as no one was sneaking him *special* treats, all would be well. If they got him high, well, I'd cross that bridge only if it was necessary.

"What are you drinking, honey?" Thelma asked me as she pulled out a chair to set her heavy tote on.

"The virgin daiquiri sounds right up my alley. If it's actually virgin."

"It's the only thing virgin about the meeting today," Dylann tossed in, an eruption of giggles following from several members. It was now that I noticed her #Team-Darius T-shirt. *Coincidence, Kira. It's just a coincidence.* Plenty of book heroes were named Darius.

Beckett nodded my way, assuring me he would watch Husker so I didn't have to worry about him sneaking out the front door after a chipmunk as everyone else filtered in. I focused on attending to the coffee pot, pulling out cups, cream, sugar, and stirring spoons as everyone settled in.

The bells chimed overhead a few times, welcoming

the last few members, and Aspen with the rest of the cupcake delivery.

"I hope you don't mind if I join you," she said to everyone.

"Pull up a seat, sweetie," Lotti offered. "Did you read the book?"

"I sure did," she said.

"What book—"

"Beckett, are you staying, honey?" Dylann asked, as though they were old friends. Had they met?

"We have extra chairs," Thelma said, her offer sounding more like a demand that was hard to evade.

I glanced at Beckett, catching his gaze and holding it for a few seconds longer than I should, considering the number of comments from the peanut gallery about the two of us.

Friends. Just friends.

"I should warn you," I said to Beckett. "This group reads mostly spicy romance."

"Think I can't handle it, Red?"

I offered a shrug, pretending I wasn't affected by the nickname I was coming to like a little too much.

"You've been warned." I turned my attention to the table. "Who wants coffee?"

"We have margaritas too," Dylann reminded the group.

"You look right at home here," Beckett said as I poured a couple cups of coffee for Betty and Carlos.

"It was home." I let out a soft sigh as I scanned the familiar room. "For a long time."

"Maybe you should—"

"Would you two hurry up and join us? I want to talk about that sexy vampire, Darius."

"You mean *Mateo*," Lotti said.

"You can have that grumpy-ass vampire. I'm Team Darius all the way."

I froze, my eyes no doubt doubling in size. The air in my lungs froze.

"You know Mateo?" Beckett asked me, his voice low.

It had to be a coincidence. The only person here who knew I was Diana Davenport besides Beckett was Aspen, and she was sworn to secrecy. But as I slowly scanned the table, I found copy after copy of *Forever Forbidden* laid out in front of several book club members. Most of them had colorful tabs sticking out the sides. They'd not just been well read, they were well annotated.

"Did you—"

"Me?" Beckett shook his head. "But something tells me your secret was never really a secret."

"Fucking hell, is she going to pass out?" Thelma said. "Beckett, make sure you hold on to her before she hits the damn floor."

"I told you we should have warned her," Dylann said, her tone a mixture of annoyance and apology as she played with the layers of necklaces hanging around her neck.

"Come join us, *Diana*," Lotti cooed, pulling out the empty seat next to her. She was easy to spot in her bright yellow and pink windbreaker suit. I followed the blur of color, feeling as though my feet were floating.

"Guess you have some fans," Beckett whispered to me. Was his hand on the small of my back? That would explain the pool of heat gathered there. Heat that was slowly spreading to other parts of my shaky body. I felt the swish of Husker's tail against my leg as he trotted beside me toward the table, and allowed that to ground me. Because all Beckett's touch was going to do was take me that much further from reality.

"You should sit down before you hit your damn head on a bookshelf and get a concussion," Thelma insisted.

"How did—" I looked at Aspen, and she shook her head.

"We've known for a long time, dear," Betty said as I fell into a chair beside Lotti.

I suddenly wished I still drank, because a margarita sounded really nice right about now.

I stared at the paperback copy of my latest book in front of me, in some combined state of shock and awe. I picked it up and examined the brilliant details my designer crafted into this cover. I hadn't ordered physical copies of my own books in almost two years, despite Lila's insistence that I sell signed copies from my website. If it weren't for her, I wouldn't even *have* a paperback option online. After I recovered from the epic shock of all this, I owed her a phone call.

"How long? How long have you all known?"

"Your mother never *meant* to tell us," Carlos said, adjusting his thick, purple-rimmed glasses.

"My mom?" Of course, I told Mom that I wrote a book. She begged me to do a book signing at her shop, but I swore her to secrecy until I was ready.

She passed the day before I was going to tell her I would.

"It was her turn to pick a book," Lotti explained. "She didn't tell us it was yours. Not at first."

"But dammit, we *devoured* that book like the fucking delectable dessert it was," Thelma added.

"Your mom was so proud of you that the truth practically burst right out of her," Carol Ann added, her smile soothing.

"She was . . . proud of me?" I didn't consider my first book to be very good at all. It sold well enough, but I figured it was because that first book set up the entire Veltori universe. My first series was . . . rough at best.

"Of course she was proud," Carol Ann said, her eyes shiny. "We all were."

"We all *are*," Thelma corrected.

"When's the next one coming? I'm dying to know!" Lotti gushed.

The swell of love that surrounded me evaporated in a single stuttered heartbeat. I didn't know how to tell the group that there would never be another Diana Davenport book. It seemed like a shitty way to end their final book club meeting at Brenda's Book Nook. I wished like hell I could give them another one. I wished the characters hadn't gone on an extended vacation, refusing to talk to me. Or that the words hadn't dried up, no matter how many days I put my butt in the seat and tried to write anything at all, only to be met with a blank page night after night.

"Stop fucking pestering the girl," Thelma chided. "The next book will come when it's ready. Isn't that right?"

Beckett's gaze penetrated from across the table, but I couldn't bring myself to meet it.

"Right."

"For now, let's talk about that sexy vampire, Darius, and his very talented tongue," Carlos insisted.

The group erupted in chatter about *Forever Forbidden*. I, as the author, was instructed to sit quietly and not give a single opinion, or answer any questions, until they were finished with their very lengthy discussion. I thought Beckett would get a little squirmy with all the free-flowing sex talk, but he seemed to be enjoying himself.

I was enjoying myself. The way they talked about my characters as though they were old friends—or in some cases mortal enemies—warmed a place deep in my soul.

For the first time in over a year, I felt the inkling of a story forming. A whisper from a character I hadn't yet met. Maybe it was wishful thinking, but I discreetly slid a pad of paper toward me anyway, and scribbled a note on it. *Mateo needs a woman who challenges him.*

I turned the pad over, and when I looked up, Beckett's gaze was trained on me as though he knew exactly what happened.

I spent over an hour answering questions about the Veltori universe, not just from this book, but from all of them. I'd forgotten about some of the side characters, ones I once intended to write spin-off series for. Maybe, just maybe, this *wasn't* over yet.

I wanted to believe that so badly.

"You should move home, Kira," Lotti insisted. "That way, we can help you brainstorm."

"She doesn't want our fucking help," Thelma chided.

"I don't want any spoilers," Betty said. "But I'd love it if you moved back. We all would."

My gaze kept snagging on Beckett's, which only confused me more. Because the more I thought about it, the more I wanted to be back in Bluebell Springs.

"But what would I do here?" The question slipped out as easily as it did last night, before I could wrangle it back down my throat. But this time, the first suggestion was not to write more books.

"Take over the bookstore," Carlos said, as though it was the most obvious answer.

"Oh my—*yes!*" Lotti all but squealed.

The entire book club went a little nuts.

"That would be so perfect!"

"Your mom would love that."

"It would be so full circle."

"Do you *want* to own a bookstore?" Aspen asked from the opposite end of the table, effectively silencing the group.

"I don't know anything about running one," I admitted.

"We do," Thelma said.

"You do?"

"I used to help your mom with the book buying," Dylann said. "I'm a little rusty, but I'm not useless."

"I worked part time just so I could read the advance copies," Thelma added.

"I worked on the weekends," Betty added. "And planned the story hours for the kids. I really miss doing that. Margene cut that program a month after Brenda left us."

"Fucking Margene," Thelma muttered.

"I still think we need to organize a manhunt," Dylann said, matter-of-factly. "Frank says he might know a guy."

"We are not hiring a hitman."

Dylann shrugged. "Just an idea."

"My husband can help with the accounting stuff," Carlos said. "At least to start."

"I might know a thing or two as well." I looked over my shoulder to find Grandma Connie standing near the register. I had no idea when she slipped in, or how. Had to be the back door. How long had she been standing there? Was she totally mortified that I wrote vampire smut? My cheeks heated to inferno levels.

"Come take a seat, Connie," Dylann insisted. "I'll pour you a margarita."

"Sorry I'm late," she said to the group, her gaze landing on me at last as she pulled out a copy of *Forever Forbidden* from her tote bag. "I—I didn't know if I—"

"We understand," Carol Ann said, her tone filled with compassion. "We know it's hard."

"That's not an excuse," Grandma Connie said. "Not anymore. I owe you all an apology."

"For what?" Lotti asked.

"I feel responsible for what's happening. If I'd stepped up and taken over—"

"Connie, you do not get to blame yourself. We won't fucking allow it," Thelma insisted, folding her arms across her chest. "Margene Miller fooled us all. The only thing you're guilty of is believing in someone who stabbed you in the damn back with a pickaxe."

Grandma Connie swiped at her tears as Husker nosed the back of her arm, causing her to laugh. "You know I brought you some asparagus," she said to him, fishing a baggie of vegetables from her tote as Dylann slid her a margarita across the table.

"Would you really be willing to work here again?" I asked Grandma Connie after she took a hearty sip, trying my best to keep my question as delicate as possible. When Mom was still here, Grandma Connie was in the bookstore daily. But, to my knowledge, she hadn't stepped foot in Brenda's Book Nook since the day of Mom's accident.

"Only if it's what you want, Kira," she said to me. "Margene left your father in a financial mess. It would be an uphill battle from the get-go. I won't ask you to sink that kind of money into a store just to preserve your mother's legacy."

What *did* I want?

I knew what I didn't want.

I didn't want to live in Omaha anymore.

I didn't want to be cut off from the people who mattered most to me.

I didn't want to just exist.

I didn't want to play it small ever again.

I caught a whiff of Mom's floral perfume and nearly started to cry. But this time, the tears were happy. This bookstore may have started out as Mom's dream, but it was integral in shaping me into the author I'd become. Whether or not I ever wrote another book, this place was special to me. Too special to let it go if I could do something to stop it. And for the first time, I realized I was not alone.

"You all understand that I don't know what I'm doing here?"

"We're here to help you figure it out," Dylann said.

"All of us," Lotti promised.

"And we're ready to put our money where our mouths are," Thelma said, pulling out a checkbook and waving it.

"What?"

"We want to invest, dear," Lotti said, as though this entire conversation was premeditated. Hell, maybe it was.

I glanced at Beckett. He was wearing one of those sexy half smiles that turned me into an instant puddle of goo.

"You already know you'll have a pretty great landlord. Just saying." He shrugged, causing a fit of giggles to erupt from Lotti and Carlos.

"But my dad—"

Dylann refilled her plastic margarita cup, pushed back her chair, and pointed to the door. "Looks like we're taking a field trip to the hardware store." She looked at me. "If you're in, that is."

Happy tears trickled down my cheeks.

"I'm in."

THIRTY
HUSKER

I smell bacon.
Mom, hurry up.
There's bacon downstairs.
Mom.
Mom.
Mom.
"Okay, okay! I'm up."
Yay!
Move faster.
You're going too slow.
I want bacon.
Why is Mom reaching for her phone?
The bacon will be all gone if we don't go right now.
Mom, hurry up.
"I need to call Lila."
Lila?
Is Lila here?
I should look out the window.

Is Lila outside?
"Sorry, Bubbies. She's not here."
Is Lila downstairs eating bacon?
"Do you think I'm crazy?"
What is crazy?
Am I crazy?
Does crazy mean more bacon?
What's that smell?
Sniff, sniff, sniff.
It's more bacon.
Mom, we have to hurry!
Grandpa Dale's going to eat all the bacon.
"I know you'll be happier here."
Mom, you're moving too slow.
Can we go downstairs?
Before all the bacon is gone?
"I think I'll be happier here too."
I'll be happy with bacon.
But we have to go before it's all gone.
"Unless the bookstore goes under—"
Mom, now!
"You don't have to be so pushy about it."
Is Mom mad?
No, Mom is laughing.
Mom, this is serious.
There's bacon.
Downstairs.
"You want bacon, don't you?"
OMG, Mom!
"Did you just roll your— No, that's impossible."
Open the door.

Open the door.
Open the door.
"Go on."
I'm free!
Bacon, here I come!

THIRTY-ONE

BECKETT

"I KNEW there were a lot of boxes up here, but holy hell, I had no idea there were *this* many."

Kira pressed her fingers into both temples as we stood at the entrance to the upstairs apartment. Her hair was pulled back into a ponytail, her arms were covered in dust, and she wore a bedazzled #TeamMateo T-shirt one of the book club members gifted her yesterday. She looked ready to tackle anything, but the bags under her eyes suggested she didn't sleep much last night.

"These are all books?" I asked.

"Yeah, looks like it."

"I'll get them moved downstairs," I said, reaching for my phone and shooting both Luke and Connor a text to see if they were free to stop over to help, promising some of the lunch I brought the army of helpers currently down-stairs doing inventory.

"Don't you have a job?" The twinkle in her Colorado

blue sky eyes suggested teasing, but the warm smile spread across her lips showed gratitude.

"I'm on my lunch break."

"Long lunch break," Kira pointed out, opening a box and pulling out a paperback to examine it.

I'd been at Brenda's Book Nook for almost two hours. Long enough for the group to decide the name of the store would stay the same, no matter how many changes they decided to make inside. It sounded like a lot to undo all of Margene's unpopular *improvements*.

"My boss is pretty lenient."

"Sounds like a good boss," she said, flipping to the copyright page. Her carefree smile fell into a frown.

"What?"

"This *new* book is four years old. It's been upstairs since Mom died." Kira gripped the book so tightly her knuckles turned white. It seemed as though she were fighting the impulse to rip the book in two.

I was fighting the impulse to gather her into my arms.

As much as I wanted to comfort her, I knew where that would lead. It was a fucking miracle we didn't end up making out the other night before Nana interrupted us. Or more. How many times had I caught Kira staring at my lips—wetting her own in invitation—since the book club meeting just yesterday afternoon?

"Fucking Margene."

That seemed to be the new mantra around here. I didn't fully understand the mess that woman left in her greedy wake, but I understood enough. I made a mental note to chat with Nana about a PI again before she left. If she didn't know one, I had other military buddies who might.

"You okay?" I asked, tucking my hands into my pockets so they behaved.

"Yeah. It's just . . . overwhelming."

"Understandable."

"Mom never kept books up here."

"No?"

"Not books for the store. Just ARCs."

"What are ARCs?"

"Advance reader copies, for books that hadn't come out yet. Publishers sent them in hopes Mom or anyone else working at the bookstore would read them. Then, when the books did release, they could talk about them to customers," Kira explained. "Getting to read my most anticipated books early was one of my favorite things about this store. It felt like I was part of a secret club."

I scanned the room, counting at least a dozen stacks of boxes.

"These can't all be ARCs?"

"No. These appear to be boxes of books for the store that never got unpacked." She moved about the room, weaving her way through the stacks, and searching labels for clues. "I just don't get it. Someone had to carry these *up* here."

Considering the back room downstairs was also full of similar boxes, my best guess was that someone moved the oldest boxes upstairs to make room for the new.

"I just can't fathom why Margene would hide boxes of books instead of putting them out to sell." Kira shook her head. "If she was so hell-bent on stealing from Mom's store, you think she'd want it to make the most money possible."

I followed her toward the back of the room, to the window that overlooked the street. It was dusty, and the blinds had seen better days. But the lone window let in a fair amount of light. Light that revealed a heavy layer of dust on almost every surface. Except one random rectangle on the floor. One large enough for a sleeping bag and a dog.

Fuck, she really *did* sleep up here that first night.

It felt like months since I jumped into Ghost Lake to rescue Kira.

Luke and Connor have talked about her for years. That's why it feels longer.

"What did your mom use this space for?"

"Relaxing," Kira said, a smile forming once again. I felt the heaviest of her tension uncoil. "She came up here to read a book or take a nap, or to brainstorm her next display. Mom loved creating displays."

"What will you use it for?"

Kira turned a slow circle, her gaze scanning the area. "I always thought it'd make a cute studio apartment."

"You want to live up here?"

She shook her head. "Not anymore. Husker's spent enough time cooped up in an apartment. And this one doesn't even have a balcony. But it might make a cute writing loft. You know, for someone who's actually writing books."

I had no conscious memory of stepping close to Kira, only the knowledge that I was now near enough to touch her elbow. The gentle contact felt more like grabbing an electric fence, but I held on despite the strong current. "I saw you making notes."

"Making notes and writing a book are two very different things."

"Maybe."

Her eyes sparkled at the easy challenge I offered. It was the same spark I noticed when she scribbled her first note during the book club meeting yesterday—the first of at least half a dozen. I felt certain Kira had another book in her. Hell, I suspected she had dozens more. She just needed to believe it, too.

"How would you decorate it?" I asked.

"It needs bookshelves," she said thoughtfully. "Built-ins across that long wall." She motioned to the wall opposite the bathroom and kitchenette. "Some to the ceiling. Some just halfway so there's surface space. I'd put a big, fluffy couch over there. One with an ottoman big enough for Husker to sleep on if he wanted. And a big, L-shaped desk over there with a whiteboard above it. Oh, and string lights."

"Lights?"

"Yeah, like white Christmas lights. All along the ceiling, like a cozy border. But unlike the ones downstairs, these would actually work."

"I can fix this space up," I offered.

"It's not exactly a top priority," she said, sighing. She turned her attention to a box beside her, and opened it. "Or a priority at all. It may not be in my budget for a while."

"At the very least, you deserve a fresh coat of paint and some updated flooring," I said. Nana would likely smack me upside the head for getting too involved, but I had no intention of making Kira pay for a single renovation or upgrade. It might be a few weeks before the sale was final, but I had liberties as the new landlord. "I'd do the same even if I were leasing to someone else."

Kira trained her gaze on me, the look suggesting she saw right through my lie, but wasn't calling me out for it. Good thing, too, considering I had plans that exceeded a simple facelift. If the book club could open their wallets, I could too.

"We need to talk about the store space, too."

"Everyone has great ideas," Kira said, referring to the gaggle of book club members who were ready and willing to invest in the bookstore. "But a lot of those ideas add up."

"It's a good thing you know a general contractor who won't charge you an arm and leg."

Kira set down the latest book she fished out of a box near the kitchenette, and looked at me. "Why are you doing this, Beck?"

"Doing what?"

"Going out of your way—" Kira froze, her eyes widening with panic. I followed her unmoving gaze over my shoulder to the stack of boxes behind me, discovering a large wolf spider perched on top.

"Guess I should add an exterminator to the to-do list." Kira didn't break a smile or eye contact with the critter. "Why don't you head downstairs?"

"And leave you with Charlie?"

"You two know each other?"

"This isn't funny."

I didn't bother hiding my smile as I slowly turned,

shuffling away from the spider so I could make a plan to remove it without startling it back into hiding.

"It's a little funny."

"Stop laughing." Kira smacked my arm with the back of her hand. "It's not—*ahhh!*"

She jumped me.

One second Kira was standing beside me, her fearful gaze locked on the spider. The next, her body was wrapped around me like a pretzel.

Her arms had a death grip around my neck. Her thighs gripped my hips like a vise, awakening everything below my belt. I was too distracted by the floral scent of her shampoo to think straight. To fight the impulses taking over. Fuck, I couldn't think about anything other than the way her body was suctioned to mine. How it might feel if we were to shed all these fucking annoying layers—

"Is she gone?" Kira whispered against my neck.

"She?"

"Female spiders kill off their man after they mate with him. I'm pretty sure it's a she spider."

"You're thinking of a praying mantis."

"Stop laughing," she said, gently pounding her fist into my back as I held her to me. I selfishly didn't want to put her down. There was nothing *just friends* about the chemistry crackling between us, or the way her body perfectly and warmly fit against mine like two perfectly shaped puzzle pieces. "And it's true. Some female spiders actually *eat* their mates once they're done with them."

"How do you know this?"

She pulled her face from the crook of my neck. Several strands of her ponytail got caught in my beard, and she pulled them free. Those fiery fingertips left a blazing trail in their gentle wake.

"Book research."

I could put her down.

I *should* put her down.

But then I'd have to admit the spider disappeared into the shadows after she screamed. At least, that was the excuse I clung to.

"Do your heroes always save the day?"

"Only when it comes to spiders," she said, one corner of her mouth tipping up. Fuck, I wanted to press my lips to that spot. To trace my tongue along the seam of her mouth until she opened for me. Would she taste like frosting? Or caramel iced coffee? "My heroines don't need a man."

"But you write romance?" I asked, confused.

I fought to keep a blank expression, as she slowly peeled herself from my body. As she lowered her legs, my hand accidentally grazed her ass, and I sucked in a breath. It took every ounce of restraint I had not to grip her hips and yank her back against me. But that would be a point of no return. I was barely hiding how badly I wanted her beneath my zipper. If I pressed her into me now—

"Beckett?"

I turned away to adjust myself. "Yeah?"

"Where's Charlie?"

"Good question."

She leaned into me, her hand gripping my arm, her floral scent—*lilac?*—invading my senses as her fingers curled, fingernails pressing through the cotton of my sleeve.

"You *lost* Charlie?"

"I still don't understand why you named a spider."

"It's not her fault she's a spider," she answered, as if that cleared it up.

"Why don't you go downstairs?" I suggested, nodding toward the open door. "I'll handle the boxes."

"Are you going to carry me to the other side of the room?" She scanned the room diligently, no doubt searching for her nemesis.

"Is this your favor?"

"What?"

"The favor you won playing darts."

"I'm not using an open-ended favor to cross a room. Even a spider-infested one."

She started to walk away, but I caught her by the wrist and yanked her back to me. I scooped her into my arms, enjoying the way her laughter vibrated against my chest.

We made it halfway across the room before I heard the heavy footsteps on the stairs. I couldn't make out what the man was saying, but I wasn't the only one who recognized the grumpy baritone.

Kira scrambled out of my arms, her feet touching the floor three seconds before Luke and Connor appeared in the apartment.

"Wow, what a fucking mess," Connor said, scrubbing a hand through his shaggy hair.

"What are you guys doing here?" Kira asked, her voice raspy, as though we were nearly caught with our pants down instead of just horsing around.

"We were summoned," Luke said, nodding to me.

"Hey, some woman in a sparkly dress is downstairs," Connor said to Kira. "Says she's your assistant?"

"Lila!" Kira gushed, running for the door without a backward glance.

My shoulders tensed as I waited for Luke to chew my ass out. Did either of Kira's brothers catch me carrying her across the room? The door was open, which in retrospect, was probably better. Implied we had nothing to hide.

"All these need to go downstairs?" Luke asked, surveying the towers of boxes with what I could only describe as contempt.

"Yeah."

Luke hefted three and headed back downstairs, Connor following his example.

The tension uncoiled from my shoulders, but barely. I shouldn't feel relieved because Kira's brothers didn't catch us in a position we had to explain. I wasn't that fucking guy. If I needed that reminder, this was it.

I could help her *and* keep my distance. It was what I had to do. But how? I had no fucking clue. Because with each passing day, I was falling a little harder for Red. One of these days, if I wasn't careful, I might reach that point of no return.

Hell, it was entirely possible I already had.

THIRTY-TWO
KIRA

"LILA?" I practically screamed her name from the back of the store when I spotted my PA holding court with the book club at the community table. She was hard to miss in her shimmering pink sundress adorned in white flowers. The woman wore confidence like it was her second skin. I admired her so much for it.

"Kira!" She rushed to me, running in wedge sandals like it was nothing out of the ordinary.

"What are you doing here?" I asked two seconds before she threw her arms around my neck and squeezed the remaining air from my lungs.

"I was worried. You never called me back."

"I'm sorry. There's been a lot—"

"You're *buying* a bookstore?" she asked, her tone both excited and accusatory as she relinquished her hold on me so she could level me with an expectant stare.

"Surprise." I offered her a forced, cheesy smile hoping

it would lessen her disappointment that I waited to tell her.

"You're moving back home, then?"

Guilt twisted a knot inside my stomach. I meant to call her back while I was walking Husker on the trail the other day, right before I discovered those blocked voicemails. Then again this morning, but there was an incident with Husker and bacon.

"I was going to call you—"

"I'm so excited for you!" She threw her arms around me again. Apparently, breathing was overrated today. "How soon are you moving?"

"I hadn't really thought about it yet."

I had a couple of months before the lease was up on my apartment, and I wasn't eager to head home and deal with packing. Not when there were a million things that needed to be done here at the bookstore to prepare it for a soft opening, and then for a grand re-opening a few weeks later. Until this mess was semi-sorted out, we agreed to stay closed. Plus, the idea—however remote—of running into Travis made going back to Omaha very unappealing.

"The sooner the better, don't you think?"

"You sound eager to be rid of me," I joked.

"You say that like it's even possible."

"Where are you staying?"

"I booked the cutest little cabin. It's walking distance from the store—and that amazing bakery you've told me so much about. I might have stopped for a cupcake or three on the way over. Those things are dangerous."

"I really did mean to call you back."

"You don't need to keep apologizing to me. You've

obviously been busy here. I'm so excited for this next chapter!"

"Really?"

"Really. And when you're ready, I can help you pack. Or I can hire packers so you can stay here and focus. One question."

"Yeah?"

"Who is Margene, and why do we want to burn her at the stake?"

"Long story," I said on a heavy sigh. "I'll fill you in tonight. Grandma Connie already invited you to dinner, I'm assuming?"

"She offered me a room too, but it sounds like there's a full house. You didn't tell me you were staying in the same place as that yummy handyman who rescued you from the lake."

"I didn't?"

"Don't worry. He's all yours."

"I'm not—"

"Have you told her yet?" Lotti called from the front.

"Told me what?" I asked.

"Oh! I'm so excited!" Lila grabbed my wrist and pulled me toward the front, where half a dozen book club members huddled around one particular hardcover book I didn't recognize. "I have a special surprise for you."

"You do?"

"That's really why I came. This deserved an in-person reveal."

"What does?"

Thelma handed over a hardback book with a deep purple cover that shimmered when it caught the light. The edges of the pages were a soft lavender that complemented the cover well, some intricate pattern printed on them. I didn't recognize the book until Lila placed it in my hands.

"I swear, I didn't tell anyone you were Diana Davenport," Lila said.

"We outed you the second we saw that *gorgeous* book," Carlos cooed.

"I meant to show you first, but then I tripped—"

"And we basically stole it from her," Lotti said, her tone unapologetic.

"This is *mine?*" Tears sprang to the corners of my eyes, threatening to fall. But I held them back for fear they'd land on this beautiful work of art and cause water damage.

I examined the book, stunned by the detail. It was a completely different design than the paperback cover. No people. Just designs. Roses surrounded a dagger in the middle, one central to the plot of my latest book. The title was foiled in silver, and so was the blade of the dagger.

"It's a special edition," Lila explained. "Do you like it? Please tell me you like it."

I glanced up, catching my friend biting her bottom lip as though I might tell her I hated it.

"Like it?" I shook my head. "Lila, I *love* it."

The silence evaporated in a heartbeat, excitement erupting around the table.

"It's a fucking work of art."

"It's perfect!"

"Imagine if *all* your books had special editions?"

"Do you have any more?"

"You should order some for the store!"

"Oh! Your mom would be so proud."

"It's so damn pretty I can hardly stand it."

Lila and I looked at one another and laughed. A couple of those tears I'd tried to keep at bay finally escaped, but they were happy tears. God, I wished Mom were here to see this.

"How did you do this?"

"Well *I* didn't do this. I worked with Tatiana on the design. And she recommended a printer who specializes in special editions. So, I had one made." Lila bit down on her bottom lip again. "If you like them, I can put in a larger order."

"Them?"

"I thought it was only fair to do the whole series," she said, pulling three additional books from her oversized tote bag and passing them around. "And when you finish Mateo's book, we can have a special edition cover made for that book, too."

My stomach dropped to the floor, reminding me I had a really terrible conversation ahead. But if anyone deserved to know the truth about the end of my writing career, it was Lila Quinn, the woman who stuck by me through my lowest lows.

"How long are you in town?"

"As long as you need me. Believe it or not, I actually have a little marketing experience specific to independent bookstores."

"We're keeping her," Dylann announced.

"You do?" I asked, surprised. Did she tell me before and I wasn't listening?

"Back in my college days," she said, waving it off like it was no big deal.

"She also mentioned she's really good at coordinating events," Grandma Connie said. "Like, *author* events."

Thankfully, my brothers chose that moment to storm into the room with another load of boxes. The book club chatter turned from oohing and ahhing over special editions, to muttered curses about Margene once again. We'd been inventorying the books on the shelves all morning and hardly made a dent. They were, of course, completely disorganized. The groans at the sight of additional books were justified.

"Where do you want these?" Connor asked after Luke set down a stack toward the back.

"Wherever you can find room."

Beckett came next, carrying three boxes that strained his glorious muscles. His biceps stretched his shirt sleeves and made his tattoos pop. Tattoos I still very much wanted to memorize better. The only one I got a really good look at the night he held me in my bed was the one on his forearm that looked like a unit crest. The rest were blurry in my memory.

"Sweetie, you're staring," Lila whispered against my ear.

I spun around, facing the table. I busied myself examining the four different special edition books. They each had their own unique objects, but the design and coloring were similar.

They were gorgeous.

They were also an incomplete set.

Beckett's earlier words echoed. *I saw you taking notes.*

Maybe I could try—*just try*—to write Mateo's book. There was a time when it was the book I was most excited to write of the entire series. It felt wrong to leave one of my favorite characters without a happily ever after . . . even if I planned to make him work really hard for it. Maybe the conversation with Lila could wait until I knew for sure.

"Lila, dear," Lotti asked, her tone sounding innocent as ever, despite it raising the hairs on the back of my neck. "How long would it take you to get a large order of these beautiful books printed?"

"How large of an order are we talking?"

"How many people do you think would show up for Diana Davenport's first in-person signing?"

I froze, the book I held nearly slipping from my hands. I just found out yesterday that my secret author identity had never really been secret. At least, not with the book club. But that didn't mean I was ready to go public. Or do an in-person event where readers would ask me by the dozens when the next book was coming.

"You look a little green, dear," Dylann said.

"I can't—"

"You *can*," Grandma Connie said, her tone the perfect medicine to soothe my fears. My rising heart rate started to fall.

"We don't mean to push," Betty added. "But imagine how well our grand re-opening would go if we paired it with Diana Davenport's first book signing?"

"With these exclusive special edition books readers can only get here," Carlos added.

Lila looked at me, her expression a mixture of sympathy and excitement. "All you have to do is show up with a pen and smile, babe. We got the rest."

"Your mom would love it," Lotti said, her words delicate yet excited. As though she didn't want to guilt me into saying yes but still kind of hoped her tactic worked.

I jumped at the loud *thud* a stack of boxes made when Beckett dropped them near the back.

"Sorry," he said, sending me an apologetic grin.

"Beckett, come here," Thelma insisted.

Lila gripped my wrist, squeezing until I met her gaze. *Does he know?* she mouthed.

I nodded.

Apparently, my nod gave Lila permission to go, well, full Lila.

"Beckett, we want your opinion on something," Lila said sweetly, reaching for the special edition of *Forever Forbidden*, my personal favorite of the bunch. "What do you think of this book?"

Beckett took it from Lila, as my heart pounded loudly in my ears. I didn't know why his opinion mattered to me. Just because he knew my secret author identity that I suspected was not going to stay secret much longer, the chances he'd ever pick up a Diana Davenport book on his own were slim at best. He wasn't my target reader. It shouldn't matter. And yet, it did.

I braced, expecting the worst.

"This is your book?" he asked, his sparkling eyes betraying genuine excitement.

"Lila had them made," I said sheepishly, as though I were speaking to some junior high crush instead of a man I'd come to consider a friend. And I was doing it in front of an audience.

"This is amazing, Kira," Beckett said, the approval in his tone sending ripples of warmth throughout my body.

My shyness evaporated, morphing into something else entirely as the memory of sliding down that hard body only a few minutes ago came rushing back to me.

"Thanks," I said, lucky I was able to choke out that single word.

"We want your opinion on something else," Thelma said, sounding like she meant business.

"Yeah?"

"We think Kira should do a book signing," Lotti offered. "To coincide with the grand re-opening."

Beckett trained his gaze on me in a way that made the chatter of the people around me muffled and quiet. The background went a little blurry. It was as though there was only Beckett, me, and the special edition book in his hands. "How do you feel about that?"

"Me?"

"You are the author," he said, a smile tugging at one corner of his lips.

I wanted to tell him all my fears. That I'd never done an in-person signing before. That I feared no one would show up and I would let everyone down when they realized I wasn't as big a deal as they thought. That if anyone did show up, they'd mock the very books that made me an author.

He stepped closer, lowering his voice. "Sometimes, the things that scare us the most are the ones most worth doing."

Another *plop* of boxes startled me from the intimate moment. Several sets of eyes locked on the two of us, and the heat of a blush crept up my neck.

"Well?" Dylann asked expectantly.

"Okay," I said quietly.

"Okay?" Lila repeated.

"Okay, I'll do it."

Lila squealed. Lotti clapped. Thelma spewed a string of approving curses. Grandma Connie looked as though she might cry, but in a good way. Excited chatter erupted around the table, the book club already making plans.

But it was Beckett's simple smile that spoke the loudest.

There was nothing but genuine support in his expression.

"Beck, get your ass back here," Luke called across the room. "We're not doing all the grunt work without you."

With one last lingering look, he hurried back to help my brothers with the rest of the boxes.

He's different, an inner voice whispered.

More than going public or doing my first signing, that mere thought was the scariest of them all.

THIRTY-THREE
BECKETT

Flashing red and blue lights bounced off the glass of the new living room window I installed earlier this week, drawing my attention to the police cruiser rolling to a stop out front of the Kniffen Street house.

My chest tightened with dread at the sight of Luke's SUV. Was he here to harass me about spending too much time at the bookstore? Or did he somehow find out about that kiss? Sure, it was last weekend, but it felt like yesterday. Like moments ago. It also would be like him to hold on to the knowledge long enough to make someone squirm.

I tensed.

Until Nana hopped out of the passenger seat, a giant smile spread across her face.

Luke waved at me, waiting for Nana to reach the front porch before climbing back behind the wheel and killing the lights.

"I see you conned him into a ride-along after all," I

said, shaking my head in amusement. Nana had a way of getting what she wanted from almost anyone. I think she enjoyed figuring out what made someone tick. What it took to not only convince someone to give in to her wishes, but to also have fun while doing it.

Even if Luke was scowling now as he drove off, I'd bet my bank account that grumpy ass had fun with Nana riding shotgun during his patrol.

"Did you doubt it?" Nana had been wearing Luke down one family dinner at a time. He insisted he didn't offer ride-alongs. Nana took his challenge to heart.

"I'm smarter than that."

Nana raised an eyebrow, as if to ask, *are you?*

"Did you have a good time?"

"It was a boring fucking day. Typical small town. Not even a speeder to pull over. But he let me turn on the siren to scare a couple of elk off the road, away from traffic."

Mischief sparkled in Nana's eyes. She could be a hardass, and often was. But she also knew how to let loose and have a little fun—something she had proven with this family since she arrived.

Two days ago, she convinced Connor and Opal to take her out on the boat they rarely used. Joe invited her on a property sale tour yesterday, which resulted in at least one offer made. He wasn't even looking for property himself. Quite possibly it was the house on Blue Spruce Lane I mentioned, and no longer had the funds to acquire. And last night, she convinced Connie to tag along with her to bingo, where she proceeded to win the big jackpot. Nana didn't have any use for a hundred and fifty dollars when she had millions in the bank, so she donated it back to the Legion.

I didn't have to feel guilty about the hours I worked. Nana didn't have much time to spend with *me*.

"You want to see the place?" I offered, waving my hand to the open front door.

"I'm here, aren't I?"

I gave her a quick tour, explaining my vision, since there wasn't much to show for it right now.

"This is the first property that's needed a total gut job, but the location can't be beat. Whether I rent it short- or long-term, I think it'll pay for itself pretty quickly."

"I thought you'd be a little further on this house by now," Nana said as we headed back downstairs. Because I'd been spending extra time at the bookstore for the past couple of days, I was behind schedule, and Nana knew it.

"I know it's just a shell right now, but—"

"I'm leaving," she said abruptly.

"What?"

"I didn't stutter."

"You just got here."

"It's time for me to go."

"When?"

"Tomorrow morning."

"Do you need a ride—"

"Connie's going to take me to the airport," she said, waving a hand to dismiss my offer. "You clearly need to stay put and keep working."

"Is this about the bookstore?"

"This is about the redhead."

"She has a name, you know."

"I'm worried you're getting too attached, and you haven't even signed the purchase agreement." Nana waved off my next concern. "Joe's good for it. The deal will go through. But bear in fucking mind that you're not even technically the owner yet. Your wallet's the other thing you should be keeping in your damn pants, at least until it's official."

Good thing I didn't tell Nana about my plans to completely renovate the bookstore apartment. I spent most of last night crunching numbers and finding room in my budget to give Kira the writing loft of her dreams. But on top of the bookstore, Karl Hayes was also expecting an offer on the Ghost Lake cabin this week. As soon as I talked to Kira and was one hundred and ten percent certain she was okay with me buying it, I'd make one.

All number crunching last night proved was that I was in over my head. I went from making careful, pragmatic decisions with my investments to rushing into too many things at once. Nana was right to be concerned. I only got this impulsive when the redheaded curse was enacted.

And yet, the knowledge of that did little to give me pause.

Would it matter if I told you I'm not a natural redhead? Kira's words whispered in my mind.

I couldn't shake this feeling that every decision I made involving Kira Mason was *right*. It didn't feel like the reckless excitement of my past poor decisions. It felt like *home*. But I didn't dare try to explain that feeling to Nana. She'd ask if I fell and hit my head when no one was around, and insist I go to the hospital in case I had a concussion.

"Where are you off to next?" I asked instead.

"I know you're deflecting," she said, heaving out a sigh. "But if you must know, I'm headed to Richmond."

"Richmond?"

"Someone needs to straighten out that sister of yours."

I hadn't heard from Madeline in a few days. I took that as a good sign, but judging by the grim expression on Nana's face, I should have detected the warning in my sister's silence.

"What did she do now?"

"She bought your parents a house."

"Shit."

"Shit is right."

"Kyle's okay with that?"

"Kyle didn't know." Nana shook her head. "If I can give you any piece of advice, Beck, it's that you don't keep secrets like this from the one you love. They can do a lot of damage."

A sinking feeling hit me in the gut. All this time I was caught up in Kira and the bookstore, Madeline had been crying out for help. I thought Kyle would keep her grounded. Keep her from doing anything reckless. But if she went behind his back—

"He hasn't left her," Nana said. "*Yet.*"

"I should go."

"No," Nana said quickly. "I know you mean well, but you'll just make it worse. You can't keep coming to her rescue. You've been doing that all your life. Madeline created this mess. It's not yours to clean up."

"But it's yours?"

"I'm just going to hand her the broom," Nana said.

Frustration welled inside me. What if I had given in

and allowed my parents to move into the vacant property? Worst case, they trashed the place, and I eventually had to evict them to renovate the house again. But at least Madeline's fucking marriage and finances wouldn't be on the line.

"Anything I *can* do?"

"Yeah," Nana said, folding her arms across her chest. "Stop making impulsive decisions. I raised you better than that."

"Nana—"

"I mean it, Beck. Look, I like the girl."

"Woman," I corrected.

"I like her. She's accomplished a lot for herself. She's got grit. Maybe even reminds me a little of myself sometimes. But getting mixed up with her is a bad fucking idea."

She didn't have to spell it out. There were Luke and Connor to consider. They might not take too kindly to me dating their sister. Not to mention the rest of her family, who basically accepted me into their clan without question. I was about to be Kira's landlord—a clear conflict of interest. If I pursued her and it didn't work out, several bridges I built since moving to town would turn to ash. I might not be welcome in Bluebell Springs at all if things went south. Then what?

I was tired of picking up my life every two to three years and starting over, something the redheaded curse was famous for enacting. Being in Bluebell Springs made me realize more than ever that I was ready to settle.

I was ready to settle *here*.

Here, where I could wake up to the sun rising over the

mountains each morning. Where I could count on a friendly smile when I needed one. Where I had deep bonds with friends who were like brothers to me.

Bluebell Springs was the closest place I'd ever known to a real home, and I didn't want to fuck that up.

"She's also a wounded animal," Nana added softly, patting my arm. "And wounded animals are unpredictable. The last thing I want is for you to get your heart broken again. There's a lot more collateral damage to consider this time."

This time.

She didn't have to say it out loud. She was referring to my most recent redheaded nightmare. The one where the boss's daughter went a little crazy when I turned down her advances. All because I was friendly and helpful to her, not realizing until it was too late that she read into my kindness. Took it for something it wasn't and accused me of leading her on. The dramatics were . . . extensive. Thankfully, her father didn't fire me on the spot, but we both agreed it was better if we went our separate ways.

But what was growing between Kira and me, it was unlike anything I'd ever experienced before.

"What if this time is different?"

Nana looked me dead in the eye, her tone serious as she said, "Then keeping it in your fucking pants for a good long while won't change that."

THIRTY-FOUR
HUSKER

Mom's here! Mom's here! Mom's here!
"She's taking you to the lake."
Opal, you give the best head scratches.
More head scratches, please.
The lake?
"She's a little stressed out."
Stressed?
"You'll be good today, right?"
I'm always good.
"Yes, you're always good, Husker."
Is that a treat in your pocket?
Sniff, sniff, sniff.
Opal giggles are my favorite.
"Sit."
Plop.
"Take it nice."
I'll take it really slow.
There.

"Good boy."

Num, num, num.

Is that the front door?

Run, run, run.

"Has he been good?"

Duh, Mom.

I'm always good.

"He's been good."

See, Opal knows.

"Thanks for watching him."

"I thought you'd be working?"

Nana?

Nana, do you have treats?

"She doesn't have treats, Husker."

Opal, how do you know that?

What if they're in her pocket?

"I'm just taking a quick break while the weather's nice."

"Beckett going with you?"

New Best Friend?

Is he here?

I'll look out the window for him.

Where is he?

"What? No."

"Good. He doesn't need distractions right now."

Nana sounds grumpy.

Is she grumpy?

Maybe she's hungry.

Someone give Nana pizza.

"I'm not distracting him, if that's what you're worried about."

Mom sounds grumpy too.

Opal, we need to order pizza.

Right now.

Everyone's grumpy.

"How about another treat?"

Okay, Opal.

"Can you give me high ten?"

Oh, this is my favorite trick.

Plop.

Lift both paws.

Paw Opal's hands.

"Good boy!"

Num, num, num.

"I like you."

Nana likes Mom?

It doesn't sound like Nana likes Mom.

I don't know about Nana.

"But?"

"But Beckett's been through a lot. I don't want to see him screw up a good thing over a bad decision."

"Bad decision."

Mom's shaking her head.

Why is Mom shaking her head?

Does she mean no pizza?

No, that can't be right.

"Beckett is a grown man, capable of making his own decisions."

"Everything all right in here?"

Grandma Connie!

Do you have pizza?

Or snacks?

Any snacks will do.

"I was just picking up Husker."

Hey, that's me!

"Going to the lake, then?"

Grandma Connie doesn't sound grumpy at all.

I bet she remembered to eat.

"With Lila."

"Lots to discuss about the store I assume?"

Grandma Connie, are you going to the store?

"Yes."

"Strange place for a meeting."

Nana still sounds grumpy.

"I do my best thinking on the lake."

It's true.

Mom is way more chill at the lake.

Unless she falls in.

Mom, don't fall in this time, okay?

"We'll see you for dinner?"

Dinner?

Grandma Connie, did you say dinner?

"Yes. C'mon Husker."

But Mom, what about dinner?

"It's not time yet."

Are you sure, Opal?

"Be a good boy, okay?"

I'm always a good boy!

"Yes you are, Husker."

THIRTY-FIVE
KIRA

SUNLIGHT WARMED my skin as I lay back on my paddleboard. Husker sat at the edge, perched and attentive like the captain of our board. I allowed my fingers to dangle, dipping them into the water as I floated in the middle of Ghost Lake with Lila. The clear sky overhead was the prettiest shade of blue, the water calm, with sprinkles of kayakers and paddleboarders, all content to keep to themselves. Summer days didn't get more perfect than this in Bluebell Springs.

Moving home felt *right*.

It felt like the peace I'd so desperately been seeking since I moved away.

"Okay, we can get the books in five weeks," Lila said from Connor's borrowed board. "It'll be cutting it close, but I got you a deal on shipping."

"You know, the point of being on the water is to disconnect," I reminded her. We'd been working around the clock at the bookstore. With the help of several book club members, we inventoried every last book, identifying the oldest ones we'd use for a sidewalk sale that preceded our soft opening next week.

"I'm putting away my phone," she said in surrender.

"And put it on silent."

"You know I can't do that."

"I think the biggest flaw of this local lake is that they insisted on having a cell tower nearby," I mumbled. "You *do* know how to relax, right?"

"Ordering four thousand copies of your special edition books and getting them here on time with a shipping discount *is* relaxing to me," Lila said, shooting me a cheeky grin to match her tone.

"I still think you ordered too many."

"You thought a hundred of each was too many," Lila shot back.

"What if no one comes?"

"Nope," Lila said firmly. "You do *not* get to worry about that. That is my job. And I've been waiting two years for this opportunity. Trust me, I'm not going to mess it up."

At the sound of an engine, I forced myself to sit up. It wasn't loud, but it was distinct. Uncle Karl would drive that old beater truck until the wheels literally fell off. We all joked that the day it quit working, he'd retire from his auto body shop and spend all his free time trying to bring the old Ford back to life. It was so strange to see him out at the cabin twice in the span of a week when he spent a decade avoiding it.

I wondered if today was the day he finally sold it.

"You okay?" Lila asked.

"Yeah, I am." Though, the idea of buying the family cabin, of living on Ghost Lake and being able to paddleboard any time I wanted had its appeal, it wasn't practical. Taking over the bookstore was no small feat. Dad promised to get things as close to the black as possible after the sale of the building closed. But we both knew it wouldn't be enough. I needed to set aside every spare dollar I had to revive Mom's store. I told Beckett as much yesterday, and gave him my blessing.

"You know, after your sexy handyman buys that cabin, you can still visit," Lila said, her tone nearly as suggestive as her waggling eyebrows.

"It's not like that," I said quickly, remembering Pauline's minor warning about Beckett making bad decisions.

Ugh, why did I want her to like me so much? Maybe if I dyed my hair dark brown, she'd have a change of heart.

"And why not?"

"Gee, let me count the ways."

"You're a romance author, Kira."

"So?"

"It's your job to figure out how to make forbidden romances not just work, but flourish into a happily ever after."

"There is no romance," I insisted, the word feeling far too intimate for my taste. "Not for me. Not ever again."

"I know The Asswipe did a number on you, but he does *not* get to determine whether or not you find love. *Real* love."

"Have you been talking to Luke?" It was the safest piece of what she said to focus on.

The idea of love still felt . . . broken. Something possible for others, but unattainable for me. Sure, I was attracted to Beckett. Very fucking attracted. And there was little doubt he was attracted to me. But that didn't mean there was a future there beyond friendship. And love? Yeah, that was farfetched. Maybe my characters fell for one another fast, but fate wasn't just accepted in the type of romance I wrote, it was expected.

"I mean it, Kira. You deserve to be happy."

"I'm working on it, in case you missed the memo. Bringing Mom's bookstore back to life is making me very happy."

"He's a good man," she said, doubling down.

"Then *you* should date him."

Lila giggled long and loud, alerting Husker. He popped to standing, his head tilting at that severe angle that would forever make him irresistibly adorable. When we decided to take a break for the afternoon, it was mostly for his sake. He'd been spending all his time at the farm because I was worried he'd bump into a stack of books and end up buried beneath them.

"What's so funny?"

"You, babe." She shook her head. "You're so full of shit."

She wasn't wrong, but I wasn't going to admit that out loud. "Are you dating anyone?"

"Not at the moment." She unfolded her legs and dipped her feet gingerly into the lake. "In fact, I've deleted all my dating apps. I'm on a hiatus."

"What happened?"

"Thirty-nine first dates and zero second dates. That's what happened."

"That's rough."

"I never liked dating apps."

The very idea of downloading one made me shudder. I met Travis on a dating app. A complete stranger. Someone who could pretend to be whoever the hell he wanted because no one I trusted knew him. No one could vouch for his character.

But a lot of people could vouch for Beckett.

As though the mere thought of him manifested the man, a black truck pulled up and parked beside my Jeep. I pretended not to notice, but Husker damn near lost his shit and started to pace on what little surface he had.

"Oh, buddy," Lila said as he started to whine. "You got it bad, too, huh?"

Beckett waved to us, and my entire body heated in a way that couldn't be blamed on the direct sunlight. His smile was fuzzy from this far out, but I could see it in my mind, clear as though he were sitting across from me on the paddleboard. I hadn't told anyone about the forbidden kiss on the dock. A kiss that could never happen again but forever changed something inside me.

At least it would be good writing fodder.

"Are you sure you two haven't slept together?" Lila pressed.

"No."

Though, if my brothers hadn't stormed into the book-store apartment when they did the other day, I might have made a very poor decision. Because when I slid down Beckett's body, I discovered just how many parts of him were hard.

"But you want to."

"When did you say those books were coming?"

Lila giggled again, a little softer this time. "Nice try. I know you better than that."

I stared at her for several beats, wondering if it would be the worst thing in the world to confess to the woman who became my closest friend during my darkest hours that I kissed Beckett. But before I could make that determination, Husker lost his balance and caused my board to wobble.

"Not again!" I shrieked.

I grabbed my dog two seconds before he face-planted into the water, jerking him to my chest. I held on tightly as the board rocked as if we were hit by a rogue wave in these otherwise calm waters.

By some miracle, when the board stilled, we were both still on it.

"It might be time to head back," I said to Lila, wishing we could take the rest of the day off. But we purposely took our break in the middle of the day to enjoy the best of the weather, with the plan to return to the bookstore later this afternoon and keep working. Dylann promised to teach me about the buying process so we could get new, bestselling titles stocked as soon as possible.

"We don't have to rush," she said, reaching for her paddle.

"Beckett is busy." I watched him disappear a few

minutes ago into the tree-covered trail that led to the cabin to meet Karl.

"Tell that to Husker."

We looked at each other and laughed.

"How's the next book coming?" Lila asked, as though she were inquiring about the weather and not the topic I was hell-bent on avoiding.

"It's not."

"Not *yet*."

"Not at all."

"No," Lila said, her tone friendly but firm. "You do *not* get to let The Ass Weasel determine your future. He lost that right a year ago."

Despite the warm sun on my skin, a chill rushed through me, causing goosebumps to run riot up and down my arms. Her perceptiveness was downright frightening at times. "It's not like I haven't *tried* to write," I said, hoping I didn't sound too defensive but certain I did anyway.

"*Keep* trying."

"I don't know if I can write anymore, Lila. I mean it."

"You're just stuck."

Dear God, I hoped that's all it was. I remembered the notes I scribbled on a piece of paper, about giving my next book hero a woman who challenged him. But since that small spark of inspiration, there was nothing.

"Mateo won't talk to me," I admitted. "I have no clue who the heroine is. It's radio silence in the Veltori world."

"Except for all the moaning they do at all times of the day and night," Lila teased.

I laughed. "I'm not going to apologize because my characters enjoy having great sex."

"All except one, currently."

"Poor Mateo," I mumbled.

"Babe, you know I wouldn't push you if I thought you weren't happy anymore, right?"

I smiled at her. "I know."

"Writing is in your blood. It'll come back. Inspiration could be anywhere. You just have to keep your eyes—and your heart—open."

My gaze flickered back toward the cabin in the trees. The same one Husker had been zeroed in on since he spotted his new best friend. Beckett walked the property with Karl, and though I wasn't an expert body language reader, I was willing to bet the sale of the cabin was a done deal.

"It's so weird to see Uncle Karl out here after he avoided the place for a decade."

"But it's nice, right? It's too sad to think that little cabin has been empty more than not."

"Yeah."

"You should help him fix it up," Lila suggested.

"I'm not the handy one."

Lila flashed me a wicked smile, wiggling her fingers suggestively. "Handy, handsy. It's the same thing, right?"

I looked away, unable to fight the smile that spread across my own lips as I imagined the two of us all alone in that cabin. Out here, no one would ever have to know. Except, I did own a flashy red Jeep that the locals would quickly come to recognize as mine, now that I was staying in Bluebell Springs for good.

Maybe Pauline was right to be stern with me.

Friends, Kira. Just friends.

But that mantra was starting to sound a whole lot like the bullshit it was.

Friends. Some *benefits?*

"You're totally screwed," Lila said in a fit of giggles.

She wasn't wrong.

THIRTY-SIX
BECKETT

I spotted a nose wedged between the table and my elbow about two seconds before the cold, wet thing rubbed against my skin. Not quite enough time to hide the flinch that followed.

"Husker," Kira said, her tone a gentle warning.

He ignored her and pushed his nose closer to the table, moving my arm further out of the way to better accommodate him.

I broke off a piece of crust and looked to Kira for permission.

"Might as well," she said, reaching for her glass of strawberry lemonade.

I focused on the pizza crust so I didn't stare at the way her lips suctioned around the straw. It didn't matter that Nana warned me to keep things professional and platonic with Kira. Or that her brothers—my two best friends— were also seated at the patio table outside Pizza Patty's.

My imagination went fucking feral when it came to Kira and what she could do with those lips.

I blamed it on the spider incident. The one where Kira ended up wrapped around me like a pretzel.

Husker snatched the pizza crust from my hands, tail wagging in victory, as though it were the first piece he conned anyone out of tonight. It wasn't.

"When are we moving you home?" Connor asked Kira.

"What's this *we* shit?" Luke chimed in.

"Do you hate me that much?" Kira fired back at him.

"I don't hate you," Luke mumbled, reaching for his glass of iced tea as he scanned the patio.

"Could've fooled me," Lila said, stirring her blue raspberry lemonade with a straw.

"I'm a man down with Johnson on vacation. I might not be able to take off work," Luke said. He was one of three full-time police officers in Bluebell Springs. The rest of his force were part-timers. But that still seemed like a shitty excuse.

It was the only reason I piped up with, "I can help."

"That would be lovely," Lila answered as Kira pulled her phone from her purse.

"I'll fucking help," Luke muttered.

"Then why couldn't you just say that?" Kira scrolled through her phone as though searching for something.

"You sure it's a good idea to move home?" Aspen teased as she helped herself to another slice of mashed potato pizza. Turned out, it really was one of their most popular choices. "You two might kill each other."

"We'll be fine as long as she doesn't get drunk and roast the town again."

"You mean if she doesn't publicly call you out for having a stick up your ass?" Aspen shot right back.

"I don't drink anymore," Kira said to Luke, sounding exasperated. As though they'd gone round and round on that subject and gotten nowhere.

"So you say."

"I believe her," I said before I could remind myself to stay out of this family feud. Luke gave me a strange look, then shot one back to Kira. Fuck, I should've sat next to anyone else tonight. But too late for that. Instead, I leaned into my defense. "Look, being around an alcoholic changes you. It certainly changed me."

"Alcoholic?" Luke repeated, looking confused for once in his life.

"Where have you been, man?" Connor asked in disbelief.

"What do you mean, exactly?" Luke asked Kira, as though he were interrogating her. I loved the man like a brother, and I'd still take a bullet for him. But fuck. I was getting tired of his shitty attitude when it came to his sister. The man could hold a grudge longer than anyone I'd met.

Kira let out a heavy sigh, setting her phone down. Lila offered to search for the email she was seeking, and Kira nodded permission before focusing on Luke.

"You want to know why I don't drink anymore, Luke? It's because I watched over and over again as one drink turned into two. Then six. Then *thirty*. And no, that is *not* an exaggeration. That's how many beers come in a thirty-pack. Pretty easy to count when no one else is drinking them. I watched how his personality changed with each drink. I stopped drinking because I knew if *I* wasn't sober, I wasn't safe."

For once, Luke didn't have anything to say.

"I take full responsibility for getting involved with him," Kira said. "For moving to another state to be with him. For staying way longer than I ever should have in that sorry excuse for a relationship. And yes, I take *full* responsibility for the mean things I said the last time I ever touched a drop of alcohol. I'm really sorry I brought up the whole jilted at the altar thing when I had the microphone. I know I hit a nerve, and that was totally uncalled for and unfair. But like it or not, I'm moving home. So you can accept my apology or not. I have Mom's bookstore to save. I'm going to be too busy to care what you think anyway."

Luke sat there, looking a bit stunned.

Three people started to talk at once. Not that I could make out what any of them were saying. Not that it mattered. Because in the middle of their talking on top of one another, Husker let out a rare but loud bark that silenced the entire table.

Every head turned, watching as he pointed at the table with his nose, as though he were hunting pizza and couldn't for the life of him figure out why we weren't more concerned about the leftovers sitting ignored on the table.

The heavy tension broke the instant I tossed him another piece of crust he caught easily, causing the entire table to burst out in laughter. Luke included.

Husker tilted his head at that sharp angle, as though

saying, *Silly humans. Don't you know pizza is the answer to everything?*

"I'm sorry, Kira," Luke finally said as the laughter died, sounding like he meant it. "I didn't know."

"None of you knew," she said. "That was my fault."

"Babe?" Lila said to Kira.

"Yeah?"

"How soon were you planning to move out of your apartment?"

"Not for a while yet. I want to focus on the bookstore for now. I have two months left on my lease."

"You must have read that wrong."

"Read what wrong?"

"You don't have two months. You have two *weeks*."

Kira grabbed her phone back from Lila, reading the email. "Shit."

"I could help next weekend," Connor offered.

"That's our soft re-opening," Kira said, shaking her head. "I really should be here for that."

"You can't reschedule?" Luke asked, sounding more helpful than asshole for once.

"Every day we drag our feet on re-opening, we lose money. We'd be open already if we didn't have all those old books to deal with." She explained about the sidewalk sale they planned for early in the coming week.

"I bet the book club could handle that sale without you here," Aspen said.

"I'm off Tuesday and Wednesday," Luke offered, surprising most everyone at the table. Except Husker. He was too trained on the remaining pizza to care about anything else, including the chipmunk that lingered nearby. "It'd have to be a turn-and-burn trip."

"That's in, like, three days," Aspen said.

Kira's eyes glazed over in what looked like panic. I shifted her strawberry lemonade closer to her hand, and she took it.

"Kira, babe, I got this," Lila said.

"You do?"

"I'll head back tomorrow, round up the girls, and get your place packed up. Don't worry. They're cheap. They work for wine. We'll have everything ready to go when you show up on—"

"Tuesday afternoon," Luke said. "We'll get an early start."

Lila looked to Connor first.

"I can make that work."

"Me too," I added.

It was a good thing Nana left yesterday and was currently dealing with my sister's mess, because she'd surely slap me upside the head for volunteering my help in this situation. I only signed the purchase agreement on the cabin yesterday. I still needed to move in. And Joe promised the paperwork for the bookstore building would be ready Monday. Not to mention, the Kniffen Street house wouldn't install its own kitchen cabinets. But I would figure it out, because being there for Kira mattered more.

"Got room for one more?" Aspen offered.

"Really?" Kira asked, looking not just at her cousin, but everyone around the table. Her eyes were shiny, as though she might cry.

"We got you, babe," Lila said, like it was the most obvious thing ever.

The urge to reach my hand to Kira's thigh and give it a gentle squeeze in reassurance was strong, but it would not go unnoticed. Even if her brothers didn't catch it, someone sitting nearby would. So I snuck a piece of ground beef to Husker instead.

"Is The Asswipe going to show up and cause a scene?" Luke asked, sounding for once more protective brother and less dick.

"I doubt it," Kira said, grabbing a second slice of pizza, but leaving it untouched. Much to Husker's apparent disbelief. He wedged his way between us and promptly shoved at the back of her arm with his nose. "Hey! That's my *boob*."

Lila and Aspen laughed. Luke and Connor groaned. I, on the other hand, got a strong visual of that *boob* cupped firmly in my hand. A very distinct image that had blood rushing below my belt. *Not fucking now.* I reached for my drink and gulped.

"Do we need a U-Haul?" I asked, desperate to distract my rampant thoughts.

"Got one booked," Lila announced, setting her phone to the side and reaching for another slice of arugula pizza I couldn't bring myself to try. "You'll pick it up in Omaha."

"So, this is really happening?" Kira said, her words almost too quiet to be heard.

"You already took on the bookstore," Aspen said, pulling cash from her purse and setting it on the table as she scooted out of her chair. "Seems kind of silly to commute."

"Aspen, babe, put your money away," Lila insisted.

"I can't let you pay—"

"I'm about to put all of you to work." Lila picked up the cash and handed it back to Aspen, holding out her hand until Aspen caved. "You can absolutely let me pick up the tab tonight."

"Headed out?" Connor asked Aspen.

"Duty calls," she said, likely referencing the bakery.

"Take a couple of slices for Owen," Kira insisted.

"He's good," she said. "He and my dad went fishing. I don't think he'll come back hungry."

"Owen's like the son he never had," Luke muttered.

Several sets of eyes locked, but no one said anything about Thoren. Not directly. They didn't have to.

"Guess you'll be moving into the cabin soon?" Luke asked me. I couldn't tell by his tone whether he was simply shifting conversation, or wondering how soon I would no longer be staying across the hall from his sister. Better to err on the side of caution.

"Soon, yeah."

"Let me know if you need a hand," Luke added.

"Don't really have much to move," I admitted.

"Then I'll bring the housewarming pizza."

Husker perked at the mention of his favorite word, as though he forgot there were leftovers on the table or that his belly was probably stuffed so full he might turn into a pizza.

I tossed him a pepperoni, stalling because I wasn't ready to leave yet. Not with Kira sitting next to me, her leg so close to mine that the heat radiating off her skin threatened to burn mine. Another inch and we'd be touching. Skin on skin.

Fuck, I needed to leave.

I needed to get moved into that cabin, and away from temptation.

And as soon as Kira was officially relocated to Bluebell Springs, that's exactly what I planned to do.

THIRTY-SEVEN
KIRA

"You sure are handy with that drill," Lotti cooed as Beckett hung brackets above the display window. The book club had unanimously agreed that we should hang a curtain until we were ready for the grand re-opening to keep people from being nosy. So Lotti had sewn a set of curtains from the cutest book-themed fabric. They were the perfect backdrop for the new sign in the window: *Stay Tuned for our Next Chapter!*

"Lotti, let the man do his job," Thelma scolded.

"What? I'm just complimenting a job well done," she said innocently, batting her fake eyelashes.

"He's not going to get the job done if you keep pestering him," Thelma chided.

I exchanged a look with Carlos, who was currently hovering behind his husband's back at the computer, and we both fought a fit of giggles.

Moments like this, I knew I made the right decision.

I wasn't alone.

I had an army of people not only ready to help, but excited to bring Brenda's Book Nook back to life.

We'd been working our asses off, but nostalgia was high as we shared countless memories that included Mom. There were plenty of tears, but so many more laughs. I hoped Mom was smiling down on this mismatched group of book lovers, laughing right along with us.

"The curtains turned out great, Lotti," I said.

"Thanks! I've been saving that fabric for a couple of years, waiting for the perfect project."

"I'm honored to have them here."

"So, I have some bad news, and some terrible news," Patrick said from behind the computer at the register. His grim tone squashed the happy mood instantly. Carlos had convinced his accountant husband to not only review the books for Brenda's Book Nook, but to stay on for the first month to help set the store up for success. The grim expression on Patrick's face made me wonder if he was regretting his offer. "Which news do you want first?"

"Just hit me with it," I said.

"There are more outstanding invoices than we originally thought," Patrick said, his tone an apology. Not that he nor anyone else huddled at the bookstore tonight had a thing to be sorry about.

"Why am I not surprised?" I muttered.

"How much damage are we talking?" Thelma, one of the primary new investors, asked.

"Twelve grand."

"Total?" Carlos asked.

"On top of the eight thousand we already accounted for," Patrick said. "So, twenty total."

"Fucking Margene," Thelma muttered before she remembered Opal was at the back of the store. My niece had the choice to hang out at the bookstore with me or at the hardware store with her dad and grandpa while they did inventory. She was here, curled up on a beanbag—one so worn it needed replacing before we re-opened—reading Husker a book about Colorado wildlife. If she noticed the cursing, she didn't acknowledge it. "Sorry," Thelma apologized.

"What's the *terrible* news?" I asked hesitantly.

"Some of these vendors have already sent you to collections."

A knot coiled in my stomach, making me regret my earlier decision to order nachos from the Mexican restaurant down the street.

Collections added an extra layer of complication we didn't need.

"Maybe we don't tell my dad about this," I said to the group.

Dad had been by earlier to chat about the state of the business. He'd kept the utility payments current and used his savings to shore up the outstanding payroll. But he couldn't do more until the sale of the building was final without dipping into his retirement fund—which I was absolutely not going to allow him to do. Even after the sale, paying off the second mortgage was the priority. If, and only if there was anything left, he'd help pay off the outstanding debts.

Because he hadn't officially signed over the business to

me yet, he tried, once again, to talk me out of doing this. To let him file bankruptcy before trying to save Mom's store bled me dry. He even suggested closing Brenda's Book Nook so I could start a brand new business of my own.

But I just couldn't.

I was already in this. I made a commitment not only to the book club members, but to myself. And to Mom. Brenda's Book Nook was the next chapter in my life. After the last few years that nearly broke me, and the last year I spent merely existing, I was ready for my life to have purpose again. Saving the bookstore that shaped my childhood seemed like a pretty damn good way to accomplish that.

"I hope your mother is haunting Margene's ass," Thelma muttered.

"She is," Opal piped up, causing everyone to turn their heads to the back where she sat with Husker. "Karma is catching up to her."

Sometimes, my eight-year-old niece said the oddest, yet most profound things. I couldn't help but hope she was right. But even if it were wishful thinking, it warmed a spot in my heart to know she felt such conviction.

"Good," Thelma said.

"Karma's going to bite her right in the behind," Lotti said. "With shark's teeth."

"How does that look?" Beckett stood back from the display window now covered by a set of curtains that reached the raised landing. He'd drawn them closed, ensuring they were the right fit.

"It's perfect," Lotti said. "And just in time, too."

Tomorrow morning, I was heading to Omaha with my

brothers, Beckett, and Aspen to pack up my former life into a moving truck. But the book club was showing up in force for a large sidewalk sale. Dylann, Betty, and Carol Ann were around town today hanging flyers. Lila—despite all the packing—was blasting the sale all over social media.

Our goal was to clear out as much of the oldest inventory as possible, even if it meant selling them for next to nothing. There wasn't a single book in the store that was returnable due to its age. Whatever didn't sell, we would either put in a bargain bin, or donate.

"Are you all sure you'll be okay without me for the next couple of days?" I asked for at least the third time tonight.

"I say this in the most loving way possible. But would you please stop trying to control everything and just let us do this, honey?" Carlos pleaded.

"We've got your back," Lotti reassured.

"She's right. Plus, you haven't seen hustle until you've witnessed Dylann work a crowd. I dare anyone to make it past the store without buying at least one book when she's on shift," Thelma added.

"It'll be fine," Beckett said, offering me one of those easygoing smiles that had the ability to short-circuit my brain.

I still couldn't decide how I felt about his offer to help with the move. Luke and Connor could handle loading the truck on their own. But selfishly, I wanted him there. "Are you sure you can step away from all the work you have to do?"

He placed his hands on my shoulders and locked his gaze with mine. "It's two days, Red. Not two months."

Tingles skittered down my arms from the contact. They skittered into other places down south as well, which made it hard to maintain eye contact. The room did that weird thing again, where everything and everyone around us blurred and muffled. It would be so easy to close what little distance remained between us. To feel his hard body pressed against mine.

I studied his Glacier National Park T-shirt to keep my eyes off his lips.

"I don't want to get on your Nana's bad side any more than I already am."

"Nana'll come around."

He sounded so sure of himself. I wanted to believe him. But I was playing with fire, and we both knew it. So, I stepped back until his hands fell away and the room refocused.

"Opal, honey, you about ready to go?" I called to my niece.

"Five more pages," she hollered back.

"What do you want me to do about the outstanding invoices?" Patrick asked. "The new ones?"

"I'll move some money over tonight. Get them paid this week if we can."

"Sweetie, you have investors too," Carlos reminded me. "You don't have to take on the financial burden alone."

"I know," I said, averting my gaze from Beckett's. "And I appreciate that. But trust me. There will be plenty more things to invest your money in. Let me worry about getting us back in the black."

After a quick huddle to go over the plan for the sidewalk sale once more, we called it a night. I waited as Thelma, Lotti, Carlos, and Patrick filed out.

"You okay?" Beckett asked as we waited for Opal to finish reading Husker his book. Odd, considering he never sat still long enough for me to read him more than a paragraph of anything. But that dog kept glancing between Opal and the book, almost as though he understood her.

"Overwhelmed, but okay."

"You need to unwind some of that stress," Beckett said, his voice low. I couldn't decide if I was imagining the suggestive part, but I was too tired to talk myself completely out of it.

"Any suggestions?" Not too tired to flirt, apparently.

"I can think of a few." Beckett traced my jaw with a single finger. I didn't remember him stepping so close. Or was I the one? When his finger reached the bottom of my chin, he tilted my face up, bringing our lips dangerously close to one another.

"Do they involve that mouth of yours?"

"What would you want me to do with my mouth?" he asked, his voice low. The gruffness in his tone caused a ripple of pleasure to travel the length of my body. It settled between my legs, because I knew exactly where I wanted that mouth.

"We're ready to go!" Opal announced, the clap of the book she was reading the return to reality I needed.

I stepped back just as Husker rushed us, wedging himself between Beckett and me. I, of course, was stuck with his booty. He looked up at the counter, where Mom used to keep a container of treats. I made a mental reminder to fix that next.

"You could also try writing," Beckett said, shifting to a suggestion that was more kid-friendly at Opal's approach.

"Maybe," I said, though any attempts I made at Mateo's book still fell flat. I wasn't as convinced that Diana would *never* write another book again, but I certainly didn't feel confident enough to set a release date for the next one.

"Maybe the two go hand-in-hand," Beckett said. "Or is it mouth to—" He purposely didn't finish his sentence, but his flickered gaze did. My core tingled with want. I wanted so badly to revoke the *no benefits* part of our friendship.

What's stopping you?

"Your next book will be your best one yet," Opal said, her young tone all matter-of-fact, as though her opinion was a simple-known fact.

"I hope you're right."

"I am."

"That's sweet of you to say."

"I didn't say it."

I exchanged a glance with Beckett, who seemed as confused as I was.

"Who did?"

"Grandma Brenda."

Opal clipped Husker's leash to his collar and led him to the door. As though her words didn't just completely shake me. I glanced back to the paranormal romance section, where I last smelled her perfume. Maybe it was wishful thinking.

Or maybe Mom knew something I didn't.

"Is she—" Beckett asked, nodding at Opal.

"What?"

He shook his head. "Never mind. We should get back to the farm. It's late, and we have an early morning."

With one last look at the store, I flipped the lights off. A hint of Mom's perfume lingered by the front door. But whether she was really there, or I just wanted so damn badly to believe she was, was up for debate.

THIRTY-EIGHT
HUSKER

Mom got her suitcase out.
Where are we going, Mom?
I better circle the bed so she doesn't forget I'm here.
"Husker, calm down, buddy."
Calm?
What's that?
Pace, pace, pace.
"I have to make a super quick trip."
Trip?
Where are we going?
Will there be pizza?
Don't leave without me.
"Hey, it's okay."
Mom stopped packing.
To pet me.
Oh, no.
She's trying to hug me.
I don't like hugs.

Ugh, hugs!
Mom, you're squishing me.
Why are you squishing me?
"I'm only going to be gone one night."
Gone?
Where are we going?
"You're going to stay with Grandma Connie."
Grandma Connie has the best asparagus.
Does she have asparagus now?
Or bacon?
Maybe we should check.
"Opal will be here too."
I love Opal!
Wait.
Why are you putting stuff in your suitcase?
Where's my stuff?
Am I going?
I'm going too, right?
You can't leave me behind.
I want to go.
"Husker, buddy."
New Best Friend!
He has a good laugh.
New Best Friend, Mom is packing.
Did she tell you where we're going?
"Is he always like this?"
Am I always the bestest?
Yes.
Yes, I am.
"There's a reason I didn't pack until this morning."
"We could bring him."

Yes!

New Best Friend, where are we going?

"This is how he acts when I pack one bag. Can you imagine what he'd be like packing up an entire apartment?"

Apartment?

I like my balcony.

And my treats are there.

But I like Grandma Connie's house better.

Pace, pace, pace.

"Husker."

Yes, New Best Friend?

"Want to go outside?"

Outside?

Yes!

Let's go!

"Thank you."

New Best Friend, what's taking so long?

Why are you looking at my mom so long?

Come on.

I better push New Best Friend's legs so he moves.

He seems stuck.

Let's go!

Let's go!

Let's go!

"Okay, we're going!"

Finally!

THIRTY-NINE
BECKETT

"Is that everything?" Lila asked, looking around the empty apartment. Aside from a couple of garbage bags of trash and a few odds and ends that would also end up in the dumpster, Kira's Omaha apartment was fully packed up and loaded in a U-Haul.

It was official.

She was moving to Bluebell Springs.

I'd see her every day.

Fuck. I'd see her *every* day.

"That's it," Kira said, her gaze scanning the open-concept space and landing on a small, sealed box she labeled as trash, on the kitchen counter. With the way she kept glancing at it, I had to wonder what was inside.

Lila let out a long yawn.

"I can't thank you enough," Kira said to her friend, hugging her for several beats. Pathetic to say I was a little jealous. Not of Lila. But of the hug.

Since Kira tackled me during the spider incident a

week ago—I didn't have the heart to tell her I hadn't located Charlie yet—we were careful to avoid most physical contact. Definitely the kind of physical contact that had our bodies pressed together. It was for the best, considering the electric current that crackled between us even from across the room. We didn't have to speak it into existence. We both knew it was there. But dammit, I missed the way her curvy body fit so perfectly against mine.

"I'm going to miss our coffee dates," Lila admitted. "But I'm so excited for your next chapter."

"Me too," Kira agreed, her eyes shiny.

"Don't you dare cry," Lila playfully scolded. "I'll see you in a few weeks, when your books show up."

"I hope you know, the book club officially nominated you as our author event coordinator."

"Just the book club?" she teased.

"Oh, me too."

"I'll be back and forth as much as I can."

"I'm starving," Luke announced as he, Connor, and Aspen reappeared in the hallway outside Kira's open doorway.

"I know just the place," Lila said.

"Why don't you guys go ahead?" Kira said. "I'll get the last of the trash, and meet you at Maximino's."

"You sure?" Aspen asked, fighting a yawn.

"I'll stay and help," I offered.

Luke flashed me a look, but it was short-lived due to his hangriness. "Let's go," he said, about-facing toward the elevator.

"You don't have to stay," Kira said quietly.

"I know." I locked eyes with her, assessing whether she wanted to be alone or if she wanted me to stay. I didn't want to encroach on her space, but the idea of leaving her by herself when The Asswipe could show up unannounced didn't sit well with me. She assured all of us the odds were low, but that also meant they weren't zero.

"I'm going to do one last walk-through," Kira said as the others piled onto the elevator.

I nodded, grabbing a couple of trash bags and taking the stairs. I waved the others off as they filed into Lila's car, and went back inside for another load.

When I returned to the apartment, I found Kira standing in front of the same small box on the kitchen counter, visibly shaking.

"Is there a bomb in there or something?" I teased, hoping to calm the tension pouring off her in waves.

"Not quite," she said, sniffling through a forced smile, drawing my attention to the redness in her eyes. Hell, had she been crying?

"Hey, if you don't want to move, we can unload that truck right now—"

Kira sputtered a laugh through the tears. "It's not that." She wiped beneath her eyes with the back of her hand. "It's . . . hard to explain."

I leaned against an adjacent counter, giving her space but staying close. "You want to try?"

She took a deep breath and released it slowly. "A couple of weeks after I broke up with Travis, he showed up *bearing gifts* for my thirty-second birthday."

I made a mental note to learn her birthday the first chance I got. But for now, I just listened.

"I asked him not to contact me. After everything I went through with him, I thought it was the least he could do for me. But, of course, he didn't like that. He tried everything to get me to take him back. When I ignored the influx of phone calls, voicemails, and texts, he decided to show up at my apartment with presents. I didn't let him in, but he left them outside my door when I refused to answer."

"I'm guessing he didn't come over much?"

Kira let out a *ha!* "He was always too good to spend time in my apartment, since he had a perfectly good house. It was his way of punishing me for not moving in with him. God, I'm so fucking thankful I never caved on that."

The urge to reach for her, to pull her gently into my arms and hold her, overwhelmed my senses. I gripped the granite counter behind me, hoping it was enough to root me in place as she continued.

"He went out of his way for my birthday. Bought me all these gifts that were so specifically me. I know that sounds sweet, but after the couple of birthdays before this one . . ." She shook her head. "Let's just say, his idea of giving someone a present was to make them feel guilty for wanting one at all, and eventually taking them to a store and telling them to pick their own. And then acting like he did you the greatest kindness ever."

"Geez." I had a whole helluva lot more to say on the matter, but I kept my thoughts to myself so Kira could finish.

"It was infuriating getting this stupid box of presents. It proved he was paying attention the whole time, but never wanted to put in the effort until it might benefit him.

But it was too late to matter. I donated all the gifts to a shelter. But he also wrote me a letter." She opened the box and pulled out a single envelope with a folded-up sheet of yellow legal pad. "The only reason I've held on to it is because I wanted to burn it. But they kind of frown upon setting fires inside apartments."

"I imagine they do."

"I'm not taking it back to Colorado with me," she said, dropping it into the box and closing the flaps. "I don't want that negativity following me. I guess the dumpster is as good a place as any for it."

"No," I said, pushing off the counter.

"No?"

"You want to burn it, we're going to burn it."

"But how?"

"You leave that to me." I grabbed another load of trash.

Together, we emptied the apartment of the remaining garbage in two trips. Lila had promised to send in cleaners tomorrow, so Kira propped the small box beneath her arm as she locked the door for the last time.

We rode the elevator down in charged silence. I wanted to hold her hand, to touch her lower back, to put my arm around her and tug her against me. But since I couldn't do any of those things without setting off a chain reaction neither of us might be strong enough to fight, I did the next best thing. I drove us to a spot just past the edge of town and pulled over on the side of a gravel road surrounded by cornfields.

"I don't understand," Kira said.

I reached across her lap for the glove box and retrieved a lighter. Did I mean to graze her thigh when I did? Fuck,

I couldn't pretend it was an accident. I was desperate to touch her, even if for a single seemingly innocent moment. "C'mon," I said, pushing my door open and hopping out.

The small burn barrel I'd forgotten to remove from my truck bed was buried beneath the totes we'd stacked there, but I managed to dig it out. I intended to leave it at the Kniffen Street house to make more room for Kira's things, but I stayed late to hang curtains at the bookstore last night and forgot until we were fifty miles down the road. Connie would insist there were no such things as coincidences.

I set the barrel up in front of the truck, firmly in gravel. It was oversized for just a letter, but it would do the trick.

"Here," I said, holding out the lighter to her.

She took it from me, her fingers grazing mine. The embers sparked to life. The simple touch a warning that if we started this fire, it would be next to impossible to extinguish.

"It was a weird fucking letter," Kira mumbled, pulling it from the envelope. She thumbed the lighter and held the flame to the corner of the yellow paper. It caught quickly, licking across the page until it was nearly engulfed in flames. She dropped it into the barrel. "And now it'll be ash."

We stood in silence as the letter and its envelope dissolved into dust. Her stoic expression morphed into relief, and a single tear rolled down the side of her cheek.

I waited until the flames extinguished, and poured water into the bottom of the barrel to be certain the fire was out. Kira leaned against the side of the truck, looking up at the star-filled sky in what I could only describe as relief as I cleaned out the barrel and stowed it.

In silence, I joined her, leaning my back against the truck.

But before I could look up at the stars and compare them to the Colorado night sky, Kira flung herself at me. One moment we were beside one another. The next, her body perfectly molded with mine. She reached for the back of my head with both hands and yanked me down for a kiss I had no power or desire to fight.

Our lips moved together as one, as though they had a thousand kisses to learn this rhythm. I traced my tongue against the seam of her lips until she opened for me, allowing our tongues to dance.

Fingernails pressed against the back of my neck, her breasts pushed against my chest, and those fucking perfect hips arched right into me. If she doubted my attraction to her before, there was no hiding it now. Blood rushed south, making me hard as a fucking rock in two heartbeats.

I slid my hands down her back, over her hips, and onto her firm ass.

"Fuck, Kira," I groaned between frenzied kisses, lifting her until she wrapped her legs around my waist. I spun us, placing her back against the truck, and continued tasting those delicious lips.

Hands roamed greedily as our kiss deepened. A hunger I'd never experienced stirred to life inside me. It wasn't the impulsivity I'd experienced with women in the past. It was more profound, and it roused something primal within me. I didn't understand what the fuck was happening here. But one thing was clear: Kira Mason was my kryptonite.

She rocked her hips against my length, and I damn near went blind.

I slid my hand inside her shirt, just above the hip. The skin-on-skin contact sent a lightning storm of sensation throughout my body. I raked my fingers slowly toward her breast, desperate for the feel of those perfect globes in my hands but not willing to rush this.

As my fingertips grazed lace, a shrill ring cut through the air.

"No," Kira groaned, dropping her forehead against my chest before she slowly slid down my body. She reached through the open passenger side window for her phone. Aspen's name appeared on the screen.

We were taking too long, and everyone knew.

Well, fuck.

"Hey," Kira said, answering on speaker. "We're heading there right now."

"Did you take the scenic route?" Aspen teased.

A blush surged up Kira's neck, and dammit, it made me feel smug.

"Had to fix a loose cupboard door," I said.

"That's a new one," Aspen said, as though seeing right through the bullshit lie. But somehow, I suspected she'd keep our secret. In fact, she might just be the ally I needed when it came to that bookstore apartment. I made a mental note to chat with her about it later.

We gave Aspen our orders and Kira hung up the phone.

"Sorry," she said to me.

"For what?"

"I shouldn't have kissed you. *Again*."

"Maybe I like it when you kiss me."

"Beckett," she said, pleading in her tone as she rested a hand on my chest as though it were the most natural thing to do. I wasn't even sure she was aware she did it until she looked at her hand and pulled it away. "You know why we can't."

"I know." It didn't stop me from staring at her lips like I was a starving man sizing up his first meal in days.

"Just friends," she said, though conviction was missing from her tone.

"Friends," I half-heartedly agreed.

"Friends. No benefits."

I tucked a strand of hair behind her ear, purposely dragging my fingertips along her jaw.

"That's too bad," I said, my gaze zeroing in on her mouth. I took a big step back before I gave in and kissed her again. "Because I'm really enjoying these benefits. I think you are, too."

FORTY
KIRA

"Dammit," I cursed as I discovered *another* bookshelf on its last leg. It was a miracle it hadn't crumbled before I offloaded all the books. But it too, like eight others so far, would have to be completely replaced. Just another expense that would burn through the pool of money I collected from my savings and the investments of the book club members.

At least the sidewalk sale went well in my absence. Dylann apparently was pure magic when it came to sweet-talking strangers on the street. Of the twenty-two hundred and eighteen books we identified, almost twelve hundred sold.

It wouldn't be enough to pay the balance of outstanding invoices, considering we were running a buy-two-get-one-free sale and not a single book was selling for double digits. But the money earned this week would make a dent.

Small wins.

I pulled another set of books from the shelf, stacking them on the table behind me. Since I gave everyone the night off, the stacks I was pulling off the shelves wouldn't be sorted until tomorrow. But it only felt right that I work a couple of late nights to make up for my quick trip to Omaha.

This was the first time since I opened the bookstore for the book club meeting just shy of two weeks ago that I had the store all to myself.

It looked nothing like it had.

Books were piled everywhere, sorted into categories. Most shelves were empty; the rest would be by the end of the night. Some, like the one that held a variety of travel books in the back, were good for little more than tinder. So many of them would need to be replaced.

"What else could go wrong?" I mumbled.

A flicker of an image flashed in my mind. A feisty woman, emptying the shelves of a shop. What kind of shop? I couldn't tell from the cloudy vision. Was it potions? I heard the woman mutter, "What the fuck else could go wrong today?" and knew she was the heroine I'd been waiting to meet—Mateo's mate.

Holy hell.

Where did that come from?

I pulled my phone from my back pocket, opened my Notes app, and jotted it all down. As I typed the final line of dialogue, I heard the rattle of the lock.

I could count on one hand the number of people who had a key to the bookstore, and none of them were a threat. But I tensed nonetheless, unable *not* to brace for the worst.

Maybe someday, I wouldn't be afraid of every goddamn thing.

It wasn't until my gaze snagged on Beckett's easygoing smile that I relaxed.

"Red, what are you still doing here?" he called back to me, closing the door behind him and flipping the deadbolt.

My pulse skipped and stuttered at the sound of his voice. My traitorous nipples pebbled at the very sight of him. Or maybe it was from the memory of me jumping him a couple of nights ago on that deserted country road. The way he kissed me so fucking thoroughly that I felt it in every single cell of my being. The way his hands roamed my body possessively.

I was so fucked when it came to Beckett Campbell.

So very fucked.

"I'm working," I shot back, spinning away from him and continuing to empty the last couple of shelves. "What are you doing here?"

"I need to take some measurements."

"For what?"

"For the new flooring."

I grunted under the weight of some European travel books from the shelf, and stacked them on the table. "You don't have to do that, Beckett."

"I know."

"Then, why are you? And don't give me that bullshit line about doing that for anyone else who rented from you."

"Because it needs to be done," he said simply, weaving through the precarious piles of books until he was in my corner. The ceiling was lower here, making the space feel more confined. Mom used can lights to lighten up the cramped area, but most of them had burned out because Margene had been too lazy to change out lightbulbs.

Fucking lightbulbs.

I wanted to be mad about it, but I was having a really hard time focusing on my anger with Beckett this close to my orbit.

"That space might not get used for a long time," I said, focusing on the books still on the shelves.

"It's empty right now," he said. "Now is the best time to get it done."

"I can't pay for it."

Beckett came closer, folding his arms over his chest as he leaned against the edge of one of the sturdier shelves. "Do you think I'm doing it so you *owe* me?" There was a hint of something in his tone, as though I'd offended him.

"Sorry," I said, apologizing more out of habit than anything. "I'm just used to . . ." I let my words trail off as I reached up on tiptoe for a book lying flat on the very top of the shelf. Who the hell put it up there?

I felt Beckett move more than I saw him, as though I sensed his energy pulling to mine like a magnet. He came up behind me, not touching, but the heat of him swirled between us like an untamed flame.

I started to look back, but thought better of it. If I met that intense gaze head-on, I'd probably just suction myself to him again. And though the thought of that was very, very tempting, it would only further complicate things.

Beckett reached above me for the book, capturing it easily.

He held it out in front of me, and I took it.

"Thanks," I said in what equated to barely more than a whisper.

"Kira," he said, his voice low against my ear. His hot breath tickled my neck as his fingertips grazed my side. It was a barely there touch, but it scorched the skin beneath my cotton shirt all the same. "I never do anything expecting you to owe me for it. Sooner or later, you'll realize I'm telling the truth."

Just as he started to pull his hand away from my hip, I reached back and shackled his wrist. This was a very stupid idea, but tonight I was past caring. I was so damned sick and tired of one thing after another going wrong. Tonight, I wanted one thing to go right. I wanted—*needed*—him to touch me. I needed to sate this burning desire for him, consequences be damned.

I moved his hand beneath my shirt, placing his palm flat against my stomach.

"Kira," he said, his whisper a warning this time.

"Please." Was I begging? Yes, the fuck I was. But in this moment, I didn't care. "Please, Beckett."

"Please what?" he said, his voice a low, sexy growl that instantly ignited every nerve ending in my body.

"Please *touch me*."

I guided his hand further north, reminded of the interruption that kept him from cupping my breast on that country road. If Aspen hadn't called—if I'd left my phone on silent—how far would things have gone that night? The wetness pooling between my legs suggested *all the way*.

"Where?"

"Everywhere."

"You're sure?" he asked, fingertips lingering on the

very edge of my bra. My nipples ached for him to reach up.

"Yes," I panted.

"Then, Kira?"

"Yes?"

He pulled away my guiding hand. "Be a good girl and keep your hands on that bookshelf."

I nearly came at his command.

Holy hell, Beckett Campbell had a secret dark side.

A super *sexy* dark side.

And I was here for it.

Future Kira could worry about the repercussions.

Kira of Right Now needed to experience this freshly uncovered, wicked side of Beckett Campbell.

I gripped the edges of the sturdiest bookshelf, bending forward as Beckett slid a hand over the fabric of my bra. I whimpered at the delicious contact, craving more. I arched into his touch, wishing the fucking lace prison would evaporate.

He slid his other hand up the side of my shirt and back down before dipping inside. The man was set on torturing me as he moved leisurely up my body, taking his time caressing my skin with his fiery touch. Until finally, after what felt like hours, his second hand joined the first. Then both my breasts were in his capable hands. He kneaded them, gently yet greedily.

"Fuck, Red."

"Fuck is right," I panted.

One hand disappeared, but before I could complain, the clasp of my bra slackened.

"Was that move part of your military training?" I teased.

"That move was all me, Red." Both of his hands gripped my hips, and I pushed my ass against him. He groaned as I grinded against his hard length. Those capable hands slid up my sides and gripped my bare breasts as though they were the only handholds on the side of a cliff.

"Fuck me, Kira," he groaned, teasing my nipples with pinched fingertips as he continued to massage my boobs. "I've been thinking about your tits since that first day I saw you." His confession came in hot whispers against the shell of my ear. "When you were soaking wet from falling in the lake. Your nipples"—he squeezed them both—"were poking through that sorry excuse for a shirt you were wearing."

I was so fucking turned on.

Had a man *ever* made me feel this desired by doing so little?

He released his hold on my right breast, his hand moving south. I gasped as his fingers played at the waistband of my shorts.

"Who the fuck wears shorts all the time in a *mountain* town?" Beckett growled. "You've been killing me with those long legs."

"I have?"

"Like you didn't know," he said, chuckling deeply. The low laughter vibrated against the crook of my neck as his lips pressed there. My top button popped open with the same ease as the clasp of my bra. My knuckles were turning white at the death grip I had on the bookshelf, but

I didn't dare let go for fear Beckett would stop. And I did *not* want him to stop.

Not now.

Not ever.

He slid inside my shorts, those warm fingers on a slow but determined mission. He ran them over the silk of my panties. I spread my thighs wider, desperate for him to reach his destination.

"So fucking wet," he said, his tone pure primal approval. He stroked softly, applying the perfect pressure to my button. I rocked my hips gently with his motion, afraid I'd spontaneously combust at any moment. His touch was fucking fire, and I was the short fuse to a bomb about to go off.

I moaned as he slid his hand up, and dipped it beneath the silk.

I cried out when his rough, callused fingers made contact with my clit.

"Do I make you wet, Kira?"

"Isn't that obvious?"

His laughter was one of my favorite sounds. He kissed my neck, biting down gently. "I could mark you. Like Darius," he offered in jest.

Had Beckett Campbell *read* my book?

No. He just remembered the characters the entire book club were still talking about.

"Just like that scene in the library," he said against my ear.

Fuck, he had.

"Beck . . . I'm going . . . going to—"

He pulled his hand away seconds before I was due to explode.

"What the—"

"What did I tell you?" he said.

Fuck. I'd dropped a hand from the bookshelf without realizing it. I replaced it instantly, desperate for him to finish me off. I *needed* this release. I needed him to give it to me.

"Please," I begged, turning my head over my shoulder to meet his gaze. It was liquid heat.

I parted my lips in anticipation.

He kissed me the same moment he dove back into my pants. There was nothing slow about his movements this time. His hand moved savagely through my folds. He slipped a finger inside me, and that was it. I clenched, bracing for the powerful orgasm. I cried out as my climax fucking wrecked me.

My body shook violently.

I gripped the bookshelf so hard I heard a crack.

Beckett held me to him, one hand on my breast, one anchored between my legs, as wave after wave of pleasure pummeled me. He held me until my body stopped jerking from the euphoric intensity of it all.

"That was the sexiest thing I've ever fucking witnessed," Beckett said, kissing my temple. "Next time," he said, dragging his hands leisurely across my body as he pulled them away, "I want to *taste* you as I make you come."

FORTY-ONE
KIRA

NEXT TIME.

Beckett implied there would be a *next time*, and it was making it impossible to focus on anything else. Including the sketch right in front of me with my rough ideas for a new store layout.

Had I ever had an orgasm I felt in my entire fucking body?

No.

Until last night, I didn't think they were possible. I'd written about them, convinced they were pure fiction. I'd had orgasms before. Good ones, too. But until Beckett got hold of me, I had no idea what I was missing. Every time I so much as glanced at the empty shelf where the travel section once lived, my entire body tingled from the inside out.

What happened last night couldn't happen again.

We both knew that.

Yet he implied there would be a next time.

"You all right, dear?" Lotti asked, a knowing smile on her face that said I wasn't wearing a blank expression.

"Fine," I said. Or, I attempted to say. I had to clear my throat and try again. "I'm fine."

"Sure, you are," Thelma cackled, reaching for a donut on the community table we gathered around to discuss the changes. With the number of shelves that were total losses and the rest currently empty, we decided it was the perfect time to make some changes with the overall layout of the store.

"Do you think we should move the children's section to the front?" I asked.

Carlos lifted his gaze from the store's laptop, adjusting his purple-rimmed glasses, and said, "Lotti looks like that when she's fantasizing about Mateo."

Lotti shrugged her shoulders, no hint of apology in her carefree smile. "It's true. I do. Ooh! Are you writing his book yet?"

"Just started, actually."

I never thought I'd utter those words about this particular book. I was convinced my ability to write anything more than a check had shriveled up and died. But after that mind-blowing orgasm, inspiration seemed to ignite. I went back to the farm and straight to my room, pulled out my laptop, and wrote as though the words possessed me.

Would this first chapter ever see the light of day? It was too early to tell. But the spark I felt at the keyboard was like an old friend welcoming me home. God, it felt good.

Maybe one of Mateo's hidden talents in this book was the ability to give his mate magical orgasms.

"You sure it's just Mateo?" Thelma asked, her playful tone more accusatory than curious.

"Have you picked a release date?" Lotti asked hopefully.

"Not yet."

"You should announce one at the grand re-opening," Carlos suggested.

Panic seized me, and my smile dropped.

"Maybe," I said noncommittally.

One rough chapter was a far cry from a finished book. I had no idea whether last night was a fluke or if the rest of the pages would fall into place at all. It was entirely possible I was high on orgasm energy and would never write chapter two.

Beckett can help with that.

"I bet I know who you're thinking about," Thelma said.

"Does anyone have ideas for our first window display?" The desperation to change the subject before Beckett's name was dropped was palpable.

"I thought we agreed on a Diana Davenport display," Carlos said.

"For the grand re-opening," I answered. "But do we want to do something different for the soft launch?"

After some discussion and adjusting of our original timeline, we determined we needed two weeks before the inside of the store would open to the general public. That was the amount of time Dylann estimated was necessary to order the most recent releases and bestsellers and get them on the shelves. Until then, we'd continue occasional sidewalk sales.

"It's that sexy handyman, isn't it?" Lotti cooed.

"He has a name, you know," Thelma said. "And he's a general contractor, not a handyman."

"Oh, I think he's plenty handy," Lotti went on, unbothered by Thelma's corrections. "I bet Kira knows exactly *how* handy."

I nearly fumbled my water tumbler at the playful accusation. Oh, I knew all right. I knew *very* well how handy Beckett Campbell could be. And yet, I was desperate to see what other talents he had. Particularly, ones with that tongue. What I didn't understand was how all of *them* knew it. Was I that obvious? Was it written all over my face?

"I have some bad news," Dylann said, emerging from the back office. She moved a pair of reading glasses from the bridge of her nose to the top of her head. "Brenda's Book Nook is basically blacklisted from ordering books."

The abrupt announcement caused a harsh shift in the air. Any fantasies I'd been playing in my mind went blank.

"From where?" I asked, a sinking sensation settling in my stomach.

"From damn near everywhere." She marched up to the table and yanked a jelly donut from the box. "Fucking Margene."

"We can't order books?" I asked, hoping I heard her wrong. I had to have misheard her, because if we couldn't order books, we didn't stand a chance. No one would want to shop at our bookstore if we didn't carry the latest releases. "*Any* books?"

"All of the publishers have cut us off," she explained,

pulling out a chair and plopping into it. Her heavy necklaces jangled in protest.

"But we've paid all of them. Aren't we current now?"

"Too little, too late, I'm afraid. Not to mention, Margene was apparently selling new releases days before they came out. Some of those publishers are still quite pissed about it." Dylann wore a defeated expression, one that caught around the table. "Ingram closed our account, so that's been a whole other mess."

"Ingram?" It sounded familiar, but Lila would be more familiar with it than me.

"It's the major book distributor," Dylann explained. "If we had to, we could order solely from them for now. Focus on rebuilding our relationships with publishers over time. But it means our profit margin will be slimmer. Our terms were definitely better working directly with the publishers."

"Still sounds better than not being able to order books at all," Lotti said.

"I'm working with a rep to set up a new account, but it might take a few days to get past the red tape," Dylann said. "We might have to push the soft opening."

I sank my teeth into a glazed donut, but the sweet treat did little to ease the sour pit in my stomach. The longer we pushed the soft opening, the longer it would be before we had any notable cash flow. In the meantime, the bills would continue to stack up. Everyone was currently working for free, but that couldn't last. I wouldn't allow it to last.

"What can we do while this gets sorted out?" Carlos asked.

"We can figure out the new layout," Thelma said, nodding to my sketch. "That'll give us an idea of how many bookshelves we're going to need to order."

"Or build," Lotti suggested. "Think Beckett could help us with that?"

I almost said no, but everyone was looking at me so damn expectantly. As though they knew if I asked, he would say yes in a heartbeat.

"I'll talk to him," I finally said. "But let's research all our options. Beckett's got his own business to run."

"Maybe he just needs some extra incentive," Lotti said, wriggling her eyebrows.

"Lotti!" Carlos scolded.

"Just ask him for a favor," Lotti said. "It's up to you whether you want to return it."

Beckett did owe me a favor, from the night of beating him at darts. But now that he gave me one of his potent full-body orgasms, I wasn't so sure I wanted to use the favor on something so . . . boring.

"Down, Lotti!" Thelma chided.

"What else do we need to figure out?" I asked.

"Updating this godawful decor Margene brought into the store," Dylann insisted.

"I propose a bonfire to burn anything and everything associated with Satan's mistress," Thelma said.

"I second the motion," Carlos agreed.

The table erupted with plans of heading to Mexico—a popular topic of conversation these days. While they argued about the best way to hunt down a fugitive, I studied the sketch I'd made of a new layout. One that was similar to Mom's since Margene basically rearranged the entire store and obliterated some of my favorite parts. I added circles for cushy chairs, squares for dog beds, and designated an area for authors to set up signing tables. The reading nook was also high on the list.

I chewed on the top of my pen as I reconsidered Carlos' earlier suggestion to announce a release date for Mateo's book during our grand re-opening. I didn't even have a title yet.

I could hear Beckett's voice in my head: *Sometimes, the things that scare us the most are the ones most worth doing.*

"Oh, what the hell," I mumbled.

"What's that, dear?" Lotti asked.

"Nothing."

Before I could talk myself out of it, I picked up my phone and sent a text to Lila.

FORTY-TWO
HUSKER

Tap, tap, tap.
What's that noise?
Tap, tap, tap.
Mom, don't you know it's bedtime?
Tap, tap, tap.
Big stretch.
Full-body shake.
Tap, tap, tap.
Mom, are you working?
It's bedtime.
Tap, tap, tap.
"Sorry, Bubbies."
Ooh, booty scratches.
All is forgiven.
"I'm almost done for tonight. I promise."
Okay.
Because it's bedtime.

Circle, circle, circle.
Plop.
I'm going back to sleep now.
Tap, tap, tap.
Zzzzz . . .

FORTY-THREE
BECKETT

"The butterscotch oak was definitely the right choice," Aspen said approvingly as she surveyed my work in the bookstore apartment. Unbeknownst to Kira—who was currently helping Connie in the garden at the farm—I enlisted the help of both Aspen and Lila. When I finally revealed this space to Kira, I wanted it to be everything she imagined it could be, and more. But one brief description before the encounter with Charlie wasn't enough to go on. I needed reinforcements.

"Good. I think so, too. And the paint color?"

I'd been nervous about the color, worried it would turn out too dark and make the space feel small. But the tone, *mapped blue*, complemented the floors well. The best part: it matched the color of Kira's eyes.

"It's perfect, Beckett. Seriously."

We moved around the apartment, and I asked questions with each space we discussed. Backsplash for the kitchenette, finishes for the bathroom, where to install can lights for extra illumination.

"I thought I might add lighting inside the shelves too," I said, remembering a picture I found online. "Is that too much?"

Aspen stared at me for several beats, a smile growing. "You really care about her, don't you?"

"Yeah, I do," I said, running a hand over the back of my neck. It's not as though Aspen hadn't picked up on that since I asked for her help a week ago. But admitting it face-to-face like this felt more fucking vulnerable than I wanted it to.

"She cares about you, too."

"She does?" The question fell out before I could rein it back in, my unconscious half step forward with the words noticed by both of us at the same time.

Aspen glanced from my boot to me with an amused smile.

Fuck, the last thing I needed was to sound like some hapless teenage boy tripping over his own two feet when it came to the homecoming queen.

"I mean, I—"

"If you're in this—and I think you are—you'll need about three times the patience you're anticipating. Her trust was shot to hell until there was nothing left of it. It's going to take some time for her to heal again. To trust again. You get me?"

"Yeah, I do."

Nana's analogy about Kira being a wounded animal was perhaps the best nugget of wisdom she offered before her departure. Even if the context was a little different, the core of the meaning was the same. Kira would need time to trust I was who I said I was. To trust that my feelings were genuine. And I'd give it to her.

"I know you helped her burn the letter," Aspen said.

The letter. In Omaha. I cleared my throat, wondering what else she knew about that trip.

"You're a good guy, Beckett. Better than I gave you credit for."

"But?"

"No buts."

"Unless I misstep, right?"

She patted me on the arm, the way my sister sometimes did. "*Now* you're getting it."

We discussed the apartment some more. Where I planned to start next—the bathroom because it'd take the longest, and might require asking for help. The less I had to tell Luke and Connor, the better. I could explain fresh paint, new flooring, and some trim. But I couldn't explain a fully furnished writing loft with built-in bookshelves that lit up. Better to have them help now before I fixed up anything else.

"You'll have to tell them eventually," Aspen pointed out.

"I know."

"But you tell them too soon, and you'll spook Kira."

"Don't I know it."

"I think she's going to love it," Aspen said.

"Any advice?"

"On the apartment, or Kira?" The twinkle in her eyes said she already knew. "You can never really do *too much* for Kira. Not when she's so used to settling for table scraps on the best days. But she also needs to know she can fly with her own wings. Don't try to fix her problems, just support her while she sorts everything out. If you're lucky —and hella patient—you'll get the girl in the end."

Heavy footsteps sounded on the stairs and we both froze.

"Too heavy to be Kira," Aspen whispered.

"Sorry to barge in on you kids." Joe Mason appeared in the open doorway, surveying my work in one slow scan. "Well, I'll be damned. Looks like a new place."

"I think Kira's going to love it," Aspen said.

"Kira?" Joe repeated.

Shit. I hadn't really discussed this with Joe. I mentioned I was sprucing up the apartment when I purchased the paint from the hardware store a couple of days ago, but not why. And I certainly omitted the part about a complete renovation with furnishings.

"I know we haven't officially closed yet—"

"Does she know?" Joe asked.

"No," Aspen answered for me. "It's a surprise. So you're sworn to secrecy, Uncle Joe. Got it?"

Joe nodded.

"Now that that's settled, I'll let you two boys chat. I have to run. Owen's grilling steaks."

Joe and I stood there in silence, both looking around the empty space. I wondered how he saw it. Did he see the new life breathed into it? Or did he picture the past, when his wife hid away up here to read? Did he hate the changes I made?

"You care about her, don't you?" he asked me.

"I do." No point in lying. Kira might not be ready for a

relationship right now, but a feeling deep in my gut told me one day that would change. *Patience*, Aspen had advised. A whole helluva lot of patience.

"I'm glad you're the one buying the building. Gives her the best chance of making it."

"She will," I said.

"You sound pretty confident."

"I haven't known your daughter long, but I've known her long enough to recognize her unmatched resilience. If anyone can save the bookstore, it's Kira."

That brought a slow smile to Joe's lips. "I certainly hope you're right, son."

Son.

The single word threw me off balance, like a friendly punch to the shoulder. How many times had I desperately wanted to hear my own dad call me *son*, just once? But he, like my mother, was too busy wishing they never had a son at all.

"What else you have planned up here?" Joe asked.

"More than I probably should," I admitted.

Joe's smile doubled in size. "I know a guy who can get you materials at cost."

"You don't have to—"

"I want to."

There was no point in arguing, so I simply said, "Thanks."

"Now, tell me what you have in mind."

FORTY-FOUR
KIRA

THE DRY RATTLE of the doorknob left me puzzled. I didn't remember locking the door to the bookstore apartment. In fact, I distinctly remembered leaving it *unlocked* so Beckett could paint this week.

I was overwhelmed by the sheer number of tasks we needed to accomplish before our soft opening next week and wanted a quiet escape. Just for a few minutes.

I took a deep breath, but the thoughts ran rampant anyway.

Thankfully, Grandma Connie worked her magic and repaired a severed relationship with one of the major publishers. Turned out, she had an old friend still working as a book rep, and called in a favor. It wasn't as much progress as we hoped, but having some recent releases and bestsellers was certainly better than having none. The books, however, would arrive before the bookshelves I ordered. We might only have a day or two to assemble the new shelves and stock them. It all left me feeling a little . . . dizzy.

Because there was absolutely no time to head to the lake today, I sought the solace of the empty apartment to clear my head.

Except the damn thing was locked.

Maybe Beckett locked it out of habit.

I went back to the office, searching my purse for my set of keys, and headed back up the stairs. But when I inserted my key into the lock, it didn't fit.

"What the—"

After a struggle ensued to pull my key out of the lock, I tried the other key. The only other key I had for the bookstore. But it, too, was rejected.

It made no sense.

I'd been using the same keys since I snuck into the bookstore my first night back in town, almost a month ago. Not once did they give me an issue with any of the doors.

Until now.

Did Beckett change the locks?

No. Why would he do that without telling me?

Besides, he wasn't technically the landlord yet. I doubted Dad would give him authority to change the locks until the sale was final.

I pulled my phone from my back pocket and called Dad.

"Kira, everything okay?"

"My key to the apartment isn't working."

"The new one?"

"What new one?"

"I had the locks changed right after Margene . . ." He

didn't finish that sentence; he didn't need to. "I figured you picked up your keys weeks ago. Otherwise how— Oh, sorry. Gotta run, honey. Need to help Mrs. Cappers with some paint."

The line went dead before I could say anything more.

New keys?

I vaguely remembered an odd exchange with Luke that first night he found me in the apartment. But it didn't make sense. I was one hundred and ten percent certain nothing was unlocked. I used keys to get inside both the back door to the store *and* the apartment inside.

I hurried down the stairs, making a beeline for the front door, ignoring the half dozen questions shot at me by various people as I rushed by them. I went outside, pulled the door closed, and used my key to lock it.

Or tried to.

But it wouldn't fit in the lock.

"What the hell?" I muttered.

"Kira?" Lotti asked when I cracked open the door to examine the lock mechanism. "Everything okay? You look a little frazzled."

"Lotti, can you lock this door when I close it?"

"Sure."

"Thanks." I pulled the door closed, waited for Lotti to flip the deadbolt, and tried my key again.

Same result.

Lotti waited for my signal to unlock it, looking curious as ever.

"You okay?" she asked. "You look a little green."

"Kira?" Grandma Connie asked.

"When did Dad change the locks?"

"Right after he found out Margene left town. Almost two months ago, now. Why?"

I felt my body overheating.

It was a really shitty time for a panic attack.

There had to be a logical explanation. But whatever it might be, my overloaded brain just could not process it.

"Nothing."

I returned to the office and closed the door, leaning my back against it. I was already overwhelmed. This was just . . . too much. My breathing was labored, as though I'd been running. The truth was there, but I couldn't seem to accept it. It was one thing to smell Mom's perfume from time to time. Quite another to accept she was playing locksmith from the grave.

The edges of a panic attack clawed its way in, but I fought it down.

I would *not* break down.

Not here, in front of an audience.

I reached for my purse, knocking over a small framed photo on the desk. When I went to right it, I froze. The gold frame contained a picture of me in my college graduation outfit, Mom next to me. Her smile beamed so brightly it was damn near blinding. She was so happy I got a degree in English Lit, even if I had no intention of teaching. Back then, I only dabbled with the idea of being an author. I'd drafted some stories, most of them messy and incoherent. The degree was a frivolity. The accounting minor was what saved me when I searched for jobs.

"Mom, I don't understand," I whispered to the frame as tears threatened to fill my eyes.

I waited, hoping the scent of her perfume would tickle

my senses and bring me comfort. But the office smelled as it always had—of old books and a hint of lavender from the air diffuser.

Maybe a quiet drive through the mountains would soothe me.

I shouldered my purse, but before I could sneak out the back door, I ran into Grandma Connie.

"I need some air," I told her.

"Everything okay?"

"Yeah. It's just . . ." *A lot.* But I couldn't complete my sentence without falling apart.

"Be careful," she warned. "The water is extra choppy today."

"I'm not—"

Thelma summoned Grandma Connie to the front counter. I took the opportunity to slip out before anyone else expressed concern, and headed to Ghost Lake.

FORTY-FIVE
BECKETT

"You KNOW, for a guy who said he didn't have much to move, you sure have a lot of shit," Luke commented as he set a large tote next to the couch.

"Less than your sister did," I pointed out.

"Yeah, and we'll have to move all that again when she finds a place to live," Luke grumbled.

We moved the majority of Kira's things into the storage unit three down from mine. She was planning to stay with Connie and Dale until the bookstore got solid legs under it.

It was why I took Karl up on his offer to move in before the official closing date on the cabin. I didn't trust myself around Kira, but I wasn't about to be disrespectful to the people who took me in for the better part of four months. If I slept at the cabin, the temptation to sneak across the hall would be eliminated.

"That should be the last of it," Connor announced as a

strong gust of wind slammed the screen door shut for the third or fourth time. He set down an end table in the living room.

The lakeside cabin looked different from the first time I saw it, yet still the same. Connor and Luke helped me empty the place of Karl's furniture, and retrieve what little I had from my storage unit. The green carpet, wood-paneled walls, and decades-old bathroom fixtures would eventually get upgraded, but those projects were far down on my list.

"You going to survive out here, cooking your own meals again?" Luke ribbed.

I *would* miss Grandma Connie's cooking. But I was looking forward to cleaning up the old charcoal grill and putting it to good use.

"I'll hardly be here," I admitted. I was behind schedule on the Kniffen Street house, but if I put in some long days, I could catch up. *If you stop focusing so damn much on the bookstore, you'd be on schedule,* Nana's voice echoed in my head.

I checked my phone on impulse, but I hadn't heard much from her or Madeline since Nana caught a flight out of Denver almost two weeks ago. Only a few texts to know she arrived safely.

I sure as hell hoped no news was good news.

"You need any help with that house?" Connor offered.

"Maybe next week when I start on the kitchen. This week is painting, and I only have one sprayer."

"How's the sale on the bookstore coming?" Luke asked.

"We close middle of next week."

"Any regrets?"

I studied my best friend, wondering if his question was more than a surface-level inquiry. With Luke, it was hard to tell.

"No. It's a solid investment."

"Think Kira can do it?" Connor asked Luke.

"I don't know," Luke said, his tone more honest than cynical. "I hope so."

"I think the odds are in her favor. She has a lot of help," I chimed in.

"You've been spending an awful lot of time—" Luke's phone rang, effectively cutting him off. He was in plain clothes today, due for a day off. But as the police chief, he was always on call. Judging by his hardening expression, it was work.

"Shit, got to run. Some idiot ignored the warning and went kayaking on Glimmerstone Lake."

I glanced out my new living room window, noting the choppy water. The wind was gusting north of fifty miles per hour, according to the coffee drinkers I'd bumped into earlier. It made for rough waters. At the big lake, I suspected it would be worse.

"I'd offer to help you unpack," Connor said, glancing at his watch, "but I need to pick up Opal from summer camp."

"I'm good," I said to them both. "Dinner's on me whenever you're free."

As the brothers drove away in their separate trucks, I stared out the window and watched the waves rippling across the otherwise quiet lake. No one was out on it today. The locals obviously knew better.

Silence quickly filled the cabin. I'd always been a sort of lone wolf, but the quiet was already deafening.

I threw a set of sheets in the stackable washing machine—the newest appliance in the entire place—and set to unpacking, hoping to drown out the silence. I considered calling Madeline as I worked, but her lack of communication likely meant she was pissed at me. Probably convinced I'd sicced Nana on her. It might be best to hold off until I talked to Nana to get an assessment of what was going on.

I filled the dresser and closet with clothes, the linen closet with a set of towels, and the pantry with a few items I picked up at the grocery store earlier. But the house still felt . . . empty. The walls were bare—the family photograph taken down before I was given the keys.

It was missing something.

Kira.

I tried to shake away the thought, but a new one popped in to join it.

And Husker.

I imagined her laughter as I cooked dinner, trying not to burn the food because she was bare-legged and wearing only my T-shirt. Husker, of course, would be stationed in the doorway waiting for handouts, those sonar-level ears at the ready for anything.

I moved the sheets to the dryer, and went for the living room curtains next. I wasn't sure whether a cycle in the washing machine would help them or not, but for now, it would have to do.

I was antsy.

I resisted the urge to head into town. It didn't matter what destination I set out for. I'd end up at the bookstore.

Aspen's advice echoed. *Don't try to fix her problems. Just support her while she sorts everything out.*

So instead, I went out to my truck to retrieve the last of my things, mostly a dirty load of laundry I'd start after the curtains were finished. But as I closed the back door, a glimmer of shiny red caught my eye through the thick of trees.

A red Jeep.

Kira.

I tossed the laundry bag into the back seat of my truck and headed down the narrow dirt-packed trail to the boat dock. As the waves rocked almost violently against the shore, I picked up my pace. Surely she and Husker weren't on the water today.

Except, I spotted Kira standing on a paddleboard a good twenty yards from the boat ramp, paddling away from shore. She wobbled as she fought the choppy waters. I didn't see Husker on the board or in the water, and it didn't appear that Kira was looking for him. That brought me a small sense of relief because Kira always put him above her own safety. On a day like today, that could be a deadly impulse.

She wasn't wearing a life jacket.

I'd never seen Kira wear a life jacket on Ghost Lake. I was told she was a good swimmer. But *good* didn't guarantee she was strong enough to fight water moving this quickly. My fists balled at my sides. *What the fuck is she doing?*

I didn't realize I was kicking off my shoes until I saw her fall in.

I didn't wait to see if she resurfaced.

I dove in and swam.

FORTY-SIX
KIRA

I was shivering from head to toe as Beckett carried me to his cabin, too frozen to argue that I could walk.

I didn't want to walk.

Not if it meant surrendering his warmth.

The warmth I shouldn't want but now craved all the damn time.

"What were you thinking, Red?" His scolding was gentle and filled with concern. *Real* concern.

Ah, fuck, I was falling for this guy.

"I needed to clear my head." It was a partial truth, but I didn't tell many people about Mom visiting me in my dreams. Beckett wouldn't understand why I had to get on the water to find her.

Not that I did find her.

And now my paddleboard was lost at sea.

Well, shit.

"We need to get you warmed up," Beckett said, sounding much too serious for my liking. I could think of plenty of ways I enjoyed being warmed up by Beckett Campbell. But his tone told me this was not the time to test those waters.

"This looks different," I said, noticing the furniture change. And where were the curtains for the living room window?

"I'm all moved in."

"Oh."

"Worried you're going to miss me, Red?"

"You can put me down now."

Deflection was my only defense. Well, that and my chattering teeth. Fuck, that water was colder than I remembered. I didn't plan on falling in, but I also knew better than to get on a fucking board when the waters were that rough. I was a strong swimmer, but I was also out of practice.

Beckett set me on my feet in the kitchen, just outside the cramped bathroom.

"Where's Husker?"

"At home, with Grandpa Dale. You didn't think I'd take him out on the lake today, did you?"

"So, the lake was safe enough for *you*, but not your dog?"

"Gee, *Dad*, I didn't really think of it that way." Except, of course, I had. I swayed from side to side, feeling suddenly dizzy. Automatically, I reached for my head, though I didn't remember hitting it.

"What's wrong?"

"Nothing."

"Kira."

"I'm fine."

"You're obviously not."

My teeth were chattering again. "I'm fucking cold," I shot back.

"Take off your wet clothes."

"Say it like you mean it," I teased, pulling off my thin hoodie that seemed to weigh twenty pounds. Why did he let me come inside with dripping wet clothes?

"Kira," he said, his tone a warning as he stepped into the outdated bathroom and turned on the shower.

"I'm not the only one who needs warming up," I pointed out, scanning the way his T-shirt and shorts clung to his body. I bet every last inch of him was fucking perfection, even when it was cold.

"Stop undressing me with your eyes and get your ass in that shower," he insisted.

"What about you?"

"What about me?"

I pulled off my tank, then my shorts, standing before him in a miserably wet bra that did not match my panties. Because I didn't think today would be the day Beckett Campbell got me naked.

"You're cold."

"Trust me, I'm warmer than you think."

My gaze dropped right to his crotch. What I saw there had me feeling suddenly warmer inside. I was exhausted from pretending I didn't think about this man every damn minute of the day. Tired of acting like I didn't want him all the time. And right now, I had no energy left for self-control. *Fuck it.* I lifted my eyes to his and reached behind my back to undo my bra.

"Kira—"

"Warm me up, Beck." I let the bra fall to the floor. "*Please.*"

"That shower isn't big enough for the both of us," he said, his tone regretful as he seemed to struggle with where to look. His gaze kept landing on my breasts, and my nipples puckered right up in approval.

I bent forward, pulling off my panties.

"Fuck," he hissed.

As I rolled back to standing, I ran my hands along his legs, stopping at the waistband. "I bet we can make it work."

"Have you ever actually showered out here before?" Despite his concerns, he pulled off his shirt. His sculpted chest was painted with the tattoos I'd been wanting to memorize up close. Maybe today, I finally would.

I tugged down his shorts and boxers together, reaching a hand between his legs to guard his shaft as the last of his clothing fell away.

He groaned at my touch.

I whimpered at the feel of him in my hand, relishing in the way he grew firmer at my touch.

I no longer needed the hot shower. My internal body temperature had shot right the hell up to lava hot. I gently stroked him as he guided us under the spray of hot water.

He wasn't wrong. This stand-up shower was impossibly small. But I wanted—*needed*—to be this close to him. I was so damn tired of fighting this pull between us. I didn't understand it, but I no longer wanted to. I simply wanted to give in.

Beckett gripped the back of my neck possessively as our lips crashed together. I continued to stroke his cock as he reached a hand to my ass and squeezed. Our kisses were savage. Desperate. Hungry. Our tongues wrestled for dominance as he slid his hand to my hip and lifted my knee to his waist.

I braced my toes on a plastic lip of the shower, moaning as his hand slid beneath my thigh. His thumb strummed my sensitive button, his rhythm perfection.

"I don't have any girly body wash," he said.

"So?"

"You're going to smell like a man."

"You mean like you." *Like pine needles.*

The pressure of his thumb increased, and I nearly lost my footing. But Beckett held me against him, his grip reassurance that he wouldn't let anything bad happen to me. He brought me right up to the edge with that single fucking thumb. I dug my fingernails into his shoulder.

"I'm going to—"

"Not yet," he said, pulling his hand away and lowering my leg.

"What the hell?" I huffed.

Beckett reached over my head for a bottle of men's body wash and a loofa that looked brand new.

"Don't worry, Red. I'm going to make you come."

"Really?"

"Really." He lathered the loofa and turned me around so my back was to his chest. He pulled back my hair to expose my ear, lowering his lips to the shell. "I want to make you come so damn hard you leave your body."

I shivered, but nothing about me was cold anymore. Oh no, this was a sinful shiver of anticipation.

I leaned into Beckett as he lathered my body in his

woodsy, spicy body wash. His length pressed into my lower back. If this shower were bigger, I'd bend over and beg him to take me from behind.

Beckett hung up the loofa and used his hands to work in the bubbles, taking his sweet time with each caress. Those rough, callused hands slid up my stomach and cupped my breasts.

"In case you weren't aware, you have great tits."

"Oh, yeah?"

"I've been thinking about them since I made you come in the bookstore."

I whimpered as he teased my pebbled nipples with his index fingers, reaching behind me to move his cock between my legs.

"Kira?"

"Just let me play," I pleaded, spreading my folds so I could press his length against my clit. He groaned as I rocked my hips against him.

"I'll let you play, Red," he said, grabbing my tits firmly. "But you're not allowed to come until I tell you. Is that understood?"

God, I loved this dominant bedroom side of Beckett.

"Kira?"

"I understand."

"Good girl."

I stroked him against my sensitive flesh until my toes curled, and I cried out in warning. It wasn't just his hard length that felt so fucking good between my legs. It was the way his body enveloped me against him. The way his lips teased the crook of my neck, teeth scraping my skin. The way my breasts fit perfectly in his big rough hands.

"I gotta—gotta stop!" I panted.

Beckett yanked himself from me two seconds before I lost control.

"How would you punish me?" I asked as he turned off the water.

"What?"

"If I came too early. How would you punish me?"

His hazel eyes were drenched with heavy desire, the intensity in his gaze almost too much to handle. Fuck, that gaze alone could make me come if I wasn't careful.

"Kira Mason, are you asking me to spank you?"

A full-body quiver erupted at his words.

Am I?

"I—I don't know. Maybe?"

"Maybe next time, Red."

"Next time?"

He stepped out of the shower, reaching for a towel and using it to dry me off while I watched the water drip from his body. I studied the tattoo of the unit crest. "What is that one from?"

"Later."

"Later?"

"We can talk later, Red."

He scooped me into his arms, me only half dry and him all the way wet, and carried me to the bedroom. There was only a set of sage green sheets, no blanket. That was the last detail I noticed before he lowered me to the bed and slid down my body, settling his face between my legs.

Beckett's tongue and mouth worked in perfect harmony.

I gripped the pillow behind my head with both hands,

desperate to watch him play but unable to keep my eyes open.

Had anything *ever* felt this good?

"Beckett," I groaned.

"You close?" he asked, his words vibrating against my sensitive flesh.

"So close."

Everything intensified. His pace, the pressure, the building pleasure.

"I'm—I'm almost—"

"Kira?"

"*Mmm?*"

"Come for me."

I exploded at his command.

Beckett fused his face to my pussy, showing not a single ounce of mercy as I came so hard I thought I'd shoot right off the bed and leave a hole in the ceiling. My toes and fingertips tingled as they gripped for purchase. I felt as though I'd been blasted off like a rocket and was now free floating into space, fueled on euphoria.

Beckett crawled beside me, cupping my cheek and kissing me so sensually it threatened to short-circuit my brain.

I didn't know if I'd catch my breath before sunset, but I reached my hand between us, circling it around his length.

He groaned.

"Beckett?"

"Yes, Red?"

"I want you inside me."

"Are you sure?"

"Yes."

Beckett rolled onto his side, pulling open a nightstand drawer.

"You really have settled in," I teased.

"I wanted to be prepared," he said, tearing at the foil packet.

"Prepared to have a woman in your bed?" A hint of jealousy wormed its way in, and I wondered how many women there might be now that Beckett was out here all alone. But I had no right to be jealous when I was the one fighting this. Right?

"Prepared to have *you* in my bed."

"You knew this would happen?" *Shut up, Kira. You're ruining this.*

"No," he admitted, kissing my forehead as he climbed on top of me. "But I really fucking hoped it would."

He pushed apart my thighs with his knees and lowered himself to my entrance. I held on to his shoulders as he nudged inside.

His lips met mine, and I sank into the sensation of it all. The feel of him inside me. The way my body craved his touch. How I couldn't seem to get close enough to him, no matter how tightly I wrapped myself around him. I met him thrust for thrust, desperate for more.

"Fuck, Kira," he growled against my ear.

"Come inside me," I pleaded.

He kissed me harder as he pummeled into me over and over. Pleasure built in my core once more. Fuck, was I going to come—*again?*

I exploded once more.

And Beckett came right after me.

FORTY-SEVEN
BECKETT

"I'm supposed to be at the bookstore," Kira said, her head on my shoulder as she lazily traced fingertips over my chest. Her clothes were currently in my dryer, and I hoped it took all damn day for them to dry.

"The only place you need to be is right here, naked in my bed."

I kissed her forehead, mostly because I could.

She draped a leg over mine and nestled closer. She was so fucking wet, and I loved how it felt against my thigh.

"Did you know my keys don't work?"

"What?"

"My keys. For the bookstore. The ones I've had since Mom died. They just stopped working."

"I don't think that's how it works."

"I've been using them since I came back," she said, tracing her finger over the outline of a panther tattoo on my chest. "My keys worked yesterday."

"Maybe you have both sets?" I guessed.

Kira hesitated, and I glanced down to see her biting her bottom lip.

"What is it?"

"If I tell you something, will you promise not to think I'm crazy?"

"You're a redhead. Crazy kind of comes with the territory."

Except, her blonde roots were growing out enough to bolster her claim about not being a natural redhead. But it didn't matter if she allowed her natural color to grow out fully. She'd always be Red to me.

"Beck, I mean it."

"Tell me," I said, caressing her arm.

"I think my mom let me in."

"Your mom?"

"I know it sounds crazy."

"No, not really." I wasn't superstitious, and I didn't have a strong belief in ghosts. If I did, I wouldn't have bought a cabin I planned to gut which could summon the wrath of a ghost. From the stories I'd been told, Grandma Pebble didn't sound like the kind of spirit I wanted to tangle with. "How else can you explain it?"

"The first night I was in town, I unlocked the back door and the apartment door. With my key. It was just after midnight. Luke showed up just before five that morning, claiming the silent alarm was recently tripped. Do you know of any alarms that trip five hours later?"

"No."

"I tried to go upstairs."

"When?"

"Today."

I tensed, relieved that she hadn't been able to get inside. Otherwise, she'd see the boxes and stacks of materials I acquired over the past few days. I wanted the final reveal to be a surprise. Something she couldn't try to talk me out of doing. But if she got a sneak peek, my plans might be thwarted. I'd have to find a reason to keep her out of the apartment.

"That's why I left. I was just so . . . overwhelmed. I mean, how could Mom . . ."

"You could have drowned, Kira. If I hadn't seen you fall in—"

"I know," she said, sounding regretful. "Sometimes I don't think. I just—I just wanted to talk to my mom and she wasn't at the bookstore. Not today."

She'd told me about a dream she had. One that caused her to pack her things and drive straight to Bluebell Springs, now more than a month ago, without even warning anyone she was coming.

"The last time I ignored Mom in a dream, it was bad."

"What happened?"

"She warned me to leave Travis," Kira said, tracing the outlines of my tattoos as she spoke. "Like, in this crazy, dreamlike way, she showed me how to escape. She showed me the way out. But I thought he'd changed. I thought *I* could help him change. I didn't listen to her, and . . ." She took a deep breath, and I waited. "He was drunk. Very drunk. It was his birthday. I never should've gotten in the car, but I did. He was in one of those weird moods, like he wanted to push all his limits. Like he wanted to challenge death."

Anger burned inside my chest. I could already see where this story was headed. I was all too familiar with the disregard someone like that, drunk off his ass, had for other human life. Especially someone he cared about.

"He almost wrecked, right into the back of a big truck. I don't know how he missed it. I swear, he has this way of cheating death that just seems so unfair."

"Were you hurt?"

"No. I still don't understand how we didn't— But anyway, a cop saw him and he got arrested. I should have left then, when he was in jail. But I wanted so damn badly to tell him off to his face. To let him know how much he hurt me. So, I waited for him to get released—his mom always bailed him out. And then, he was so remorseful. Promised things would be different. Talked about buying me a ring. And I fell for it."

"My dad was good at manipulating my mom, especially when he was hungover. She called it his *sweet* phase. But all it ever amounted to was a bunch of empty promises so she wouldn't yell at him. A few days later, he was back to doing the same thing."

"Do you still talk to them?"

"No, I've been no contact for years. But my sister . . ."

"She still has hope?"

"Yeah." I stroked her shoulder, eager to shift the conversation away from my family. "You know what I think it all means?"

"What?"

"That you're in the right place."

"Then, why would my mom lock me out of the apartment? I just wanted to see how the new paint and flooring turned out."

"Maybe she knew I wasn't done." It was a half truth. "So be patient."

Kira let out a soft giggle. "Maybe."

"How is everything else coming along?" I asked of the bookstore.

"It would be a whole lot better if the bookshelves weren't delayed." She let out a sigh. "But they're still supposed to show up before the soft opening. Did you know the book club wanted me to ask you to build new ones?"

"I could have."

"Your grandma already has it out for me. I don't need to take more of your time than I already have."

"I like it when you take my time."

Kira looked up at me, as though searching for the truth. It irritated me that she struggled to take me at my word, but it wasn't her fault. Her trust had been fractured. I traced her jaw with my thumb, silently vowing in that moment to do everything I could to help her rebuild it. I drew her in for a kiss that lingered. She shimmied up my leg, her wetness smearing my hip.

Blood rushed south, awakening my cock for another round.

"What's this tattoo about?" she asked of the panther on my chest.

"It's in honor of a buddy I lost."

"Lost?"

"To war."

"Oh. I'm sorry."

"Me, too."

She straddled my hips, sitting back as she studied my ink.

Fuck, she was beautiful.

Her curvy body was a wonderland I wanted to memorize. I yearned to yank her down to me, so I could get one of those tits in my mouth. But I restrained the urge, and allowed her to ask about each and every tattoo, relishing in her fascination.

"The unit crest?" she asked.

"It's the unit I deployed with. The one your brothers and Thoren were in."

"Do you miss it?"

"The Army?"

"Yeah."

My cock stood at attention, pressed against her ass. It was getting harder to think straight, because all I could focus on was how fucking good it felt to be inside her. How badly I wanted to be there again.

"Sometimes," I admitted. "But I was ready to move on."

Kira leaned back, reaching a hand behind her and gripping my shaft. "You have another condom?"

"In the drawer."

She leaned forward, dangling those tits in my face as she fished a rubber from my nightstand. I watched in rapt interest as she lifted her hips, placing my cock in front of her parted legs, and rolled on the condom.

"How did you become a contractor?" she asked, lifting her hips and sinking slowly onto me.

"I've been helping build and renovate houses off and on since high school."

She slowly gyrated her hips, nothing hurried about the way she was enjoying me inside her. Fuck, I could watch this all day.

"Since high school?"

"My dad worked a deal with our neighbor to get me a job young. Neighbor was a builder." It was getting harder to concentrate on what I was saying. The only thing I could seem to focus on was the way Kira kept sinking her pussy onto my shaft one slow roll at a time. Her wetness. Her heat. Her perfection. "My dad—and I use . . . the term loosely—just wanted the . . . the extra money."

"You didn't get to keep your own money?"

"Not at first."

"But?" Kira pressed a finger to her clit, and I watched in rapt interest as she slowly played with herself, as though we had all the time in the world to enjoy one another. I reached my hands to her hips.

"But the builder caught on and gave me a raise—one he never . . . never told my dad about. So, I at least got to . . . got to keep the difference."

"Is that why you joined the Army?" Kira asked, leaning forward and stealing a kiss as she sank down all the way, burying me deep inside her channel and holding me there. Fuck was there any better feeling than *this*? What I wouldn't give to just get fucking lost in this sensation and live here.

"I joined after college—" I cradled her dangling tits in my hands. "—to get away from my parents, once I knew my sister was taken care of. Kept helping build . . . builders on the side, on weekends." I groaned at the feel of her wet heat wrapped around my length, finding it harder to concentrate by the second.

"You love it?"

"Yeah, I guess I do." I firmly massaged her tits, drawing one nipple into my mouth.

Kira let out one of those soft, sexy whimpers, grinding herself against me with my cock still fully seated inside her.

I took the other nipple into my mouth and scraped my teeth against it.

She cried out, grinding harder.

I gripped her hips and held her against me. Guiding her in just the right way. I wanted to feel her climax with my cock buried inside her.

"Fuck me, Beckett," she cried out as she exploded on top of me.

"With pleasure." I rolled her over, sinking right back inside that sweet channel as her orgasm held on, pummeling into her until I was coming too. The intensity of my climax nearly blinded me. My entire body jerked above her. Fuck, this was unreal.

I'd had good sex before. Great sex.

But this?

This was levels beyond any of it.

I stared into those deep blue eyes, relishing in her sated smile and tangled, freshly fucked hair. I dropped my lips to hers, savoring a kiss that threatened to bring on round three. I wasn't sure I had the stamina for it, but fuck, I wanted to find out.

Except my damn phone chose that moment to ring. As

much as I wanted to ignore it, I didn't want to risk Luke or Connor showing up and finding their sister naked in my bed. Sooner or later, I'd have to tell them, but not like this.

"Sorry," I apologized, turning over my phone on the nightstand to see who was calling. "It's my sister."

"Madeline?"

"Yeah. She doesn't usually call without sending a dozen texts first."

A twisting feeling in my gut warned me I should answer, despite how badly I wanted to ignore the whole world and give Kira another orgasm that would leave her unable to walk straight.

"Answer it," she said.

"Hey, Madeline."

"Hey Beck. Busy?" The nervous tremor in her voice was unlike her, and it raised my Spidey senses. Something was definitely up.

"Everything okay?"

"Um, yeah. I'm actually in town."

FORTY-EIGHT

HUSKER

Mom's home!
She's been gone forever.
Mom's home!
I thought she was never coming back.
Mom's home!
"Easy there, Husker."
What's easy, Grandma Connie?
Mom's home!
Did you see?
That's her Jeep.
That's my Jeep, too.
Can I go outside?
I need to go get my mom.
Mom's home!
"Can you take him outside?"
Yes, Grandpa Dale!
Take me outside to see Mom.
"C'mon, Husker."

Click.
My leash is on.
Now I can go outside.
Sniff, sniff, sniff.
Is that a funny walking bird?
He's in the garden.
Grandpa Dale, that funny walking bird is in the garden.
I don't trust her.
"*Leave it, Husker.*"
But Grandpa Dale, she's looking at me funny.
"*Husker, leave that chicken alone.*"
Mom!
You're home!
Mom, there's a funny walking bird.
Right there!
I need to get it!
"*You know you're not supposed to chase the chickens.*"
But Mom!
"*You're out late.*"
Who's late?
"*I needed some air.*"
Mom, why is your face a funny color?
And why do you smell like New Best Friend?
"*Everything okay?*"
"*Yeah.*"
Mom?
Grandpa Dale?
Mom?
Why is no one talking?
Why is no one paying attention to the funny walking bird?

"*I better get Husker inside before he gets on Connor's shit list.*"

What's a shit list?

"*Kira?*"

"*Yeah?*"

"*You're not in this alone, you know.*"

Mom is smiling.

That's good.

Maybe I'll get a treat.

Mom, can I have a treat?

"*I know.*"

Mom, why do you smell like New Best Friend?

FORTY-NINE

BECKETT

"What are you doing here?" I asked my sister when I spotted her out on the deck of Kat's Place. She picked a table by the water, which was why it was easy to find her.

"Wow, I'm happy to see you, too, Beck." She stood, giving me a hug.

I hugged her back and felt her wilt in my arms. Shit. Was she going to cry? I should have insisted she meet me somewhere more private. But I didn't know if she had a car or if she'd be able to make the trek out to the cabin without blowing a tie rod if she did.

"Where are the twins?"

"Kyle took them to his parents' place."

"Oh."

"It's not what you think." When she pulled back, there were no traces of tears, but she wasn't wearing her usual dramatic makeup. She waved at the server and ordered a draft beer. Madeline was unaffected by the alcohol problem in our family. She could handle a single drink and not crave another. She was never tempted to drown her sorrows with it.

"Then, fill me in."

"Nana showed up."

I nodded.

"Which you knew, of course."

"I didn't send her."

Madeline let out a laugh. "I thought you did at first. I was so pissed at you, too. You could have warned me she was coming, you know."

We both knew I couldn't. "You bought a house?"

The server brought Madeline her beer, me a glass of iced tea, and an order of fried pickles for us to share. My sister waited until we were alone again to explain.

"I bought it for a dollar."

"A dollar?"

"It was one of those auction houses."

"A foreclosure?"

"I thought if Dad had a project, he'd stay out of trouble. For a while, it worked. The house was a complete pit. Barely above condemnable."

It made sense why my sister went radio silent for so long. She considered the problem handled. I didn't have to ask what happened. I was too intimately familiar with the pattern Madeline seemed dead set on ignoring.

"You and Kyle okay?"

"Yeah. He was pissed, of course. But I sold the house."

"Already?"

"I sold it to Mom for a dollar."

"Why Mom?"

"Dad's in jail again."

The casual tone killed me every time. This was not fucking normal. I understood that well before moving to Bluebell Springs and being absorbed into the Mason/Weston clan. How did Madeline not know this?

"You don't want to know what for?" she asked.

I somehow managed to swallow a sigh that swelled from the basement of my soul. "Don't care."

"Yeah, I guess that's fair."

I shot her a look, surprised by her reaction. This conversation usually took a different route. Was it too much to hope that Madeline had finally come around about how shitty our parents were? Maybe Nana got through to her after all.

"Don't take this the wrong way, but why are you *here?*"

It wasn't like my sister to show up anywhere unannounced. What made her a good attorney was her calculated and planned approach to life.

"Kyle and I agreed we need a fresh start. One far, far away from Mom and Dad."

Excitement and dread warred for the top spot. I would love nothing more than to have my family close. To see the twins all the time. To take Kyle fishing. For Madeline to experience what a healthy family dynamic was like. But if our parents followed them here, I didn't know if I could forgive Madeline.

"You look like you swallowed something sour," she said. "You don't want me to come."

"I do."

"Relax. I'm just here scoping it out as an option."

"But you came alone."

"Kyle agreed to a fresh start, but he's still pretty pissed about the whole thing."

"Understandably so."

"Gee, thanks."

I took a long sip of my iced tea, scanning the deck out of habit. I didn't see anyone I recognized in more than passing. I still couldn't help but wonder how long it would take for a rumor to circulate that I'd been on a date with a strange woman. Odd that it didn't even bother me. *Huh.* Maybe small town life had officially grown on me.

"Are those . . . scratch marks?"

"What?"

"On your neck. Did you get a cat? No. You're allergic. If a cat did that, you'd be hospitalized by now."

"I probably just scratched it on a piece of plywood or something. Been working a lot."

"You're a terrible liar, Beck. Always have been. Who is she?"

Fuck, this was not the conversation I wanted to have with my sister an hour after I finally had Kira in my bed. I was still sorting out the jumbled thoughts in my head without also trying to articulate them out loud. There was a very real possibility I was falling in love with her. Maybe I already had. But that was not a topic I was comfortable discussing with Madeline.

"It's nothing."

"I know you better than that. You don't do casual. It's definitely *not* nothing."

"How long you planning on staying in town?"

"A week. Maybe a little longer."

"You were able to take that much time off work?"

"I'm kind of on an extended vacation." Her eyebrows lifted a fraction. How much did Nana tell her? "And you still didn't tell me her name."

"I'm not telling you her name," I said. "What happened at work?"

"So, there *is* someone. I bet she's the redhead Nana mentioned."

A mischievous smile formed across her lips. Fuck. This was never good. Madeline liked to meddle, especially when she was bored. And if she was here without any work to do, without kids or her husband to fuss over, she was definitely going to meddle.

"Difference of opinion. Nothing you need to concern yourself with. Are there any law firms in Bluebell Springs?"

I refused to acknowledge the redhead comment. "Don't act like you haven't already researched that. Where are you staying?"

"A little birdie told me you recently purchased a two-bedroom cabin. I thought I'd stay with my big brother. Help make sure you don't enact another redheaded curse."

Double fuck. There'd be no sneaking Kira over with my sister hanging around. I highly suspected Nana encouraged this sibling reunion. "That little birdie was Nana."

"Serves you right for not warning me she was coming to pay me a visit."

"She wouldn't have shown up if you didn't buy a house for our pathetic excuse for parents without telling your husband," I pointed out.

"I'll need a ride."

"How did you get to town?"

"Uber."

"From Denver to Bluebell Springs?"

"No, from the North Pole. Duh, from Denver." She swiped the last fried pickle from the basket before I could take it. "I didn't think you'd mind. Nana said everything in town is within walking distance."

"Not from the cabin."

"So, I'll ride with you."

"I'm hardly home."

"Because of some bookstore? What's *that* about?"

"If you're staying with me for a week, I'm putting you to work."

"I'm a terrible laborer," she said.

"Don't remind me."

"Seriously, Beck. Tell me about the bookstore. Nana said you bought a million-dollar commercial building."

I emptied my iced tea, pushing up from my chair.

"Where are you going?"

"Home."

I left a twenty on the table and walked away, wondering what special hell I was in for with my sister in town. I loved her to death, but her timing couldn't be worse. The last thing I wanted Kira to think was that I only wanted her for sex. And with Madeline attached to me at the hip for the next week, I couldn't fathom getting Kira alone long enough to talk about what today meant.

But my sister left to her own devices was definitely the bigger risk.

FIFTY
KIRA

I REFRESHED the link for the bookshelf shipping information, hoping for an update. Despite the delays I'd already been notified about, the two dozen shelves I ordered were supposed to be here today. Yet I hadn't received a confirmation text from the shipping company that they were on their way.

"No update?" I grumbled.

Husker perked his head from the dog bed I tucked behind the front counter. Most days, I left him at the farm due to the excessive number of book stacks littered around the store. I could just see him getting excited and knocking them over with an enthusiastic butt wiggle. Not only would it create more work, but I didn't want him to get buried underneath them.

Today however, the store was quiet. I gave everyone the morning off in anticipation of a late night of bookshelf assembling, promising to update them the minute I had one.

When things were quiet, Husker tended to nap.

I searched the order confirmation email for a phone number. I was not in the mood to have a chat with a robot.

Before I could locate one, the bells jingled overhead.

I almost forgot Dad rehung them last night while the rest of us were sorting the remaining books into *keep* and *donate* piles. I looked up, expecting to see one of the book club members or a family member. But I didn't recognize the tall, slender woman with wavy chestnut hair who walked in.

"I'm sorry, we're not open."

"I can see that," she said, extending a smile as she scanned the mess.

"We're re-opening next week."

"I'm not here to buy a book."

My patience was running a little thin, on account of the bookshelf fiasco and a lack of sleep from a late night of writing. "Is there something else I can help you with?"

"I just wanted to meet you."

Okay, this was starting to feel uncomfortable.

"I didn't catch your name."

"No, you didn't."

I reached for my phone, ready to text Luke. I'd bribe him with a free lunch if I needed him to stop by and defuse . . . whatever situation this might be.

"I'm sorry, ma'am, but we're not open."

The woman visibly shuddered. "Please don't call me that."

I held onto Husker's collar as he started to rise. He was the friendliest dog I knew—he'd probably fawn all over a burglar, especially if they were smart enough to bring treats—but my Husky mix looked like a German Shepherd. Some days, that worked in my favor. I wondered if today would be one of them.

"If you come back next week—"

"Oh, I doubt I'll still be here then."

A million possibilities rushed through my mind about who this woman might be. Was she one of Diana's crazy superfans who might threaten to kidnap me if I didn't finish Mateo's book? Was she Travis' new girlfriend, searching out the *crazy ex* for herself? Or was she—

"I'm Madeline."

"Madeline."

"Beckett's sister."

"Oh," I said, a sense of relief flooding my nervous system, and cooling it off. "I'm sorry if I was being rude."

"You didn't know who I was, so it's fair."

Madeline approached the counter. Her makeup was minimal, but it was expertly applied. It paired well with her denim shorts and loose floral blouse. She didn't *look* like she hated me. But she hadn't had a chance to size me up for herself.

I waited until she saw Husker to let go of his collar. He trotted around to her, and she extended her hand for him to sniff. I relaxed a little more.

"I didn't mean to barge in. I was surprised the door was unlocked, actually. I just wanted to see the building my brother bought."

"And meet me?" I reminded her.

"Yes."

"Did Pauline send you?" I asked, half teasing, half serious.

"Not exactly," Madeline said, leaning her elbows on the counter. "But she did mention you."

"Probably all bad things," I muttered.

"She's just looking out for Beckett. Same as me."

"Because of the redheaded curse?" I supplied.

"You've heard, then."

"A little."

"Beckett's got a big heart, but he tends to place his trust in the wrong people. At least, when it comes to women."

"So, you came to see if I was one of the *wrong people*."

"Yes."

Her honesty made me like her a little more.

"We're just friends," I told her.

"I doubt that," Madeline shot back, a knowing twinkle in her hazel eyes. The same color as Beckett's. The resemblance was easier to spot, the longer she stood on the other side of the counter. "But I'm not here to lecture you or anything. You two are grown adults. What you do—or don't do—is none of my business. So long as you aren't taking advantage of my brother."

"Is that a threat?"

Madeline shrugged. "Does it need to be?"

"No."

"Then, it's not."

The bells chimed overhead again, and Husker sprinted to the front door.

Beckett walked in, carrying two coffees—one of them iced. "I see you two have met."

"We were just having a little chat," Madeline said,

pushing up off the counter and taking the warm coffee from him.

"Madeline," he said, his voice a low warning.

A little late, considering his sister already had her cards on the table, but still kind of sweet.

"She's right," I chimed in. I didn't need Beckett getting in the middle of whatever this was. I could handle his sister, even if I did have something to hide. I was done being pushed around. "We were just chatting."

"Ready to go?" Madeline asked Beckett.

Beckett set the iced coffee on the counter and gave me a wink. "I'm taking her to the Kniffen Street house." To Madeline, he said, "You do know I'm putting you to work, right?"

"I thought of it as more of a supervisory position."

"It's not."

"We'll see."

"Everything good here?" Beckett fished a treat out of his pocket and Husker plopped his butt down in anticipation.

"Yep." I forced a smile, hoping he bought it.

I was not about to admit I had an issue with bookshelves in front of Madeline. I didn't need to give her any reason to think I was taking advantage of her brother. I understood her protective nature. I felt the same way when it came to my brothers. But I didn't care for her snap judgment.

"Just getting some work done while it's quiet," I said.

"If you need anything—"

"Thanks," I said quickly, glancing at Madeline, who was already at the door.

Beckett's gaze lingered on mine. For a moment, I forgot we had an audience. The wicked gleam in his eyes brought me back to the cabin, where he gave me so many orgasms I lost count.

"See you at family dinner tomorrow, Red."

FIFTY-ONE
BECKETT

CONNIE AND DALE's house was filled with conversation, laughter, and as many people as they could fit around the extra-large farmhouse table. Madeline won them over with ease, offering to help Connie prepare the massive meal that produced enough food to feed an army. She was like Nana in many ways, able to fit right into whatever crowd she stumbled upon as though she'd been there the whole time.

She declined Connie's offer to stay in the guest room I'd occupied. Too bad, because I missed having Kira in my bed these past few days.

I scanned the dining room for Red.

Husker's nose appeared next to Grandma Connie's plate, but there was no trace of Kira.

I carried a stack of empty plates to the kitchen, rinsed them off in the sink, and slipped out the back door in search of her.

When I didn't find her on the patio near the firepit, I

turned my attention to the dirt-packed trail I watched her travel down with Husker a couple of weeks ago. Or had it been longer? Time was an elusive creature when it came to Kira Mason. I felt as though I'd known her for months. Years. Lifetimes. And yet, it'd only been a few weeks since the day I found her at Ghost Lake that first time.

"Beck?" I heard her voice before I spotted her on a bench tucked away in a grove of trees, just before the trail started.

"Hey. You okay?"

"Not really." She let out a heavy sigh, and I joined her on the bench. It was private enough that I might get away with a kiss, but too close to the house to risk it. Any number of people might stumble upon us, and then what?

I hated that whatever was brewing between us was a secret. But until Kira was truly ready, it had to be that way. I didn't want to put any unfair pressure on her when she clearly had enough on her plate as it was.

"What's wrong?"

"Those bookshelves I ordered for the store? To replace the ones we dumped last week?"

"Yeah?"

"They were supposed to be here yesterday. I tried talking to someone at the company, but I got the runaround about them being delayed."

"How delayed?"

"They're not coming."

"At all?"

"I just got an email from the distributor canceling my order." She stared off at the mountains, her expression blank. "Apparently, they had a fire at their distribution center and my dozen bookshelves were incinerated."

"Fuck."

"Fuck is right." She turned to me then, and the shininess I expected to see in her eyes was missing. In its place was quiet determination. "Remember that favor I won beating you at darts?"

I'd actually forgotten until now, but I nodded anyway. "Yeah?"

"I'd like to collect. If it's not too much trouble."

"What do you need?"

"Bookshelves. At least a dozen. All built before the grand re-opening in two weeks. It's not ideal, but I have a plan to hang a curtain to hide the construction at the back part of the store so we can still do our soft opening in the front section, day after tomorrow."

"You don't—"

She bent one knee and tucked her foot beneath her opposite thigh. "I was hoping to use my favor for something more . . . enticing. But desperate times and all . . ."

I scanned the area, looking for the threat of eavesdroppers. I'd hear a conversation if two people approached, but I could easily miss the light padding of footsteps because the wind would drown them out. When I was convinced the area was clear, I leaned closer. I reached a hand toward her cheek, playing with a strand of hair that escaped her loose ponytail. "You don't need to use a favor for that, Red."

"I don't?"

"If you want me to make you come, all you have to do is ask."

Her cheeks reddened instantly, and dammit did it cause my blood to rush swiftly south.

My gaze dropped to her lips, tempting me to make good on that promise right now. But we both knew it was playing with fire.

"And save your favor," I added.

"You won't—"

"Of course I'll help with the bookshelves. But I'll be recruiting help, so it doesn't seem fair to let you cash in that favor when I can't do it alone."

I dragged my fingers along her jaw, wishing so fucking badly that I could kiss her. Just as I was about to say fuck it and do it anyway, Husker ran straight for us.

"Husker? Where's your leash?" Kira grabbed his collar seconds before he spotted his elusive chipmunk friend diving under a boulder.

"Sorry!" Madeline called, running behind, leash in hand. Of course it was Madeline. She was damn near as bad as Nana about me and Red. I knew she was looking out for me, but I was a little exhausted from all the over-protectiveness.

"I didn't realize he'd dart right out the door."

"He likes to go for the chipmunks. Or the chickens, if one gets out," Kira explained, taking the leash from my sister and clipping it on Husker's collar.

"I'll be more careful next time," Madeline said. "Anyway, it's time for dessert. Grandma Connie wants everyone inside because we're apparently celebrating a birthday."

"We are?" I asked.

"Connor," Kira answered, pushing up off the bench.

"And don't be surprised you didn't know. He doesn't like anyone knowing. He puts Christmas as his birthday on his social media profile because he thinks he's clever that way."

I waited until Madeline headed back toward the house before I leaned my lips against Kira's ear.

"Remember, all you have to do is ask."

FIFTY-TWO
HUSKER

Sniff, sniff, sniff!
New Best Friend, I like riding in your truck.
Except, you forgot to roll down the other window.
Let me just press my nose against it to make sure.
Yep.
It's closed.
New Best Friend, why are we stopping?
I smell treats!
Sniff, sniff, sniff!
These are the best treats!
With frosting!
"Should we head inside, Husker?"
Inside?
Where there are so many treats?
Yes!
Zig-zag, zig-zag, zig-zag!
"Someone's excited!"
Who said that?

New Best Friend, do we know that lady?
"He likes his treats."
Treats?
Where?
"C'mon, Bubbies. Inside the bakery."
Sniff, sniff, sniff.
Is Tango here?
I smell him.
I don't see Tango.
Where is he?
"Hey, Beckett. What can I get you?"
Aspen!
She makes the best treats ever!
With frosting!
"Iced coffee."
"For Kira?"
Hey, that's my mom's name!
"Am I that obvious?"
"Yes. But I'm not complaining."
"Better get a treat for this guy, too."
"Hey, Husker!"
Aspen!
I'm hanging out with New Best Friend today.
Mom says she doesn't want me to get buried under books.
Do you have treats?
"Very food motivated, that one."
"You don't have to tell me twice."
Num, num, num.
"Here. Some for the road."
"Thanks."
"How's the project coming?"

Something's under the counter.

Sniff, sniff, sniff.

Oh, bonus treat!

"I think it'll be done in time for the grand re-opening."

"In two weeks?"

"If you think you can make that work?"

Work?

I don't want to work.

Who wants to work?

"Husker, you've already had a treat."

More treats?

Thank you, New Best Friend!

Num, num, num.

Best treats ever!

"I'll have all the finishing touches ready to go by then."

"Thank you, Aspen."

"I'm glad I was right about you."

"How's the cabin?"

Aunt Wendy!

Do you have treats too?

What's that smell?

"I'm all settled in."

Sniff, sniff, sniff.

It's a tiny dog.

Why is the tiny dog in that lady's bag?

It's so small.

"Husker, she's not a toy."

Aspen has toys?

"We better go before there's a scene."

Go!

Let's go!

Where are we going, New Best Friend?
I see you, tiny dog.
I've got my eye on you.
"Don't forget the coffee."
"Thanks!"
"Beckett?"
"She's going to love it."
"I hope so."
Let's go!

FIFTY-THREE
KIRA

WHEN THE BEEP of the delivery truck backing up to the front door of Brenda's Book Nook echoed, everyone inside the bookstore froze mid-conversation and stared at one another. After a few beats of excitedly charged silence, the group burst out in delighted squeals. Well, Thelma gave more of an enthusiastic grunt.

"They're here!" Dylann announced, clapping her hands together. Maybe it was the reflection of the light on the lens of her readers, but I swore her eyes were shiny.

Everyone rushed to the front door.

Thanks to Carlos' connections with the town council, we were given express permission to allow the first delivery truck to unload from the front of the building—something not typically allowed in Bluebell Springs' downtown area.

Since the back room of the store was filled with building materials for the new bookshelves, and the back half of the store behind the massive curtain was a construction zone, the easiest option was to offload these boxes through the front door. Plus, Lotti suggested it might create a stir among locals and tourists alike if a delivery truck was in their way outside Brenda's Book Nook, and impossible to miss.

"Are you ready for this?" Grandma Connie asked, meeting me behind the small mob that were all honorary Book Nook employees.

"I think so."

She gave me a side hug. "Me too."

Aside from our delivery driver and his dolly, only Carlos and I carried individual boxes inside—I did not need anyone injuring themselves before the soft relaunch tomorrow. It warmed a spot inside me to know Beckett would help if I asked, but it was more important to me that he take Husker for the day.

It still seemed surreal.

A man hanging out with *my* dog without me.

It made me want to believe this could work. Maybe after the craziness of the store's grand re-opening subsided, I could consider something . . . *more* with him.

Or maybe I was just fucking horny and needed another of his potent orgasms. I was more than a little sexually frustrated, considering Madeline just left this morning and I had yet to get Beckett alone since she showed up last week. I could also blame my characters, who were most definitely getting more action than me.

"This is going to be perfect!" Lotti cooed. "We'll have so many new releases for tomorrow!"

We decided to do our soft opening on a Tuesday. I

forgot that publishers released on that day of the week. Being an indie author, I released on whatever day felt right. Which reminded me, I owed Lila a text.

"Look at the copyright page!" Carlos held a hardcover book out to Betty. "Isn't that the most glorious thing you've seen all day?"

"We actually have *current* books!"

I was still amazed Mom's bookstore survived as long as it did, with how poorly Margene Miller ran the place. It was a miracle it was still here to save.

And save it, we would.

There was no other option.

I pulled my phone from my pocket to shoot Lila a quick text about the release date for Mateo's book—I had finally picked one. But before I could, another text caught my attention.

> Beckett: Husker can have frosting, right?

Attached was a photo of my dog, wedged between the two front seats of his truck, a smear of blue frosting across his muzzle as he looked straight out the window. He looked very much like he did on a paddleboard. Alert, like he was the captain of a ship, even if he was currently in the back seat. Only half of Beckett's face was in the photo, but it was enough to reveal that panty-melting smile he wielded so effortlessly.

> Kira: Some frosting is fine.

> Kira: Too much, and you'll get to see a whole new side of him.

Beckett: Got it.

Beckett: Did the books arrive?

> Kira: Yes! I'm so relieved!

Beckett: Maybe we should celebrate ☺

A tingle of warmth shot right to my core. With that innocent smiley face, Beckett might simply mean celebrating with sweet treats. But who said frosting couldn't be applied . . . other places? A rush of heat hit me as I imagined Beckett licking blue frosting from my nipple.

Before I could test those waters and text him something naughtier about said frosting, another text came through.

Unknown: U moved kare bear?

A knot tangled in my stomach the instant it appeared. My hands started to shake, but I willed them to still. I would *not* let Travis ruin this day for me. I would never let him ruin another day for me, ever again.

I blocked the number and deleted the text.

"Kira?" Grandma Connie called. "We're ready to start filling the shelves."

I slipped the phone back into my pocket, refusing to give The Asswipe a single second of my energy. That part of my life was over. I had a new life now. A life I loved. People in it I loved.

Did I *love* Beckett?

Because that question was far too complicated to answer, I ignored it completely and met the ladies at the front to fill our shelves for a soft launch.

FIFTY-FOUR
BECKETT

WHEN I DROPPED Husker off at the farm, I was surprised not to see Kira's red Jeep in the driveway. It was late; late enough that Husker was struggling to keep awake, despite his best efforts to fight his heavy eyelids. Although that might be attributed to his eventual sugar crash.

Connie was already in bed, and Dale was snoozing to episodes of *M*A*S*H* reruns in the living room. I left Husker by Dale's recliner, curled up on a dog bed, and snuck out the door.

> **Beckett:** You okay?

I waited for a couple of minutes, but there was no response.

I hadn't heard back from Kira all day. Not after I sent her a text about celebrating the books arriving this morning. Not after I sent her another picture of Husker "helping" me renovate the Kniffen Street house, which amounted to Husker stationed at the sliding glass door watching a chipmunk while I installed vinyl planking in the living room.

I was concerned.

I drove to the bookstore, not surprised to find a faint glow in the curtained window. I parked beside her Jeep on the side of the building and walked around front.

"Kira?" I called out, entering and locking the door behind me.

"Back here," she replied, sounding tired but not in distress.

The tension I carried in my shoulders relaxed.

I paused at the filled bookshelves in the front of the store, amazed at the vibrant displays. The group had been at work all day, preparing for what Kira called a soft launch. The doors would be open to customers, but there'd be no big announcement about it until the grand re-opening in two weeks. I didn't know much about bookstore setups, but it felt like they'd set themselves up for success, despite all the setbacks.

None of this would be possible without Kira's conviction. Her drive and dedication. I wondered if she had any idea how much of a force to be reckoned with she really was.

I moved behind the terrycloth curtain we hung to divide the open part of the store from the construction zone, but I still didn't see Kira.

I did, however, spot a faint light coming from the back area.

The office.

"Are you still working?" I asked, stopping in the doorway.

She sat at the desk, rubbing both hands over her face. Her red hair was piled into a high messy bun. One tank top strap hung to the side, revealing that dragonfly tattoo again. I wanted to ask her about it. Did it mean anything? Or was it a spontaneous walk-in tattoo from a girls' weekend trip?

Before I could ask, my gaze zeroed in on the strap of her red lace bra.

Fuck.

I forced my gaze around the office instead, noting framed pictures, book quotes, and a filing cabinet that was on its last leg. But I didn't need to see those puckered nipples to visualize them. The way they looked teased between my fingers as I entered Kira's hot, wet channel.

"I'm almost done."

I cleared my throat. "It's late."

"I know. Where's Husker?"

"He's watching *M*A*S*H*."

Kira's eyes widened, as though she was just now processing how late *late* really was. She leaned forward, pulling her phone from the back pocket of her denim shorts. I tried not to stare at the way her ass popped when she arched her back, but I was only a man.

A man who was fucking crazy about this incredible, hardworking, talented, beautiful woman.

I wanted to tell her.

The words begged to be released from my clamped lips, but I forced them to stay put. Once the grand re-opening and her first book signing as Diana Davenport were over, I'd show her the finished apartment upstairs.

And lay it all on the line.

Until then . . .

"Beck?"

"Yeah?"

"If you're going to stare at my ass, the least you can do is touch it."

Our gazes locked and held. There was exhaustion in her blue eyes, but there was also mischief.

"I'd apologize, but it would be a lie," I admitted, scrubbing a hand over the back of my neck.

"I'm sorry I missed your texts. I silenced my phone earlier, and we just got so busy—"

"You're fine. I wanted to make sure you were safe."

"How are you even real?" The question that escaped her lips was so quiet I barely heard it. "Beck?"

"Yes, Red?"

"You remember that thing you said to me when we were outside on the bench the other night after family dinner?"

Blood rushed below my belt. I knew damn well what she was talking about, but I enjoyed making her work for it. "You'll have to refresh my memory."

She pushed the rolling chair aside and stood. "You don't remember?"

"I might."

Kira leaned back against the desk, bracing her ass and both palms against it. "You're going to make me say it, aren't you?"

"Say what?"

She rolled her eyes, but it was playful. Suggestive. Seductive.

"You said if I wanted you to make me come, then all I had to do was ask."

I pushed off the doorframe and closed the door behind me. There wasn't much room in the cramped office, but we'd make do. Seemed we were good at making the best of tight spaces.

"Then, what are you waiting for? Ask."

"Beckett?" she purred my name, gripping the edge of my T-shirt and tugging me to her. "Will you please make me come?"

"With pleasure."

I cupped her cheek and drew her in for the kiss I'd been desperately craving since the day she left my cabin. Despite my best efforts to find time alone with Kira while my sister was in town, Madeline was more concerning when left to her own devices. I had to stay close to keep an eye on her.

I didn't just want Kira.

I fucking *craved* her.

My hands slid down her body until my thumbs caught in the waistband of her shorts. I quickly undid the button and tugged down the zipper, revealing a pair of red silk panties. *A matching set.* Another day, another time, I'd admire them more. But tonight, I gripped them with her shorts and pulled them to her ankles.

"Lean back," I insisted as she tugged her tank top over her head.

"Like this?" she asked, pressing her palms into the side of the desk and spreading her legs wide for me.

"Exactly like this." I unhooked her bra and tossed it aside.

"Why am I the only one who's naked?"

"Because you're the one who's coming, Red." I slid my hand around the back of her neck. "Now, be a good girl and just enjoy what I'm about to do to you."

I lifted her ass to the edge of the desk, spreading her wider and stepping in between her legs. My thumb swirled circles around her swollen button as we made out like that night on the side of the country road. She moaned into my mouth as I plunged a finger inside her. Then two. I sawed at her pussy, not slowly, but methodically. Reveling in her sexy whimpers and the way those fingernails dug into my biceps as she edged closer to that delicious climax.

Kira raked greedy fingers up the back of my neck, kissing me like I was the oxygen she needed to survive.

She came apart hard.

"That's it, Red."

Her body convulsed against mine, her channel contracting around my fingers. Fingers I really fucking wished were my cock.

Apparently, she had the same thought, because her shaky hands tugged down the zipper of my jeans and reached inside.

"Red," I growled.

"Please?" she pleaded.

"I don't have a condom with me."

"I'm on birth control," she said, pushing my jeans and boxers over my hips. "I'm clean."

"I am too."

"Then, please?"

"You're sure?"

Kira pulled my shaft to her drenched center, stroking me through her wetness. She locked her fierce blue gaze with mine.

"I want you to come inside me, Beckett."

I drew her in for a wild, untamed kiss as my cock slid perfectly into her depths. It felt so fucking good to be inside her that I could hardly fathom this was reality. That anything else was ever enough.

Her legs snaked around my waist, and I slid my hands to her hips as I set a savage pace. We held onto one another as though there were no other choice. I kissed her so hard I worried I'd bruise her lips. But she didn't allow me to back off as she dug her fingernails into my shoulders and I slammed into her over and over.

I held out until the moment Kira exploded, and then I stopped fighting it. I came so hard I left my fucking body.

When the world finally stilled around us, we both noticed the mess we created. The books, papers, and trinkets strewn all over the floor and desk, as though a windstorm had blown through. One of the desk legs cracked, and I pulled Kira into my arms seconds before it gave.

"I'll fix that," I promised, kissing her again.

"That doesn't count as my favor, right?" she teased.

"No, Red, it doesn't."

"Good." She kissed me once more. "Because I'm saving it for something really good."

FIFTY-FIVE

HUSKER

Sniff, sniff, sniff!
These boxes smell funny.
Mom, what's in all these boxes?
They're really big.
Sniff, sniff, sniff!
"Are these the special editions?"
What's a special edition, Grandma Connie?
Special edition treats?
They don't smell like treats.
"I think so—"
"Surprise!"
Lila!
Hey, Mom, Lila's here!
I like Lila!
She's one of my favorite people.
Mom, did you know Lila's here!
"Husker, are you excited too?"
I'm excited, Lila!

What are we excited about?
"You're a few days early."
"You didn't think I'd let these babies show up without me,
did you?"
Babies?
Babies smell funny.
But they taste good.
Are there babies in these boxes?
Maybe that's why they smell funny.
Hey, let me get in on this hug.
I need to wedge myself right—
—there.
"Husker, buddy, I'm not going anywhere."
Lila giggles are nice.
"He missed you."
Lila, what's in the boxes?
"Can we open them?"
Yes, I agree with Grandma Connie.
Can we open the boxes?
"Husker, you know they're not treats, right?"
Treats?
Did someone say treats?
Where are the treats?
"Sorry."
Why is Lila sorry?
"There are treats over there."
Yeah, what Mom said.
"Hold on, buddy."
But treats.
Over there.
I need the treats over there.

"Okay, okay. You win!"

I win!

Treats!

Over there!

Treats for me!

Treats right here!

"Here you go."

Thanks, Lila!

Num, num, num.

Did you put one in your pocket?

I think you put one in your pocket.

"Let me get the box cutter. It's in the office."

Grandma Connie, where are you going?

"I hope you don't mind that I'm early."

"Why would I mind?"

"I didn't want to interrupt . . . anything."

Mom, why are your cheeks turning a funny color?

"What do you mean?"

"Oh, please! I'm your best friend, Kira. I can read you easier than a book."

Lila, is there a treat in your pocket?

I saw you put a treat in your pocket.

Sniff, sniff, sniff.

"Husker, hold on, buddy."

Okay, Lila.

But hurry, please.

"It might be something."

"I knew it!"

Knew what?

That there's a treat in your pocket?

That isn't new.

Lila, can I have the treat?
Please, please, please?
"It's a good thing you're cute."
Lila thinks I'm cute!
Treat!
Num, num, num.
"You have to tell me everything."
Grandma Connie, did you go get treats?
"I'll tell you later."
"You better."
"Let's see what these beauties look like!"
Do they look like treats?

FIFTY-SIX
KIRA

"You look like a rock star," Lila squealed, clapping her hands together. "Do you love it?"

I stared at myself in the full-length mirror, stunned at the end result. I couldn't take any credit. The long, wavy hair and dramatic yet elegant makeup was all Lila's doing. Her talents knew no bounds, apparently. She found the formfitting black dress, too. But not just any black dress—one that shimmered with my movements. Discreet, but definitely a statement piece.

"You don't think this is too much? It's just a book signing."

"*Just* a book signing?" Lila scoffed. "Don't you *dare* minimize this special day. Your fans have been waiting for years to meet you. Embrace your badassery, babe. Because you've earned this."

My heart pounded in my chest, thundering in my ears.

Today was the day.

The grand re-opening of Brenda's Book Nook.

And Diana Davenport's first ever public appearance.

Though Lila refused to tell me how many tickets she sold, she did share that they were all sold out.

How many people were waiting to meet me? Twenty? Thirty? A hundred?

After today, my face would be plastered on social media. My identity would no longer be a secret.

As nervous as I was, I had to go through with this. The book club had worked tirelessly these past several weeks. So had my family, building the bookshelves so the store could be fully open today.

I still wasn't convinced I was a household name in the book world, but Diana Davenport had made enough of a dent that she just might help save a very important bookstore. One that meant a great deal to so many in Bluebell Springs.

Anxiety or no anxiety, I had to be brave.

"Where's Husker?"

"Beckett's got him."

"He was here?"

Disappointment hit hard, threatening to worm its way into my already rampant fears of the day. Why did Beckett stop by to pick up Husker but didn't even say *good luck* to me?

"Turn that damn frown upside down, babe. Your lovesick puppy came looking for you. *I* chased him off."

"Why?"

"Because you need to focus right now. And if I let him near you in this dress, it'd already be on the floor." She fidgeted with my hair a little more, meeting my gaze in the mirror. A wicked smile spread across her bright red lips. "And anticipation makes for crazy good sex later."

My cheeks flushed, but I didn't try to hide the reaction. Lila knew nearly everything now. In fact, she helped me sneak over to Beckett's cabin a couple of times since her arrival so we could have some alone time. I claimed it helped me relax, but we both knew I wasn't telling the full truth.

I wasn't just having a little friends-with-benefits fun with the man.

I wasn't just falling for him.

When it came to Beckett Campbell, I was pretty sure I was all the way in love with him.

That scared the ever-loving shit out of me, of course. But I was working through the panic. One of these days, when things were more settled and the fate of the bookstore was stable, I might even be brave enough to tell him. Brave enough to take a chance on love again.

"You ready to go?"

"Ready as I'll ever be for something I swore I'd never do." No matter what happened today, there was no turning back. On the way out the door, I caught the faintest whiff of Mom's floral perfume. Whether imagined or real, I accepted it as the good omen I so desperately needed. "Let's go before I try to run away."

FIFTY-SEVEN
BECKETT

"You did good, Beckett," Aspen said, scanning the bookstore apartment one last time for any final detail we may have missed.

"Really damn good," Alyssa agreed, fluffing one of the throw pillows for the cozy corner sectional. Some color Aspen called *dusty rose*.

"Couldn't have done it without some help."

"If Kira doesn't beg you to marry her and give her babies when she sees this, there's no hope for you," Alyssa added.

"That good, huh?" I said on a chuckle.

"This has been her dream since she was nine," Aspen explained. "I don't think she figured out she wanted to be a writer until college, but she always talked about it when she was a kid. I'm sorry to say you've probably set the bar pretty high for yourself. You'll have a hard time topping this."

The room sparkled with all the twinkle lights along

the ceiling and tucked into the custom bookshelves, which were painted white, at Lila's insistence, and filled mostly with decorative items. Filling them with books, I was informed, was something Kira would want to do.

"The flowers aren't too much, are they?" I asked of the enormous bouquet of local wildflowers resting on the L-shaped writing desk near the window. A desk I custom built. I considered red roses, but I felt those might send too strong a message. Even if I was planning to ask her to make what had been growing between us official.

"The flowers are perfect," Aspen reassured me.

"Nervous?" Alyssa teased.

"Hell yeah, I am."

"Good," they said in unison. Husker looked up at them, seeming to agree.

I hoped they were right. Because after Kira closed the bookstore today, I planned to bring her up and show her. I planned to tell her I was falling for her and didn't want to sneak around anymore. I wanted her to be my girlfriend.

I wanted to tell her that I loved her, but I didn't want to move too fast, too soon. I was sure about her, and that was all that mattered to me. I would wait as long as I needed for her to meet me in the middle.

"What do you think, Husker?"

Husker tilted his head at that sharp angle, and we all laughed.

"I think that means he approves," Alyssa said.

"Or he just wants the treat in your pocket," Aspen added.

Husker perked at the word *treat*. I didn't know if I'd ever met a more food-motivated dog in my life. After I showed Kira her new writing loft—and broke it in if she so desired—I'd take us out for pizza. Her, me, and Husker.

"Here you go, buddy," I said, extracting a treat from my pocket. One of many I had stashed for the day. I waited for him to finish chomping before I clicked the leash back on his collar. "Now, let's go support your mom on her big day."

FIFTY-EIGHT
KIRA

I DON'T KNOW what I was expecting when we turned onto the main strip downtown, but a packed line three blocks long for Brenda's Book Nook was not it. The string of people stretched clear past Gift Shop Alley, all the way back to Bert's Shirts.

"Are they—"

"All here for you, babe."

I covered my agape mouth with both hands, stunned at the sight. Certain I was dreaming. Maybe I overslept but no one had bothered to wake me because not a single fan showed up.

"There's a reason Carlos gave the town council a heads-up about the event so everyone could prepare for this influx of people. You're not just saving the bookstore today. You're helping all the local businesses, too."

"Me?"

"Yes you. You don't hit the top ten in the entire store and *not* draw a crowd," Lila pointed out.

My pulse doubled, then tripled. Panic threatened to undo me before Lila even turned into the alley. I closed my eyes and focused on my breathing. Even if I was terrified to face them, I had to do this.

For Mom.

For my hometown.

"You're one hundred and ten percent certain on the release date for Mateo's book?" Lila asked as she put my Jeep in park.

"Yes." I didn't have to think about that one. I wasn't finished with the first draft yet—those two main characters were really damn horny for one another, but my readers loved the sex so I didn't pull it back—but I was confident enough in the story to stick to the date I chose. The words were flowing easily. My editor was booked. My cover was already designed. Everything was falling into place for an early fall release.

I hoped it helped the bookstore stay in the black during the quieter winter months.

"Let's do this."

We slipped inside the back door, and I made my way for the designated author signing area. One we planned to keep set up all year round. Lila already had a schedule booked out three months in advance for guest author signings. But today, it was all mine.

A banner taller than Luke advertised Diana Davenport as the vampire romance queen. There were purple balloons, a table filled with stock, and more swag than I thought possible for the readers to take home with them—bookmarks, stickers, magnets. Lila had truly thought of everything.

My eyes landed on the cookie cake in the center of my signing table. One outlined in dark purple frosting that read: 'HAPPY COMING OUT DAY DIANA DAVENPORT!'

"It's funny, right?" Thelma asked, sidling up to me and dropping a hand to my shoulder.

"Yes," I said, laughing. Tears sprang to the corners of my eyes.

"Hey, it's just a cookie cake," Lila said in warning. "Don't mess up your eye makeup already."

"We're so proud of you," Dylann said, giving me a hug.

"You look *hot*!" Lotti cooed.

"Yeah, you do," Carlos agreed.

"I'm so impressed, honey," Dad said, giving me a rare hug. "Mom would have loved this."

"You think so?"

"Yeah, I do."

"You clean up decent," Luke said, dressed in uniform. He agreed to do security. I didn't think it was necessary, but I was outvoted. Either way, I was happy to have him here.

"Gee, thanks."

"Aunt Kira, you're so pretty!" Opal rushed me in a hug, and I had to steady a hand on the bookshelf behind me. Luckily, every bookshelf in the store was nice and sturdy, thanks to Beckett and my brothers.

"Thank you, sweetie."

"You remind me a lot of Mom," Connor said.

"I do?"

"She would've done everything it took, too." He patted me on the arm before following Opal to the front of the store, where we'd relocated the children's section. My niece gushed at the new setup and immediately dropped into one of the new beanbag chairs.

"You're going to rock this," Alyssa said, surprising me.

"You came?"

"Don't act like it's such a shock. Of course, I came." She grabbed me in a hug. "This is your big day. I wouldn't miss it."

"Thank you," I said to her.

"I hope I made enough cupcakes," Aspen said, joining the hug.

"You two are the best."

"Don't cry, or we'll all cry, and Lila will get mad at us for ruining your makeup," Alyssa said, all of us laughing.

"C'mon," Aspen said to Alyssa. "I need help with the cupcakes."

"I thought we already—*Oh.*"

"You look beautiful." I heard Beckett's voice before I saw him. Caught sight of Husker's tail before I felt the warmth of Beckett's breath on my neck. "You're going to do amazing today."

I turned to meet his gaze, and the room went fuzzy around us.

"Thanks. Thank you for every—"

"Husker, no!" Lila moved the cookie cake before Husker could take a bite out of it, but his nose was covered in purple frosting.

"I better take him," Beckett said, reaching for my hand and squeezing it. "Good luck today."

I watched him slip out the back, and nearly forgot

what today was all about. Until Grandma Connie asked, "You ready to do this, sweetie?"

I scanned the bookstore slowly, as though taking in all the recent changes for the first time. The new bookshelves filled to the brim with colorful books, the dog beds and comfy chairs scattered throughout, the reading nook restored, the twinkle lights overhead all in working condition. It was a dream come true. Mom's bookstore brought back to life with my own flair added to it.

"I'm ready."

"Okay, I'm letting them in!" Thelma announced.

The click of the deadbolt releasing echoed in the large space.

That was the last moment of quiet I had for hours.

Fans poured in one after another, all smiling, all excited. I signed hundreds of books, took dozens of photos, and answered countless questions about the Veltori world and my upcoming plans.

It lit up my soul in ways I never expected.

I lost track of time. Had it been minutes, hours, days?

My cheeks ached from smiling, and my hand was cramping. But the atmosphere inside the store was warm, inviting, exhilarating. Just the way Mom would have wanted it to be.

FIFTY-NINE

HUSKER

Sniff, sniff, sniff.

Zig-zag, zig-zag, zig-zag.

Sniff, sniff, sniff.

All these people.

They smell funny.

Oh, that lady smells good.

I think she has a treat in her pocket.

"Husker, c'mon, buddy."

New Best Friend, where are we going?

"Going to grab coffee?"

Uncle Luke!

"Figured Kira could use a refill."

"I'll join you."

Sniff, sniff, sniff.

Zig-zag, zig-zag, zig-zag.

"Turned out pretty great, huh?"

"Did you really doubt your sister?"

"Not anymore."

Sniff, sniff, sniff.

Ewwww.

Oh no.

That's the bad smell.

Hey, New Best Friend.

The bad smell.

Uncle Luke.

The bad man is here.

Sniff, sniff, sniff.

Ewwww.

"Husker, hold on, buddy."

We can't hold on.

We have to get back to Mom.

Turn around.

Mom needs us.

Sniff, sniff, sniff.

Ewwww.

"I'll get you a treat, don't worry."

Treat?

Yes, I want a treat.

But the bad man.

We need to get to Mom.

Right.

Now.

"Husker's acting weird."

"Might be overstimulated."

Now I know why Mom says boys are stupid.

Except, I'm a boy.

I'm not stupid.

The bad man.
He's here.
Turn around.
We need to go back.
Now!

SIXTY
KIRA

"It's okay. I'm not in line," a male voice cut through. "I just need to get inside quick. I know the author. She's my girlfriend."

The blood in my veins ran cold at the sound of that hauntingly familiar voice. My entire body stiffened at the sight of Travis squeezing his large frame through the open doorway.

He looked disheveled, his wrinkled button-up shirt partially untucked, and his jeans scraped up as though he'd tripped and his knees skidded across dirty pavement. His eyes were bloodshot, and he'd shaved his head. It made him look meaner. Colder.

What the fuck was he doing here?

At first, I thought I was imagining it. Until the lovely lady I was signing a set of books for asked, "Who is that guy? He looks like one of your villains."

"Right," another in line behind her agreed. "Like that guy Vincent Veltori unalived for touching his mate."

"He looks meaner in person."

Not imagining it.

What the actual fuck?

"He's not supposed to be here," I said to the curious women near my table. "And he is *not* my boyfriend."

Travis stumbled his way through the crowd, his sights set on me. It was obvious he'd been drinking. How much was anyone's guess.

Where the fuck was Luke?

"I'll go find your brother," Thelma muttered low, patting my shoulder before she disappeared.

My first impulse was to cower. To feel guilty for the success of today, because it would make *him* feel bad. As if his failures and shortcomings were somehow my responsibility. How many times did Travis tear me down from a high moment simply because he was jealous? How many times did he make me believe I didn't deserve my success? That it was nothing more than a fluke?

The crowd lined up outside proved otherwise.

Fear turned to anger.

I pushed back from my chair, determined to stand my ground, both figuratively and literally.

"No," I commanded, so loudly Travis actually stopped in his tracks and gaped at me in shock. I spotted Luke in the doorway, along with Beckett. About fucking time. "You do *not* get to come here and ruin my day."

"Kare bear—"

"Call me that again, and it'll be the last thing you *ever* call me." Okay, so making death threats in front of my police chief brother and dozens of camera phones was probably not the wisest course of action, but I was beyond caring. Travis had stolen enough from me. I was done allowing him to take one more damn thing. "This is the only time I'll say this nicely. You need to leave."

"But I came here to see you—"

"If you want to stay, it's your funeral." I stared him down and held my ground, despite the way my entire body was shaking.

"What are you talking about?"

"I'm done being silent." I folded my arms over my chest. I caught sight of my brother hanging back, ready to step into action, but allowing me to have my say. Beckett and Connor were both at his side, looking equally pissed. "If you want to stay, I'm telling them everything."

"You're nothing without me. All this," he said, using his arms to make an exaggerated sweeping movement that nearly knocked him on his ass. His pitiful expression hardened into the cold monster I remembered. "This is because of *me*. You wouldn't have any of it if it weren't for me. I'm the reason this all happened. You *owe* me."

"Did you write the fucking books?" Thelma piped up.

God, I loved that woman.

"This was all me *despite* you. Despite you constantly putting me down. Despite you telling me my success was a fluke. Despite you making me believe I had to hide who I was because no one would accept me if they knew I wrote vampire smut."

"She writes excellent vampire smut," Lotti chimed in.

Several readers agreed in earnest.

"I never—I mean—I helped you—"

"You didn't *help* me," I fired back. "If anything, you hindered me. You constantly tried to hold me back. It's a miracle I was able to write at all with how much you constantly tore me down. But that's over now. I'm not going to protect you anymore."

For once, Travis was speechless.

"You are not welcome in my bookstore. You are not welcome in my town. You are not welcome in my life."

The final piece of his mask fell, and in its place was pure hatred. It was the same rage I saw the day he cocked a fist in my face. If I ever wondered whether I exaggerated things in my head, I didn't now.

"It's time to go," Luke said, grabbing him by the arm. Travis tried to shrug him off until he noticed who had him. He was a lot of things, but stupid enough to get arrested was not typically one of them. He valued self-preservation above all else. "Is that alcohol on your breath? Tell me you didn't *drive* here."

Okay, maybe not *stupid enough to avoid arrest.*

Travis struggled against Luke, but Connor and Beckett quickly jumped in. Together, the three wrestled him into submission. Husker let out a sharp bark. *Good boy, Husker.*

The remaining crowd watched in rapt attention. And when Travis was pushed through the open doorway, back outside, everyone erupted in cheers.

"Thatta girl!"

"Diana Davenport is a badass!"

"Yeah, she is!"

Husker rushed to me, Opal running after him, leash in hand. I didn't care that he'd get blond hairs all over my black dress. I knelt and squeezed him in a hug, one he didn't try to squirm out of for a solid five seconds.

"You're such a good boy, Husker."

With a deep breath, I prayed for Mom to help me get through the rest of this day. I clung to the adrenaline rush with a death grip, the one that made me feel empowered and brave. It was the only thing that would hold me together until the store closed. Once I locked the door, *then* I could fall apart.

SIXTY-ONE
BECKETT

"Have you seen Kira?" Connie asked me, scanning the mostly empty bookstore. The doors had closed an hour ago, everyone making quick work of resetting the store so they could open for regular business tomorrow morning. Somehow in all the chaos, Kira had slipped away.

"I thought she left?"

"She sent Husker home with Connor and Opal half an hour ago," Connie said. "But I thought she was still here."

My gaze zeroed in on the door to the back room. The one with the staircase to the upstairs apartment. I locked it, of course. But she'd been using her new keys. I hoped she was there, and not out at the lake. I wanted to blindfold her and make the reveal extra special, but I'd take a spoiled surprise over jumping in a cold lake in the dark any day.

"I'll go look for her."

"Thank you, dear." Connie patted my arm. "Beckett?"

"Yeah?"

"I saw what you did for her." She nodded her head upward. "Upstairs."

I nodded, because I didn't know what else to say.

"You're a good man. I hope Kira realizes that."

It warmed my heart to have her blessing. "She's been through a lot."

"Obviously."

We both chuckled, but tension hung in the air anyway. Travis was sitting in a jail cell twenty miles down the road because he was stupid enough to get behind the wheel of his car while intoxicated. Luke arrested him before he could put his keys in the ignition and hurt anyone.

He was safer in jail than anywhere else.

Bastard.

All I could think was, *Husker knew.* The one time that dog forwent treats to get back to his mom, I should have known something was amiss.

"Good luck," Connie said.

I slipped into the back, and up the stairs.

The door was locked, as I expected. I had a key, but I knocked first and waited.

Nothing.

I knocked again. "Kira? Are you in there?"

The deadbolt clicked open and the door pulled back slowly. "Hey, Beckett. You might as well come in."

Her red-rimmed eyes were puffy, her makeup smeared. Her hair was pulled back into a low messy bun. The strong, fierce woman I watched stand up to her worthless ex appeared fragile and broken.

I closed the door behind me and reached to gather her into my arms.

Kira flinched and took a step back.

Fuck, I hated that.

I stuffed my hands in my pockets instead. "Sorry."

"It's not your fault," she said, her voice hoarse. "You're amazing, Beckett."

Double fuck. I recognized that tone, and it caused me to brace.

"I can't believe you did all this for me," she said, waving her hand to indicate the whole room.

The twinkle lights gave the studio apartment a soft, magical glow. But this moment was anything but soft or magical. I could feel her tension as strongly as if it were my own.

"I'm going to pay you back," she said.

"No, you're not."

She flinched again, drawing attention to the harshness in my tone. But dammit, I was so fucking over her thinking I did things so she owed me.

"I'm not *him*, Kira," I said firmly.

"I know."

"Do you?"

"This is too much."

"It's not half of what you deserve," I shot back.

"I can't do this, Beck. I'm sorry. I just . . . can't." The defeat in her cracked voice made my anger fuel hotter. If Travis were stupid enough to step foot in Bluebell Springs ever again, Luke would have to arrest me for what I'd do to him.

"You deserve to be happy," I pressed, resisting the urge

to reach for her. To touch her. To cup her face and insist she look me in the damn eyes. "You deserve everything you've worked for, and so much more. Don't let that asshole ruin that."

"That's not what's happening here," she said, sounding less fragile and more determined.

Good. That fire I'd come to know still burned within her. She just had to believe it, too.

"You need space?"

"Yes. No. I don't know. I can't do this. I'm not cut out for this. It's better for everyone if we just go back to how things were before I kissed you on that dock."

"Better for who?"

"Your grandma and your sister were right. You're a really good man, Beckett. And the last thing you need is me complicating your life any more than I already have. You deserve better."

"Kira—"

"Please, Beck. Please, just go. Don't make this any harder for me than it already is."

Every impulse demanded I stay and fight for the woman I loved. The woman who pulled me in from the first moment I spotted her on that paddleboard in the middle of Ghost Lake with her quirky dog. But impulses had gotten me nowhere in the past.

I did cup Kira's cheek then, gently. I waited until she met my gaze and said, "I'll give you all the time and space you need, Kira. But make no mistake. I'm not going anywhere. When you're ready, you know where to find me."

I dropped a long kiss to her forehead and did the hardest fucking thing I'd ever done: I left.

SIXTY-TWO
KIRA

A HARD KNOCK pounded at the apartment door, and Husker perked up from his new favorite napping spot— the oversized sectional.

Luke.

Who else would knock like he wanted to execute a police raid? Husker popped off the couch as I saved my manuscript.

"I'm coming," I called, as Luke knocked again.

"Took you long enough," my brother said, sounding as grumpy as ever. The familiarity of it all was oddly comforting. I struggled to find comfort these days; my fault for pushing away the man I was definitely in love with.

But I stood by my decision.

Beckett deserved better than the broken, unhealed version of me. He deserved a woman who could love him with her whole heart. I didn't know that my heart would ever *be* whole again.

He deserved someone who could appreciate his grand gestures. Not freak out because of them.

"You brought me iced coffee?" I asked, raising a suspicious eyebrow at the offering. "Am I in trouble?"

"That depends. Did you do something that'll piss me off?"

"The bar's not really set that high, so you'll have to tell me."

I reached for the coffee, but he pulled it out of reach. "What are we, twelve?"

"You need a shower."

"Gee, thanks. I didn't realize that."

He wasn't wrong. I hadn't showered in three days. Hell, I hadn't left the writing loft apartment in three days, except to take Husker out. And most days, I was lucky enough to have someone volunteer during store hours.

When I told the book club that I was finishing Mateo's book—true story; I was—they all but insisted I let them run the bookstore while I stayed up here and finished. Bribing them with advance reader copies probably helped my case some.

Lotti offered to lock me in the apartment until I was finished, but, despite her cheerful tone, that felt a little too *Misery* to me.

"Promise me you'll shower if I let you have this," Luke said.

"Fine, *Mom*."

We stared at one another for several beats, expressions blank. Slowly, a hint of a smile tipped one corner of his mouth.

"You *can* smile."

"Don't get used to it." He handed over the coffee. "I thought you'd want to know that The Asswipe made bail."

My muscles instantly tensed. I wasn't surprised. Mommy Dearest probably bailed him out. But what did that mean for me?

"That took longer than I expected."

"I want you to get a protective order, Kira."

I bristled. I *hated* being told what to do. But in this case, he was right. And he wasn't the only one saying it. Aspen, Alyssa, and Lila were in unanimous agreement. I didn't think anyone who cared about me would let me know peace until I finally caved. And I was blessed to know that the number of people who cared was too high to count. Just another indication that moving home was the best decision.

"Okay."

"I'll go with you to the courthouse to file one," Luke offered, taking a seat on the sectional. I sat too. "If you want."

"You'd do that?"

"Why does that surprise you?"

"I don't know. Because you usually act like you hate me. Or maybe it's just your natural grumpiness. I can't always tell."

"I'll always look out for you, even if you piss me off."

"Such a sweet man. How are you still single?" *Shit.* I braced, waiting for him to frown. It wasn't meant to be the jab he likely thought it was.

"It's a mystery that's stumped the world."

I let out the breath I'd been holding.

"It was a long time ago," Luke said, referring to his ex

leaving him at the altar. "I don't cry myself to sleep about it."

"Anymore?" I teased.

"Don't push your luck."

"Are we okay?" I asked him.

"Yes, Kira."

"Hug?" I asked, a purposely cheesy grin spread across my face.

"Only *after* you take a shower."

"Fine. After I finish my coffee."

Luke scanned the apartment, as though he was just seeing it for the first time. Beckett outdid himself with the details. I was told my friends helped, but I knew it was because he wanted me to have the best. I wondered how much my brother knew about this secret project.

"You talk to Beckett?" Luke asked, as though reading my mind.

Eerie, but okay.

"No. Not . . . lately."

Not since the night of the grand re-opening, when I told him I couldn't see him anymore. But that didn't mean I didn't reach for my phone all the damn time, my fingers itching to shoot him a text. He respected the space I clearly needed, but it wasn't bringing me the peace I hoped.

"You should."

I eyed my brother suspiciously. "Why are *you* encouraging this?"

"You two aren't exactly subtle," Luke said, his tone a grumble.

"Oh." I bit down on my bottom lip. "Well, it's not going to work out."

"What did he do?"

That my brother immediately took my side over that of his best friend warmed a spot inside my heart I didn't realize was still frozen. Maybe people could change. People who wanted to anyway.

"Beckett didn't do anything," I said.

"Then, what's the problem?"

"Me, dummy. I'm the problem, it's me."

"Then get your head out of your ass. Beckett's a good man."

"That's kind of the problem."

"Maybe your girlfriends will coddle you, but I'm not going to tolerate your fucking pity party. I've known Beckett for the better part of a decade. I've seen that man fall for women before, and hard. But I've never seen him fall for someone like he has for you. If you screw this up, I will have no choice but to lock you up on an insanity charge."

"That's harsh."

"Did you think I was a soft kind of guy?"

"Maybe somewhere deep down in there."

"If you won't do it for you, do it for me. I'm getting tired of his ass moping around." Luke scratched Husker on the head, pushed to his feet, and headed for the door. Hand on the doorknob, he looked back and said, "Take a damn shower first."

SIXTY-THREE
BECKETT

"You're finished?" Madeline's face lit up through the phone screen as I shared the good news. I spent the past week working late into the night to finish the Kniffen Street house. It was the best distraction I had from Kira.

I missed the hell out of her, but I knew she needed space.

Patience, Aspen warned me, time and time again.

But no one warned me how fucking hard *patience* would be.

"I just have a few finishing touches left, but you can start packing your bags."

"We've been packing since I got home," Madeline admitted.

"Of course you have." I flipped the camera, walking the house to give my sister a tour. It was the perfect size for their family, and included an extra bedroom in case the family grew while they were here.

I didn't offer the rental to her until earlier this week,

but my sister didn't seem the least bit surprised when I did. She already had a job lined up with a local attorney's office. Kyle planned to be a stay-at-home dad while he explored new career options. They were moving to Bluebell Springs, whether or not I agreed to be their landlord. This just made things more seamless.

"You promise our sorry excuse for parents don't know anything about where you're moving?"

"Beck, if you're worried whether or not I've finally learned my lesson, I have. Our parents won't change. I see that now. It fucking sucks, but I swear to you, I get it," Madeline said as squealing erupted in the background.

One kid screamed. The other started crying. Who was who was anyone's guess until a little boy ran streaking in the background. The squealer.

"Don't mind them. It's bath time. Kyle drew the short straw tonight."

I couldn't wait to have my niece and nephew close. To see them all the time, and watch them grow up. I didn't even mind the tantrums.

It made the ache to start my own family grow deeper.

But if I wasn't starting a family with Kira Mason, I wasn't interested in starting one at all. That woman had me mind, body, and soul. She was it for me. I didn't know how I knew, I just *knew*.

It pained me not to reach out. Not to ask if she was okay. I even avoided family dinner this past week, risking the wrath of Connie Weston, because I didn't want Kira to feel as though she couldn't go.

"You okay?" Madeline asked, frowning.

"Yeah, just thinking."

"About the redhead?"

"She has a name, you know."

"She still not talking to you?" Perhaps the most surprising turn of events this past week was telling my baby sister about my love life. Or lack thereof, at the moment. I didn't realize how much I held back from her in the name of protecting her. I didn't want her worrying about me, because all I knew was worrying about her.

But Madeline didn't need my protection. She was one of the strongest women I knew. And sometimes, she even surprised me. Like when she offered up a number for a PI to hunt down Margene Miller in Mexico.

"Not yet."

"She will."

"You sound so sure of yourself," I teased, hoping to lighten the mood.

But the ache in my heart wasn't fooled. I missed the hell out of Kira. I missed her laugh. I missed that mischievous twinkle in her eyes. I missed the feel of her lips pressed against mine. The way she looked tangled in my sheets. The way she dug her fingernails into my skin when she came apart. I missed all of her.

"She loves you, Beck. She's just scared."

"Of me?"

"No. She's scared of losing herself."

Well, damn. That made a whole helluva lot of sense.

"How did you get so wise?"

"We always knew I was the wise one. That's why I became the lawyer."

A bloodcurdling cry rang out, and Madeline's eyes fell closed as she took in a deep breath.

"You have to go?"

"I really wish I didn't. Bye, Beck." She ended the call before I could say the same.

I stared at my phone for long seconds that stretched into even longer minutes, willing Kira's name to flash on the screen. I ached for that woman. Always would.

"Patience," I reminded myself.

Just as I set the phone down, it dinged.

Kira: I want to collect my favor now.

Kira: Meet me at the boat ramp in an hour.

Kira: Please.

SIXTY-FOUR
HUSKER

Mom, do I really have to wear this stupid thing?
"Husker, if you stop squirming, it'll be easier to get your life jacket on."
But all the other dogs will make fun of me!
Mom!
Click.
"There, all good to go."
Go?
Are we going?
Where are we going?
Are we going on the lake?
I don't want to get wet.
But I want to find that stupid pondweed.
I have a score to settle.
Mom, are we going?
Hurry up!
"We have to wait."

Wait?

Go?

Wait?

Go?

Which one is it, Mom?

"Here, have a treat."

Oh, treat!

Num, num, num.

"I hope he shows."

Mom is worried.

Here, Mom.

Scratch my booty.

It'll help.

Scratch, scratch, scratch.

"Maybe I waited too long."

Okay, fine.

You can give me a hug.

But make it quick.

I already look ridiculous.

"Thanks, Bubbies. You're the best."

I am the best!

Wag, wag, wag.

What's that sound?

I hear something.

I hear a truck.

It's New Best Friend!

New Best Friend!

New Best Friend!

"Calm down, Bubbies."

Calm?

Who can be calm?
I haven't seen New Best Friend in forever!
Where has he been?
New Best Friend!
New Best Friend!
New Best Friend!

SIXTY-FIVE
KIRA

MY PALMS GREW sweaty at the sight of the black truck pulling into the clearing. I watched Beckett park beside my Jeep, feeling my throat suddenly go dry.

He came.

But did I wait too long?

My heartbeat pounded in my ears as he stepped out of his truck in his usual T-shirt and jeans. Maybe I should have warned him to wear shorts. The man had to be tired of soggy jeans when it came to me and this lake.

I had Husker by his leash, but I let go of the handle when he spotted Beckett. He raced to his favorite person, looking a little ridiculous in his bright yellow and black life vest as he ran, but if he was self-conscious about it, he didn't show it. He nearly took Beckett out at the shins. Luckily, the man had learned to brace for impact.

"Hey, Husker."

My heart melted at the sight of him crouched down and greeting my dog as though he were his own.

If I had any doubts left over, they evaporated in this moment.

"Hey," I said as he approached, leash in hand.

"Hey," he said, his smile hesitant but still there. Like a constant.

Beckett was my constant.

I still didn't fully understand what I did to deserve him, but I was done pushing him away. I wetted my lips, willing my frayed nerves to calm as I found the words I'd been rehearsing all day. It'd only been a week apart, but it felt as though a decade had lapsed since I last saw him.

"You doing okay, Red?"

"I love you, Beckett."

Shit. Okay. Not the way I planned this. But, well, shit. It was out there now.

I rubbed my sweaty palms on the back of my shorts, looking at the hard-packed rocky ground, the calm waters, the two paddleboards I set up. At Husker. Anywhere but *at* Beckett.

"Let me try that again—"

"I love you too, Red. But I think you already know that."

"What?"

When did Beckett close the distance between us? How was he standing right in front of me when I didn't even remember him walking up to me? Dammit, this had to be a dream. A really good dream, but a dream. A dress rehearsal. Fuck, I didn't want to do this a second time.

"Did you really have any doubts about the way I feel about you, Kira?"

Beckett reached for my cheek, and my entire body

hummed to life. As though winter was giving way to spring.

Okay, not a dream.

Thank God.

Except, I just blurted my feelings without apologizing. Without explaining myself. Without—

"You don't need to overthink this," Beckett said gently, caressing my temple with his thumb. "I told you I wasn't going anywhere. That I would be here when you're ready. So, there's just one question to answer: Are you ready?"

I flickered my gaze to meet his, wondering how the hell it was possible a man like Beckett Campbell existed.

"I'm ready."

He drew me in for the kiss I'd craved since I told him to go. I sank into him, wrapping my arms around his neck and dragging him down to me as our bodies molded into one. Holding on too tightly because I refused to ever let him go again.

"I'm sorry, Beck," I said when we came up for air. Which was only because Husker was impatiently whining and wedging his way between our legs, letting us both know he was not enjoying being left out.

"You don't have to apologize, Red."

"I hurt you, and that wasn't fair. I wish I could just show up as this completely healed version of myself that never let anything knock me down, but that's not realistic. It felt really fucking good to tell Travis off. But that doesn't mean I'm not a little battered and bruised. But I want to try again. I want to put myself out there, and well, I kind of already did that—"

"Kira?"

Shit, I was rambling. "Yeah?"

"I'm battered and bruised, too. In case that escaped your mind."

"The redheaded curse," I said, laughing.

"Yeah."

"Just so you know, I think I'm leaving my hair red. It's really grown on me."

"Good. Because I'd call you Red even if your hair was green."

"Green?"

Beckett's smile stretched his cheeks and lit up his eyes, reminding me of its potency. If we didn't get on the water soon, I might do something reckless like tackle him and take him right here on one of the paddleboards.

"All I'm saying is that I'm all in," Beckett said.

"I am, too."

He kissed me again, and this time even Husker's insistent wedging wasn't enough to slow us down. Beckett's warm hand roamed up inside my shirt, settling on my breast. His thumb brushed over the peak of my nipple, and I whimpered.

"I fucking love that sound," Beckett said, his words a near growl. "I love making you *make* that sound."

"We could go back to the cabin," I suggested, snaking my hands up the back of his neck.

"Yeah?"

"But it'll have to be after we get on the lake," I said, nodding at Husker, who was pacing around us in circles, his leash wrapped around our legs. "He's been cooped up all week while I finished my book. He deserves a little adventure on the water first."

"You finished your book?"

"I did."

"Number twenty-six." Beckett kissed me again. "I'm so damn proud of you, Red."

My entire body flushed from the compliment. "Well, you certainly helped with the inspiration."

"Good. I hope I help inspire many more books to come."

"I think that's a fairly strong possibility." I kissed him once more, and then proceeded to untangle us from Husker's leash before someone on the other side of the lake saw us making out and called my brother to report an indecent exposure.

I turned to the boards before I remembered Beckett was wearing jeans.

"Did you want to grab shorts?"

"Nah."

"Really?"

"I've gotten pretty used to swimming in jeans when it comes to you, Red."

I gave him a flirty shrug. "I've gotten used to getting you *out* of wet jeans."

"Are you planning to fall in the lake today?" Beckett asked, a twinkle in his hazel eyes that I hoped would always be there.

"God, I hope not. That water's fucking *cold!*"

EPILOGUE
KIRA

"I brought margaritas!" Dylann announced as she walked through the front door, pitcher in hand.

"I don't drink," Carol Ann said from the table.

"That's why I brought virgin daiquiris," Lotti chimed in.

"And I have enough cupcakes to put an army in a sugar coma for three days," Aspen said, holding up the covered tins as evidence.

"You got the coffee pot going?" Carlos asked me from the other side of the front counter.

"You know it. I'll bring you a fresh cup when it's done brewing."

"You're the best."

The chatter grew as more members arrived and settled in around the community table. We left it in the same spot it always was, right in the middle of the store. Our group had grown by a few members since our grand re-opening two months ago, but thankfully, we could still fit everyone around the table. Today, however, we were holding a special meeting for the original book club members only.

Brenda's Book Nook flourished since Diana Davenport's first official in-person signing. The financial books were strongly back in the black, and we were confident we could make it through the slower winter months, since Lila hooked us up with online ordering. We could now ship books to anywhere in the world.

The store was thriving, the book club was happier than ever, and I was still amazed that *this* was my life. Words flowed more than they didn't. I liked to tell Beckett he was my muse—and some days he definitely was—but he liked to remind me that burning that letter back in Omaha was really what set me free. He was simply here to support me while I soared.

"You need anything before Husker and I head out?" Beckett's low voice vibrated against the back of my neck as he pressed his lips to my skin.

"You don't want to stay?" I teased, scratching Husker's head as he leaned heavily against my leg.

"I've already read the book," he said, kissing me on the lips. "And I got a personal one-on-one interview with the author."

My body heated at the memory of *discussing* my book while we were naked and tangled in his sheets. Though I still lived with Grandma Connie and Grandpa Dale, I spent more nights at the cabin than I did with them. Beckett and I had talked about moving in together, but if I learned anything, it was that there was nothing wrong with taking things slow. I was no longer wrapped up in the end result. I yearned to enjoy the journey.

"You have room for one more?"

Beckett and I both looked to the door in surprise.

"Pauline?" I looked at Beckett. "You didn't tell me your grandma was coming."

"I didn't know."

I moved around the counter to greet her, but Beckett caught me by the wrist and laced his fingers through mine. We walked to meet her, together. I braced for her disapproval.

"Nana, I didn't know you were coming."

"Of course you didn't," she said, giving Beckett a hug.

I stood, frozen beside him. I hated that I wanted so damn badly for this woman to like me.

"How long are you in town, Pauline?" I asked.

"Haven't decided."

"Where are you staying?" Beckett asked.

"With Madeline."

It was still strange having Beckett's sister in town, but also nice. She warmed up to me more quickly than I thought possible, considering how distrustful she was with me upon first meeting. Though this newfound friendship might be courtesy of my dog. Husker loved the twins. Especially when they dropped food or sneak-fed him snacks.

"Do you want to join us?" I offered, motioning to the table.

"I'd love to, though I have to admit, I haven't read the book yet."

"Technically it's not out until next week," I said. "But I can get you an advance copy if you'd like."

"That would be lovely, dear."

Dear? Did Pauline just call me *dear*?

"I actually have some news," she announced, "about Margene Miller."

The chattering at the community table turned to a low hum as several sets of eyes looked at Pauline expectantly.

"Did you say Margene Miller?" Thelma asked. "Or Satan's mistress? They sound a little similar."

"She's been apprehended."

The group went dead silent, no doubt from shock or fear of having misunderstood what Pauline said. Though we still regularly cursed Margene's name, we'd given up on actually finding her and bringing her to justice.

"In Cozumel," Pauline added.

"I knew it!" Dylann said. "She talked about Cozumel all the damn time."

"What happens now?" Carlos asked, adjusting his purple-rimmed glasses.

"She's sitting in a jail cell waiting for a court date," Pauline said.

"Did you hire a PI?" Beckett asked her, looking as surprised as I felt.

"Better. A bounty hunter."

"You know a bounty hunter!" Lotti cooed, pulling out a chair. "Do tell!"

Pauline focused on me, making me feel both naked and loved at the same time. It was a very confusing feeling.

"There's nothing I hate more than a spineless cheat. You tell your father I have a fantastic lawyer on standby."

"Wow, I don't know what to say."

"*Thank you* is fine," Pauline said.

Tears welled in the corners of my eyes and I threw my

arms around Pauline before she could escape me. I think I startled the woman, but so be it.

"Thank you. You have no idea how much this means to me."

"You're family now," she said.

"Family?" A tear trickled down my cheek, emotion swelling inside me.

"I don't say that lightly. So don't fuck it up and get on my bad side."

I let out a laugh, but I knew how serious she was.

"Now, who's pouring me a margarita?" Pauline asked, turning to the table.

"Me!" Dylann volunteered. "And we want to hear all about how this handsome bounty hunter captured the devil incarnate."

"I think they're going to be distracted for a little bit," I said, wiping another happy tear from my cheek. "You thinking what I'm thinking?"

"That we should go tell your dad the good news?" Beckett answered.

"Oh," I said on a blush. "That's probably a good idea too."

"What were you thinking?" he asked, low against my ear.

"That we could sneak away upstairs. But we should really go tell my dad about Margene. He'll want to know."

Beckett clicked the leash onto Husker's collar. "For the record, Red, I'm *always* thinking about sneaking off upstairs with you."

A full-body tingle skittered up and down, settling in my core. Making me wish we could hit the pause button so

I could enjoy some alone time with the man I loved more than I thought possible. We'd make up for it later.

"We'll be back," I said to the group before I surrendered to temptation and dragged Beckett upstairs. "We're going to tell Dad."

Beckett laced his fingers through mine again, and we headed down the block to the hardware store. Husker walked in front of us in his usual zigzags. The sun warmed my skin and I looked up to the clear blue sky. I hoped Mom heard the good news too.

Half a block down, Husker yanked hard on the leash.

"Chipmunk?" I asked.

"Your brother," Beckett said, nodding toward Luke. He stood near the curb, dressed in his police uniform, typing quickly on his phone. He looked grumpy, but it was hard to tell by his frown alone if he was in a bad mood or just a normal one.

"Are you giving someone a virtual parking ticket?" I teased.

"No," Luke answered, sounding extra sour. Guess it was a bad-mood day. "Just arguing with a fucking *Karen* about my pet policy."

My brother owned a duplex in town, lived in one side and rented out the other. At family dinner last week, I remembered him saying his long-term tenants moved out recently. He floated the idea of short-term rentals during the summer and early fall months. I wondered which this was.

"What kind of pet?" I asked.

"A dog."

Husker tilted his head as if to ask *what's your problem with dogs?*

"What's the issue?" I asked. "You like dogs."

"We spent two days replacing all the baseboards the last dog ate," Beckett said to me.

"She's trying to convince me her dog isn't a chewer, but she's doing a shitty job," Luke said, shoving his phone into his uniform shirt pocket.

He lifted his sunglasses to the top of his head, his eyes looking weary. As though he'd been losing sleep. Over his pet policy?

I should leave well enough alone, but I couldn't resist. "How so?"

"Failing service dog training doesn't exactly fill me with confidence. If it weren't a month-long rental and the end of tourist season, I'd have blocked her ass by now. I don't have time for this shit."

"Can you make her pay a pet deposit or something?" I suggested.

"Money doesn't buy back time," Luke grumbled. "What are you two doing out and about? I thought there was a highly anticipated book club meeting happening right about now."

"Margene's been caught," I told him, a smile stretching my cheeks. "She's in jail."

"You're serious?"

"Apparently, Nana has bounty hunter friends. Who knew?" Beckett added.

"We're going to tell Dad the news. Want to come?" I asked.

Luke's phone dinged again, and the look of frustration

that instantly etched his expression was borderline comical.

"Fuck, I've got to deal with this lady. Apparently, she's already in town. I'll catch up with you guys later. I want to talk to Pauline when she's free."

Husker watched Luke stalk across the street to his cruiser, his head still tilted as though he couldn't figure out what one of his favorite people had against dogs.

"That should be interesting," I said of my brother, the wheels turning in my head. An idea for a new book about feuding neighbors of the opposite sex unfolded in my imagination. I yearned to jot the thoughts down before they evaporated, but I'd left my phone at the bookstore.

"I can see the romance writer at work," Beckett said, handing me his phone. It was already open to a Notes app.

Another reminder that I was one of the luckiest women in existence to snag a man this good. A better man than I could have created in any of my romance novels.

"Have I told you lately that I love you?" I asked.

"Not since this morning." He lowered his mouth to the shell of my ear. "Right after I made you come."

BONUS EPILOGUE
BECKETT

Amidst the falling snow, a mass of blond fur leapt through the air in front of my living room window. If it wasn't for the tall, pointed ears and long, curled tail, I might have dismissed the blur as a deer.

Husker.

Kira warned me he loved the snow, but until last night, any snowfall we saw this season had yet to stick. His obsession was something I'd yet to witness, but now, a solid six inches coated the ground. More where it drifted closer to the house. Husker obviously sought out the deeper mounds for his enjoyment.

I chuckled, watching him bob up and down in the drifts, simultaneously biting at the softly falling snowflakes.

But where was Kira?

"Shit." I rolled off the couch, slipping my feet into boots in record time.

I flew out the front door, but before I rounded the

cabin to retrieve Husker, I spotted Kira dragging a massive box along a path I'd yet to shovel. I completed another renovation late last night, and was determined to enjoy a day off. Which accounted for my laziness and the covered path. In my defense, Kira was supposed to be locked in her writing loft until dinnertime.

My head swiveled between the two. Husker seemed preoccupied, pouncing over and into snowdrifts. But his leash was missing.

"He's fine for a few minutes," Kira called over her shoulder.

My attention shot back to her, dropping immediately to that cute ass wrapped in denim. One that popped each time she yanked the tall box backward, toward the cabin. Her hair, still red, was longer than it was when we met this past summer. It dangled halfway down her back as she struggled with the box she dragged.

"Beckett? Little help?"

I forced a hard blink as I jogged over to assist her. It was so easy to lose track of time and space when she was in my orbit. I could spend hours simply admiring her sexiness. And *everything* about Kira Mason was sexy.

"What is that?" I asked, glancing once more at Husker as I caught up to Kira. The enthusiastic pup continued leaping through the drifts, his flight risk appearing low.

"A Christmas tree."

I crouched to the ground, lifting the edge she'd been dragging through the snow. "But it's not even Thanksgiving yet."

"Your point?"

"Why is—" I cut myself off before the question fully formed, because the significance of this gesture hit home.

The last time Kira shared her Christmas tree with another, he ripped her heart right out of her chest and stomped on it.

A bubble of anger grew beneath my rib cage as I recalled the story she told me about Travis punishing her for spending time with family out of town by undecorating her seven-foot tree. Like the fucking Grinch on steroids, he packed up the ornaments, the lights, and the garland. After disassembling the tree and shoving it back into its box, he left it all in the hallway of her apartment for her to discover when she returned home later that night.

God, I was glad The Asswipe wasn't stupid enough to set foot in Bluebell Springs since Luke arrested him this past summer.

If Kira was bringing her Christmas tree to the cabin, it meant something.

Something big.

Almost a month ago, I slipped a cabin key onto her key ring. The longing for her to move in set in the day I unpacked my own things months ago. But I forced myself to be patient. Deep down, I knew she belonged here with me. Husker, too. But it had to be her decision.

I casually made the offer for her to move in that night I gave her a key, after we were both high on lovemaking and orgasms. But I made it clear it was an open invitation, to be accepted if and when she felt ready.

This Christmas tree meant we were one step closer.

"Something you should know about me," she said as I

flipped us around so I could get the door. "I really love Christmas."

Once inside, I propped the box against the couch.

Kira was panting, her cheeks tinted pink. "Is this a bad time to tell you there's more in my Jeep?"

I gripped the bottom of the flannel coat she wore—*my* flannel coat—and tugged her to me. I cupped her rosy cheek, stroking her chilled skin with my thumb. I had several ideas of how I could warm her right up. All of them involved us both naked.

"You want to put that tree up today, don't you?"

"Can I?"

Fuck, the way she bit her bottom lip just did something to me. "Yes, Red."

"You don't have to help me—"

I tilted her head up until her blue gaze locked with mine. "I *want* to."

"Really?"

"Really."

I drew her lips to mine, meaning to kiss her softly, sensually. I still had decorations to retrieve, and there was the matter of Husker outside without a leash. If he spotted a deer, we might end up spending the rest of our day tracking him down.

But then she dug those fingers into the back of neck, arching her body into mine, and dammit if I didn't forget everything but the way we molded together in perfection. I slid my hand to the small of her back, and gripped her tighter. I fucking loved being close to this woman.

"Guess you really like Christmas, too," she said, her

eyes sparkling as she cupped her hand over my bulge. I was already hard. Of course I was.

"I'm not a grinch, if that's what you're worried about, Red."

"Good. I think Santa's more the good girl type anyway."

She pulled my mouth back to hers, her tongue sliding against mine. I tugged the zipper of her flannel jacket down, sliding it off her shoulders when it opened. My hand slid beneath her sweater and layered tank top, on a mission north.

"Maybe you should sit on Santa's lap and tell me all about it," I said, my words a near growl. Red brought out the primal, possessive side of me. Every damn time.

"That can be arranged—"

A *thunk* against glass snapped both our heads to the living room window. Husker stared in, his head tilted at that crazy angle. The glass was fogging around the nose he pressed against it.

"I better get him before he has a squirrel moment, and bolts," Kira said.

I headed to her Jeep, not surprised to find four totes sprinkled in a layer of dog fur labeled *Christmas Tree Decorations.*

When I carried the last one inside, Husker had made himself at home on *his* couch, looking as though he'd been thoroughly rubbed down with a towel. Stripped down to jeans and a tank top, Kira was bent over a green tote filled with lights.

"I hope these still work," she said, reaching to plug one strand into an outlet.

I came up behind her, placing my hands on her hips.

"You're staring at my ass, aren't you?"

"So what if I am?"

She wiggled her butt, pressing it back against me. A hint of red lace peeked out from the top of her sliding jeans. The temporary effects of the cold outside were no match for the warmth she filled me with now. Blood rushed south once again, making me hard as a fucking rock.

The strand of lights lit up in full, bringing a smile to Kira's face.

My dick throbbed.

"I thought we were putting up the tree," she said, bending back over. *Purposely* popping that ass in my direction this time.

"The tree's not going anywhere, Red." I leaned over her slightly, just enough to rub my palms down the front of her thighs. My thumbs grazed the bend of her legs, dangerously close to her center.

Husker grumbled from the couch, hopping off and taking himself to the bedroom.

We both laughed at his retreat.

"Poor guy just wants a nap," I said.

"He wanted an excuse to claim the bed before we did."

I flattened a palm against her ass, giving it a firm squeeze. "Guess I'll just have to fuck you out here, then."

Kira looked back over her shoulder, desire heavy in her eyes. "I'm not stopping you."

I reached a hand around to the button of her jeans,

undoing it. She fumbled the string of lights in her hand, dropping them.

"Keep working on the lights," I insisted, dragging down the zipper. My fingers brushed against the lace. I bet it was nice and damp between her legs.

She reached over to plug in another strand of lights, but only half of them illuminated. "Damn," she murmured.

"One of them might be loose," I suggested, reaching a finger inside her jeans. "Better check them."

"And if I don't want to?"

"Then, I might have to put you on Santa's naughty list." I hooked a finger against her wet panties, thoroughly enjoying her whimper of pleasure as I hit that special spot.

"What happens if I'm on the naughty list?" She wriggled her ass at me in invitation.

I dipped my finger beneath the lace, sinking into her sopping wet folds and circling her button. She gripped the edges of the green tote and lightly gyrated her hips to my rhythm.

"You'll get coal for Christmas."

Kira looked back at me, rolling her eyes.

"Well," I said, tugging down her jeans to reveal the red lace panties beneath them. "You could negotiate terms."

"Or you could just spank me now," she insisted.

"You really want to be spanked, don't you?"

"So what if I do?"

Slowly, I pulled the red lace down until her panties hovered just below her pussy. I stood behind her, sliding my hands from her hips to her firm cheeks. I dug my fingers into the edge of her bottom and squeezed. She let out a soft moan that had me aching to free my cock.

I would take her from behind soon enough.

But first, I wanted to enjoy this moment.

I sawed two fingers between her legs, rubbing her clit.

"Beckett," she panted, my name a plea to carry out her wicked desire.

I lifted my other hand and gently swatted her butt.

Her body wobbled, a moan of delight escaping her throat as she gripped the tote tighter. "More," she panted.

I inserted a finger into her channel, and smacked her ass again.

"Harder," she insisted.

"You want me to spank you *harder*?"

"Yes!"

I leaned over her, bringing my lips close to her ear. "Then, be a good girl, and touch yourself."

She reached one hand between her legs as I pushed a second finger inside her channel. I waited several seconds, building anticipation, before I brought my other hand to her cheek a little harder this time.

"Oh, my—*yes*!" she cried out.

"You like that?"

She nodded vigorously, rocking her hips to the motion of my fingers inside her. "More."

"Your ass is going to be as red as your hair if I keep going," I teased.

"Good."

"Do you want me inside you while I spank you, Red?"

"Yes!"

"Keep touching yourself," I demanded as I pulled my

fingers free and yanked down my jeans and boxers. I lined up my hard length between her legs, pushing through her wet folds. She reached for me, pressing me against her until I was coated in her juices.

I pushed my tip into her entrance, and she sank back onto me.

The pleasure was blinding—every fucking time. There was no better place to be than buried inside the woman I loved more than life itself.

I swatted her bottom as I thrusted into her, and she cried out in ecstasy. A second time, and she exploded. I gripped her hips, pummeling into her as she came. In seconds, I was coming apart with her. I held her to me as wave after wave of ecstasy rippled through us.

When she finally stilled, I pulled free.

"Wow," she said, a sated smile on her lips as she turned around to face me in nothing but her tank top. "*That* was fun."

"You liked that, huh?" I said, fixing my jeans.

"I always thought I would."

"Wait, you've never—"

Kira shook her head.

"I've written about it. Darius Veltori's mate? She *loves* getting spanked." She retrieved her red lace panties and slipped them on. "But I've never tried it before myself."

"I have to say, that surprises me a little. You've been pretty enthusiastic about it since the first time I got you naked."

"I've never been with anyone I trusted this much."

Her words were so quiet I almost couldn't make them out. But truth lingered in her eyes, and it warmed a spot deep in the recesses of my heart. I would happily spend a lifetime earning this woman's full trust, if that's what it took. That she trusted me enough to let me into this very private desire of hers meant more to me than she could possibly comprehend.

"I love you, Beck," she said, reaching for my hand.

"I love you, too."

"I'm ready."

"Ready?"

"To move in."

My heart stuttered and skipped, because I was certain I misheard her. What if I was passed out on the couch, daydreaming this?

"You're sure?" I asked.

"If the offer still stands, that is."

"Of course it does." I pulled her into my arms, hugging her tight against me. "I would love nothing more than to fall asleep every night next to you. To wake up and see your face every morning."

"What if I drool? Or snore—"

"You definitely snore."

"I do not!"

I cupped Kira's cheek, drawing her gaze to mine. "You do," I said. "But I don't mind. It's cute."

"Cute," she repeated, as though the word were sour on her tongue.

"Take the compliment," I insisted.

"Weird compliment, but okay."

I drew her in for a long, sensual kiss. A kiss filled with promises of the future. Promises of *our* future.

"You know this means you'll be waking up every morning to dog breath, too, right?"

"Definitely not as cute, but yes, I'm aware."

"Good, because we're a package deal, Husker and me."

I hugged Kira against my chest, holding her close. Soaking in her warmth and the perfect way her small frame fit against me, like the puzzle piece I had been missing until that day I jumped into a cold lake after the redheaded stranger.

"I wouldn't have it any other way, Red."

HUSKER

For those of you who are curious, Husker is based on a real dog. A dog I didn't deserve but was lucky enough to have in my life for ten and a half years.

He really did fit in a cat carrier beneath the seat of the plane when I adopted him at nine weeks old. He was known to steal freshly picked asparagus right from my grandma's garden. He prided himself on treeing squirrels. The only way he rode in my car was to pace my back seat like a caged lion, sniffing out one window than the other every two seconds. He enjoyed being on a paddle board, but definitely not in the water. And he was absolutely obsessed with pizza.

He passed suddenly and unexpectedly in August of 2023, leaving a gaping hole in my heart. Making him a character in this book brought me so much joy.

ABOUT THE AUTHOR

Caroline Stone is a steamy contemporary romance author who writes heartfelt stories with depth.

Her books are heavy on the romance, family—real and found, friendships, real life issues, and a whole lot of laughs. You can rest assured you'll always find at least one four-legged friend trying to steal the spotlight.

Though Will Bark for Pizza is the debut for Caroline Stone, this seasoned author has been publishing for over a decade and has 160+ published works. She also writes as Jacqueline Winters (sweet, Hallmark-style, just kisses romances) and Kali Hart (short & sweet with plenty of heat romances you can fit into your busy life.)

She is a dog mom, Army veteran, sweets-obsessed gym lover, survivor, and—most importantly—a hopeless romantic and dreamer.

OTHER PEN NAMES

Enjoying my writing style? Have you tried my other pen names?

Jacqueline Winters writes sweet, Hallmark-type, just kisses romances. Her most popular series is the Finding Love in Alaska series.

Find her books at authorjacquelinewinters.com

Kali Hart writes short & sweet with plenty of heat. These are romances short enough to squeeze into a lunch break, binge before bedtime, or breeze through in a long afternoon. Her most popular series is the Mountain Men of Caribou Creek.

Find her books at kalihartauthor.com

www.ingramcontent.com/pod-product-compliance
Lightning Source LLC
Chambersburg PA
CBHW031731180726
48283CB00005B/1458